Pamela Sadadi Y... Christian Education ... fiction prompted he... romance. When she's ... busy wife, mother an... ....g basketball, cooking or planning her next vacation. Pamela lives in Alberta, Canada with her gorgeous husband and adorable, but mischievous son and daughter.

USA Today bestselling author, **Trish Morey**, just loves happy endings. Now that her four daughters are (mostly) grown and off her hands having left the nest, Trish is rapidly working out that a real happy ending is when you downsize, end up alone with the guy you married and realise you still love him. There's a happy ever after right there. Or a happy new beginning! Trish loves to hear from her readers – you can email her at trish@trishmorey.com

Melanie Milburne read her first Mills and Boon at age seventeen in between studying for her final exams. After completing a master's degree in Education she decided to write a novel and thus her career as a romance author was born. Melanie is an ambassador for the Australian Childhood Foundation and is a keen dog lover and trainer and enjoys long walks in the Tasmanian bush. In 2015 Melanie won the HOLT Medallion, a prestigious award honouring outstanding literary talent.

Romantic Escapes

Romantic Escapes:
Venice

PAMELA YAYE

TRISH MOREY

MELANIE MILBURNE

MILLS & BOON

First Published in Great Britain 2022
by Mills & Boon, an imprint of HarperCollins*Publishers* Ltd,
1 London Bridge Street, London, SE1 9GF

www.harpercollins.co.uk

HarperCollins*Publishers*
1st Floor, Watermarque Building,
Ringsend Road, Dublin 4, Ireland

ROMANTIC ESCAPES: VENICE © 2022 Harlequin Enterprises ULC.

Seduced by the Hero © 2015 Pamela Sadadi
Prince's Virgin in Venice © 2019 Trish Morey
The Venetian One-Night Baby © 2019 Melanie Milburne

ISBN: 978-0-263-30468-8

MIX
Paper from
responsible sources
FSC® **C007454**
www.fsc.org

This book is produced from independently certified FSC™ paper to ensure responsible forest management.

For more information visit: www.harpercollins.co.uk/green

Printed and Bound in Spain using 100% Renewable electricity at CPI Black Print, Barcelona

SEDUCED BY THE HERO

PAMELA YAYE

Chapter 1

"Surely you can't be *that* dumb." Dionne Fontaine heard the scathing retort leave her mouth and wished she could cram the words back down her throat. Not because she felt guilty for losing her temper, but because the novice life coach with the Dolly Parton–like cleavage had burst into tears.

Her vice president and friend, Sharleen Nichols, glared at her as if *she* were the problem, and Dionne wondered if she'd been too harsh. Considering all of the facts, Dionne determined her next move. Sharleen and Annabelle Clark had arrived at her office ten minutes earlier, during her morning meditation time, and although she'd been annoyed by the interruption, Dionne had given them her undivided attention. She was the CEO of Pathways Center, the head woman in charge, and she prided herself on being accessible to her employees. Even starstruck life coaches who put themselves in compromising situations with male clients.

"Annabelle did nothing wrong," Sharleen insisted, her tone matter-of-fact. "It's not her fault Ryder Knoxx propositioned her during their free consultation yesterday. She shouldn't be blamed for *his* poor judgment."

Feeling contrite, Dionne spoke in a sympathetic tone. "Entertainers are notorious womanizers with no conscience. Since it's obvious Mr. Knoxx has a crush on you, I'll assign you to another client and pass the aging rock star on to a more seasoned life coach."

Panic flickered across her face. "No. Don't. I like him, and we have a lot in common."

"This isn't about you, Annabelle. This is about doing what's best for our clients."

Her shoulders drooped, and she slid down in her chair, as if she were trying to disappear into the plush, soft fabric. "But we clicked," she whined. "Ryder thinks we're kindred spirits."

Of course he does. He's trying to get into your pants, and you're too stupid to realize it.

Dionne struggled to control her temper. It was a challenge, especially in light of everything that had happened at the center in recent months, but she maintained her cool. "Your goal as a life coach is to encourage and support clients through their problems and issues, not become their BFFs."

Annabelle started to speak to argue her point, but Dionne silenced her with a look. Her Southern drawl was charming, but she was a pain in the ass and she wanted to get rid of her. "Life coaching is about helping people improve the quality of their lives without expecting anything in return," she continued. "It's imperative you act professional at all times, and don't, under any circumstances, accept money, gifts or favors from clients."

"Does that mean I can't attend the world music awards with Ryder next month?"

"That's *exactly* what it means."

"But—"

"But nothing," Dionne snapped, finally losing her patience. The more time she spent with Annabelle, the less she liked her, and she suspected the only reason the university graduate had applied to Pathways was to hook up with a celebrity. "You've only been working here for three months, and since you started it's been one problem after another..."

Sharleen tried to interrupt her, but Dionne was on a roll. She didn't believe in biting her tongue or sugarcoating the truth. She always spoke her mind. "I'm all for a woman using her physical assets to get ahead, but you need a make-*under*. Tone down the eyeliner, lay off the hair spray and, for goodness' sake, cover your tits. This is a place of business."

Sniffling, Annabelle cleaned her plump, tearstained cheeks with the back of her hands. "You're right, Mrs. Fontaine. I'm sorry. I'll do better, I promise."

"You better, or you're fired."

Sharleen winced as if she were in pain, but Dionne pretended not to notice.

"Pathways is my life, and I won't let you or anyone else destroy my agency."

Nodding, Annabelle rose to her feet and straightened her low-cut, belted dress. "I better head back to my office. My next session starts at ten, and I need time to prepare."

Annabelle hustled through the open door and closed it behind her.

Dionne was glad to see her leave. "You never should have hired her," she said, reaching for her oversize mug and raising it to her lips. "She's young and immature, and so damn gullible. It's hard to believe she's twenty-seven years old."

"Annabelle's a good life coach."

"That remains to be seen."

Sharleen released a deep breath. With her flawless complexion and delicate features, she'd always been a pretty girl, but since meeting race-car driver Emilio Morretti, she'd stepped up her fashion game. No longer self-conscious about the scars on her arms and legs she'd suffered in a tragic house fire, she'd traded in her dark suits for vibrant designer outfits. The oversize bow on the neckline of her red A-line dress was eye-catching, and her pearl accessories enhanced the femininity of her look.

"You're being too hard on her," Sharleen said.

"And you're being too nice."

"Leave everything to me. I'll mentor her and show her how to be a great life coach."

Dionne admired her optimism. Appointing Sharleen as her VP was the smartest thing she'd ever done. She hoped they'd be friends and partners for many years to come.

Not if Emilio Morretti has his way, whispered her inner voice.

The sports legend had proposed to Sharleen on her twenty-eighth birthday, and three weeks later she was *still* floating on air. Standing on the podium after winning the World Series All-Star Race, Emilio had stunned her friend—and the 1.5 million viewers watching worldwide—by popping the question on live TV. The happy couple were planning to exchange vows in Venice, Italy. Although Dionne had tried talking Sharleen out of getting married in December, her friend was determined to tie the knot in just three months' time. She was convinced Emilio was "the one," and she was so anxious to jump the broom, it was all she could talk about. Dionne only hoped Sharleen wouldn't one day regret her decision—

Like me, she thought sadly, swallowing hard. *If I had known then what I know now, I never would have married Jules after dating for only six months.*

"Annabelle has the requisite skills," Sharleen continued. "She just needs to put what she's learned in the classroom into practice, and I'm confident she can—"

"Well, I'm not. I think she's a liability, and I want her gone." Taking a sip of her green tea, she kicked off her Gucci pumps and reclined comfortably in her zebra-print chair. Dionne loved her office. It was bright, welcoming and feminine, just like her. She'd spent a fortune decorating it, and was thrilled her interior designer had brought her vision to life. Star-shaped chandeliers hung from the ceilings, teal walls evoked feelings of calm, her Versace furniture reeked of glamour, and the burgundy carpet was pillow-soft.

"Give Annabelle another chance. This is her first coaching job, and she's still finding her footing," Sharleen explained. "I believe in her, and you should, too."

Dionne drank her tea, gave some thought to what Sharleen said. "I liked you better when you were single," she teased, hoping to lighten the mood with a joke. "You used to be tough and tenacious, but now that you're in love you're a total softy."

A smile brightened Sharleen's face. It was obvious she was thinking about her fiancé. It took everything in Dionne not to roll her eyes to the ceiling when her friend sighed dreamily and gazed longingly at her engagement ring. It was the size of a golf ball, encrusted with diamonds, and it was the most beautiful piece of jewelry Dionne had ever seen.

"I can't help it," Sharleen said with a giggle. "I'm so freakin' happy, I feel like dancing in the streets. I want to share my happiness with everyone I know."

"I'm thrilled for you, but your romance is bad for business."

"Bad for business?" she repeated, arching an eyebrow. "In what way?"

"Because of you, our female life coaches are secretly hoping to make a love connection with every wealthy client, and as a result are breaking the employee conduct rules."

"My feelings for Emilio have nothing to do with him being famous, and everything to do with who he is as a person. He makes me feel special, as if I'm all that matters…"

They all do in the beginning, but it doesn't last. Trust me, I know what I'm talking about. I've been married twice.

"If Emilio lost everything tomorrow, it wouldn't change how I feel about him. I'd live with him in a cardboard box if I had to." Happiness warmed her face, and she laughed heartily. "But enough about me and my amazing fiancé. How are you doing?"

Dionne finished her tea and put down her mug. "Great, fantastic, couldn't be better."

"I know the last few weeks have been tough on you, what with your in-laws bad-mouthing you to the press and the construction delays at the Seattle and LA offices, but I'm here for you, Dionne. You don't have to deal with those issues alone."

"Thanks, Sharleen, but I'm fine, really."

"I don't believe you…"

What do you want me to say? "My whole world is falling apart, and if I didn't have Pathways to keep me going, I'd probably have a nervous breakdown"?

"It isn't healthy to keep things bottled up." Sharleen sounded wise, like a therapist counseling a distraught client. Her expression was filled with concern. "We're a team, and I have your back. No matter what. You can count on me."

Dionne shifted around on her chair and fiddled with the diamond tennis bracelet on her wrist. Every day, without fail, Sharleen asked how she was feeling, and every day, without fail, Dionne lied through her teeth. She didn't want to talk about Jules or their contentious divorce proceedings. Not with Sharleen. Not with anyone. Working helped Dionne forget her hurt, her failures, and she'd rather suffer in silence than pour out her heart. She admired Sharleen and thought she was an exceptional life coach, but a woman desperately and madly in love wasn't the right person to confide in. Neither were her two older sisters, Mel and Lorna, who both just didn't understand what she was going through.

No one does—that's why I keep my feelings to myself. Her gaze strayed to the window, and she peered outside. Pathways Center was in an attractive plaza filled with glitzy boutiques, cafés and beauty salons, but what Dionne loved most about the location was the hustle and bustle of Peachtree Street. Growing up in a large family, she'd always thrived in chaos, and having her business in a high-traffic area fueled her creative juices.

"We'll get through this together. You have my word." Sharleen reached across the desk and touched Dionne's hand, giving it a light squeeze. "If you need anything, just ask. I'm here for you, and so is the rest of the Pathways family. You've built a fantastic team, and any one of our colleagues would be glad to listen if you need to talk. We're a hundred percent behind you, Boss."

Dionne opened her mouth to thank Sharleen for her support, but she couldn't find her voice. She wasn't one to cry, but her friend's words made her eyes tear, and the room swam out of focus. *Good God, what's wrong with me? I'm an emotional wreck, and it's only ten o'clock.*

"How did your meeting go yesterday with Jules and his attorney?" Sharleen asked. "Are you any closer to finalizing the terms of your divorce? Have you finally reached an agreement you're both satisfied with?"

I wish, but he's determined to screw me over. Dionne's gaze fell across the picture frame on her desk. The photograph had been taken Labor Day weekend at her childhood home, and every time Dionne looked at the picture of her loved ones, her heart ached. In her culture divorce was frowned upon, something her deeply religious Somali father was vehemently against, and Dionne felt horrible about the pain she'd caused her family. Her parents adored Jules; so did her siblings, and every day her mother implored her to kiss and make up with her estranged husband.

No way, no how, she thought. Her Prince Charming had turned out to be a frog, and she was sick of playing the role of the dutiful wife. They were finished, over for good, and there was nothing Jules could say to convince her to reconcile. Their marriage had been stained with insults, name-calling and lies, and Dionne was ready for a clean break.

"Nothing's changed. Jules is still as stubborn as ever and…"

Dionne suddenly closed her mouth, stopping herself from saying any more. Even though she knew the divorce was for the best, discussing the demise of her marriage always made her emotional. Scared her emotions would get the best of her, and she'd end up bawling all over her Escada pantsuit, Dionne turned toward her computer monitor and typed in her password. "I have to finish my speech for the Seattle Leadership Conference, so let's touch base later."

"It's Thursday, remember? I'm off at noon."

"Hot date?" Dionne teased, playfully wiggling her eyebrows.

"You know it." Sharleen cheered and danced around in her chair. "Emilio's taking me to Fiji for the weekend."

"Again? But you guys were there Labor Day weekend."

"What can I say? My fiancé likes spoiling me, and I'd be a fool to stop him."

Enjoy it while it lasts, because things will change. They always do, and not for the better.

"I'll be back on Sunday, but call if you need me."

"Why bother? You never answer your phone after hours."

Her eyes twinkled, and a smirk curled the corners of her glossy lips. "You wouldn't either if you had a man to wine you and dine you."

"It's a shame Emilio doesn't have a twin," Dionne joked, laughing.

"He doesn't have a twin, but he does have five *very* single, *very* handsome brothers. Want me to hook you up?"

"Hell no!" she shrieked, fervently shaking her head. "The last thing I need is another lying, cheating man in my life. I'm better off alone."

"Not all men are dogs, you know."

You're right, they're not, but the good ones are rare and harder to find than the exit at a corn maze. Dionne hadn't dated anyone since leaving Jules and moving out of their marital home, and she had no intention of putting herself out there anytime soon. Her focus was on building her business and spending time with her family. They wouldn't hurt her, wouldn't betray her trust—

"You and Jules have been separated for almost a year," she pointed out. "Wouldn't you like to do something *besides* work? You're a great catch, Dionne, and there are plenty of eligible, successful men who'd love to date you."

"I'm not interested. I like my life just the way it is, thank you very much. I have my business, my family and my friends, and that's more than enough."

"Well, if you change your mind just let me know."

I won't, so don't hold your breath. Unconditional love

is a myth, and the notion of living happily ever after is a fairly tale.

The phone sounded, and Dionne sighed in relief. She was tired of talking about men, namely her good-for-nothing ex, and wanted to get back to doing what she did best: running her business. Dionne hoped it was her divorce attorney calling with good news, and placed her hand on the receiver to signal the end of their conversation.

Thankfully, Sharleen took the hint and rose from her chair. "Have a good weekend," she said, marching towards the door. "Don't work too hard."

Back in CEO mode, Dionne sat up tall and cleared her throat. Even though her marriage was in shambles, she looked forward to coming to work every day and enjoyed connecting with clients. "Dionne Fontaine speaking," she said brightly, turning away from her computer screen. "How can I help you?"

"You can start by returning the money you stole from me."

Her eyes narrowed, filled with hate. Damn. It was Jules. *Again.* How many times did she have to tell her assistant not to put his calls through? Her ex could be persuasive, charming even, but still Lily worked for *her*, not Jules, and now because her assistant was a softy, she was stuck talking to her estranged husband. The man who'd made her life a living hell for the past year. Her first impulse was to hang up the phone, which is what she usually did when he called, but this time she didn't. "I have nothing to say to you. Quit calling me at work. I'm busy."

"Return my money. You stole from me, and I want every cent back."

Dionne played dumb, pretending not to know what he was talking about. She was, of course, aware of what Jules was referring to, but she wasn't going to argue with him about the six-figure donation she'd made to the Atlanta

Children's Shelter just days before she filed for divorce. *If you can spend thousands of dollars at the strip club, then I can give thousands of dollars to a worthy cause.*

"This has gone on long enough," he snapped, his voice taut with anger. "You made your point. Now, move back home before I change my mind about giving you another chance."

"This isn't a game. We're through, and there's nothing you can say to change my mind."

"You don't mean that. Think of all the good times we've had."

What *good times? We argued constantly, and you betrayed me over and over again.* For five years, they'd lived in comfort and affluence, but it was time to end her marriage and move on with her life. Her parents couldn't talk her out of it; neither could her in-laws, and in the time they'd been separated, she'd never once regretted her decision.

"Every marriage goes through rough times," he said. "Don't let your insecurities ruin us."

"It was your lies that destroyed us, not me."

"We need to talk, *alone*, without our attorneys. What time will you be home?"

Her stomach twisted into knots. Was Jules in her house? Was he calling from her master bedroom? Snooping through her things again? Last Friday, she'd arrived home to find Jules in her living room, and if she hadn't pretended to call the police with her cell phone, he'd probably still be demanding she withdraw the divorce papers.

"If you keep harassing me I'll file a restraining order against you."

"But I love you."

Dionne burst out laughing. Surely he wasn't serious? Jules thought if he poured on the charm, she'd be putty in his hands, but his attempt to sweet talk her was so pathetic she rolled her eyes to the ceiling. His moods changed as often as the weather, and she'd always been on guard around him. She never knew what to expect, what would set him off, and hated how he used to take his frustrations out on her. "You don't love anyone but yourself. That's how it's always been, and you'll never change."

"If you come back home I'll buy you a Porsche, a new mansion, anything you want…"

Dionne tuned him out, losing interest in his smooth, slippery speech. Instead of trying to fix the problems in their marriage, Jules had put all his time and energy into running his family's construction business, Fontaine Enterprises. To this day Dionne felt as if she'd never truly known him. He had a temper, but it was his lies and infidelities that had destroyed their relationship. Despite his family pedigree and accomplishments, Jules was the most insecure man she'd ever met, and Dionne had no respect for him.

"Is this about money?" she asked.

Jules barked a laugh, and the sharp sound pierced Dionne's eardrum.

"Of course this is about money. With you it always is. Call off the divorce and I'll increase your weekly allowance by ten thousand dollars. Will that make you happy?"

Disgusted, Dionne stared down at the receiver with contempt. Jules was showing off, talking big, but she knew the real reason he was calling, why he was blowing up her phone day and night. Jules had political aspirations, dreams of being the next mayor of Atlanta, and feared a divorce would tarnish his perfect image. Dionne didn't give a rat's ass about his public persona. Reconciliation wasn't an option, never would be. It wasn't in his DNA to be faithful and honest, and she was tired of making excuses for his poor choices. Their marriage was broken, irrevocably damaged, and nothing could change that. "You know what would make me happy, Jules? A divorce. So revise your initial offer, or take your chances in court in November."

"I made you a generous offer, and I'm even willing to overlook the money you stole from me." His voice was terse, colder than ice. "If you embarrass me or my family in court I'll make your life a living hell, so I strongly suggest you think long and hard about your decision."

Dionne broke into a cold sweat and couldn't stop her hands and legs from shaking.

"Imagine what would happen to your business if the truth came to light."

Panic drenched her skin. Dionne had one regret in life, and it wasn't eloping at nineteen with her first husband; it was confiding in Jules about her past. He was threatening to tell the world the truth about her rags-to-riches success story, and his threats were weighing on her. On the surface, she appeared to be strong, but she was stressed out about the divorce and her future.

"You're not a self-made woman. You're a fraud, and if you don't do what I say, you'll suffer my wrath…"

Dionne was afraid of losing everything she'd worked hard for, but she refused to buckle under the weight of her fear. Jules didn't control her anymore, couldn't tell her what to do, and she was sick and tired of arguing with him. "This conversation is over."

"Like hell it is. It's not over until *I* say it's over. You hear me?"

"Goodbye, Jules. See you in court."

Without a second thought, Dionne dropped the receiver on the cradle, pushed all thoughts of her estranged husband out of her mind and got back to work.

Chapter 2

Two weeks. That's how long security specialist Immanuel Morretti had been trailing Dionne Fontaine. Always from a distance, he kept a low profile and blended into the background, wisely hiding himself in the crowd. He'd followed her husband's instructions to a tee, and was surprised to discover everything Mr. Fontaine had said about his estranged wife was true. She was curt, demanding and obsessed with her looks. Beauty treatments, shopping sprees and spa days were the norm. She loved dining at chic restaurants filled with socialites and celebrities.

Parked under a lamppost in a black Ford Expedition with tinted windows, Immanuel watched the front door of Pathways Center, keeping his eyes trained on the brick building in the middle of Peachtree Plaza. His company, Mastermind Operations, specialized in physical, personal and cybersecurity, and his surveillance division was in such high demand he'd had to hire additional staff last week. Since opening Mastermind Operations in Atlanta three months earlier, he'd been working nonstop—meeting prospective clients, training staff and creating innovative ad campaigns. But since Jules Fontaine had insisted Immanuel personally take on his case, he'd had no choice but to clear his schedule and leave his business partner, Malcolm Black, in charge. Jules Fontaine was not someone you refused, and Immanuel knew working for the esteemed CFO could open doors for him.

Immanuel had committed Dionne Fontaine's daily routine to memory. He'd collected a wealth of information since "meeting" her, but he hadn't uncovered anything incriminating yet. Her husband was convinced she was having an affair with a younger man, and he wanted physical evidence before their November court hearing. That gave Immanuel eight weeks to prove his worth to Mr. Fontaine, and he would.

Yawning, Immanuel leaned back in his seat and rubbed the sleep from his eyes. He'd been sitting in his truck for hours, but had used his time away from the office wisely. He'd read his emails on his BlackBerry, returned phone calls and spoke to his assistant at length.

His BlackBerry sounded, flooding his truck with light. Pressing Talk, he put his cell phone to his ear and greeted his cousin. "Hey, Nicco, what's up?" Immanuel lowered the volume on the radio. "How's married life treating you?"

"Great, coz, I couldn't be happier. You have no idea what you're missing."

"I think I do, and I'll pass. Marriage isn't for everybody, and it damn sure isn't for me."

"I felt the same way until I met my baby," Nicco said good-naturedly. "You'll change your mind once you meet Mrs. Right. You'll see."

Immanuel shook his head, snorted a bitter laugh. "Mrs. Right is a myth, so don't bet on it."

Nicco chuckled, and Immanuel did, too. He didn't talk

to his cousin often, only a couple times a month, but whenever they did, he had a good laugh. Now that he was living in the States, he planned to reconnect with his relatives, starting with Nicco and his brothers, Demetri and Rafael. He was looking forward to getting to know them better.

"How's Hotlanta treating you? Finally settled in, or still living out of boxes?"

Regret tormented his soul. After last year's scandal, he'd had no choice but to close down his offices in Venice. But not a day went by that he didn't think about his family, especially his grandmother, Gianna. They were close, and despite the mistakes he'd made in his past, she'd always been his most fervent supporter. "Dante found me a bachelor pad in Brookhaven, and as of last night I'm all moved in," he said. "I'm starting to like Atlanta—"

"Liar. You're homesick and anxious to return to Venice, aren't you?"

"Far from it. I have my hands full at the office and more work than employees." Immanuel had done his research, taken the time to explore the market, and realized the Peach State was an entrepreneur's dream. It had one of the strongest economies in the United States, and was home to prominent, influential businesspeople. Within months of opening Mastermind Operations, it was *the* agency to the stars. Thanks to his cousins' numerous connections, celebrities and entertainers were flocking to his agency for protection, and business couldn't be better. He had twenty-five employees on his payroll, and planned to double that number by the end of the year. He gave his staff the freedom to be themselves, encouraged them to think outside the box, and was reaping the dividends of trusting his team. Immanuel was contemplating opening a second location in Georgia, and had commissioned his younger brother, Dante Morretti, to find another property in Savannah.

"It sounds like business is booming. Tell me more."

Immanuel did. He told Nicco about his five-year plan, his latest ad campaign and the Fontaine case. It was the big break he'd been waiting for, and if everything went according to plan, he'd be doing business with Fontaine Enterprises for years to come. The Atlanta-based, family-operated company was one of the premier construction companies in the state. It owned dozens of local businesses and had plans to expand into other American markets.

"Jules Fontaine of Fontaine Entreprises? He's a big fish. How'd you meet him?"

"Through a mutual friend."

"I'm glad things are working out for you," Nicco said, his tone filled with warmth and sincerity. "And I'm looking forward to seeing you in December."

"You're coming to Atlanta for the holidays?"

"No, I'm going to Venice for Emilio's wedding. Aren't you going?"

Immanuel raked a hand through his dark brown hair, searching his brain for a suitable excuse. His sister, Francesca, had called him weeks earlier with the news, and as she chatted about Emilio and his fiancée, Immanuel got the sense that his brother had changed his life for the better. He was proud of him, but he didn't want to reunite with the superstar. "I can't go to the wedding. I have to work." He added, "You're an entrepreneur. You know how it is."

"Nothing's more important than family, Immanuel. Never forget that."

That's easy for you *to say. Your kid brother didn't screw your fiancée.*

"I called Emilio yesterday to congratulate him on his engagement, and he sounded great, all excited and amped up. His fiancée is obviously a miracle worker, because the last time I spoke to Emilio he was an emotional wreck."

And for good reason. Immanuel thought of Lucca, and

pain stabbed his chest. His nephew, an adorable five-year-old with curly hair and wide, expressive eyes, had died in a tragic pool accident at Emilio's Greensboro estate. The last time he'd seen his brother was at Lucca's funeral, and Immanuel cringed when he remembered the cruel things he'd said at his nephew's grave site. He'd let his anger and resentment get the best of him, and knew deep down he owed Emilio an apology. But he wouldn't attend his December wedding. Just couldn't do it.

"Coz, I have to go…" Nicco trailed off and didn't finish his thought.

Immanuel heard children's voices, laughter and a door slam.

"I told the kids I'd take them to Chuck E. Cheese's, and they're getting impatient."

"No worries, Nicco. Check you later."

"I'll call you next week. Love you, man."

Immanuel ended the call and plugged his cell phone into the charger. He picked up his energy drink and took a swig from the can. He glanced at his Rolex watch and frowned. Mrs. Fontaine usually worked until six o'clock, but it was seven forty-five, and he still hadn't seen any signs of her. Stretching, he leaned back in his seat and drummed his fingers absently on the steering wheel. Minutes later, the lights went out in Pathways Center, and the front door opened.

And there she was. The most beautiful woman he'd ever seen: Dionne Osman Fontaine. Immanuel bolted upright and peered through the windshield. The sidewalk was her stage, her own personal runway, and as she strode toward the parking lot with an air of confidence, desire shot through his veins.

His temperature soared to unimaginable heights. An erection grew inside his jeans. Immanuel was so aroused, so turned on by the sight of her, explicit thoughts crowded

his mind. Thoughts of kissing her, caressing her and ripping the clothes off her sexy, curvy body. It happened
every time he saw Mrs. Fontaine. His physical reaction
to her embarrassed him, made him feel like a pubescent
kid, rather than a thirty-nine-year-old man worth millions.

As he watched her, he took note of Dionne's graceful
walk. She moved seamlessly, with a grace all her own.
Every hair was in place, and her milk-white coat and black
pantsuit made her look glamorous. He found it hard to
believe she was thirty-five years old. She had the youth
and vitality of a college-aged woman and the taut, toned
shape to match.

Images of Dionne clad in a purple mesh top and span-
dex shorts were engraved in his mind. Four mornings a
week, Dionne took a spin class, and watching her at the
small downtown studio was the highlight of his day. The
master life coach was exactly his type—strong, smart, independent, vivacious—but she was a diva. Someone who
yearned for fame and fortune, and he was through hooking up with shallow, materialistic woman obsessed with
the high life. *And besides, she belongs to another man.
My client.*

His eyes trailed her every move. Petite, with creamy
mocha skin, almond-shaped eyes and righteous curves, it
was no surprise that everyone on the sidewalk stopped to
stare. Her scarlet lips made her mouth look tempting, inviting, and thoughts of kissing her ruled his mind.

Knock it off, chastised his conscience. *Dionne's married to Jules Fontaine—a man who could ruin you in this
town—and if you ever cross the line you'll regret it.*

Immanuel nodded to himself, knew it was true, but continued admiring the Somali-born beauty with the exotic
look. Dionne had her briefcase in one hand, her purse in
the other and her cell phone pressed to her ear. What else

was new? She was addicted to her iPhone and couldn't go five seconds without checking it.

You're a fine one to talk, argued his inner voice.

Curious, he cocked an eyebrow. Immanuel wondered who Dionne was talking to. It was someone special. Had to be. Her eyes were bright, and her smile was radiant. Was her lover on the phone? The man her ex was convinced she was having an affair with? Immanuel hadn't found any evidence of her infidelity and suspected Mr. Fontaine was wrong about his estranged wife being promiscuous. She worked nonstop, even on weekends, and spent her free time at home—alone—not in bars and nightclubs.

Dionne stopped at the rear of her Lexus and popped open the trunk. Immanuel put on his seat belt and turned on the ignition. He didn't want to lose her in the parking lot, and reminded himself to follow from a distance as she exited the plaza. His cell rang, and he glanced down at the center console. His grandmother's phone number appeared on the screen. But he didn't have time to shoot the breeze, so he decided to let the call go to voice mail.

Immanuel looked up just in time to see a short figure clad in dark clothes approach Dionne. He scanned the man's face. The stranger had a desperate look in his eyes, a wild, crazed expression that was frightening, but Dionne was too busy talking on the phone to notice. He was pale and built like a defensive lineman. Immanuel read him like a book, sized him up in ten seconds flat. The guy was a thug, a no-good punk who'd rather rob than work, the most dangerous type of criminal. Immanuel had to act fast.

Sensing what was about to happen, he threw open his car door and took off running across the parking lot. The cold autumn wind sliced through his black button-down shirt, chilling his body to the bone, but he didn't stop. Couldn't. It was a matter of life and death, and he had to reach Dionne before the bastard attacked her, or worse, tried to kidnap her.

His breathing was heavy, ragged, and his heart was beating out of control. Feeling a surge of adrenaline, Immanuel ran faster, harder. Bent on reaching her, he dodged cars and wide-eyed strangers as he raced through the parking lot.

Immanuel heard Dionne scream, watched in horror as the man grabbed her and shook her violently. His stomach fell, plunged to his feet, and anger shot through his veins. What happened next stunned him. Dionne didn't comply with her assailant's demands, instead deciding to fight back. Kicked, punched, scratched at the stranger's eyes and face.

"Stop!" Immanuel shouted. "Get away from her. Let her go!"

The stranger knocked Dionne to the ground, grabbed her purse, and jumped into her car. Seconds later, he started the engine and sped out of the parking lot in her silver Lexus SUV.

Immanuel wanted to chase him down and kick his ass for assaulting a defenseless woman, but he couldn't leave Dionne alone. He didn't stop running until he reached her side. She was unconscious, lying motionless on the ground. Her face was swollen, her bottom lip was cut, and her designer clothes were stained with dirt.

Struggling to catch his breath, Immanuel dropped to his knees, gathered Dionne in his arms and searched the parking lot for help.

Chapter 3

Pain racked Dionne's body, stabbed every inch of her five-foot-two frame, making it impossible to move. She tried to open her eyes, but couldn't. Her limbs were cold, shivering uncontrollably, and her forearms ached. *Where am I?*

Sniffing the air, she detected the faint scent of flowers, and a delicious, masculine cologne that evoked thoughts of French kisses, red wine and dirty dancing. *Cologne?*

Panic soaked her skin. Her head felt groggy, as if she'd had one too many cocktails last night during happy hour. *Did I have a one-night stand? Did I follow some guy home from the bar? Am I lying in bed with him right now?* Dionne deleted the thought, refused to believe it, not even for a second. She'd never hook up with a random stranger, and besides, she'd worked at the office late last night, not gone for drinks at her favorite martini bar with her sisters.

Listening intently, Dionne soaked in the world around her. She heard the buzz and whirl of monitors and machines, a TV blaring, felt a coarse material rubbing against her skin. An intercom came on, and realization dawned. *I'm in the hospital. Why? What happened? Was I in a car accident? Did I crash my Lexus*— Before Dionne could finish the thought, memories flooded her mind. Leaving her office…someone sneaking up behind her…fighting him off…the crippling blow to the head.

Dionne struggled to get air into her lungs. It felt as though a bowling ball were sitting on her chest. Taking a deep breath, she broke free of the violent images holding her hostage. She wouldn't think about it. Wouldn't allow her attacker to victimize her in the privacy of her thoughts. Holding herself tight, she told herself she'd survived, that everything was okay. She was alive, safe, and he couldn't hurt her anymore.

With great difficulty, Dionne forced her eyes open. The room was bright, the air still and quiet. She lifted her blanket and gasped when she saw the cuts and bruises all over her body. The wristband on her left arm listed her name and health care number. More questions remained. Dionne continued to take in her surroundings. A wooden chair sat at the foot of the bed, a crystal vase overflowing with roses was displayed on the side table, and a tall, slim man in a black power suit stood in front of the window.

Dionne narrowed her gaze, sized him up. She needed to know who the stranger was and why he was in her hospital room. *Was he a cop?* Giving herself permission to stare, she admired his profile. The man was a force. A six-foot-six Adonis with olive skin, a full head of jet-black hair and a lean physique. He had specks of salt in his goatee and an imposing presence. He was a man of influence, someone who made things happen, who wasn't afraid of taking swift and decisive action. Dionne guessed he was in his thirties, but wouldn't be surprised to learn he was older. *Is he a doctor?* she wondered, noting his designer threads.

The stranger must have sensed her watching him, because he turned toward the bed and met her gaze. The faint scar along his left cheek only enhanced his rugged, masculine look, and his piercing blue eyes were lethal weapons.

A slow, easy smile crept across his lips.

Dionne's heart skipped a beat, drummed in her ears. She instantly recognized him, knew exactly who the drop-dead sexy stranger was. He wasn't a doctor. He was a Morretti. Had to be. No doubt about it. He had a straight nose and a strong jawline, and looked like an older version of Emilio.

Months earlier, before things went south with her employee Brad McClendon, Dionne had researched Mastermind Operations online. She'd planned to hire Immanuel Morretti's security company to help Brad find his estranged wife and sons. But since Brad had quit and taken his celebrity clients with him, she'd changed her mind about helping him reconnect with his family.

Dionne thought hard. She never forgot a name or a face and recalled everything she'd read about the Italian businessman on his agency's website. He'd spent five years in the Italian military in the special forces division, and had worked for a decade as a personal bodyguard before opening his security business in Venice. On the website, she'd seen pictures of Immanuel with dignitaries, celebrities and high-ranking government officials, and according to the Italian newspaper *La Repubblica*, his agency was second to none.

"Good morning, Mrs. Fontaine."

He spoke with a thick Italian accent, one she was sure drove women wild, but his expression was one of concern. Questions stirred her curiosity, made her wonder why Emilio's brother was in her hospital room. Did Sharleen send Immanuel over to check on her after hearing about her attack? Is that why he was there?

"How are you feeling?"

Dionne cleared her throat and found her voice. "I'm

sore, and more than a little confused," she admitted sheepishly.

"My apologies. Let me introduce myself. I'm—"

"Immanuel Morretti," she provided, pulling herself up to a sitting position.

Surprise showed on his face, coloring his eyes. Immanuel looked rich, like the kind of man who dined nightly on wine and caviar. He carried himself in a dignified way. Thanks to her master's degree in psychology, Dionne was skilled at reading people, and instinctively felt the security specialist was someone she could trust. "You're Emilio's brother and the CEO of Mastermind Operations."

"You're a World Series racing fan?" he questioned, fine lines wrinkling his forehead. "I never would have guessed it."

"Emilio's engaged to Sharleen Nichols, the VP of my life coaching center. I've gotten to know him over the last few months. He's a great guy, and he treats Sharleen like gold."

Dionne watched his face darken, saw his jaw clench tight, and wondered what was wrong. *Are the brothers still estranged? Is that why Immanuel looks pissed? Because I complimented his brother?*

"Can I get you anything? Something to eat or drink, perhaps?"

"No thanks. I'm fine," she replied, shaking her head. "Where am I?"

"At the Atlanta Medical Center. You were robbed outside of your office last night."

Her eyes grew moist, and her lips trembled, but she willed herself to keep it together. "I remember," she said quietly. "But why am I here? I'm fine."

"You were unconscious when I arrived on scene."

"You were there? You saw what happened?"

"Yes, Mrs. Fontaine, I did." Immanuel glanced away

and slid his hands into the front pocket of his pants. "I was shopping at Peachtree Plaza when I heard a commotion and ran over."

"You scared off the assailant… You—you saved my life."

"No, I didn't. *You* did." His gaze was filled with awe, and it seeped into his tone. "To be honest, I came to rescue your attacker. You gave him one hell of a beating, and I was scared if I didn't intervene you'd kill him."

Dionne beamed, feeling a glimmer of pride at his words. "Serves him right for attacking me. He's lucky I forgot my pepper spray at home, or I would have emptied the entire bottle on him."

Like his voice, his laugh was pleasing to her ears and brought a smile to her lips.

"You're a brave woman, Mrs. Fontaine. A woman of incredible strength and heart, and you should be very proud of yourself. Few people would have been able to fight the way you did, and I'm blown away by your courage."

Moved by his words, she soaked up his praise. "Please, call me Dionne."

"Only if you call me Immanuel. All my friends do."

Her thoughts returned to last night, and dread flooded her body. Dionne was curious about what had transpired after Immanuel arrived on scene, and was hoping he could fill in the blanks for her. "What happened after I blacked out? Did the mugger steal my purse?"

"Yes, I'm afraid so, and your Lexus as well."

"Oh, no. My whole world was inside my purse. My wallet, my address book, my iPad." A chilling thought entered her mind. "The mugger knows where I live. What if he's at my house right now? Lying in wait?"

Immanuel strode over to the bed and took her hand in his. He was a calm and comforting presence. Having him nearby made Dionne feel supported and less afraid. She

didn't know if it was because he looked like Emilio—
a man she thought was considerate, compassionate and
kind—or his warm disposition. But she liked his touch
and drew strength from him. "I don't have a security system at my new place. I've been meaning to install one,
but I've been so busy with work I haven't had the time."

"I know it's upsetting, but try not to worry. The police
are investigating…"

*What good will that do if the mugger attacks me in my
sleep?*

"I hope you don't mind, but I took the liberty of calling
one of my technicians to change the locks at your house
and office," he explained. "And if you'd like, he can also
install voice-activated alarm systems at both locations."

"How do you know where I live?"

"I'm a security specialist. That's my job."

Dionne felt a wave of relief wash over her. "Thank you,
Mr. Morretti. I appreciate it. At least I know the crook isn't
in my house, robbing me blind." She was glad Immanuel
was there. "Have the cops identified my attacker? Do they
know who he is? Have they found my car?"

"No, not yet, but they assured me they're working hard
on the case."

"Where's my cell phone? I need to call my family or
they'll be worried sick."

Immanuel released her hand and stroked the length of
his jaw. "I'm not sure if detectives recovered it at the scene,
but you can ask them when they come to take your state-
ment—"

The door swung open, and a slender fiftysomething
nurse burst into the room. Her shoes squeaked as she approached the bed, and her frizzy white hair flapped around
her face. "Good day, Mrs. Fontaine. How are you feeling
this glorious afternoon?"

"Afternoon?" Dionne repeated, confused by her words. "What time is it?"

Immanuel checked his Rolex watch. "It's twelve fifteen."

"I've been sleeping for more than fourteen hours?" she asked, unable to believe it.

"You experienced a traumatic event last night and suffered a mild concussion," the nurse explained. "You need your rest, and for the next few days you'll have to take it easy."

Dionne didn't need rest; she needed a stiff drink, something with a shot of Patrón in it. But she knew her serious, no-nonsense nurse would never honor her request. "I'm thirsty," she said, touching her throat. "May I please get a cup of green tea?"

"Of course. Just let me check your vitals first. I wanted to do it earlier, at the start of my shift, but you were sleeping soundly and I didn't want to disturb you."

"You need your privacy," Immanuel said. "I'll wait outside."

No. Dionne opened her mouth to ask him to stay, but he was gone in the blink of an eye.

"Why did you fight back?" Detective Sluggs asked with a bewildered expression on his fat, fleshy face. "You could have been kidnapped, or worse, killed."

"No, *he* could have been killed, because I wasn't going down without a fight."

The emergency room doctor, a twentysomething brunette with Prada eyeglasses, scrunched up her nose. "I see cases like this every day, and it always amazes me that people are willing to risk their lives over something as trivial as a car."

"It's not about the car," Dionne shot back, annoyed that they were giving her a hard time about the choices she'd made last night. "I work hard for the things I have, and no one has the right to take them from me. *That's* why I fought back."

The doctor and the detective had entered her room ten minutes earlier, just as she was finishing lunch. But five minutes into the interview Dionne had already decided she didn't like either one of them, especially Detective Sluggs. He was curt and condescending, and his head was so shiny it looked as though it had been polished with Pledge. Dionne couldn't wait for him to leave. She'd had a busy morning and needed to rest. With the help of her nurse, she'd called the credit card companies, requested her accounts be canceled, then called her parents. She didn't tell them about the attack or that she was at the hospital, and had to cut the conversation short when her mom told her to make amends with Jules before their November court date.

"Fighting back only makes things worse," Detective Sluggs said. "You should have given the mugger your purse, handed over your car keys, and gotten the hell out of the way."

Dionne hit the veteran detective with a cold, dark stare. *Why does Detective Sluggs have to be such a jerk? Why can't he be sympathetic and understanding like Immanuel?* Taking a deep breath, she asked the question burning the tip of her tongue. "Is that the kind of advice you give your wife?"

"I'm not married."

Why am I not surprised? Of course you're single. You're a chauvinist pig, just like my ex.

"If you had cooperated with the perp, you wouldn't have been hurt," he continued, his tone thick with condemnation. "Next time you're tempted to do something heroic, don't, because it could cost you your life. A lot of these criminals are addicts, and the last thing you want to do is antagonize someone high on crack or crystal meth."

"Detective Sluggs is right," the doctor agreed, fervently nodding her head. "It's better to lose your car than to be beaten in the streets."

Dionne hung her head, stared down at her hands. Were they right? Had she acted reckless last night? Tears rolled down her cheeks, splashed onto her cheap blue hospital gown. But when Dionne heard Immanuel's voice in her head, she slapped them away.

You're a brave woman, Mrs. Fontaine. A woman of incredible strength and heart, and you should be very proud of yourself. Few people would have been able to fight the way you did, and I'm blown away by your courage.

"You shouldn't have been on your cell phone. That was your first mistake."

Her head whipped up, and her eyes narrowed. She felt her blood pressure rise, with the urge to smack Detective Sluggs upside his lumpy bald head. Orange *wasn't* the new black, and since Dionne didn't want to be arrested for assaulting a cop, she wisely kept her hands in her lap. "Are you saying the attack was *my* fault? That I'm to blame for what happened?"

Detective Sluggs made a sympathetic face, but his gaze was dark, and his voice was filled with accusation. "Perpetrators prowl the streets looking for people who are distracted, and you made yourself an easy target…"

Dionne pursed her lips so she wouldn't end up doing something stupid like cursing him out. Although she was annoyed, she gave the detective the floor to speak. And did he ever. He went on and on, spewing his opinions.

"I suspect this was a random, drug-fueled attack, but I want to cover all the bases." He flipped open his white spiral notebook and scanned the first page. "Mrs. Fontaine, do you have any enemies? Anyone who might want to hurt you or scare you?"

Do I have any enemies? Yeah, the entire Fontaine fam-

ily. Jules's older sister, Adeline, had never liked her, and the feeling was definitely mutual. The executive accountant was a control freak who wasn't happy unless she was calling the shots, and Dionne couldn't stand her. There was no love lost between Dionne and her in-laws, but they had nothing to do with the attack. "No, no one I can think of," she answered truthfully. "My husband and I are legally separated and in the process of getting a divorce, but Jules would never do anything to hurt me."

"Don't be so sure. Divorce brings out the worst in people."

Desperate to change the subject, she asked, "Where's my cell phone?"

"We found it smashed to smithereens in the parking lot last night."

Disappointment flooded her body, but the loss of her iPhone was the least of her problems. Anxious to end the interview and leave the hospital, Dionne addressed her doctor. "Have my test results come back?"

"Yes," she said, glancing at the sheets of paper attached to a metal clipboard. "Your CT scan was normal, and you don't seem to have any lingering effects from the concussion. But I'd like you to see the hospital psychologist before I discharge you."

"No, thank you. I'm fine."

"I strongly advise you not to leave. You suffered a traumatic event less than twenty-four hours ago, and it's imperative you speak to a professional to discuss the attack."

"I concur," Detective Sluggs said, stroking his bushy mustache with tender loving care.

Dionne glanced from the detective to the doctor and rolled her eyes to show her frustration. They were giving her a headache, and she was anxious to get away from them. Determined to leave the hospital, whether or not the doctor signed the discharge papers, Dionne searched the room for her clothes. Her Escada pantsuit was probably ripped and dirty, but it was all she had. Besides, she wasn't going to a black-tie event at the W hotel; she would be headed to her office. By the time she arrived at Pathways Center, her staff would be gone for the day, so she wouldn't have to worry about anyone seeing her bruised face.

"I have to return to the precinct, but if you remember anything else about the attack, don't hesitate to contact me." Detective Sluggs promised to be in touch and left the room.

Finally. I thought he'd never leave. Dionne checked the time on the clock. Immanuel should be back any minute now. For some reason, the thought of seeing him again excited her and made a smile balloon inside her heart. He'd spent the entire afternoon with her, and talking to him about her career had momentarily taken her mind off the assault. Though he was serious and soft-spoken, he made her laugh and told amusing stories about his life in Venice. He'd offered to go to the store for her, and Dionne eagerly awaited his return, because once he arrived with the items she'd requested, she was leaving. She was tired of being in the hospital and was anxious to leave, but first she had to get Dr. Pelayo off her back. "I don't need to talk to anyone," she said, speaking calmly, in her most serious voice. "I have a master's degree in psychology, and I know what to do to preserve my mental health. Now, kindly bring the discharge papers so I can sign them and leave."

The silence was so loud it drowned out every other noise in the room. Sunshine seeped through the window blinds, filling the drab, boring space with light, but it did nothing to brighten Dionne's mood. She was frustrated that Dr. Pelayo wasn't listening to her and was losing patience.

"Very well," the doctor said after a long moment. "If you insist."

"Thank you, Dr. Pelayo. I appreciate everything you and your staff have done for me."

"I'll have the discharge papers waiting at the front desk within the hour. Who will be picking you up and driving you home?"

Confusion must have shown on Dionne's face, because Dr. Pelayo continued.

"Someone has to pick you up upon discharge and escort you out of the building," she explained, tucking her clipboard under her arm. "The policy was put in place decades ago to ensure that all patients at Atlanta Medical Center remain safe after their stay—"

"I'm not a child," Dionne argued. "And I won't be treated like one."

The intercom came on, and the women fell silent.

Sitting in bed, doing a slow burn, Dionne pictured herself jumping out her fifth-floor window and running away from the hospital. *Who do I have to bribe to get the hell out of here?* she wondered, trying to keep her temper at bay. *And who came up with this stupid discharge policy? It's the dumbest thing I've ever heard, and I won't adhere to it.*

"I have to release you into the care of a loved one, preferably someone who can stay with you for the rest of the day." Dr. Pelayo's face softened with concern. "Victims often feel fearful after an attack, so it's important you're not alone over the next twenty-four hours. Isn't there a friend or family member I can call to pick you up?"

"I don't want anyone hovering over me. I'd rather be alone."

"I understand, Mrs. Fontaine, and I'm not trying to be difficult, but it's hospital policy, and if I break the rules I could lose my job."

Disappointed, Dionne collapsed against the pillows. *Will this nightmare ever end?*

Chapter 4

Dionne had no argument left in her and reluctantly gave up the fight. Arguing with Dr. Pelayo wasn't helping her cause, so she considered her options. She thought of calling a taxi to pick her up, but remembered she had no purse, no wallet, no money. Phoning her assistant or one of her senior life coaches was out of the question. She didn't want anyone to know about the attack and hoped to keep it a secret. Sharleen was in Fiji with Emilio, her sisters were home with their kids and her parents were at work. Though retired, they both worked part-time to stave off boredom, but Dionne knew if she called them they'd drop everything and rush to the hospital. The problem was, she didn't want them there. She felt ashamed, embarrassed that the mugger had attacked her, and wanted to put the whole ugly incident behind her as quickly as possible.

"Please reconsider calling your husband," Dr. Pelayo urged. "I understand that you're separated, but you need his love and support now more than ever."

No, I don't. I need a glass of Muscat and a hot bubble bath.

"Tragedies have a way of reminding us what's important in life and bring us even closer to the people we love. I think your husband would want to be here with you."

A sharp knock on the door drew Dionne's gaze across the room. Immanuel entered in all of his masculine glory and nodded politely in greeting. Dionne stared at him. So did Dr. Pelayo. The physician was wearing a dreamy expression on her face, one that indicated she was head over heels in lust. Immanuel had that effect on everyone—nurses, housekeeping, doctors—and seemed oblivious to the commotion he caused whenever he entered a room. That made him all the more appealing in her eyes.

"Sorry I took so long to return. Traffic was crazy on the freeway…"

He spoke quietly in a smooth, sexy tone. His voice was seductive, his cologne, too, and when their eyes met Dionne had to remind herself to breathe. He moved with confidence, like a man who had the world at his feet—and he probably did.

"How are you feeling?"

Better now that you're here, she thought, but didn't say. Immanuel was the calm in the midst of the storm, and Dionne was glad he was back. "Almost as good as new."

Immanuel was holding a shopping bag in one hand and a garment bag with the Gucci logo in the other. He placed both items on the bed. "These are for you. I hope you like them."

"What's all this? All I asked for was shampoo and body wash."

"You're going home today, and I figured you'd need something nice to wear."

The shopping bag was filled with sweet-smelling toiletries, everything from deodorant to scented oils and perfume. Dionne unzipped the garment bag, and a gasp fell from her mouth. A navy pantsuit, and a silk scarf were inside. Inside the shopping bag was a shoe box with black red-heeled pumps.

Dionne couldn't believe it, thought she was dreaming with her eyes open. How did Immanuel know her size? Who'd told him that Gucci was her favorite designer? She'd tried on the same outfit last week at Saks Fifth Avenue, but couldn't justify spending thousands of dollars on clothes when Jules was fighting her about money. Touching the lapel of the jacket, she admired the intricate design along the collar of the white ruffled blouse, then quickly re-zipped the bag. "Immanuel, I can't keep this. It's too expensive."

"It's a gift."

"But it cost forty-five hundred dollars."

"It doesn't matter," he said, his tone firm. "You had a rough night, and I think you deserve to leave the hospital in style. Don't fight me on this."

Dr. Pelayo's eyes lit up, and Dionne knew the physician was impressed. So was she. Not because of the staggering cost of the outfit, but because Immanuel—someone she'd just met—had done something kind for her, something her ex never did. Jules had relied on his secretary to buy her gifts, even had her sign the cards on his behalf, regardless of the occasion. *If Jules had been more thoughtful and attentive, our marriage wouldn't have fallen apart—*

"Have you been discharged?" Immanuel asked.

Dionne blinked and broke free of her thoughts. "No, not yet, but I'm working on it."

"Is there anything I can do to help?"

Before Dionne could answer, Dr. Pelayo told Immanuel about the hospital discharge policy and expressed her opinion on the matter. "Mrs. Fontaine is going to need a lot of emotional support in the coming weeks, so it's imperative she reach out to her friends and family for help," the doctor explained. "I'm trying to convince her to call her husband."

Immanuel turned to Dionne.

The heat of his gaze left her breathless and tingling all over. Dionne smoothed a hand over her hair, and winced when she felt tangles in her wavy dark locks. *Is that why Immanuel's staring at me? Because I look a hot mess?*

"Is that what you want? For Dr. Pelayo to call your husband?"

Hell no. Knowing her response would raise eyebrows, she swallowed her retort and shook her head. Dionne wasn't calling Jules, and she wished Dr. Pelayo would stop pressuring her to do so. Besides, Jules would never come pick her up. Work was all that mattered, all he cared about, and that would never change.

"I can drive you home."

Dionne met his gaze. "You can?"

"It would be my pleasure."

"Are you sure?" she asked, moved by his words. "You've already done so much for me, and I'd hate to inconvenience you."

"It's no inconvenience at all. I live in Brookhaven too, remember?"

"That's right, we're neighbors, I forgot." Dionne wanted to break out in song. Now she wouldn't have to bother her family to pick her up, and no one would ever know about the attack. Immanuel Morretti was a hero, a stand-up guy with a heart of gold, and Dionne was grateful for everything he'd done for her in just a short period of time.

A shiver whipped through her body. It frightened her to think what would have happened if Immanuel hadn't come to her rescue last night.

"I'll be back in an hour," Immanuel said, glancing at his gold wristwatch. "I'll go home, swap my McLaren for my SUV and meet you at the front desk at four."

"You don't have to go to all that trouble. I'm just grateful for the ride."

"Are you sure? It's a small sports car, and I don't want you to be uncomfortable."

"I'm positive," she said, blown away by his thoughtfulness. Dionne returned his smile, deciding right then and there that Immanuel Morretti was the most considerate, compassionate man she'd ever met, and she liked him immensely. "I don't know how I'll ever repay your kindness."

"You don't have to. I'm a Morretti, and we're not happy unless we're rescuing someone," he said with a hearty chuckle. Immanuel touched her hand and gestured to the door with his head. "I'll be in the waiting room. Take as long as you need."

As Immanuel and Dr. Pelayo exited the room, Dionne saw the doctor make her move. Resting her hand on his forearm, she leaned into him and spoke in a sultry whisper. *Is she giving him her number? Asking him out? Inviting him over for drinks?*

Dionne sat up and tossed aside the blanket. She told herself she didn't care, and that it was none of her business what they were talking about. But if that were true, then why did she want to jump out of bed and wrestle the pretty doctor to the ground?

"Sorry for making you wait, but I'm ready now."

Immanuel glanced up from the September issue of *Entrepreneur* magazine, saw Dionne standing beside the water dispenser in the hospital waiting room and felt the magazine fall from his hands. Desire careered down his spine and shot to his groin. Immanuel heard his pulse in his ears, pounding, thumping, and he swallowed hard.

Immanuel recognized he looked foolish, sitting there with his eyes wide, staring at her, but he didn't have the strength to turn away. Women who carried themselves with poise and grace had always been his weakness, and Dionne was the epitome of class. The Gucci pantsuit was made for her, created for a woman with her delicious shape. Her fresh face only enhanced her natural beauty.

"Immanuel?"

At the sound of his name, Immanuel snapped to attention. He picked up the discarded magazine, chucked it on the side table and rose to his feet. Smoothing a hand over his suit jacket, he crossed the room toward her. He started to speak, but her floral fragrance tickled his nostrils and his thoughts went off track. The hairs on the back of his neck shot up, and sweat immediately soaked his pale blue shirt. Her beauty was striking, and everything about her appealed to him—her confidence, her resilience, the way she carried herself. Over the years he'd provided security for pop stars, actresses and supermodels, but none of them could compete with the master life coach. But it was more than just her looks. She was a woman of strength and tenacity, and he greatly admired her. She'd fought for her life last night, gone toe-to-toe with a man twice her size, and survived the harrowing ordeal. "Dionne, you're gorgeous."

"It's Gucci," she said with a dismissive shrug. "*Everyone* looks great in Gucci."

"Your beauty has nothing to do with your outfit and everything to do with your smile."

A flush crept over her cheeks. "Thank you, Immanuel. You're very sweet."

And you're stunning. He remained quiet, cautioned himself not to speak his mind. Immanuel was glad he could help Dionne, but he didn't want to freak her out by coming on too strong. She had a presence about her, an intangible quality that intrigued him, and he was looking forward to spending the rest of the afternoon with her. Isn't that what Dr. Pelayo had suggested? That he keep an eye on her? Immanuel planned to follow the doctor's orders, though he wondered how Dionne would feel about him being at her house. "Shall we go?"

"Absolutely. I've been ready to leave for hours."

Walking down the hallway, Dionne moved at a slow, easy pace. She seemed to be favoring her right side, so Immanuel rested a hand on her back and led her into the waiting elevator. She smelled of lavender—his favorite female scent. They were standing so close, he wanted to take her in his arms and crush his lips to her mouth.

Guilt consumed him. Dionne was still legally married, which meant she was off-limits. Putting the moves on a vulnerable woman would be a boneheaded thing to do, so he dropped his hands to his sides. His infatuation with her was spiraling out of control, but Immanuel was determined to control his libido. *I'm horny as hell, but that's no excuse to put the moves on another man's wife,* he told himself, tearing his gaze away from her bottom. *I won't cross the line.*

On the main floor, Immanuel led Dionne past the hospital gift shop, through the lobby and out the sliding glass doors. His car was parked at the curb, and when he opened the passenger door for Dionne she smiled her thanks and slid inside.

Minutes later they were off. Having followed Dionne home from work countless times before, Immanuel knew where she lived, but since driving straight to her house would raise suspicions, he asked for directions. Dionne gave him her address, then turned her face to the window. She obviously didn't want to talk, so Immanuel didn't pester her with conversation. She'd suffered a traumatic ordeal, and despite her outward display of calm, he sensed that she was scared to go home. Immanuel didn't blame her. Her attacker was still on the loose, and the police had no leads.

"It's weird not having my cell phone," she said quietly, glancing in his direction. "I keep putting my hands in my pocket, expecting it to be there, but it's not."

"That's normal, especially for someone who uses their phone as much as you do."

"How do you know I use my phone a lot?"

Immanuel searched his brain for a suitable response, came up empty, and said the first thing that came to mind. "Most people do," he said with a shrug. "Myself included."

"My family thinks I'm addicted to my cell, especially my mom, but she's old-school and doesn't understand the nature of my job. I run my own company, so it's important to be available for my staff and clients…"

Immanuel didn't want to miss anything she had to say, so he turned off the radio and gave her his full attention. It was a challenge, with their arms touching and her heady perfume sweetening the air. But he listened closely and filed information away in his mental Rolodex for a later date.

"How long have you had your business?"

Pride filled her eyes and seeped into her tone. "It will be ten years in January."

"That's a remarkable feat. Most small businesses don't survive the first two years, so you're obviously doing something right."

"Damn right I am," she said. "I'm working my ass off!"

And what a nice ass it is.

"Well, if the life coaching business doesn't work out you can always become a boxer. You have one hell of a right hook."

Dionne cracked up. It did his heart good to hear her laugh. Talking to her about Pathways Center was obviously the way to go, so he asked questions about her business.

"What's your secret?" he asked, wanting to hear more

about her journey to success. The research he'd done on Dionne revealed that she was also a best-selling author and motivational speaker. She charged five figures for every speaking engagement, and was one of the most sought-after life coaches in the nation. "How have you managed to create a successful life coaching business when so many others have failed?"

"Hard work and perseverance are the keys to my success. I wouldn't be here today if I'd wavered, even for a second, about my life's purpose."

"Do you have plans to expand your business in other markets?"

The smile vanished from her lips. "My clinics in LA and Seattle were supposed to open this past summer, but construction has been delayed indefinitely."

"That's ridiculous," Immanuel said, shifting gears as he switched lanes. "Who's the builder, and why haven't you sued them for breach of contract?"

"Because my hands are tied." Her voice broke, cracked with emotion, but she quickly regained her composure. "This project was in the works long before I filed for divorce, but if I'd known my ex would deliberately sabotage the project, I never would have used his family's construction company. The project has been on hold for months, and work probably won't resume until the divorce is finalized."

"How long have you been separated from your husband?"

"Almost a year. Out of respect for his family, I agreed to keep quiet about the separation, but once I filed for divorce the story hit the newspapers and things turned ugly…"

Immanuel frowned. His thoughts returned to weeks earlier. During an hour-long meeting with Jules Fontaine, the businessman had called his estranged wife a conniving manipulator who used her looks to advance her career.

He claimed he'd kicked her out of their Buckhead estate once he'd learned of her infidelity. Immanuel liked having all of the facts and sensed that Dionne was telling the truth. She didn't bad-mouth her ex or blame him for their failed marriage. He respected her for taking the high road.

"Do you mind stopping at the AT&T store on Town Road?" she asked. "I'm expecting several important calls this afternoon, and I'll go crazy if I don't get a new iPhone."

"I don't know," he teased, faking a frown. "Dr. Pelayo ordered me to take you straight home, and I'd hate to get on her bad side."

"Don't worry. What she doesn't know won't hurt her."

Immanuel chuckled. "No problem. We can go anywhere you want."

At the intersection, he turned left and found a parking space in the plaza. They entered the store, and Dionne immediately selected the latest iPhone model, and then approached the cash register.

"With the extended warranty, that comes to $649," the clerk said.

Dionne nodded. "Charge everything to the account on file. I'll be keeping the same plan."

"In order to do that I'll need to see two pieces of ID."

"I don't have any ID. My purse was stolen last night." Dionne peered over the clerk's shoulder and motioned to the door behind him. "Is your manager around? I spoke to her earlier, and she assured me getting a new cell phone would not be a problem."

"I'm sorry, but she's gone for the day."

"Call her. I explained my situation to her, and she was—"

"I can't." He shrugged his bony shoulders. "Come back tomorrow with the proper ID."

Dionne spoke through pursed lips. "Go. Call. Your. Store. Manager. *Now*."

"Ma'am, you're being rude. I'm going to have to ask you to leave."

Hoping to defuse the situation, Immanuel opened his leather wallet, took out his Visa Black Card and handed it to the clerk. "That won't be necessary." He was ticked off that the guy was giving Dionne a hard time, but he didn't let his frustration show. "Charge everything to my account."

"No," Dionne argued, adamantly shaking her head. "I don't want you to pay. All he has to do is call his manager. She'll straighten everything out."

"Don't worry, Dionne. I got this." Winking, he patted her good-naturedly on the hips. That earned him a smile. His chest inflated with pride, filled to the brim. "Hang tight. We'll be out of here before you know it, and you can go home and get some rest. I promise."

To reduce the tension, Immanuel chatted with the clerk about the weather and sports. The man was a huge baseball fan and screeched like a parrot when Immanuel told him Demetri Morretti, the star slugger of the Chicago Royals, was his cousin.

"The Royals will be in town at the end of the month," the clerk said excitedly, rubbing his hands together. "I can't wait to see Demetri play. I hope the game goes extra innings."

Immanuel chuckled. "Thanks for everything, man. You've been really helpful."

"Helpful my ass," Dionne grumbled, snatching the plastic bag off the counter.

"Thanks for choosing AT&T," the clerk said. "Have a nice day."

Outside, Immanuel opened the passenger door and stepped aside. But Dionne didn't get in. "You're too nice," she said, shielding her eyes from the sun. "This isn't Venice, Immanuel. This is Georgia. You better toughen up, or people will walk all over you."

"My grandmother, Gianna, says you can catch more flies with honey than vinegar, and I think she's right. So the next time someone's being a jerk, kill them with kindness. Trust me, it works every time."

"Maybe you're right."

To make her laugh, he joked, "I'm a Morretti. I'm *always* right."

Her smile was fake, forced, and seeing the wounded expression on her face saddened him. He'd said too much. She'd been through a lot in the past twenty-four hours, and the last thing Dionne needed was someone coming down on her. But before he could apologize, she spoke.

"I'm sorry if I embarrassed you inside the store. I didn't mean to. Because I'm petite, people usually don't take me seriously, so I have to raise my voice to get their attention."

"I understand, but don't stoop to *their* level. Let them rise to yours."

"Great advice. I'm going to remember that."

"Are you ready?"

Dionne nodded, but she didn't move. Immanuel didn't either. Couldn't. Felt as if his feet were glued to the ground. Their eyes met, held for a beat. Lust exploded inside his body, threatening to consume him. Their connection was undeniable, but it was nothing he'd ever act upon. He'd been burned by love before, betrayed by a woman he'd thought was his soul mate, and he wasn't going down that road again. Not even for a dime like Dionne. He had to remember that no good could ever come of their being lovers. *That's easier said than done,* he thought.

Dionne stared at him, her gaze strong and intense. His hands itched to touch her, to caress every slope and curve on her delicious body. His pulse quickened, and his thoughts ran wild. *What would she do if I kissed her?*

Would she push me away or kiss me back? Does she feel the chemistry between us, or is it a figment of my imagination?

There's only one way to find out, whispered his inner voice.

Chapter 5

"Immanuel, are you coming?"

Immanuel blinked, just then noticing Dionne sitting in the passenger seat of his car wearing a bemused expression on her face. He inwardly winced. Damn. How long had he been staring off into space? He was out of sorts, and his pretty companion was the reason why. Maybe Malcolm was right. Maybe he *should* start dating again. Get out there and see what the Peach State had to offer. He missed having someone special in his life, and he had no chance in hell of ever hooking up with Dionne.

Immanuel got behind the wheel of his car, started the engine and exited the parking lot. He was content driving and watching her on the sly.

"Why did you relocate to Atlanta?" Dionne said, interrupting his thoughts.

"I needed a change of scenery." He'd been asked the question dozens of times and gave everyone the same answer, but this was the first time he felt guilty about lying.

"I grew up in Italy, but I went to a university out east, so moving here wasn't much of an adjustment."

"What do you think of Atlanta so far? Do you like it?"

"So far, so good. It's a fantastic city. Southern people are incredibly charming, but there's nothing quite like living in Venice."

"I agree. I traveled to Venice last year on business, and I didn't want to come home."

"I take it you enjoyed your trip," he teased, wearing an easy smile.

"I loved everything: The food, the atmosphere, the rich architecture and history, strolling along the canals at night. It was breathtaking."

I know just how you feel, because I'm in complete and total awe of your beauty.

"Did your husband make the trip as well?"

"No." Sadness flickered across her pretty, delicate features. "The more successful I got, the more problems we had in our marriage. By the time our fifth wedding anniversary rolled around, we were living separate lives. It hurts that he couldn't support my dreams the way I championed his."

If you were my woman, I'd support you a hundred percent.

"What do you miss most about Venice?" she asked.

"My family, especially my grandparents. They helped raise me, and I owe everything I am to them. We Skype every day, but it's not the same thing as being there."

"Having Emilio nearby in Greensboro must be nice, though."

If you say so. I've never been to his estate, and I have no intention of ever visiting him.

It was a short drive to Brookhaven. Ten minutes after leaving the plaza, Immanuel pulled in front of a brick colonial-style mansion. Lush green magnolia trees surrounded the property, flower beds dotted the landscaped grounds, and the front porch held a swing and bright, comfy chairs. "This is a lot of house for one woman."

"You sound like my dad. He said I should rent a smaller place, but the bigger the better in my opinion. You only live once, right?"

"That's one way of looking at it."

"No, that's the *only* way of looking at it. I work hard. After a stressful day at the office I love nothing more than coming home to my big, beautiful mansion. Don't you?"

"You're confusing me with my brother. He's the ostentatious millionaire, not me."

"Oh, that's right. You prefer to spend your money on sports cars worth half a million."

"Who told you that?"

"Lucky guess, but you *are* driving a McLaren. They're ridiculously expensive, and I bet this is just one of many luxury cars in your collection."

"You're smart *and* clairvoyant. How fascinating."

Dionne laughed, and Immanuel did, too.

"My father and grandfather were both championship race car drivers, and I developed a love of exotic cars at a very young age," he explained. "They're my guilty pleasure."

"I'm surprised you're not a race car driver yourself."

"I couldn't cut it, but after several fits and starts I discovered my passion and built a successful business that I'm incredibly proud of."

Dionne looked impressed and nodded her head in agreement. "Good for you. As long as you're happy and doing what you love, that's all that matters."

Tell that to my father. In his eyes I'm a failure, and nothing I ever do is good enough.

Putting the car in Park, Immanuel surveyed the neighborhood, searched for anything out of the ordinary. Aside from a woman powering up the block with her golden retriever, the streets were empty. Satisfied nothing was amiss, he got out of the car and walked around to the passenger-side door. As Dionne stood, he noticed the pained expression on her face. He could sense her anxiety and wondered if she was reliving the attack in her mind.

"Are you okay?"

Her eyes were sad, but she nodded. "Yes, of course."

Flowers lined the walkway, perfuming the air with their sweet, fragrant scent.

Dionne moved slowly, as if it required all of her strength, but she flashed a thumbs-up when she caught him staring at her. Immanuel watched her with growing admiration. He'd never seen anyone bounce back so fast after a violent attack, and although she was sore, he knew her spirits were strong. Dionne took her new keys out of her pocket that he had given her at the hospital, but struggled to get the correct one inside the lock.

"Allow me." Immanuel reached for the key ring, and their fingers touched. It was a warm September day, a balmy eighty degrees, but her skin was ice-cold. *She's scared. Scared because the mugger knows where she lives.* Anxious to get Dionne inside, he unlocked the door, pushed it open and disabled the alarm.

The house smelled of cinnamon and vanilla. The decor in the three-story mansion was simple but elegant. Framed photographs, African artwork and glass sculptures decorated the foyer, giving the space a luxurious feel. Hardwood floors, indigo walls and multitiered chandeliers dripping in crystals beautified the main floor, and the arched windows provided natural sunlight.

"It's good to be home," she said softly, entering the gourmet kitchen. "I was only in the hospital overnight, but it feels like weeks since I've been home."

"Are you hungry? Do you want me to make you something to eat?"

"In *my* kitchen?" Dionne laughed, as if it were the funniest thing she'd ever heard. "No thanks. I'm not hungry, just tired. I think I just need a nap."

"I don't mind sticking around until you wake up. Dr. Pelayo asked me to keep an eye on you, and I feel bad leaving you here alone."

"In *my* house?"

She sounded incredulous, looked it, too. Immanuel realized he was out of line. He wasn't her husband or family, and he had no right forcing himself on her. "I come from a large Italian family, so taking care of people is in my blood," he explained, wearing an apologetic smile. "But I'll get out of your hair and let you rest."

"Immanuel, I appreciate your concern, but I'm fine. You've done more than enough today, and you should probably go home to your family. It's almost suppertime—"

"I'm not married, and I have no children. Just a temperamental bulldog who hates me because I'm never home to play with him."

Laughing, Dionne opened the side drawer and retrieved a pen and leather-bound checkbook. "Wait a minute. I can't let you leave until I pay you." She clutched her Montblanc pen in her hand. "How much do I owe you for the clothes and cell phone?"

"Nothing. They're gifts, and I won't accept your money."

"Immanuel, that's crazy. You spent thousands of dollars on me, and I insist on paying you back."

"Thankfully, I can afford it, so please put your checkbook away."

Dionne protested, argued her case, but Immanuel wouldn't budge. He didn't want her check, not when he had more money in the bank than he could ever spend. "Italians are generous people who love spoiling their family and friends." He didn't want to offend her or come across as an obstinate jerk, so he tried to lighten the mood with a joke. "But you know who I *really* like to spoil? Strong, courageous women who fight like Jackie Chan!"

Dionne laughed, and the sound tickled his ears. A strange thing happened when their eyes met. His heart raced, and his temperature soared. His gaze zeroed in on her mouth, and the urge to kiss her was so strong, he could almost taste her lips.

"Fine, if you won't take my money, then I'll make you a hero's dinner next Friday as a token of my appreciation." Her tone brightened. "I'll make you a delicious three-course meal, and we can spend the evening getting to know each other better. I hate to brag, but my prime rib is to die for, and so is my butternut squash ravioli."

Immanuel didn't want to hurt her feelings, so he faked a smile. "That's not necessary, and furthermore I'm not a hero. *You* are."

"Your humility is endearing, but you're not fooling anyone—"

"I did what anyone in my situation would do."

"That's a lie. You bought me a designer outfit to wear home from the hospital, an iPhone 6, and a home security system. No one I've just met has ever been that benevolent."

Immanuel couldn't help but laugh. Dionne was a spitfire, a ballsy, gutsy woman with a great head on her shoulders. He found her fascinating. Few people could have done what she did last night, and the more they talked and laughed, the more he liked her.

"You're a stand-up guy, Immanuel, and now it's *my* turn to spoil *you*." Smirking, her eyes radiant and bright, she joked, "FYI, I *always* get my way. Quit while you're ahead."

Immanuel shrugged a shoulder, tried to downplay what

he'd done last night. "I have sisters, so I did what I'd want someone to do for them if they were victims of a brutal attack."

Her face fell, and the smile slid off her lips. Hanging her head, she shifted her weight from one foot to the other. "Don't say that. I fought back. I'm a survivor. Not a victim—"

Her voice cracked with emotion. Seeing her sadness, the grief that lay naked in her eyes, filled him with guilt. *I should have run faster. I should have reached her before that sick bastard knocked her to the ground.*

Immanuel moved toward her. He knew it was a mistake to touch her, but he couldn't stop himself. Her pain was profound, and he wanted to comfort her. He heard a sob escape her lips, felt her body tense, but she didn't pull away. Immanuel held her tight, close to this chest, tenderly stroking her neck and shoulders. She felt damn good in his arms, like a dream come true.

"Dionne. Dionne. Honey, where are you?"

Startled, Dionne jumped back. "It's my mom." Sniffling, she wiped her face with her hands and straightened her clothes. "I apologize in advance for what's about to happen—"

"There you are." A full-figured woman with a short Afro charged into the kitchen and wrapped Dionne in her arms. "Thank God you're all right. I was scared out of my mind."

"Mom, what's wrong? Why are you crying?" Dionne cupped her mom's face in her hands and wiped the tears from her plump brown cheeks. "Talk to me. What's the matter? When I spoke to you this morning you sounded great."

Standing in front of the French doors, Immanuel watched the exchange with growing interest. He admired the way Dionne treated her mom, how she spoke quietly to her with love and affection. And for some strange reason, seeing them embrace made Immanuel think about Emilio. *Will we ever be real brothers again?*

"I was at work, having lunch in the staff room, when I saw the story of your attack on the twelve o'clock news. I was dumbfounded, and…"

Dionne groaned in despair. For the second time in minutes tears filled her eyes. Immanuel wished he could take her back in his arms and tell her everything would be okay, but he stayed put. It wasn't his place, and he didn't want to earn the wrath of her mother. Like Dionne, her mother was petite with dark brown eyes and flawless skin. She spoke in a heavy Somali accent, and gestured wildly with her hands..

"I—I—I was on the news?" Dionne's voice was loud and panicked, thick with despair. "My clients will think I'm weak, and they'll find another coaching center—"

"The reporter didn't use your name, but I recognized your license plate number," Mrs. Osman explained. "Why didn't you say anything? Why did you lie to me?"

"Ma, I didn't want you to worry. It was nothing."

Mrs. Osman touched her cheek. "But your face is swollen, and your eyes are—"

"I'll survive. Besides, it's nothing makeup can't cover."

"I'm just glad you're okay. I don't know what I'd do if anything ever happened to you."

"Yes, you do. You'd use the insurance money to build your dream house in Somalia."

"Hush your mouth, child. Death isn't something to joke about." Mrs. Osman rested her hands on her hips and glanced around the kitchen. "Where's Jules? He should be here taking care of you. You were mugged last night, and you need him now more than ever."

Dionne groaned. "Mom, please don't do this. I'm tired.

I don't have the energy to argue with you about the sanctity of marriage and my failures as a wife."

Feeling like an intruder inside Dionne's home, Immanuel knew it was time to leave. He'd call later and apologize for leaving without saying goodbye. He turned and strode out of the kitchen, but stopped when he heard Mrs. Osman shriek. Glancing over his shoulder, he was surprised to see both women staring at him with admiration in their eyes.

"You saved my baby?"

Mrs. Osman rushed across the room and threw her arms around his shoulders. She held him so tight he feared his ribs would crack. She kissed him on each cheek, then did it again for good measure. "God bless you, young man. Thank you from the bottom of my heart."

"Ma'am, it was nothing."

Mrs. Osman furrowed her eyebrows, wearing a puzzled look. "You call saving a woman's life nothing? You're a hero, and my husband and I are forever in your debt."

Immanuel sensed it was a bad idea to argue, so he remained quiet.

"You have to join us for dinner tonight. Please, say you'll stay."

"That is very kind of you, Mrs. Osman, but I have other plans." It was a lie, but Immanuel didn't feel comfortable breaking bread with Dionne—not when his attraction to her was spiraling out of control. "All the best in your recovery. And remember what Dr. Pelayo said. Take it easy for the next few days, and don't push yourself."

"I won't, and thanks again for everything." Dionne smiled. "I'll be in touch."

Immanuel strode out of the kitchen, down the hallway and out the front door. Intent on making it downtown before the end of the business day, he hopped in his car and sped out of the cul-de-sac. In all the years he'd been working in the security business, he'd seen it all—extortion, embezzlement cases, kidnappings and even a murder attempt. After talking to Detective Sluggs that morning, he suspected someone in Dionne's inner circle was behind her attack. And the prime suspect was his new client: Jules Fontaine.

Fontaine Enterprises occupied the thirteenth floor of One Atlantic Center. The building was a national symbol of success, an iconic landmark more than three decades old. It stood fifty stories high, and was home to the most revered names in the business world. It was within walking distance of High Museum, Woodruff Arts Center, and premier restaurants, hotels and boutiques.

The lobby of Fontaine Enterprises was filled with marble and granite; everything shone and sparkled. The ten-foot windows offered unobstructed views of the city. As Immanuel approached the front desk, he straightened his navy blue Burberry tie. The receptionist, an Asian woman with fake eyelashes and peach lips, greeted him with a wide, radiant smile. "Good afternoon. Welcome to Fontaine Enterprises. How may I help you?"

"I'm Immanuel Morretti. I'm here to see Mr. Fontaine."

The receptionist opened the black leather-bound book on her desk and ran a gel nail down the right column. She narrowed her eyes and pursed her lips as if she was sucking on a lemon. "Is he expecting you?"

"Yes, of course." On the drive over, he'd called Jules several times, with no success, but the receptionist didn't need to know the truth. He had to speak to the CFO today, and he wasn't leaving Fontaine Enterprises until he did.

"I'm sorry, but Mr. Fontaine is in an important meeting and can't be disturbed."

"No problem. I'll wait."

"Very well, Mr. Morretti. Please have a seat in the waiting area." Her smile was polite, but it failed to reach her eyes. "Can I interest you in something to drink?"

Immanuel glanced over his shoulder and scanned the refreshments on the side table. "If it's not too much trouble, I'd love a cup of warm milk."

"Milk?" she repeated, wrinkling her nose.

"Yes, please, thank you."

The receptionist stood, straightened her orange A-line dress and flipped her long, silky hair over her shoulders. "Give me one moment."

"Thank you, miss. I appreciate it."

Immanuel took out his cell phone, punched in his password and scrolled through his new text messages. He pretended to be absorbed in his task, but he was watching the receptionist out of the corner of his eye. The moment she turned around, Immanuel sped through the glass doors and down the corridor. Having been to Fontaine Enterprises before, he knew exactly where to go. Confronting Jules about his suspicions could cost Immanuel his job, but he didn't care. Doing the right thing was all that mattered, and he was determined to uncover the truth.

At the end of the hall, Immanuel turned left and stopped at the corner office. He knocked on the door, then threw it open. A woman with big hair and fuchsia lips hopped to her feet and fussed with her clothes. Jules sat behind his executive desk, wearing a sly, dirty grin.

"Immanuel, what are you doing here?" Jules spoke to Immanuel, but his gaze remained glued to the brunette's ass. "I'm busy."

"I need to talk to you about Dionne. It's important."

Jules gave a curt nod, rudely dismissing the brunette with a flick of his hands.

The mystery woman fled the office and closed the door behind her. A modern mix of leather, wood and glass, the space was an extravagant display of luxury and wealth.

Certificates and awards were prominently displayed on the mounted wall shelves, but Immanuel wasn't impressed. Born into a rich family, Jules Fontaine had had everything handed to him, though he foolishly believed *he* was the reason for his success. He was a loud, opinionated prick, and if not for his charity work and million-dollar donations, Immanuel would think the man had no heart.

"I don't have time to shoot the breeze, so make this quick."

Of course you don't. You're too busy getting blow jobs from your female staff. There was something about Jules Fontaine that irked him, that set his teeth on edge. He carried himself in a smug manner, as if he owned the world and everyone in it. Immanuel couldn't figure out how Jules—a short, average-looking guy—had scored a woman like Dionne. Immanuel suspected the businessman had showered her with expensive gifts to win her heart.

"Dionne was robbed last night."

He shrugged and leaned back in his chair. "What does that have to do with me?"

"Don't you care?"

"No. She's been acting like a spoiled brat for months, and I've had enough. Hopefully, this assault will knock some sense into her, *literally*." Reclining in his chair, as if he was tanning on the beach, he clasped his hands behind his head and propped his legs up on his desk. "Her attack could turn out to be a blessing in disguise."

Immanuel's eyes thinned, and his body shook with uncontrollable rage. He felt his hands curl into fists and imagined himself punching Jules in the face. He hated men who mistreated women, and stared at the businessman with disdain.

Jules must have sensed what was coming, must have seen the murderous expression on Immanuel's face, because he now wore an apologetic smile. "Forgive me. That came out wrong. What I meant to say was that I hope this experience reminds Dionne how precious life is. I'm her husband, and I deserve to be treated with gratitude and respect."

"Did you have anything to do with the assault? Did you hire that creep to rough her up?"

"What are you, a cop now? I don't answer to you. Now, get out of my office, and don't come back until you have evidence of Dionne's infidelity." A grin claimed his lips. "And I don't care what you have to do to get it—even if you have to set her up."

A chill whipped through Immanuel's body. Everything became clear. Why Jules had hired him. Why he'd insisted he personally handle this case. His experience working on high-profile cases had nothing to do with it. Jules knew about the scandal in Venice—the one that had destroyed his business and his reputation—and thought he could manipulate him into doing something shady to frame Dionne. It was obvious Jules was a jerk, a snake of the lowest kind, and Immanuel wanted no part of his sick, devious plot. "I quit."

"You can't quit. We have a contract."

"Just watch me."

The men stared each other down, glaring at each other with contempt.

"I think you had something to do with Dionne's attack, and since I don't do business with criminals, our contract is null and void, effective immediately."

"If you screw me over, I'll run your business into the ground."

Immanuel turned and walked back through the office. He knew he was doing the right thing, making a wise decision, and there was nothing Jules could say to change his mind. "I don't give a damn what you do. I don't respect men who abuse women."

"I hired you for a reason, and I expect you to do your job."

Stopping, he wheeled around and faced Jules once again. "I'm going to ask you one more time, and this time I want the truth. Did you hire someone to hurt your estranged wife?"

"Of course not. I'd never do anything to hurt her. She's my life, my everything…"

Sure she is. That's why you're screwing other women.

"I need you to watch out for her," he continued. "Dionne has a lot of enemies, and—"

"Really?" Immanuel cocked an eyebrow. "Like who?"

"Dionne isn't the easiest person to work for, and over the years several of her employees have threatened her. Most recently, Brad McClendon."

A sour taste filled his mouth. Someone had threatened Dionne? Why didn't she tell the police? Why was she protecting her ex-employee? Were they lovers?

"Imagine how you'd feel if Dionne got hurt again and you weren't there to protect her."

That's my biggest fear.

"Stay on the case. I'll double your salary."

Immanuel was troubled, unsure of what to do. He sensed Jules was lying to him, saying what he thought he wanted to hear. It was apparent someone was after Dionne. He needed sound advice and knew who to call. "I'll be in touch."

Immanuel then turned and marched out of the office. As he strode down the corridor, his doubts intensified. He couldn't shake the feeling that Jules was playing him, and that was reason enough to stay away from the smug CFO. A meeting with his attorney was definitely in order, because the sooner Immanuel severed ties with Jules Fontaine, the better.

Chapter 6

Dionne loved Mel and Lorna and appreciated their taking time out of their busy day to visit her, but she wanted her sisters out of her house, now. They'd overstayed their welcome, and their incessant questions about the attack and Jules's whereabouts had her on edge. She woke up that morning with the intention of going to the office, but when she looked in the mirror and saw her puffy eyes and swollen face, she decided to work from home. Just as she'd entered her home office, her sisters had arrived with breakfast. As they sat down in the kitchen to eat, Sharleen had shown up with flowers and get-well balloons. Upon learning about Dionne's attack, she'd cut her romantic trip short and promptly returned to Atlanta. Dionne appreciated the sacrifices she'd made and thanked her for being a terrific friend and vice president.

The women sat at the kitchen table, eating and chatting, but Dionne wasn't hungry. Nor was she interested in joining the conversation. It was a challenge to stay awake when all she wanted to do was curl up on the couch and sleep.

Dionne yawned and stretched her sore, achy arms in the air. Tossing and turning all night, she'd had horrible dreams about the attack, nightmares so frightening she was scared to fall asleep. Dionne was nervous about leaving the house, afraid the mugger was outside lurking in the shadows. She wished Immanuel were there to protect her.

Thinking about her real-life hero—the man who'd risked his life to save hers—brought a smile to her lips. What struck her most about Immanuel, besides his good looks, was his kindness and generosity. That's why Dionne wanted to see him again, to return the favor. He'd turned her down twice, but she wasn't giving up. She wanted to do something special for Immanuel, and considered asking Sharleen for advice.

"Dionne, Mom's right." Mel reached for her glass of orange juice and took a drink. "Jules *should* be here with you. He's your husband, and you need him now more than ever."

No, what I need is for you to get off my back.

Mel was a wife and a mother of two, with caramel skin, a slender shape and ridiculously long legs. When she wasn't chasing after her toddler sons, she was doing yoga, whipping up vegan recipes and caring for her elderly mother-in-law.

"You were mugged, and that crook knows where you live." Lorna shivered, as if chilled to the bone. "You shouldn't be by yourself at a time like this. You should be with Jules, in your marital home, not going it alone here in Brookhaven. "

Dionne didn't want to talk about the attack, and she damn sure didn't want to talk about her marriage. Why couldn't her sisters understand that? Why were they being so judgmental? And why were they pushing her to reconcile with Jules? He'd called last night, supposedly to check up on her, but spent the entire conversation talking about himself. He'd been nominated for Atlanta Businessperson of the Year, and wanted her to accompany him to the award luncheon in November. As if. The event was just days before their court date, and Dionne would rather swim with sharks than pretend to be his dutiful wife.

"Jules is a good man, and if I were you I'd reconcile with him before it's too late."

Is she high? Dionne didn't want to argue. Her sisters didn't know what it was like to be in a loveless marriage, and she resented their telling her what to do, especially Lorna. The Atlanta housewife was married to a celebrity manager, the mother of three teenagers and bossy as hell. But Dionne wasn't having it. Not today. She had a mind of her own, a strong sense of self, and she wasn't taking Lorna's stupid advice. "I appreciate your concern, but my marriage is none of your business. You don't know what it was like living with Jules—"

"Dionne, spare me," Mel snapped. "I've been married twice as long as you have, and I've never once left my husband. We make it work, no matter what."

"That's easy for you to say. Francisco is a great husband and father. He'd never dream of stepping out on you. He's loyal and trustworthy. It's obvious he loves you very much."

Lorna reached across the table and patted Dionne's hand. "I'll ask Randle to speak to Jules on your behalf. They get along great, and I'm sure my husband can talk some sense into him. You'll see. You guys will be back together in no time."

"Please don't," Dionne said, shaking her head. "It'll only make things worse, and Jules will be pissed that I told you about his affairs."

Sharleen gasped. "Affairs? As in more than one? Why didn't you say anything?"

"So, Jules is sowing his wild oats." Lorna twirled an

index finger in the air and gave a dismissive shrug of her shoulders. "Big deal. Cheating is not a deal breaker."

"It's not?" Dionne and Sharleen shouted in unison.

"Not to me. As long as my husband pays the bills, respects my role as his wife and gives me a healthy weekly allowance, I don't give a damn what he does in his free time."

Stunned, Dionne couldn't speak. *What is this, the Dark Ages? Doesn't she realize how insecure she sounds?* She studied Lorna's face, searching her eyes for clues. *She's just trying to get a rise out of me, right?* Their mother had raised them to be strong, independent women, and Lorna's views about love and relationships went against everything they'd been taught.

"You know what your problem is, Dionne? You let success go to your head."

Her body tensed and anger pounded furiously through her veins. "Are you saying it's *my* fault that Jules cheated on me?" she roared. "Are you blaming me for *his* mistakes?"

"I'm not condoning what Jules did, but he's not entirely to blame for the problems in your marriage. You modern, career-driven types don't know the first thing about the opposite sex, and you've deluded yourself into thinking you don't need a man, but you do."

Sharleen dropped her fork on her plate and hitched a hand to her hip. "I disagree."

Mel snickered. "Of course you do. You're as misguided as Dionne is."

"I *can* have it all. A career I love, the man of my dreams *and* children if I choose," she said, her tone filled with pride. "Emilio added to my life, but he's not my whole life. I adore him but I had goals and ambitions long before I ever met him, and I plan to fulfill each and every one."

"You're deceiving yourself if you think you can have it all, because you can't."

"How would *you* know?" Dionne shot back. It was her life, and she wasn't going to let her sisters bully her into reconciling with Jules. He'd broken her spirit every time he lied to her, and Dionne was tired of pretending they were living the American dream. Their marriage couldn't be saved, and if Lorna didn't like that, it was too damn bad. "You got married straight out of high school, and you've never worked outside of the home."

Her gaze was dark with venom. "This isn't about me. This is about *your* failed marriages."

"Marriage is hard work, and you can't quit at the first sign of trouble."

"The first sign of trouble?" Dionne repeated, raising her voice. "Mel, don't you *dare* call me a quitter. You don't know what it's like to go to bed every night and not know where your husband is. Jules doesn't want a wife, he wants a puppet, and I can't take it anymore."

"And you shouldn't have to. No one should." Sharleen wore a sympathetic smile, but her eyes glimmered with mischief. "Cheating is a deal breaker to me, so I commend you for taking the high road. I would've doused car with gasoline and lit a match."

For the first time in days, Dionne laughed. Laughed so hard water filled her eyes. Her sisters stared at her as if she were out of her mind, but Dionne didn't care. Joking around with Sharleen made her feel good, less scared and stressed out. Her friend was a positive, optimistic soul, and her words of encouragement bolstered her spirits.

"You have to do what's right for you and *only* you."

"Thanks, girl. I really needed to hear that."

"All great changes are preceded by chaos, and I suspect this is going to be a banner year for you," Sharleen said with a wink. "Hang in there, boss. Things will get better. I know it."

"If you divorce Jules you'll live to regret it."

No one asked you, so mind your own business.

"Adeline called me last night, and we spoke at length about your marital problems," Lorna said in a somber tone, as if she were delivering a eulogy at a funeral. "She's very upset about the separation, and so are her parents."

Of course they are. They act like they're perfect, but they're not. They have flaws, insecurities and fears just like the rest of us.

"Go back home," Mel urged. "It's the right thing to do for everyone involved—"

Hearing her cell phone ring, Dionne excused herself from the table and grabbed her iPhone off the breakfast bar. The conversation was getting too heavy for her, giving her an excruciating headache, and she feared she'd soon say something she'd regret.

As Dionne exited the kitchen, she overheard Sharleen ask Mel about her wedding day. Her vice president was charming, and when Dionne heard her sisters giggle she knew they were eating out of her friend's palm.

The screen said "unknown number," but since it could be a prospective client calling to book a free consultation, Dionne took the call and spoke in a bright, confident voice. "Hello, Dionne Fontaine speaking."

Click. Dionne hung up the phone, and it rang almost immediately again. Same result. Annoyed, she wondered if there was something she could do about it. She made a mental note to ask Detective Sluggs the next time they spoke. All morning, she'd received prank calls, and it was getting on her nerves. It was probably Jules, trying to scare her. Dionne wasn't going to let him intimidate her or pressure her into returning to their marital home. She had everything going for her, and she wasn't going to let her ex call the shots anymore. It was time to stand on her own two feet, and—

Her cell phone rang yet again. Dionne froze, but when she saw the name on the screen, her spirits soared. She cleared her throat and answered on the second ring. "Hello."

"Good morning, Dionne. It's Immanuel Morretti."

A smile bloomed in her heart and spread to her lips. *That* voice. That dreamy, husky voice excited her every time. Her thoughts returned to Thursday afternoon, to the exact moment Immanuel had taken her into his arms and held her close. It was seared into her memory, and for as long as she lived she'd never forget how safe he made her feel. "It's good to hear from you," she said quietly, meaning every word.

"How are you feeling?"

"Terrific. As long as I have wine and chocolate nothing can *ever* get me down."

Immanuel chuckled. "That's valuable information. I'll have to remember that."

For a moment, Dionne forgot about her troubles—the attack, her impending court date, the argument with her sisters minutes earlier—and enjoyed her conversation with Immanuel. He was easy to talk to, a calm, quiet soul, and she appreciated his calling to check on her.

"Have you had breakfast?" he asked. "I'm at the Waffle House near the Brookhaven shopping center, and I thought you might want something to eat."

"That's very sweet of you, Immanuel, but I already ate."

Laughter exploded inside the kitchen, floating down the hall and into the living room. Dionne wondered what her sisters and Sharleen were cackling about, then moved toward the bay window so Immanuel wouldn't hear their boisterous laughter.

"You have company."

"Yes, Sharleen and my sisters came by with breakfast, but they're leaving shortly…" *So if you want to come by for a visit, that would be great.* Dionne wanted to see Immanuel again, but couldn't bring herself to invite him over for lunch. She wasn't used to making the first move, and didn't want him to think she was desperate.

"My apologies for interrupting. I'll let you return to your guests."

Disappointment filled her, but she pushed back her emotions. Immanuel had called to check up on her, which meant he cared about her, right? Feeling hopeful, she expelled a nervous breath and spoke with confidence. "Do you have plans next Sunday? I'd love to have you over for brunch. Or we can meet somewhere in town if you'd like. My treat."

Silence infected the line, and seconds ticked by on the clock hanging above her couch.

"I'm sorry, I can't. I have to work."

"I understand. Maybe next time."

"Take care of yourself, Dionne. Get plenty of rest and drink a lot of fluids," he advised. "It takes several days to recover from a concussion, so don't push yourself too hard."

"You sound like Dr. Pelayo," she joked, hoping to make him laugh.

He did, and her heart swelled with pride. Dionne felt like a teenager again—giddy, self-conscious and nervous—and Immanuel Morretti was the reason. His old-fashioned ways were endearing, and so was his Italian accent. He was the polar opposite of her ex, but that was a plus. Dionne was curious about him, wanted to get to know him better. *What does he do for fun? What are his hobbies and interests? Is he dating anyone?*

"Dr. Pelayo knows her stuff. You should listen to her."

Her spirits sank, and her shoulders drooped. Is that why

he didn't want to come over? Because he was interested in the pretty doctor?

"Bye, Dionne."

She nodded and swallowed the lump in her throat. "Bye, Immanuel. Thanks for calling."

The line went dead, and she slumped against the bay window with a heavy heart. It was times like this Dionne wished her brother, Kwame, were around. They had a strong bond, always had, and every time he called from Melbourne they talked and laughed for hours. He was a forty-year-old web designer, working abroad in Australia, and Dionne missed him dearly. Unlike her sisters, he was supportive and sympathetic and gave great advice.

"Dionne, I have to run."

"Me, too," Mel said. "The boys have a soccer game at noon, and I promised I'd be there."

Breaking free of her thoughts, Dionne followed her sisters to the front door. She could tell by their tight smiles that they were mad at her, but Dionne didn't care. She'd done nothing wrong and wasn't going to apologize for having a mind of her own.

"Kiss the kids for me and tell them Auntie loves them very much."

As her sisters got in Lorna's shiny white convertible, Dionne waved. They drove her nuts sometimes, but they were her family, and she couldn't imagine life without them. Hopefully, Mel and Lorna would be in a better mood the next time they spoke, because the last thing Dionne wanted was for her sisters to be mad at her. *I have enough on my plate as it is.*

Standing on the porch, she felt the sun on her face, the light autumn breeze. There wasn't a cloud in sight, nothing but clear blue skies for as far as her eyes could see.

Glancing up and down the block, Dionne searched for anything suspicious. *Is the mugger nearby? Is he watching me right now? Plotting his next move?* At the terrifying thought, perspiration drenched her skin in a cold sweat. Dionne focused her gaze, giving her property a thorough search. Finding nothing, she sighed in relief. Later, after her nap, she'd call the police and get an update on the case. Not knowing what was going on was nerve-racking.

Dionne returned to the kitchen and found Sharleen standing outside on the patio deck, talking on her cell phone in Italian. She'd been taking Italian language classes for months and enjoyed practicing with Emilio. Dionne guessed Sharleen was making plans with him, something wonderfully romantic. They were always calling and texting each other, and when her vice president wasn't at the office, she was out and about with Emilio. Dionne was thrilled for Sharleen, glad her friend had found a loving, supportive man who treated her like a queen.

I didn't, but I have no one to blame but myself.

"You should go in the living room and rest." Sharleen closed the patio door, joined Dionne at the kitchen sink and took the soap sponge from her hands. "I can finish up in here."

"Let's do it together. We can brainstorm new ad campaigns while we clean."

Sharleen beamed. "*Or*, we can talk about my Venice wedding."

Sharleen talked, and Dionne listened. She had questions about Immanuel—lots and lots of questions—but since she didn't want to give her friend the wrong impression, she wisely kept her thoughts to herself. "How did you find out about the attack?" Dionne asked, curious.

"Annabelle saw the story on the evening news and called me right away."

Why am I not surprised? "Juicy gossip" should be her middle name.

"You're the heart and soul of Pathways Center, so I'm glad that you're okay."

"Thanks, Sharleen. Me, too."

"Will you be in tomorrow?" Sharleen asked, returning the cleaning supplies to the closet.

"I'm going to work from home this week, but I'll definitely be in Friday."

Sharleen cheered. "Good, so we can head straight to the spa after work. I could use a hot stone massage, and I bet you could, too."

"You can say that again. It's been a hell of a week, and I can use a bit of pampering."

"I hear you. Planning a wedding in a foreign country for 250 guests is stressful. If Emilio invites one more person I quit, and we're eloping to Vegas."

Dionne cracked up, laughed out loud when her friend made a silly face.

"Do you like baseball?" Sharleen asked, sliding her cell phone into her back pocket. "Emilio's cousin Demetri plays for the Chicago Royals, and he invited us to watch his World Series game from his private luxury box. It's on the twenty-ninth. What do you say?"

Dionne opened the fridge and grabbed the bottle of juice. "I better not," she said, filling two glasses. "I know nothing about baseball, and I don't want to embarrass myself."

"You have to come. There'll be terrific food, an open bar, and plenty of opportunities to network with influential people and wealthy baseball executives."

"Why didn't you say that sooner? Networking is my specialty," Dionne said with a laugh. "Count me in. I'd love to go."

The women clinked glasses and shared a smile.

"Will Immanuel be there?"

Sharleen raised an eyebrow. "I don't know. Why? Do you like him?"

"Of course not. I'm just curious, that's all."

"I still can't believe he rescued you from that deranged mugger on Thursday. Crazy, huh?"

You can say that again, Dionne thought, exiting the kitchen. *Even crazier? I can't stop thinking about him, and last night I dreamed he kissed me.*

Dionne entered the living room and flopped down on the couch.

"I can't wait to meet Immanuel. What's he like?"

He's wordly, sophisticated and hot, Dionne thought. Taking a deep breath to calm her raging heartbeat, she opened up to Sharleen about the attack, her hospital stay, and all the kind and thoughtful things Immanuel had done for her. "I offered to write him a check when he brought me home on Friday, but he refused."

"I'm not surprised. He's a multimillionaire. He doesn't need your money."

Dionne felt her eyes widen and her jaw drop. "A multi-millionaire? Wow, who knew the security business was so profitable? Girl, we should buy shares in Mastermind Operations."

Sharleen cracked up. "I know, huh? Emilio and Immanuel's brother, Dante, is a real estate developer, and he had encouraged them to invest in the real estate market. Emilio says it's the smartest decision he's ever made." She added, "Besides proposing to me, of course."

"Okay, I get it, Immanuel doesn't need my money, but I'd still like to do something special for him," she said. "Every time I invite him over he turns me down, and it's frustrating."

"Then kidnap him. Once he's your hostage you can have your way with him."

Dionne laughed, but an idea sparked in her mind. Excitement warmed her skin, and goose bumps exploded across her chest. Dionne knew just what to do to thank Immanuel— her tall, dark and handsome hero—and couldn't wait to see the look on his face when she surprised him. She'd need a few days to arrange everything, but she was confident her plan would work. "Sharleen, you're amazing," she praised, leaning over and giving her friend a one-arm hug. "You just helped solve my problem."

"I did?" she asked, surprise coloring her cheeks. "What are you going to do?"

Dionne smirked. "Girl, if I tell you, I'd have to kill you!"

Chapter 7

Immanuel was supposed to be working. He had emails to answer, cases to review and memos to write, but he couldn't stop thinking about Dionne. He wondered if going to the gym would help take his mind off the fearless lady with the effervescent personality—

No, argued his inner voice. *You'll just obsess about her while you're at Sampson's Gym.*

His gaze landed on the wall clock hanging above his office door, and his eyes narrowed. Every day at six o'clock, he called Dionne to check in with her. Their conversations were brief, only a few minutes, but he looked forward to hearing her voice at the end of the day. It had been a week since the attack, and every day she sounded stronger and more upbeat. He'd called her cell phone twice, but with no luck. The suspense was killing him, driving him insane. Dionne wasn't his girlfriend and he had no claims on her, but he hated not being able to reach her. He felt in his gut that something was wrong and considered going to her home to check on her. *After all, we're neighbors*, he reasoned. *That's what neighbors do. They look out for each other.*

Immanuel picked up his desk phone, but he didn't hit Redial. Something held him back, preventing him from dialing. It was his attraction to Dionne, the white-hot chemistry they shared. He was playing with fire, and feared if he wasn't careful he'd end up doing something he regretted—like kissing her passionately the next time he saw her.

Dropping the phone in the cradle, he picked up the manila envelope beside the pendant lamp. The package had arrived that morning via UPS, but Immanuel still hadn't decided whether or not he was going to Demetri's game. He loved baseball and didn't have any plans that particular night, but he didn't want to go to the stadium alone. If his sister were in town she'd go to the game with him, but Francesca was in Italy visiting relatives and wouldn't be back in Atlanta until after Emilio's wedding. Immanuel thought of inviting Malcolm, but the last time they attended a sporting event together, his friend had ditched him for a voluptuous redhead and hadn't resurfaced until the end of the game.

His thoughts wandered, returning to the woman who'd starred in his dreams last night. *Does Dionne like baseball? Should I invite her to the game?* Demetri's luxury suite would be filled with friends, family and associates, and Immanuel wanted to have someone to enjoy the game with— someone witty and fun. He knew only one woman who fit the bill.

Staring out the window, Immanuel leaned back in his leather executive chair. His mind returned to last Friday, and images of Dionne filled his mind. On the drive from the Atlanta Medical Center to Brookhaven they'd talked with ease, as if they'd known each other for years, rather than a few hours. He appreciated Dionne's candor, found her honesty refreshing. Immanuel didn't have any female friends and liked hearing Dionne's take on relationships, business and pop culture.

"Man, you're a pitiful sight…"

Immanuel blinked, spotting his business partner, Malcolm Black, standing in the doorway, and straightened in his chair. He scooped up his pen and made notes on the document sitting on the middle of his desk, pretending to be hard at work. "I'm just taking a short break," he said, feeling the need to defend himself. "It's been crazy busy around here, but I've made a ton of progress on the online marketing campaign—"

"Busy my ass. You haven't done jack shit all day, and you know it."

Malcolm closed the door, marched into the office and plopped down on the edge of Immanuel's L-shaped mahogany desk.

"Man, is everything okay? You've been acting strange."

"I'm good. Couldn't be better."

"Liar! Either you're in love or you're having a nervous breakdown. Which one is it?"

Immanuel gave a hearty laugh. "None of the above."

"Good. Just checking." Malcolm turned serious, wore a pensive expression on his face. He spoke openly about staff concerns, his goals for the agency and security practices he wanted to implement for high-profile clients.

Immanuel lost his focus. He glanced discreetly at his watch, saw that it was six thirty, and decided to call it a day. No use staying at the office. His thoughts were on Dionne, and he wouldn't be able to get anything done until he heard from her.

"Mr. Fontaine made a second payment today," Malcolm said. "And it was five figures."

Immanuel groaned. Damn. That's the last thing he wanted to hear.

"I called his office to alert him of the error, but his secretary said you'd know what the additional payment was for. Fill me in."

The case was confidential, deeply personal, and Immanuel didn't feel comfortable discussing it with Malcolm. His partner sucked at paperwork and couldn't write a memo to save his life, but he was the heart and soul of the agency. Efficiency improved once the former navy SEAL took over the HR department. Everyone on staff loved Malcolm's gregarious personality. If he told his friend about his feelings for Dionne—that he was romantically interested in her—the whole office would know by the end of the week.

"Does the additional payment have something to do with Mrs. Fontaine's brutal attack?"

Needing a moment to think, Immanuel nodded absently. Annoyed at himself for not standing his ground last Friday at Fontaine Enterprises, he plotted his next move. Jules had him backed into a corner and had effectively bought his silence by issuing a second payment. Even though Immanuel suspected Jules had something to do with Dionne's attack, he couldn't prove it, and if he pissed off the CFO it could cost him his career. *I'm too old to start over again. Mastermind Operations Atlanta* has *to work. This is my last chance.*

"Mr. Fontaine is worried about his estranged wife and wants additional security for her."

"That's odd. Most divorcés pay to kill their spouses, not keep them alive." Malcolm exploded in laughter as if his joke were the funniest thing he'd ever heard. "I heard Mrs. Fontaine is a battle-ax, so I'm not surprised she has enemies."

"Who told you that?"

"One of her female life coaches. I met Annabelle a few weeks ago at Sampson's Gym, and she had nothing nice to say about her boss."

Was Annabelle the disgruntled employee out to get Dionne?

"That's not my perception of her at all. To be honest, she's one of the most fascinating, interesting women I've ever met and I've worked with some of the biggest stars in the world."

"It sounds like *someone* has a crush on Mr. Fontaine's wife."

"I'm just calling it as I see it," Immanuel said with a shrug. "Sometimes being the boss sucks. I know firsthand how stressful it is to man a successful company. You don't know who to trust, and your employees will stab you in the back without a second thought."

"This isn't Venice, Immanuel. What happened in Italy isn't going to happen here."

I sure hope not.

"I look forward to meeting Mrs. Fontaine. I heard she has a lot of celebrity clients. Befriending her could be great for Mastermind Operations."

"I think you're going to like her. She's strong, fearless and successful in her own right."

And did I mention she's ridiculously beautiful, too?

"Then assign *me* to her case, because I could use a sugar mama."

An idea suddenly came to Immanuel. It was the answer to all of his problems. He'd give Jules exactly what he wanted. He'd assign his best employee to Dionne's case to follow her until her attacker was caught. He felt a dull ache in his chest, a familiar pain. Immanuel hadn't done anything wrong; he was just doing his job, but his guilt was tremendous. *Should I tell Dionne the truth? Will she understand, or lash out at me in anger?*

"Let's split the money in half, right down the middle." Wearing an intense face, Malcolm hopped to his feet and pleaded his case with conviction. "I could use a new set of wheels."

"Another one? But you just bought a classic Mustang last week."

"A man can never have too many toys." He added with a sly grin, "Or women."

Immanuel turned off his computer. He had to get going. Anxious to see Dionne, he picked up his car keys off the desk and stood. As he grabbed his suit jacket off the back of his chair, he caught sight of his reflection in the wall mirror. He hated the scar along his jaw, hated the man who'd put it there even more. Every time he thought about that fateful night, anger consumed him. Casting aside the bitter memory, he swallowed hard. "I'm heading out now. Do you mind locking up?"

Malcolm whistled, made a show of looking at his diamond wristwatch. "This is a first. You must have somewhere important to be because you never leave the office before sunset."

His partner was fishing for information, but since telling him about his plans would inevitably come back to haunt him, Immanuel changed the subject. He loved Malcolm like a brother and couldn't have asked for a better business partner, but he didn't want anyone to know his feelings for Dionne, especially not the office gossip. "What are you getting into tonight?"

"You mean *besides* the Brunson twins?" Malcolm popped the collar on his navy blue dress shirt. "They practically begged me to come over tonight…"

Immanuel stood there listening to his business partner brag about his sexual conquest and felt a mixture of pity and disgust. *Will I turn out to be just like Malcolm one day? Is this what I want? To be a forty-five-year-old bachelor with no wife, no kids and no future?* Immanuel would never admit it to anyone, but he was jealous of his cousins. By all accounts, Demetri, Nicco and Rafael were living the American dream. Hell, so was Emilio. They had fantastic careers, success and most important, the love of good women. *What do I have?*

A big house and no one to share it with, that's what, answered his inner voice.

As Immanuel exited his office with Malcolm in tow, he thought about the last conversation he'd had with his grandmother, Gianna. He heard her soft, soothing voice playing in his mind as he stalked down the dimly lit corridor.

I'm not getting any younger, mio figlio, and neither are you. I want to see you get married before I die. Is that too much to ask?

Moved by her heartfelt plea, he'd promised to do as she asked, to look for a suitable bride, but he was no closer to settling down than Malcolm was. The past three years had been plagued with highs and lows—more lows than he cared to admit—but Immanuel was through feeling sorry for himself. His fiancée was long gone, and she wasn't coming back. It was time to move on, to find his soul mate and bring her home to his beloved grandmother. *I wish I could meet someone like Dionne*, he thought.

No, you don't, argued his inner voice. *You wish you could have her for yourself.*

The reception area was deserted, and the air held the faint scent of coffee. His stomach groaned, releasing a torrent of rumbles, but food was the last thing on Immanuel's mind. He was worried about Dionne, afraid that she'd met ill will, and—

A blinding light flashed in the reception area, drawing Immanuel's gaze across the room. A white limousine with tinted windows stopped at the curb, and the driver jumped out. He marched briskly around the car, opened the passenger door and stepped aside.

Immanuel hung his head. *Damn. What is Mr. Fontaine doing here?* The CFO had arrived at Mastermind Operations in a limo weeks earlier. *What does he want now? Hasn't he done enough? Why won't he back off, and let me do my job?*

"Looks like you have a visitor." Malcolm clapped a hand on Immanuel's shoulder and gestured to the corridor with a flick of his head. "Go out the back. I'll get rid of him."

Shaking his head, he masked his frustration with a smile. Mastermind Operations was his life, his brainchild, and he wasn't going to shirk his responsibilities because he disliked his newest client. But once he got rid of the cocky CFO, he was going to find Dionne. "Don't worry. I got this. I can handle Jules Fontaine."

Immanuel stuffed his keys into his pocket and buttoned up his suit jacket. He was quickly glancing around the reception area, ensuring everything was in order, when he heard Malcolm gasp. "Lord have mercy. Feet don't fail me now."

Immanuel looked up just in time to see Dionne emerge from the backseat of the limousine. She straightened to her full height, ran her hands along the side of her black couture gown, and glided—not walked—down the sidewalk. It was a dress intended to turn heads, and it did. Everyone on the street stopped and stared.

Time slowed, crawled to a stop. For the first time in Immanuel's life he was speechless, couldn't do anything but stare. He felt a mixture of apprehension and relief. He was glad that Dionne was okay, but the sight of her dressed to kill in a figure-hugging lace dress and knee-high leather boots took his breath away.

His eyes appraised her look, admiring every aspect of her appearance—the side ponytail, the dramatic makeup, the gold teardrop earrings that grazed her shoulders. Immanuel liked the cut of her dress, liked how it skimmed her curves and hips.

"Who is *that*?" Malcolm asked, licking his lips. "And where has she been all my life?"

"That's Dionne Fontaine."

His jaw dropped, and his eyes widened. Seconds passed before Malcolm spoke, and when he did, his voice was filled with awe. "How did Jules score a honey like that?"

Your guess is as good as mine. He doesn't deserve her. Never has, never will.

"It's an open secret that Jules cheats on her, but why? If that were my wife I'd burn my little black book, quit my job and work from home."

That makes two of us. I'd probably never leave the house again.

"Damn, she's coming this way." Malcolm raked a hand through his hair and straightened his burgundy dress shirt. "How do I look? Are my clothes okay? Do you think she'll like me?"

Immanuel chuckled, couldn't help it. His partner was losing it. Unfortunately, he knew how Malcolm felt. Dionne had that effect on him, too, and it took every ounce of his self-control not to crush his lips against her mouth every single time she smiled at him.

Dionne entered the office, moved toward him with deliberate intent. She had a lovely face and sexy lips, and her walk was mesmerizing. She always looked like a star, as if she were at a red carpet event. Tonight was no exception. Everything about Dionne's appearance excited him, made him want to kiss and stroke her.

Immanuel wiped his brow with the back of his hand. He was sweating, burning up in his tailored suit, and his throat was bone-dry. Her fruity perfume filled the air, tickled and teased his nostrils. The scent made him hanker for a cold glass of strawberry lemonade.

Her eyes were on him, watching him, appraising him, and Immanuel wondered what she was thinking. Dionne waved, blessed him with a smile, and his brain turned to mush. He couldn't think, couldn't speak, felt his pulse beating erratically.

Taking a deep breath helped Immanuel gather himself. He was a grown-ass man, a Morretti no less, and nothing could rattle him—not even a seductive woman with curves like a winding road—so he nodded politely at Dionne and slid his hands into his pocket.

Feeling confident and back in control, Immanuel stepped forward and offered his right hand in greeting. Dionne pretended it wasn't there and touched his forearm. His heart lurched, froze inside the walls of his chest, and his flesh quivered with uncontrollable need. Dionne leaned in, pressed herself flat against him, and kissed him on each cheek.

Desire singed Immanuel's skin, set his body ablaze. Her smile was dazzling, so bright it could light up the city center, and if they were alone he would've returned the gesture, kissed her hard, passionately, with fire and desire. He craved her, longed to have her in his arms and in his bed. His feelings for her were insatiable, out of control. But since Immanuel would never do anything to compromise his reputation, he tore his gaze away from her mouth and stepped back.

"Wow, Immanuel, you look amazing," she gushed. "Very dashing and debonair."

Malcolm cleared his throat and stepped forward. "I'm Malcolm Black, co-owner of Mastermind Operations," he said with a wide, toothy grin. "Welcome to the agency, Mrs. Fontaine. To what do we owe this pleasure?"

"I'm taking your partner out for dinner tonight."

Malcolm cocked an eyebrow. "Is that right? Funny, he never mentioned it."

"That's because it's a surprise."

"Sounds intriguing," Malcolm said, stroking his jaw. "Tell me more."

But she didn't. Dionne turned to Immanuel and gave him her undivided attention. Her gaze was on him, glued to his face, and she spoke in a reverent tone of voice. "This is my way of saying thank you for everything you've done for me."

"You've expressed your gratitude several times—"

"I know, but I want to do something *extra* special for you." Her eyes shimmered with excitement, and a smile warmed her moist red lips. "You have to eat, and I have to eat, so we might as well do it together. Shall we?"

"It doesn't look like I have much of a choice."

"That's because you don't."

Immanuel wanted to protest, but when Dionne winked at him he forgot what he was going to say. She was trying to impress him, to prove she had deep pockets, but it wasn't necessary. There was nothing sexier than confidence, and she was swimming in it. That's what intrigued him about her.

"Let's go. We have a fabulous night ahead of us, one you won't soon forget." The matter decided, she stepped forward and looped an arm through his. Dionne led him through the building, out the front door and to the waiting car.

The limousine driver bowed chivalrously at the waist, then opened the passenger door.

"Do you always drive around town in a limo?" Immanuel asked, cocking an eyebrow.

"I wish. My car's still MIA, so I decided to rent something fancy for our date..."

Our date? Her words echoed in his mind. *Is that what this is? A date?* A grin claimed his mouth. Immanuel hadn't been out in months. Not since his disastrous double date with Malcolm and the Brunson twins, and he liked the idea of spending some time alone with Dionne. "Do the police have any suspects in custody?"

"No, unfortunately they don't. I spoke to detectives this morning, and they assured me they're working hard on the case, but I've lost all hope of them ever finding my Lexus. It's probably been stripped of its parts and sold to a chop shop by now."

"Stripped of its parts and sold to a chop shop? Where did you learn to talk like that?"

"I watch TV. I know what's up." Dionne climbed inside the limousine, crossed her legs, and patted the seat beside her. "Get in. You can tell me about your day on the way to the restaurant, and if you play your cards right I just might give you a glass of Cristal."

"Where are we going?"

"It's a surprise."

Chuckling, Immanuel ducked inside the car.

Chapter 8

Bacchanalia, the most expensive restaurant in the state of Georgia, was praised for its Southern hospitality, celebrated for its unique seasonal menu and envied for its esteemed clientele. But what Dionne loved most about the establishment was the romantic ambience. Vintage mirrors hung from the ivory walls, bronze candelabras showered the restaurant with light, and fine china beautified the round tables. The air held a savory scent, one that roused Dionne's hunger. Her mouth watered and her stomach grumbled at the tantalizing aromas wafting out of the kitchen.

Entering the waiting area, Dionne scanned the dining room. TV personalities, the mayor of Atlanta and socialites dripping in diamonds were living it up—eating, drinking and laughing as though there were no tomorrow. The patrons were illustrious, the mood was festive, and the silver-haired piano player was so talented, diners were moving and grooving in their seats.

"Welcome to Bacchanalia." The maître d', a slim man with blue eyes, gave a polite nod. "The private dining room is ready. Please follow me."

Dionne stepped forward, but Immanuel didn't move.

"A private room?" Wrinkles creased his forehead, and a scowl bruised his lips. "This is crazy. I should be treating *you* to dinner. Not the other way around."

Unsure of what to say in response, Dionne took a moment to gather her thoughts. In the limousine, on the drive over to Mastermind Operations, she'd rehearsed her speech to perfection, yet when she saw Immanuel her confidence deserted her. It was happening again. Her skin was cold and clammy, and her tongue was stuck to the roof of her mouth.

Hurry up, urged her inner voice. *Say something or he'll leave.*

Determined to salvage their date, Dionne moved closer to him and rested a hand on his arm. Damn. Like the rest of him appeared, it was hard, muscular and firm. Dionne blinked, chided herself to focus. It had taken several days to pull everything together, and she wasn't going to let anyone—not even the guest of honor—ruin her plans.

"You can pay for dinner next time." To lighten the mood, she added, "And I suggest you save up, because I have *very* expensive taste, and a *very* healthy appetite."

Immanuel didn't laugh. His mouth was set in a frown, and his arms were crossed.

"Dionne, I don't like this. This isn't me."

"You don't like what?"

"You paying for dinner. I'm old-school, and where I come from, men pay for everything."

"Well, I'm new school, and where I come from, women can do it all, *including* pay the check." Dionne inclined her body toward his, but didn't speak until he looked right at her. "You saved my life. If not for you, I wouldn't be here today. So please don't fight me on this—"

"You're giving me too much credit. I'm not a hero, Dionne. *You* are." Pride shone in his eyes. "You're my hero! You opened a can of whoop-ass on that creep, and I bet from now on he'll think twice about robbing innocent people."

"I sure hope so, because if he tries me again I won't go so easy on him."

"Let's meet halfway," he said, sliding his hands into the front pockets of his dress pants. "You pay for dinner, and I'll leave the tip. Deal?"

Dionne patted the lapel of his suit jacket. "Immanuel, don't worry. I got it."

"I insist."

"Are you always this difficult?"

"Yeah, I am," he confessed, wearing an impish smile. "I'm a Scorpio, *and* Italian, so you don't have a chance in hell of winning this argument."

"Fine, if it'll make you happy, you can leave the tip."

"I'm overjoyed."

"No," she challenged, pointing a finger at his chest. "You're a pain in the ass."

Chuckling, he took her hand in his and gave it a light squeeze. Desire prickled her skin. Dionne felt like the belle of the ball when Immanuel wrapped an arm around her waist and pulled her close to his side. He made her feel protected, as if her well-being mattered more than anything. It was a heady feeling.

Stealing a glance at him, Dionne admired his handsome profile. It was impossible to keep her eyes off him. He had a face made for magazines, a lean, toned physique, and a voice so sexy her ears tingled every time he spoke. He looked sexy in his slim-fitting navy suit, but it was how confidently he moved that captured the attention of every woman in the room. Immanuel Morretti was the hottest thing to come out of Italy since Versace, and he was with *her*. Dionne was proud to be his date, and not just because he was a hottie. He was a gentleman, a class act, the kind of guy women couldn't help but love.

Dionne spotted a familiar face across the dining room and strangled a groan. Adeline. *Someone* must *have it out for me*, she thought, drawing in a deep, calming breath. Jules's sister was a busybody who wasn't happy unless she was telling someone what to do. The executive accountant ran a tight ship at home, and everyone in the Fontaine family, including her toddler son, knew better than to cross her. Her eyes were daggers, and her lips were a hard line. As Adeline approached, Dionne stopped and nodded her head in greeting. "Hi, Adeline," she said with a polite smile. "How are you doing?"

"Scheming gold digger," she spat, through clenched teeth. Adeline brushed past her and continued through the restaurant with her friends—two successful business women Dionne had had in her home as guests on several occasions. The pair ignored her, but they made eyes at Immanuel.

"They looked happy to see you."

"The woman in the mauve cocktail dress is my ex's sister, and we don't get along."

"Why not?" he asked, raising an eyebrow.

"We're both opinionated, headstrong women. We clashed from day one."

Entering the private dining room, Dionne took in her surroundings. It was an elegant, intimate space filled with glass vases overflowing with long-stemmed red roses and scented candles. Stars twinkled, showering the space with a faint, sultry light. The crescent moon in the night sky provided a romantic backdrop.

Immanuel pulled out Dionne's chair. "Have a seat, beautiful."

"I love fine dining, and this meal is going to be epic, so the sooner we start eating the better."

Amusement twinkled in his eyes. "Epic, huh?"

"You just wait and see."

"A Hero's Dinner?" Frowning, he picked up the glossy white card on his plate and read the personalized menu aloud. "The Good Samaritan signature cocktail sounds interesting."

"You'll love it. It's made with Campari and orange juice and tastes a lot like Negroni."

"What do *you* know about Negroni? It's an Italian cocktail that's decades old."

"I know a little somethin' somethin' about Italian cuisine. I've done my research."

"Wow, I'm impressed. There's never a dull moment when you're around, is there?"

"I feel the same way about you, Mr. Morretti. A woman can never have too many male friends, and I love how honest and grounded you are."

He cocked a brow, examined her with a critical eye. "Why do you sound surprised?"

"Because it's hard to meet a man of integrity in this day and age."

"And women are perfect, right?"

"God no!" Dionne smirked. "Just me."

The waiter arrived, introduced himself and unloaded his wooden tray. "I will be back shortly with the second course," he said in a faint British accent. "Enjoy the appetizers."

Dionne picked up her cocktail glass and raised it in the air. "I'd like to make a toast."

"The floor is yours."

"Thank you for saving my life, and for being a kick-ass fairy godfather."

Immanuel cracked up. "No one's ever called me a fairy before."

"There's a first time for everything," she teased, shooting him a playful wink.

He laughed harder, and the sound of his hearty chuckle made Dionne smile. After the week she'd had, it felt good to joke around with Immanuel. "To friendship," she proposed, fervently nodding her head. "May we be friends for many years to come."

"I'll drink to that."

They shared a smile, then clinked glasses.

Dionne tasted her cocktail, deciding she liked the spicy flavor, then eagerly sampled the Kumamoto oysters. As they ate, they discussed their careers, their favorite cities and vacation spots, and their families. Immanuel listened more than he spoke, but as they started the second course he opened up to her about his past relationships. He was a sensitive man who felt things deeply, but he wasn't a crybaby by any means. He took responsibilities for the mistakes he'd made in the past, and was determined to be a better man. Dionne admired his drive and ambition.

"When was the last time you spoke to Emilio?" she asked, wondering what had caused the rift between the two brothers that Sharleen had once casually mentioned. "Have you seen him since you returned to Atlanta?"

"No, and I don't plan to. I have nothing to say to him."

"That's harsh."

His face hardened. "No, that's the truth."

"My sisters drive me crazy sometimes, but I couldn't imagine not having them in my life. Mel and Lorna are my best friends, and I love them dearly."

Immanuel nodded his head, as if he wholeheartedly

agreed. He chewed his food slowly, as if he was savoring every bite, then reached for his water glass.

"It's sad that you guys don't talk," she said, quietly. "Do you miss him?"

"Every day."

"Then why don't you call him?"

A dark shadow crossed his face. "Because what Emilio did is unforgivable."

"I don't believe that. Everyone deserves a second chance."

"Even family members who stab you in the back?"

"Yes, even family members who stab you in the back. Your family is a gift to you, as you are to them. You need each other, especially during tough times."

Immanuel fell silent. His head was down, his face was sad, and his posture was stiff.

It was hard for Dionne to keep her wits about her when all she wanted to do was take him in her arms and hold him tight. "It might help to talk about it."

"You wouldn't understand."

"I have a Masters in psychology. Try me."

"Emilio slept with my fiancée."

Dionne choked on her tongue and stared at him in astonishment. She hadn't expected him to drop a bombshell during dinner and was stunned by his confession. To alleviate the dryness in her throat, she picked up her glass and sipped her cocktail. Dionne couldn't think of anything to say in response, and needed a moment to get her thoughts in order.

"When I caught Emilio and Valentina in bed, I went ballistic."

"I'm not surprised you lost your cool. Anyone would in that situation."

"My brother and I fought like dogs that night." Immanuel touched his cheek, winced as if in pain. "This scar was a parting gift from him."

Moved by compassion, she offered a sympathetic smile. Immanuel wore a pensive expression on his face and seemed to be in another world. *Is Immanuel thinking about his ex-fiancée right now? Does he still love her? Does he wish he were having dinner with her tonight instead of me?*

Dionne banished the thoughts from her mind and returned to the present. She didn't like talking about Jules or the problems in their marriage, but maybe if she opened up to Immanuel he'd realize that he wasn't alone. Everyone faced tough times.

"I know how it feels to be betrayed by someone you love," she said quietly, meeting his gaze with her own. "For years, I suspected my husband was cheating on me, but I didn't have proof of his infidelity until his mistress showed up on my doorstep last year demanding money."

"You must have been devastated."

"Actually, I was relieved. Knowing the truth gave me the courage to move out and file for divorce." Dionne held her head high. "I've always believed disappointments are a blessing in disguise, and every setback I've faced has made me a stronger, more resilient person."

Immanuel gripped his glass in his hands, held it so hard his knuckles turned white.

"Have you ever asked Emilio why he betrayed you?"

"He said he didn't know Valentina was my girl," he said in a pained whisper.

"That sounds plausible. Why don't you believe him?"

"Because he's a spoiled, egotistical jerk who only cares about himself."

"People change, Immanuel."

"Not my brother. He's as selfish as they come."

Dionne hesitated, struggling with her words. She didn't want Immanuel to think she was taking sides, but it was important for her to speak her mind. "I've had dinner with Emilio and Sharleen on several occasions, and that wasn't my impression of him at all. He's chivalrous and charming, and his love and devotion for Sharleen are admirable."

Immanuel stared at her with astonishment, as if she were dancing on top of the table.

"What will it take for you to forgive Emilio?" she asked, wishing he'd stop glaring at her.

He answered with a shrug. "I don't know."

Silence fell across the table. It was deafening, thick with tension, and the longer it lasted the more uncomfortable Dionne felt.

"I'm mad at Emilio, but I'm even angrier at myself for choosing someone like Valentina. I thought she was 'the one,' and I feel like a jackass for proposing to her."

"Don't beat yourself up about it. That chapter of your life is over, and now it's time to learn and grow from that experience." Dionne parted her lips and was shocked by the pitiful sound of her voice. "Consider yourself lucky. At least you don't have two failed marriages under your belt. Now, *that's* hard to live down."

Immanuel paused reflectively, seemingly giving considerable thought to what she said. "What went wrong in your first marriage?"

"I was naive, and he was a worldly older man who swept me off my feet," she explained with a deep sigh. "Our differences drove us apart, and we eventually split up."

"How long were you married?"

"Two years. I was young and dumb and had no business tying the knot."

Dionne kept her eyes down, fiddled with the gold napkin holder beside her plate. She wondered what Immanuel would think if he knew the truth. *Would he think the worst of her? Would he keep his distance?* At the sound of his voice, she blinked.

"It sounds like you've overcome a lot of adversity in your life."

"Haven't we all?"

"That's certainly true in my case."

"Are you still in love your ex? Do you want to reconcile with her?" Holding her breath, she waited anxiously to hear his response. Not that it mattered. They were friends, and that would never change.

"It's been five years since our breakup."

"That's not what I asked you."

"No, I don't want her back, but I miss her companionship." His tone was somber. "It would be cool to have someone to spend time with at the end of a long workday."

"Then get a dog. They're fun and loyal and easy to please."

Immanuel chuckled. "You're hilarious."

And you're even sexier when you laugh.

His eyes probed hers, and his gaze made her skin flush with heat. Worried she had food on her face, Dionne grabbed her napkin and wiped her mouth. It didn't help. Immanuel continued to examine her with his bedroom eyes. "What is it?"

"Nothing." He reached across the table and touched her hand. "It's hard to believe we've only known each other for a week. I feel like I've known you for years."

Me, too. Even more shocking? I dream about you every single night.

The waiter appeared, carrying a white box tied with a red ribbon on his wooden tray, and presented the gift to Immanuel. "Sir, this is for you."

"I don't understand. What's going on?"

The waiter set the box down on the table in front of Immanuel and left.

Dionne felt warm and tingly all over, excited that her plan had gone off without a hitch.

"What is it?" he asked, pointing at the box.

"There's only one way to find out. Open it."

Immanuel picked up the box, untied the ribbon and placed the lid on the table. "A Rolex Submariner 16610V?" Surprise covered his face and seeped into his tone. "Where did you get this? It's a collector's piece worth thousands of dollars."

Dionne gave him a quizzical look. "Yeah, how do you know?"

"I bought one for my dad for Father's Day," he explained, wearing an impish smile. "My dad and I rarely speak, but I wasn't going to let Emilio upstage me again this year."

"Do you like it?"

"Yes, but I can't accept it. It's too expensive."

"You have to. Your name is inscribed on the back of it."

Frowning, he took the watch out of the box and turned it over. "To Immanuel, my hero." A smile curled the corners of his lips. "Thank you, Dionne. I'll wear it with pride."

Immanuel took her hand and tenderly kissed it, and her heart skipped and danced.

Three hours and seven courses later, Dionne and Immanuel left Bacchanalia. The impeccable service, creative food and exquisite wine pairings had exceeded her expectations. As they exited the private dining room Dionne thanked the staff for a wonderful evening. Everything was delicious, from the first bite to the last. It was, without a doubt, the best dining experience she'd ever had. And the best date, too. Charming and urbane, Immanuel regaled her with stories about his travels abroad, and after their third round of cocktails they were cracking jokes like longtime friends. Conversation flowed freely from one subject to the next, and no topic was off-limits. It was midnight, well past Dionne's bedtime, but she was wide-awake, ready to talk for hours more.

"Let's go to Polaris," Dionne suggested, exiting the restaurant on Immanuel's arm. The wind whistled through the trees, the air held a crisp, refreshing scent and the sky was painted a dazzling shade of pink. "They make delicious iced coffee drinks, and the rooftop view of the Atlanta skyline is breathtaking."

"Can I take a rain check? I have an early-morning meeting tomorrow, and if I want to impress the executives at Sony Music I need to get my rest."

"Sony Music?" she repeated, arching a brow. "Are you auditioning for a boy band?"

Immanuel pitched his head back and erupted in laughter.

"I didn't know you could sing. My, my, my, Mr. Morretti, you're full of surprises."

Resting a hand on her back, he opened the back door and helped her inside the limousine. "Sony Music wants to hire a new security firm," he explained, sitting down beside her. "They heard Mastermind Operations is the best in the business, and it is."

"I *love* your humility," she teased, unable to resist poking fun at him. "It's endearing."

"And I love your smile."

Thanks for giving me something to smile about. Immanuel was impossible not to like, and it was easy to see why his security firm was in high demand. He was everything a man should be—attentive, chivalrous and affectionate—and she enjoyed spending time with him.

The traffic was light, the streets were quiet, and as the limousine cruised down Peachtree Road, Dionne reflected on their romantic marathon date. She couldn't have asked for a better night, and wished their time together didn't have to end.

"Tonight was fun. We should do this again soon, but next time *I'm* paying for dinner."

"Don't even start. Your tip was three times the cost of our meal."

Immanuel grinned, shrugging his shoulders dismissively, and Dionne knew she'd been had. That bothered her. *Was he intimidated by her success? Is that why he'd left an exorbitant tip?*

Hearing his voice, she blinked and returned to the present.

"Do you have plans tomorrow?" Immanuel asked.

"Aren't you going to Demetri's game?"

His eyes narrowed in confusion. "*You're* going?"

"Yes, Sharleen invited me," she explained. "I don't follow baseball, but since your cousin is a baseball legend, I agreed to go."

"So, you're going to the game with Sharleen *and* Emilio?"

"Is that a problem?" she asked, confused by his odd reaction.

"No." He sighed and raked a hand through his hair. "I haven't seen my brother in years. It's bound to be an awkward reunion, and I'm not looking forward to it."

"Immanuel, if Emilio approaches you at the game, be open and honest about your feelings. Try to bury the hatchet once and for all."

Nodding his head as if he was considering her advice, he stroked the length of his jaw.

"I want you to come with me to the game."

"You do?" she blurted out.

"Yes, of course. You're great company, and I think we'll have fun together."

So do I. You make me feel like a teenager again.

"We can have dinner at one of the restaurants near Turner Field, then walk over to the stadium in time for the game. What do you say?"

Dionne wanted to cheer, but contained her excitement.

She was a mature, dignified woman, not a tween girl at a pop concert. "I'd love to."

"Great," he said smoothly, wearing a boyish grin. "It's a date."

I was hoping you'd say that, she thought, smiling. *Tomorrow can't come fast enough.*

The limo stopped in front of Dionne's house, and Immanuel helped her get out of the car. Taking her hand, he led her up the walkway. His touch, his smile and the scent of his cologne put her in the mood for loving. Dionne couldn't remember the last time she'd had sex. A year? Two? Jules used to complain she was cold and uptight in bed, but his insults never bothered her. He knew nothing about tenderness and intimacy, so who was he to judge? After learning about his affairs, she'd kicked him out of their bedroom and devoted all her time and energy to work. But tonight, Dionne didn't want to edit the monthly newsletter or read client profiles. She wanted one man in her bed, and his name was Immanuel Morretti.

Her heart was in turmoil; her body, too. She was hot and cold, nervous and excited, anxious and giddy, but the strongest emotion Dionne felt was desire. She longed to touch him, to caress him, wanted to taste his lips once and for all. Struggling to keep her hands at her sides and off his chest, she tore her gaze away from his mouth and took her keys out of her purse.

Dionne unlooked the door, flipped on the lights in the darkened foyer and disabled the alarm. She turned around to find Immanuel watching her and sucked in a deep breath.

His gaze was piercing, so intense and seductive that erotic images consumed her thoughts. She imagined them upstairs in her master bedroom, rolling around in bed, kissing each other desperately. But quickly changed the channel in her mind. They were buddies, not friends with benefits, and nothing good could ever come of having a fling with him. "I'm going to make myself a cup of coffee," she said, dropping her keys on the end table. "Would you like one?"

"No. I have to go, but I'll call you tomorrow." Immanuel leaned over, touched a hand to her face, and kissed her cheek. "Thanks for dinner. And, the watch."

Disappointed, Dionne watched him jog down the steps and duck inside the waiting limousine. She waved goodbye, and once the car drove off, she activated the alarm. With a heavy heart, she walked into the living room, collapsed onto the couch and stared up at the ceiling. She'd had a great time with Immanuel at Bacchanalia, and for as long as Dionne lived she'd never forget how special he made her feel. *And* how hot and bothered.

Chapter 9

"Let's not argue," Dionne said, raising her voice to be heard above the chatter in the conference room. It was Friday afternoon, and her staff—twelve life coaches, a receptionist and three bright-eyed interns—were seated around the table discussing mandatory employee training programs. They were snacking on fruit and the homemade pastries Sharleen had brought in, and drinking coffee as if there were no tomorrow. "We can revisit the issue in the future, but in the meantime everyone please register for the December training session."

Dionne glanced at Sharleen and laughed inwardly when her vice president tapped the face of her wristwatch and mouthed, "Move it along. We have plans tonight, remember?"

"Are there any questions?" Dionne asked, glancing around the table.

Annabelle raised her hand. "Are you okay?"

Confused by the question, she frowned and shot the

blonde a quizzical look. "Yes, of course, why wouldn't I be?"

"Because you were brutally attacked a week ago—"

Dionne cut her off. "What does that have to do with our monthly meeting?"

"Some staff members were wondering if your attack has something to do with your ongoing feud with your estranged husband," she explained, leaning forward in her chair. "A lot of people think Brad attacked you, but I don't believe that for a second. Brad isn't a criminal, and even though he was wrongly dismissed, I don't think he'd be stupid enough to attack you…"

Oh. No. She. Didn't! Dionne wanted to reach across the table and smack the novice life coach for embarrassing her, but she caught herself in time and buried her hands in her lap. Anger burned inside her. Her personal life was just that—personal—and she didn't appreciate Annabelle's asking about the attack during the staff meeting. It was unprofessional and disrespectful, but Dionne didn't lash out at her.

Dionne took a sip of her chamomile tea. Over the rim of her mug, she noticed that everyone in the room was staring at her intently, passing judgment with their eyes. Since she didn't want her employees to think she was upset, she put down her mug and spoke in a confident tone.

"Annabelle, I'm fine," she said, her voice masking her frustration. "I appreciate your concern, but the Atlanta Police Department is working hard on the case, and I'm confident they'll make an arrest soon."

Interest sparked in her eyes. "So, the police have a suspect?"

Dionne ignored her, consulting her two-page agenda instead. "Let's discuss our clients." Back in control, she straightened in her chair and picked up her pen. "I'd like everyone to give a brief update about the clients you're supporting, and the challenges you've faced this week."

Silence plagued the room, and staff members shifted around in their chairs.

"I'll start." Annabelle rose to her feet. Her expression was somber, but she spoke with pride. "I had a six o'clock session last night with Ryder Knoxx at his Druid Hills mansion, and he made another pass at me."

Dionne started to speak, then remembered the conversation she'd had with Immanuel at AT&T store last week and bit her tongue. His words played in her mind, and her anger abated. *You can catch more flies with honey than vinegar.*

"Thanks for sharing, Annabelle. It can be challenging working with celebrities, and I appreciate your efforts, and your candor," Dionne said, wearing a sympathetic smile. "Let's meet tomorrow to discuss the situation further. I'd love to share some tips and strategies with you that have served me well for the last fifteen years."

Annabelle beamed. "Thank you, Mrs. Fontaine. I'd like that very much."

Within seconds, everyone was talking, openly sharing their concerns and frustrations. For the next forty-five minutes, Dionne shared advice with her staff. Problem-solving was mentally draining, but she welcomed the challenge. This was her calling, what she was born to do, and she wanted to empower her staff more than anything.

"I want to thank you all for a job well done." Dionne made eye contact with each staff member, trying to communicate her gratitude and appreciation through her gaze. This was her favorite part of the day, what she loved most about her job. She liked touching base with her team, and looked forward to connecting with them every Friday at the monthly meeting. "Because of your efforts, Pathways Center is the number one life coaching center in Atlanta, and it's going to remain that way for many more years to come, right, everyone?"

Applause, cheers and whistles filled the room.

"Staff, that will be all for today." Closing her notebook, Sharleen gestured to the papers on the middle of the table. "Please remember to submit your holiday requests to the HR department by Friday if you'd like time off during Thanksgiving. It's only a few weeks away, so time is of the essence."

Everyone filed out of the room, and Sharleen locked the door.

"Who are you and what have you done with my boss?"

Dionne laughed out loud. "What's gotten into you?"

"I was about to ask *you* the same question. I thought you were going to strangle Annabelle when she asked you about the attack, but you handled it like a pro. And you were surprisingly sympathetic when she shared her concerns about Ryder Knoxx."

"I've turned over a new leaf—"

"I'd say," she snapped, nodding her head emphatically. "The old Dionne would have given her a thorough tongue-lashing, then tossed her out the door!"

Laughing, Dionne leaned back in her chair and crossed her legs. Since the attack, she'd changed for the better. She was more patient, less uptight, and Immanuel was the reason why. He never raised his voice, treated everyone with respect and went out of his way to help others. He was a kind, gentle soul, the type of person she aspired to be. She was glad they had met. Not only was he a great friend, he was someone she could count on.

"I know I can be hard on people, especially our female staff, so I'm making a concerted effort to be more understanding," she confessed, speaking from the heart. "To make Pathways Center a success I need the support of the entire team, and since you can catch more flies with honey than vinegar, I'm killing them with kindness."

"I've been saying that for years," Sharleen said, fervently nodding her head. "I'm glad you're finally taking my advice. It's about time."

Hearing her cell phone vibrate, Dionne picked it up off the table and read her newest text message. It was from Immanuel, and as she read his message, heat flooded her body.

I can't wait to see you. You've been on my mind all day.

Her heart fluttered inside her chest. Immanuel made her feel special, as if his sole purpose in life were to please her. Since their candlelit dinner at Bacchanalia he'd been doing just that. On Sunday, he took her to see *Motown: The Musical* at the Atlanta Theater, then days later they had lunch at her favorite sushi spot, and last night he'd treated her to dessert at Sugar Shack, a quaint Brookhaven shop just minutes away from her house. They'd sat at their corner table talking about movies, music and past relationships for hours. By the time they left the café, she was dying to kiss him. At her doorstep, he'd given her a hug and a peck on the cheek, but she'd secretly longed for more. She wanted to kiss him, and yearned to feel his hands all over her body. Friendship be damned. Everything about Immanuel was a turn-on—his piercing eyes, his panty-wetting smile, the way he moved—and it was getting harder and harder for Dionne to fight the desires of her flesh.

"Why are you smiling from ear to ear?" Sharleen asked, wearing an amused expression on her face. "Did you finally sign a celebrity for our new marketing campaign?"

"No, not yet, but I'm working on it."

"Do you want me to ask Emilio to do the ad?"

Dionne couldn't resist poking fun at her friend and hid

a cheeky smile. "No, don't, it's *never* a good idea to mix business with pleasure."

"Says who? Mixing business with pleasure worked for me, and I have the engagement ring to prove it!" Sharleen laughed. "We better get going. Emilio should be here any minute to pick us up for Demetri's game, and I don't want to make my baby wait."

"You guys go on without me. I'll just meet you at Turner Field."

"But we agreed to go together, and you won't be granted access to Demetri's luxury box without us," she explained.

"I know, but Immanuel invited me to the game and I said yes."

"Immanuel!" She dropped into her chair, wheeled over to where Dionne was sitting at the head of the table and gripped her shoulders. Her face was bright, her eyes were wild with excitement, and her voice was a deafening shriek. "You guys are dating? No way! OMG, if you guys get married we'll be sisters-in-law! How cool is that!"

"Girl, slow your roll. It's not like that. We're just friends."

"Yeah, for now, but it's just a matter of time before Immanuel sweeps you off your feet."

Sadness pierced her heart, and a bitter taste filled her mouth. "I hope not, because the last time I fell in love I was played for a fool."

"This time will be different."

"How do you know?"

"Because I know you," she insisted, her tone firm and convincing. "You're smarter and wiser now, and besides, Immanuel's a Morretti, and Morretti men don't mistreat women."

Dionne smirked. "What, so you're the family spokesperson now?"

"Nope. I'm just a hopeless romantic who's a sucker for happy endings."

"Then forget about my love life, and focus on reuniting Emilio with his brother."

Her smile dimmed. "There's nothing I can do. Trust me, I've tried."

"Has Emilio tried reaching out to Immanuel?"

"Only a million times. He calls and texts him, but to no avail. Immanuel has completely shut him out of his life. No matter what Emilio does, it's never good enough."

"I know the feeling." Dionne released a deep sigh. "You heard my sisters. They think I'm to blame for Jules's infidelity and ordered me to call off the divorce and return home."

"I'm glad I don't have older siblings, because I hate when people tell me what to do," Sharleen said. "What do your parents think? Do they want you to reconcile with Jules?"

"Yes, unfortunately they do. I went home on Saturday, and my dad had some very harsh words for me. He stopped short of calling me irresponsible, but his comments still hurt."

"I'm sorry to hear that, but try not to let it get you down." Sharleen winked and gave her a one-armed hug. "I think you're fabulous, and I bet Immanuel does, too."

Laughing, the women exited the conference room. They parted ways in the reception area, and after Dionne spoke to the receptionist she grabbed the day's mail and marched out the front door. It was early evening, but the sun was shining and the air was warm.

Her cell phone rang and she put it to her ear, thinking it was Immanuel. "Hello?"

Click.

Annoyed, she stared down at the phone in disgust. The prank calls had started the day after she'd arrived home from the hospital, and had increased in frequency ever since. Her cell phone provider said there was nothing it could do and advised her to change her number. Dionne considered telling Immanuel about the calls, but struck the thought from her mind. They were both busy, with a million things to do, and she didn't want her problems to add to his stress.

Dionne glanced at her watch. She had just enough time to go home and freshen up before Immanuel picked her up for their date. An image of him clad in an Armani suit flashed in her mind, and a shiver tickled her spine. They were friends and nothing more, so why did the thought of seeing him again excite her?

Because he's kind and chivalrous and you have a lot in common, whispered her inner voice. *Immanuel treats you like a person, not an object, and it's refreshing to be with someone who appreciates your mind, not just your body.*

Dionne picked up her pace. Anxious to see Immanuel, she rushed over to her rental car, hopped inside and sped out of the parking lot.

Chapter 10

The private luxury suite at Turner Field was filled with gorgeous furniture, flat-screen TVs and a chic marble bar. Sports memorabilia lined the sable-brown walls, and glass windows provided an unobstructed view of the field. Pop music played from the mounted speakers, and when Dionne heard the opening bar of her favorite Prince song a smile overwhelmed her mouth. Years ago, when she was in graduate school, her sisters had surprised her with tickets to his Atlanta show. They'd danced all night, sang off-key to each hit and screamed like teenage girls. Dionne thought about Mel and Lorna and wondered how they were doing. She hadn't spoken to them since they'd visited her home and left in a huff, but she planned to call them tomorrow. Surely they weren't still mad at her—

"Is everything okay? You suddenly went quiet on me..."

Hearing Immanuel's voice, Dionne blinked and met his gaze.

That was her first mistake.

Touching his arm was her second.

Inhaling his cologne, her third.

Time screeched to a halt, and everything in the room faded to the background. He rested a hand on top of hers, splayed his fingers against her flesh, and her body trembled with desire. Immanuel looked at her as if she was hot, desirable, the sexiest woman he'd ever seen. His grin, the one that sparked in his eyes and warmed his lips, made her clit tingle and her panties wet.

His touch made her dizzy and her thoughts scatter, but she didn't pull away. She didn't have the willpower it required, not after all the flirting and touching they'd been doing since he picked her up at home. Dionne was drawn to Immanuel, loved being with him, and could easily spend the rest of the night playing this thrilling game of cat-and-mouse. When it came to the opposite sex, she'd always had a will of steel, more self-control than a man of the cloth, but Immanuel excited her, turned her on like no one else, and flirting with him was the ultimate rush. *Is it just a matter of time before we become lovers?* she wondered, her heart racing at the thought. *Is this the night he'll finally make his move?*

Dionne licked her lips. Her gaze left his face and slid down his ripped physique. His shoulders filled out each inch of his white mock-neck shirt. His dark straight-leg jeans were a perfect fit, and his Timberland boots gave him a bad-boy edge, one that made her nipples harden and her body quiver. Embarrassed by her physical reaction to him, she turned away and reached for her cocktail glass. "I'm good," she said, tasting her martini. "Some game, huh?"

"What game? I'm having so much fun with you I forgot who was playing."

His eyes zeroed in on her face, held her in their powerful grip. The energy pulsing between them was insane, more potent than a shot of vodka and impossible to resist.

Immanuel was the sexiest man ever, and there was an air of mystery about him that she was inexplicably drawn to.

"You look incredible tonight," he whispered. "Every night, actually."

Immanuel put a hand on her leg, and her pulse shifted into overdrive.

"Are you having a good time?"

"Of course," she said, returning his smile. "I always have a good time with you."

"Great answer."

They had sat on stools in front of the window when they arrived hours earlier, and even though Dionne didn't know anything about baseball, she was having a great time. The mood was festive, charged with excitement, and laughter abounded. "Is your cousin's fiancée here?" she asked, noting all of the attractive women in the room. "Sharleen thinks Angela's the best thing since fat-free ice cream, and I'd love to meet her. She sounds like good people."

"No, Angela's not here. She's a sports nut who likes to be close to all the action, so she watches from the stands with Demetri's overzealous fans."

Dionne heard a brash, horselike laugh, recognized it immediately and rolled her eyes. She could spot a dog a mile away, and Immanuel's business partner needed to be in a kennel. Malcolm was strutting around the room with his chest puffed out, bopping from one woman to the next, acting like he owned the place.

"This game sucks. And so does the home team," Malcolm bellowed, taking a swig of his beer. "Demetri's killing the Astros tonight. There's no way in hell they can make a comeback."

Malcolm plopped down on the stool beside Immanuel, and Dionne swallowed a groan. It surprised her the men were not only business partners, but longtime friends. They couldn't be more different. Immanuel was suave, cultured and refined, the kind of man people gravitated toward. Malcolm was loud and juvenile, the type of man women ran away *from*, not to.

"Are you ready to bounce?" Malcolm asked. "Let's go check out the 69 Club."

Immanuel's narrowed gaze and wrinkled nose spoke of his displeasure. "We're too old for that bar. Most of the clientele are underage, and—"

"Like hell I am. I don't look a day over twenty-five."

Laughter exploded from Dionne's mouth. Both men turned to look at her, their eyebrows raised. She didn't like Malcolm, but since she didn't want to make any enemies, she simmered down.

"Dionne, you enjoy having a good time, right?" Smiling with the likeness of a snake, he ogled her chest. "Want to check out a hot new club?"

His question was ridiculous. As if. *Why would she want to go to a sleazy nightclub on the wrong side of town when she'd rather be alone with Immanuel?* They'd had great conversations about life and love, and the more Dionne learned about him the more she wished he were her man. "Thanks for the invitation, but I'll pass. I'm not the club type."

Rap music began to play, and Malcolm hopped to his feet. "I'll be back in a few." He put his cell phone to his ear and swaggered off.

Dionne spotted Sharleen and Emilio standing at the bar, and waved in greeting. They made an attractive couple in their Chicago Royals attire, and were gazing at each other with stars in their eyes. "Sharleen and Emilio are here. Let's go say hi."

"I'm good here. You go ahead."

"Come on," she said, dragging him up to his feet. "Don't be like that."

"Don't be like what?"

"An old sourpuss!"

His nose twitched, but he didn't laugh.

"Fine, I'll text Sharleen and ask them to come to us."

"If Emilio knows what's good for him, he'll stay on his side of the room."

"Immanuel, no one likes a bully."

"Who are you calling a bully?"

"You," Dionne said, pointing a finger at his chest. "And it's not cool."

"I'm not a bully."

"Then prove me wrong." Dionne tilted her head to the side and wore a knowing smile. "Be the kind, chivalrous gentleman your grandmother raised you to be, and every woman in here will be eating out of your hands."

"I don't want to impress anyone but you."

"Then let's have a drink with your brother and his gorgeous fiancée."

Dionne grabbed her purse, tucked it under her arm and walked purposely toward the bar. In her peripheral version, she saw Immanuel behind her and cheered inwardly. "I thought you'd never get here," she said, approaching Sharleen. "What took you guys so long? I was worried you'd changed your mind about coming tonight."

"I wanted to be here sooner, but my boss left work early again today, and I had to lock up." Wearing a long face, she sighed dramatically. "Girl, pray for me. She's *such* a tyrant."

"Emilio, are you sure Sharleen's the one?" Dionne asked. "She's a *real* handful."

"I'm a hundred percent sure. She's my everything, and I won't live without her."

The couple melted into each other's arms and shared a kiss.

Dionne waited for Emilio and Immanuel to acknowledge each other's presence, but they didn't. Thankfully, Sharleen did.

"Immanuel! It's great to finally meet you!" Speaking in Italian, she leaned in and kissed him on each cheek. "I thought this day would never come! I've heard a lot about you—"

"None of it's true."

Stunned, Dionne cranked her head to the right and examined Immanuel's profile. His voice was filled with animosity, and his face was dark with rage. His hands were curled into fists, and his mouth was a hard line. *What can I do to help?* she thought, her gaze darting between the two men. Dionne feared if she didn't do something quick, the situation was going to go from bad to worse. She quickly linked arms with Sharleen and moved away from the bar. "We're going to the ladies' room. We'll be back in a few."

Sharleen frowned. "We are? But I just got here, and the calamari smells *so* good."

"Don't worry," she whispered. "I'll buy you some at the concession stand. Let's go."

Immanuel wanted to beg her to stay, but he couldn't get his lips to work. Damn, Dionne had set him up and he hadn't even see it coming. His eyes tracked her through the room, sliding down her delicious curves and hips. Her short Chicago Royals baseball jersey showed off her toned arms, her skinny jeans made her ass look fantastic, and her high heels elongated her legs. His mind started to scheme and plot on how to get the exotic beauty into his bed permanently.

Dionne is still legally married, reminded his inner voice. *That means she's off-limits.*

Standing at the bar with his brother—the man who'd betrayed his trust and crushed his dreams—he felt his temperature rise and his pulse pound violently in his ears. But this wasn't the time or the place to have it out with Emilio, so he turned away.

Emilio caught his arm, gripped it tight.

His body stiffened. His first impulse was to push him away, but he remembered the advice Dionne had given him at Bacchanalia and took a deep, calming breath. Immanuel hated to admit it, but she was right. His feud with Emilio had gone on long enough. It was a struggle, but he kept his anger in check. "Get your hands off me."

"Immanuel, we need to talk."

"I have nothing to say to you."

"Fine. I'll talk. You listen."

He wheeled around and was surprised to see sadness flicker across Emilio's face. He looked troubled, as if he carried the weight of the world on his shoulders. *Was Emilio genuinely sorry about what he'd done? Had he learned his lesson?* Immanuel rejected his thoughts. He knew better. His brother was just putting on a show for his pretty fiancée. Emilio had hit the jackpot, which was no surprise. His brother was accustomed to dating—and stealing—beautiful women, and Sharleen was a stunner.

"Make it quick. I want to get back to the game."

"I never meant to hurt you."

"You slept with my fiancée. What did you *think* would happen?"

"I had no idea Valentina was your girl."

Immanuel scoffed and folded his arms across his chest. "Likely story."

"It's true. I didn't see you arrive at the party together that night. I was hyped about winning another championship, and when she stepped up to me in the game room, I..."

Emilio broke off speaking, but Immanuel filled in the blanks.

"You couldn't resist her charm, is that it?"

"Immanuel, I've changed. I'm not the man I used to be."

"I'm happy to hear that, because you used to be a jerk."

"Thanks, bro. I can always count on you to keep it real," Emilio said with a wry smile.

On the flat-screen television mounted above the bar, Immanuel watched players and coaches on each team shaking hands, and knew the game was over. Demetri and his team had pulled off another impressive win, and he was proud of his cousin. Immanuel glanced around the suite in search of Dionne, but couldn't find her anywhere. *Were guys chasing her down at every turn? Had she met someone at the concession stand? Were they exchanging numbers and—*

"The things you said at the funeral..." Emilio hung his head. "They almost killed me."

"I was way out of line. I'm sorry." Immanuel looked away. Had to. Talking about Lucca, his beloved nephew, made his heart ache. Since he didn't want to have an emotional breakdown at Turner Field he changed the subject. "Congratulations on your win at the World Series All-Star Race. It was a tough course, but you made it look easy."

Surprise colored his cheeks. "You were watching?"

"Of course. You're my brother. I always want you to crush the competition." He added. "I just don't want you to screw my girl."

"Damn, bro, that was harsh."

His eyes strayed to the door, and every time it opened he felt a rush of adrenaline. He missed Dionne and wanted her back at his side. They'd known each other only a couple weeks, but she was important to him. She appealed to him in every way, and he loved to be with her.

"I heard what you did for Dionne. Good looking out, bro."

"I didn't do anything. *She* beat the mugger until he was black and blue, not me."

"You know she's married to Jules Fontaine, right? The CFO of Fontaine Enterprises."

Immanuel nodded. "I know, but they're getting a divorce."

"It doesn't take a year to get a divorce."

"What are you saying?"

"Nothing, bro. Just be careful. I don't want you to get hurt again."

Then stay away from Dionne, he thought sourly. "I'm a big boy. I can handle myself."

"We're back." Sharleen snuggled against Emilio and wrapped her arms around his waist. "Baby, I missed you."

"Not as much as I missed you. It felt like you were gone for hours."

Immanuel wanted to gag, but he wore a blank expression on his face instead. He had to find Dionne. A floral scent tickled his nostrils, and he knew she was nearby. The thought heartened him, and when he spotted her behind him, he smiled in satisfaction.

"Did you guys talk?" Dionne asked. "Is everything okay?"

"We're cool." Immanuel took her hand. "The game just ended. Are you ready to go?"

"We're meeting up with Demetri and Angela for drinks," Emilio said.

Sharleen piped up. "We're going glow bowling in Buckhead. You two should come."

"We'd love to."

"We would?" Immanuel pulled Dionne aside and spoke in a quiet voice. He wanted to see his cousin and meet his bride-to-be, but he wasn't hanging out with Emilio. It was too much, too soon. "We can't go to Buckhead. We have plans with Malcolm."

"That's fine. No worries," Dionne said, letting go of his hand. "You go hang out with Malcolm, and I'll ask Emilio and Sharleen to drop me off after bowling."

Dionne stepped past him as if the matter were decided, but Immanuel caught her around the waist. "Not so fast." He stared down at her, wishing he could taste her luscious red lips. "We came together, we leave together. Understood?"

"Absolutely," she said with a sly wink, playfully jabbing a finger in his chest. "Now, let's bowl. You better bring your A game, or you're dead meat!"

Chapter 11

"I thought I was big and bad until I went toe-to-toe with this sexy pit bull in a skirt," Demetri joked. "Angela gave me a thorough tongue-lashing that day, and two years later my brothers and teammates still tease me about our studio showdown."

Dionne laughed out loud. The baseball star and his fiancée, Angela Kelly, were a hilarious twosome. Listening to Demetri recount the first time they met was the funniest thing she'd ever heard. Immanuel was sitting beside her on the leather couch, and the sound of his hearty chuckles warmed her heart. He held her close to his side, making her feel cherished and adored. *I could so get used to this,* she thought, leaning comfortably against him. *It feels like heaven being in his arms.*

The group was at the Painted Pin, an upscale entertainment bar in Buckhead's Miami Circle. The bar had it all. Valet parking, interactive games, and comfortable seating areas with candlelit tables and attractive furniture. It was a favorite neighborhood hangout, and the patrons—a mix of tourists, college students and couples—were enjoying everything the venue had to offer. Demetri's bodyguard, an ex-marine with a boxer's build, stood at the entrance of the VIP lounge keeping the groupies at bay. Fans of Emilio and Demetri were screaming their names and snapping pictures, but the cousins seemed unfazed by the attention.

"I thought Angela was going to whup my ass when I confronted her at WJN-TV," Demetri confessed. "And that would have been a disaster, because this face is worth millions!"

Everyone at the table laughed.

"That *can't* be a true story. It sounds like an episode of a reality TV show," Dionne said, dabbing at her eyes with her fingertips. "I think you guys are pulling my leg."

"You do, huh?" Demetri winked at Angela. "Baby, show her the footage."

"Footage!" Dionne and Sharleen shouted in unison. "What footage?"

Angela took her cell phone out of her purse, tapped the screen several times, then raised it in the air. "Since you asked," she said, with a knowing smile, "here it is."

Leaning forward in her seat, Dionne stared in horror—and amusement—as an online video titled "Sexy Chicago Newscaster Goes Off on Baseball Superstar" played on the screen.

"Damn, coz, Angela gave it to you good." Immanuel shook his head as if he couldn't believe it. "Next time your manager tells you not to do something, you should listen to him!"

Demetri stared down at Angela, his eyes shimmering with love and adoration. "I'm glad I disregarded Lloyd's advice, because meeting Angela was the best thing to ever happen to me. If I had to do it all over again, I would."

Demetri hugged Angela to his side and kissed her lips.

Dionne had never met a cuter couple, though Emilio and Sharleen were definitely giving Demetri and Angela a run for their money. They couldn't keep their hands off each other, and if Sharleen moved any closer to Emilio she'd be sitting in his lap. The couples were so smitten with each other. Dionne could actually feel the love in the air.

"You guys have been engaged forever," Emilio teased. "When's the big day?"

Angela beamed. "We're getting married next summer."

"And this time I'm not letting you postpone it." Demetri's tone was firm, and his eyes were narrowed in determination. "We're getting hitched next year come hell or high water."

"Hey!" Angela shrieked, pulling out of his arms. "What's *that* supposed to mean?"

"Baby, I'm just keeping it real. I was ready to marry you last year, but you just *had* to go to the White House and interview the president and first lady for your Christmas special."

Scowling, she poked a finger in his chest. "But you told me to do it."

"Of course I did," he said with a wink. "That's what a caring, supportive fiancé does for the woman he loves, but if you postpone the wedding again I'm withholding the lovin'!"

Dionne burst out laughing for the second time within minutes, and water filled her eyes. *The Morretti men are the real deal*, she thought, glancing around the table. Demetri and Emilio were sensitive, romantic men who loved to spoil their women, and it amazed her how open and honest they were about their feelings.

"How is Rafael?" Immanuel asked. "Every time I call his cell goes straight to voice mail."

"That's because he's knee-deep in dirty diapers!"

Demetri chuckled. "He's got his hands full with Violet, and he recently found out they're expecting baby number two."

Sharleen raised a brow. "Another baby? Wow. Their daughter is only eight months old."

"They're making up for lost time," Angela explained with a laugh. "Paris wants a big family, and I have a feeling they'll be a family of eight in no time."

"What about you guys?" Emilio asked. "Do you have any plans to increase the fold?"

"No, not yet, but we're getting plenty of practice."

Angela touched Demetri's face and pecked him on the lips. "*That* we are."

The waiter arrived, dropped off another round of drinks and appetizers, and sped off.

"Are we going to bowl or what?" Emilio rubbed his hands together. "I have an ass-whuppin' with your name on it, Demetri, and this time I won't go easy on you. The winner gets bragging rights *and* cash, so put your money where your mouth is."

Immanuel barked a laugh. "I'm in! You're *both* due for a beat down, so let's do this."

Dionne watched as the men got up from the couch and stalked over to lane seven, leaving the women behind. "Dionne, how come you're not eating?" Angela asked. "You don't like junk food?"

"Girl, please. Look at me. Do I *look* like the health-conscious type to you?"

The women laughed and clinked cocktail glasses. Dionne had few female friends, and had always turned to her sisters for advice and support. But right now, she enjoyed having girl talk with Sharleen and Angela. The Chicago newscaster was full of life and positive energy, and one of the most down-to-earth people Dionne had ever met. Add to that, she looked like a superstar. Silky black hair kissed her shoulders, her makeup was flawless, and her backless purple dress was fresh off the runway.

"Immanuel took me out for dinner before the game, and I ate enough for two," she said with a laugh. "If I keep pigging out I won't be able to fit into my dress for the wedding, and I paid big bucks for my Alexander Mc-Queen gown."

"Girl, I hear you. I've gained twenty pounds since meeting Demetri, and it's all his fault. He's constantly feeding me, and I have no self-control when it comes to Italian cuisine. I love it all, especially the desserts, and my man's the most amazing cook ever!"

"Be thankful your wedding isn't six weeks away. I still have ten pounds to lose, but the more I diet the more I gain weight. It's like the universe is conspiring against me!" Sharleen said, excitement lacing her tone.

"Don't worry," Angela said reassuringly, rubbing her friend's shoulders. "You're going to be a beautiful bride, and Emilio won't be able to keep his eyes off you."

I know the feeling, Dionne thought, glancing at lane seven in search of Immanuel. She found him standing beside the scorer's table watching her and waved in greeting. He flashed a boyish smile, one that made his baby blues twinkle, and her heart leaped for joy. His gaze captured hers in a seductive grip, and all she could do was stare. Dionne rested a hand on her chest to calm her raging heartbeat, but it didn't help. Her pulse continued to race and pound.

"I love the story of how you and Immanuel met," Angela gushed. "It's *so* romantic."

"We're just friends."

"Sure you are, girl. Just keep telling yourself that."

"Angela, she's in denial," Sharleen said. "It happened to me, too."

"And me," Angela confessed, raising a hand in the air.

"Dionne, quit resisting Immanuel and join the 'He Swept Me Off My Feet' club, because once a Morretti man sets his sights on you, it's game over!"

The thought should have scared her, especially in light of her failed marriages, but it didn't. Dionne trusted her instincts and made it a point to listen to her gut feeling. Her heart was telling her Immanuel was someone special. The past two weeks had proved as much. He was unlike anyone she'd ever met, a brave, courageous man any woman would love to have.

Including you, whispered her inner voice.

Dionne heard her cell phone buzz, saw that she had a new text message from Mel and frowned. What the hell? Her sister's message was confusing, didn't make any sense.

Are you nearby? Text me when you get here.

Convinced the message was intended for someone else, she typed a message in response. Seconds later, her cell phone rang. "Hey, Mel. What's up?"

"Where are you?"

"Out with friends." Her gaze fell across Immanuel, and she smiled.

"The Fontaine Family Charity drive is tonight at Friendship House. You should be here."

Dionne was annoyed that her sister was yelling at her, but she kept her temper in check. She was having a great time with Immanuel and his family, and she wasn't going to let anyone ruin her night. "Mel, I have to go."

"So you're on your way?" Her sister sighed in relief, speaking in her usual bright and cheery tone. "Thank God. How long will it take you to get here?"

"Jules and I are getting a divorce, Mel. Our lives aren't intertwined anymore."

"You have to come. The entire family is here, and besides, it's for a good cause," she argued. "Adeline has worked tirelessly for Friendship House for decades, and she needs our support to make the charity drive a success."

Dionne nodded her head in agreement, but she didn't vocalize her thoughts. Her sister-in-law's work with inner-city youth was commendable, but the socialite was as spiteful as they come. Dionne didn't want anything to do with her. Over the years, Adeline had humiliated her countless times, and she shuddered at the memory of the tongue-lashing she'd given her last year for wearing a sleeveless dress to an event at the Fontaine family church. "Mel, I'll call you later."

She heard whispering, a shuffling sound, then Lorna's voice on the line.

"Are you with your new lover?" she demanded, her anger evident. "I spoke to Adeline, and she's very upset. She said you're flaunting him all over town. Dionne, how could you!"

Dionne stared down at the phone, stunned by her sister's words. Who did Lorna think she was? How dare she scream at her! Not wanting her friends to overhear her conversation, she excused herself from the table and left the lounge. She strode past the entrance and out the front door.

"You're jeopardizing your marriage," she continued. "Don't you see that? If Jules finds out you're hooking up with other men he'll never take you back—"

"Good, because our marriage is over, and I want a divorce."

"You don't mean that."

"Yes. I. Do." Dionne started to explain, to tell Lorna how she felt about Immanuel, but she stopped herself before the words left her mouth. She loved her sister and valued her opinion, but she didn't owe her an explanation. It was her life, her decision, and there was no way in hell she was going to the charity drive. "I have to get back to my friends. They're waiting for me."

"You're choosing some guy you just met over your family?"

"No, for once I'm doing what makes me happy, instead of doing what *you* want me to—"

Dionne didn't realize she was shouting or crying until she felt a hand on her back and heard Immanuel's voice behind her. He whispered in her ear, told her everything was going to be okay, tenderly stroking her shoulders.

"Lorna, I have to go. Bye."

Hanging up the phone, she cleaned her cheeks with the back of her hand. Dionne swallowed hard, but the lump in her throat seemed to grow, not shrink.

The wind whistled through the trees, blowing leaves in the sky, and the crisp, refreshing scent of autumn perfumed the night air. Chilled to the bone, Dionne hugged her arms to her chest.

"What are you doing out here?" Embarrassed that he'd caught her crying, she couldn't look at him, fearing she'd crumble if she did. She could feel him staring at her and attempted to dodge his gaze. "You're supposed to be inside."

"I got worried when I saw you leave and wanted to ensure you were okay."

"A hero's job is never done, is that it?"

Immanuel slid his hands around her shoulders. She felt warm and cozy in his arms, as if she were wrapped in a thick blanket. Her senses spun out of control; she was overwhelmed by his closeness, by his intimate caress. The air was electrified, perfumed with the scent of her desire. Her feelings were in tumult, her emotions, too—had been since the day she woke up in the hospital and saw Immanuel for the first time.

"Dionne, what's wrong? Who upset you?"

It was his tone, the gentle urging of his voice, that did

her in, that incited lustful thoughts. But she gathered herself and regained control. "It's not important."

"Yes it is, because you're important to me."

Dionne reluctantly pulled out of his arms. If she didn't put some distance between them she'd end up crossing the line, and the last thing she wanted to do was embarrass herself. To lighten the mood, she said, "I'm an amazing bowler. Want to see my moves?"

"Absolutely." Immanuel raised her hand to his mouth and kissed it. "Bring it on!"

Chapter 12

"If that's your take on love and relationships, you'll never meet Mrs. Right, because twenty-first century women can take care of themselves." Cradling the cordless phone between her ear and shoulder, Dionne entered the kitchen and lowered the temperature on the stove. The air smelled of spices and Italian herbs. The aroma was so enticing that she couldn't wait to eat.

Noticing the time on the stove, her eyes widened. After work, she'd gone to her evening spin class but she had so much on her mind she hadn't been able to focus. At home, her problems continued. Instead of doing housework, or packing for her upcoming business trip to Seattle, she'd flopped onto the couch, and called Immanuel. They talked two, sometimes three times a day. Their conversations lasted for hours. Chatting with him about her day always made Dionne feel better.

"All I'm saying is I liked it better when the roles were clearly defined," Immanuel said, fervently arguing his case.

"If we go out on a date I don't want you to drive, or order for us, or pay the bill, either. That's my job, not yours."

"Job? I think you're taking this whole chivalry thing too far."

"I think you're jaded and a bit cynical about men."

Hell yeah I am! You'd be jaded too if you'd been screwed over numerous times by the opposite sex. The only men who haven't played me are my father and brother.

"I love that you're a self-made woman, but I don't want you to spend money when you're with me. I got you, okay?"

Dionne winced, swallowing hard to alleviate the lump in her throat. She hated the expression *self-made woman*, and knew the term didn't apply to her. What would Immanuel think if he knew the truth? Would he think less of her? As he spoke, a frown crimped her lips. "So if I invited you to Bacchanalia again you'd say no?"

"Of course not. Smart, captivating women are my weakness, *and* you're a stunner."

"Good answer! I thought I was going to have to cut you!" she said with a laugh. One minute they were talking about their favorite pasta recipes, and the next thing Dionne knew they were having an intense discussion about love and relationships. Immanuel was an old-school gentleman who still believed females were the weaker sex, and Dionne enjoyed schooling him about career women. Talking with Immanuel took her mind off her troubles— her argument with her sisters, her stress at work, and her upcoming meeting at Simmons & Sons Law Firm. She laughed so hard at his jokes, her jaw ached. "If I ask you out—"

Immanuel cut her off. "I'll go, but I'm driving, *and* I'm paying the tab."

"That's silly. It doesn't matter who drives or who picks up the check."

"It does to me. My grandmother raised me to be a gentleman, and I take great pride in taking care of the women in my life. That's the Morretti way..."

His words impressed her, and the more he spoke about his role as a man and his duty to care for and protect women, the more Dionne wished she were his girlfriend. It wasn't the first time she'd had that thought, and probably wouldn't be the last. Loyal, sensitive men had always been her weakness, and Immanuel was everything she'd ever wanted in a man. He was opinionated and outspoken, and she loved debating with him about hot-button issues.

As Dionne made dinner, they conversed about work, getting tickets for the improv show at Comedy Club Atlanta, and meeting up with Sharleen and Emilio tomorrow night. It had been three weeks since their group date to the bowling alley, and although there was still tension between the two brothers, Immanuel was more open about seeing Emilio. He had no choice. Dionne made a point of "running into" the couple whenever they were out, and would convince Immanuel to join them for a drink. She was looking forward to having Thanksgiving dinner at Emilio's Greensboro estate.

A sharp pain stabbed her heart. This year, Lorna was hosting family dinner, but Dionne didn't feel comfortable going to her sister's home. Not after the heated argument they'd had at her parents' house last Sunday night. Since Immanuel wasn't welcome at Lorna's home, she'd decided to spend the holiday with her friends. Her parents didn't like it, thought she was being unreasonable, but there was nothing they could say to change her mind.

"How is the new car?"

"You don't even have to ask," she said, a smile overwhelming her lips. "I love it."

Last weekend, he'd picked her up at noon, and after dim sum in Chinatown they'd gone to a local car dealership. She'd fallen in love with a Mercedes-Benz convertible, and thanks to Immanuel's excellent negotiation skills she'd gotten a great deal on the sporty red car. She'd driven it home two days later, and every time Dionne looked at it she thought about Immanuel. He was a godsend, the kind of person who'd give a stranger the shirt off his back. Not a day went by that she didn't wish they were more than just friends.

"I better go," Immanuel said. "It's eight o'clock, and I still haven't made dinner."

"You should come over. The mushroom Bolognese is almost ready, and it smells divine." Dionne opened the jar of tomato sauce, poured it in the stainless steel pot and stirred slowly. "Should I set another plate at the kitchen table?"

"Can I eat in front of the TV?" he asked, his voice filled with amusement. "The home team is playing."

"I'll make an exception, but just this one time—" Hearing a noise behind her, she broke off speaking and glanced over her shoulder. The jar fell from her hands and shattered into a million pieces, sending shards of glass flying everywhere.

Her body was numb, paralyzed in fear, and a scream was trapped inside her throat. Narrowing her gaze, she zeroed in on the moving target. Someone was on her deck. The person was crouched down beside the table moving their hands in a wide sweeping motion, as if they were painting a picture. *What the hell?*

"Dionne, what's wrong? Are you okay?"

"S-s-someone's outside," she stammered, unable to believe what she was seeing. She rubbed her eyes, but the figure on her deck still remained. "He's on the patio."

"I'm on my way. Go upstairs and lock yourself in the bathroom," Immanuel instructed.

Her heart was racing erratically, but she spoke with confidence in a voice that masked her fears. "Hell no. This is *my* house, and I'm not going anywhere."

"I'm on my way. Call the police, and don't open the door unless you see a badge."

Dionne rejected his suggestion, didn't give it a second thought. "I can't call the police. I'm new to Brookhaven, and I don't want my neighbors to think I'm trouble."

"Forget about your public image and call for help."

"Immanuel, I have to go." Dionne hung up the phone and dropped it on the breakfast bar. Keeping her gaze on the back door, she moved over to the end table and rummaged around inside her purse. *Bingo!* Finding the can of Mace, she tiptoed to the back door and flipped on the patio lights. The stranger scrambled to his feet, jumped over the railing, and took off through the back yard. *Was he the only one? Was there someone else lying in wait?*

Deciding to investigate, she peered outside. She didn't see anyone. Spotting an aerosol can on the ground, Dionne unlocked the back door and stepped onto the patio. Her stomach muscles clenched, and dread flooded her body.

Dionne turned around and gasped. Cupping a hand over her mouth, she stared at the horrific image before her eyes. Expletives were sprayed on her house. Cruel, horrible words that pierced her soul like an arrow. *Who would do this? Why? What had she ever done to deserve being called a gold digger and a filthy whore?*

Hearing footsteps behind her, she whipped around, prepared to fight. She saw Immanuel running down the street and dropped her hands at her sides. Dionne felt a rush of emotion—gratitude, relief and an overwhelming sense of peace. Taking a deep breath steadied her nerves and stopped her legs from shaking. She had to be strong, had to keep it together, and willed herself not to cry.

"Dionne, what happened? Are you okay?"

"I'm fine," she lied, biting the inside of her cheek to ward off fresh tears. "He's gone. I scared him off when I turned on the outdoor lights."

Immanuel gave her a hug, held her tight, close to his chest. "Good thinking. I'm not surprised, though. You're as smart as they come."

His touch was warm and felt soft against her skin. Though it did nothing to soothe her troubled mind. Someone was after her, and she didn't know why. Was it Jules? A former employee with an ax to grind? Someone from her past she'd wronged?

"Go inside," he said, squeezing her shoulders. "I'm going to secure the property."

Dionne returned to the kitchen, saw the broken jar on the hardwood floor and grabbed her cleaning supplies from the broom closet. Her mind raced, jumping from one thought to the next as she swept and mopped. *Is Jules trying to hurt me? Is this retaliation for the divorce?*

Anger coursed through her veins. Dionne gripped the broom handle, imagined it was the perpetrator's neck, and decided she wasn't going down without a fight.

"Do you need any help?" Immanuel asked, quietly entering the room.

Dionne shook her head, emptied the dustpan in the garbage, and returned her supplies to the closet.

"Did you get a good look at the perpetrator?"

"No, it was too dark, and he was gone in the blink of an eye."

"It's not safe for you to stay here. That creep could come back."

She scoffed. She couldn't believe what she was hearing. "I'm not leaving my house."

"Yes, you are. Go upstairs and pack an overnight bag. You're staying with me."

"I won't let some sick bastard drive me away from my property."

"What if I book you the penthouse suite at the Hyatt?"

"I want to sleep in my own bed, in my own house, not at a downtown hotel."

His eyes narrowed, darkened a shade. "Are you always this stubborn?"

"Yes, as a matter of fact I am. I'm a Taurus, *and* Somali, and since you don't have a chance in hell of winning this argument you might as well quit while you're ahead!"

"Copycat." A grin claimed his mouth. "Can I at least take you out for dinner?"

"Not tonight. I'm tired, and I don't have the energy to make myself beautiful."

"You don't have to *make* yourself beautiful. You already are."

"Not in jeggings and an old T-shirt," Dionne said, gesturing at her casual clothes. "I feel my best when I'm all dolled up, and I wouldn't be caught dead wearing this in public."

"That's too bad. I like your look, especially your cute ponytail and bunny slippers."

And I love your smile.

Sniffing the air, he glanced around the kitchen. "What is that amazing smell?"

"Mushroom Bolognese. Do you want some?"

Flashing a devilish grin, he hungrily licked his lips and rubbed his flat stomach. "Heck yeah! You know I can't say no to food, especially homemade pasta. I'm Italian, and there's nothing I love more!"

Dirty dishes, empty wine bottles and bowls of junk food covered the wooden coffee table. Dionne and Immanuel were sitting in the living room, stretched out on the couch, watching the game on TV. The table was a mess, the kitchen, too, but Dionne was so full she couldn't move. She'd clean up later after Immanuel left, though she wouldn't mind if he spent the night. The thought excited her. Hours had passed since she'd scared off the vandal, but Dionne couldn't stop thinking about what had happened.

Her gaze fell across his face, sliding down his broad, muscled physique. He looked dreamy in his white ribbed shirt and loose-fitting pants, but it was the good-humored expression on his face that turned her on. He was telling her a story about the time he got lost with his brothers in Prague, and the sound of his hearty chuckles warmed her heart. "I'm glad you and Emilio are back on speaking terms. That's awesome."

"Yeah, it's cool. My grandmother's happy about it."

"Who knows? Maybe Emilio will ask you to be one of his groomsmen."

"I can't go to the wedding. I have to work."

"Work?" she repeated, incredulous. "But he's your brother. You should be there."

"I can't. Things are still tense between us, and I don't want to ruin Sharleen's big day."

"But...I was hoping you could show me around your hometown. There's so much to see and do in Venice, and I want you to be my tour guide."

"Don't worry. I have a big family. Someone will definitely step up to the plate."

Nodding, she masked her disappointment with a smile. "You're right. Emilio said Dante loves a good time, and he's already volunteered to show me around while I'm in town."

"Stay away from Dante," he warned. "Trouble follows him wherever he goes. I don't want you in harm's way."

Then come to Italy so we can be together, Dionne thought, wishing he weren't being so stubborn. Every time she thought about her trip to Venice she pictured herself with Immanuel—sightseeing, kissing and making love. Feeling her temperature rise, she pushed the thought away and dismissed his words with a flick of her hand. "You worry too much. I'll be fine."

"I have to. You're important to me."

"Then come to Venice," she said. "I want to see Italy through *your* eyes, not your brother's. And I don't want Dante's girlfriend to hate me for monopolizing his time."

"What girlfriend? My brother hasn't been serious about a girl since the third grade!"

Dionne laughed. "So, you'll attend Emilio and Sharleen's wedding?"

"I'll think about it."

His words gave her hope. "That's all I'm asking."

Chapter 13

It was midnight, and Dionne had to be at the office first thing tomorrow morning to meet with an eighties pop star struggling with depression. But instead of asking Immanuel to leave, she filled his empty wineglass with more Chardonnay, and turned up the volume on the stereo. They'd been talking for two hours, and the Sam Smith song playing in the background put her in a relaxed mood. Dionne couldn't remember the last time she'd felt this content, and although she was angry about the graffiti on her house, she refused to let it bring her down.

"Are you ready for your trip to Seattle?" he asked.

"I'm excited about the Leadership Conference, but I'm dreading the flight," she said, tucking her legs under her bottom. "Thank God for sleeping pills or I'd never travel."

"Have you finished your speech?"

"Yes, of course, and it's *really* good."

"I'm sure it is. You're an intelligent, articulate woman with a lot to offer. "

"You should come to the conference. It's a great networking opportunity, and I think you'll learn a lot."

"I'll get back to you. Let me check my schedule first, and see if I can free up some time."

Tasting her water, she watched Immanuel over the rim of her glass. A frown covered his face. He looked troubled, as if something was bothering him, and when he spoke, his voice was strained.

"Friday's the big day. How do you feel?"

Dionne raised an eyebrow. "I'm surprised you remembered."

"I remember everything that concerns you. You're my number one girl, remember?"

His words touched her heart, and a smile tickled the corners of her mouth. "I'm nervous about the meeting, but I'm trying to stay positive. Jules's attorney contacted us, so I'm hoping he's finally come to his senses and is ready to settle."

His expression was sympathetic, full of warmth and compassion.

"We've been arguing for months, and I'm sick of it. I just want it to be over so I can move on and start the next chapter of my life."

Immanuel picked up the remote control, pointed it at the stereo system and lowered the volume. "If you don't mind me asking, why has it taken almost a year to reach a settlement?"

"Because Jules wants to hurt me. That's all he cares about. I can't let him win."

Dionne surprised herself by opening up to Immanuel about her marriage, told him things she'd never told anyone, not even her sisters. He was easy to talk to, a sympathetic ear, and she was grateful he didn't judge her or minimize her feelings.

"Life doesn't get better by chance, it gets better by change, so don't be afraid to speak up for yourself," he advised. "Don't let Jules and his high-powered attorney dictate what's right for you, either. Your life is yours to create, and yours alone."

"I know, but Jules is fighting me at every turn. So is my family."

Immanuel squeezed her hand. "It's been a stressful year for everyone, hasn't it?"

Dionne swallowed hard, slowly nodded her head in agreement.

"Dante got divorced last year, and it took a toll on everyone, especially my nephew, but it was definitely for the best. There are some things you can't put a price on, like contentment and peace of mind. Dante's a lot happier now that it's just him and Matteo."

His words gave her pause, made her reflect on everything that had happened since she'd filed for divorce last year. Immanuel was right on. The divorce was stressing her out, always weighing heavily on her mind. Dionne couldn't go anywhere in her old neighborhood without people staring and whispering behind her back. She felt alone, as if no one were in her corner. She wanted to move on with her life, but how could she when Jules was being petty and vindictive?

"You have to outsmart him. Give Jules something he wants—" Immanuel answered the question she'd posed in her thoughts.

"You mean besides strippers?"

"What does he value more than anything? What does he hold dear?"

"His money, his privacy, his secrets…" An idea came to mind, and Dionne broke off speaking. She'd have to lie, and would need the help of one of her female employees to beat Jules at his own game, but it was worth a shot. Dionne was anxious for a fresh start, desperate to be free of Jules and his meddling, controlling family. If everything went according to plan, come Friday she'd be a free woman. "Immanuel, you're brilliant! I know what to do to win!"

He chuckled, then wore a lopsided smile. "I'm glad I could help."

"You're always helping me. It's like you're my good-luck charm or something."

Their eyes met, and the temperature in the room rose a hundred degrees. Sexual tension scented the air, filling the room with its sweet, intoxicating fragrance.

Dionne examined him thoroughly—his creamy olive skin, his piercing blue eyes, the intense expression on his face—and knew what he wanted, because she wanted the exact same thing. She craved him, desired him, had been dreaming of kissing him for weeks. Suddenly breathless, she waited impatiently for Immanuel to make the first move.

Seconds passed, then what felt like minutes.

Deciding to take matters into her own hands, she moved closer to him on the couch and gently caressed his soft, smooth skin with her fingertips. His scent overwhelmed her, increased her hunger. Dionne was shocked by the intensity of her feelings, how touching him made her body throb. He didn't speak. Didn't have to. The expression on his face said it all: he wanted her, too. No doubt about it.

Her heartbeat sped up; her pulse, too. Anxious to taste his lips, Dionne closed her eyes and slanted her head to the right. *He's going to kiss me! Finally! I thought this day would never come!* When nothing happened, she stared at him, baffled by his behavior. "What's wrong?"

"You're still legally married."

"I've been separated for months," she countered, her mind reeling from his words.

"In the eyes of the court you're still his wife, and I won't do something that's ethically and morally wrong."

Dionne felt her eyes widen and her lips part in surprise.

Why couldn't he be like other guys? Why did he have to do the *right thing*?

"I've been cheated on, and I'd never inflict that kind of pain on another human being."

Her skin burned with shame, and her body tensed. His rejection stung. It was so painful Dionne couldn't bring herself to look at him. *Now* she wanted to run and hide. Wanting to be alone, she stood and moved away from the couch. "You should go. It's late."

"Are you sure you don't want me to stay?" He sounded concerned, and wrinkles lined his smooth brow. "I don't mind, and I'll sleep better knowing you're safe."

"Immanuel, I don't need a babysitter. I can take care of myself."

"I know," he said with a knowing smile. "I've seen you in action."

Dionne opened the front door and stepped aside. "Get home safe."

"Thanks for dinner. Everything was delicious, especially the homemade bruschetta."

With a heavy heart, Dionne watched Immanuel put on his jacket and walk outside.

"Don't forget to put on the alarm before you go to bed."

"Don't worry, Dad. I won't."

He grinned, but Dionne didn't have the energy to return his smile.

"Workers from the Paint Doctor will be here first thing tomorrow to repaint the deck."

"Thanks for everything," she said. "I can always count on you to come to my rescue."

"That's what friends are for, right?"

Her shoulders sagged. *Friends? Is that* all *we are?*

"If you need anything just call. It doesn't matter how late."

Dionne couldn't get her lips to move, and nodded her

head in understanding. Her heart faltered when he kissed her on the cheek. Feeling light on her feet, she gripped the door handle to steady her balance. Her body was weak, desperate for him, but she exercised self-control, chose to stare at the hardwood floor instead of his juicy, sexy lips.

"Sleep well," he whispered, his soft, seductive voice arousing her needs. "And good luck on Friday. Remember what I said. Nothing is more important than your happiness."

He then jogged down the steps and disappeared into the darkness.

Chapter 14

The ninth-floor conference room in the Simmons & Sons Law Firm had vibrant oil paintings on the walls, eye-catching sculptures that beautified the glass shelves, and floor-to-ceiling windows that offered striking views of downtown Atlanta, but Dionne was bored out of her mind. Anxious to return to her office, she glanced at her watch for the second time in minutes. She was leaving for Seattle that evening, and she had a million things to do before her nine o'clock flight to Emerald City.

Folding her arms across her chest, she tapped her high-heeled shoes impatiently on the floor. Sunshine splashed through the windows, but it didn't improve her foul mood. Jules and his attorney were fifteen minutes late, and she had no choice but to wait. Dionne was sitting at the table with her attorney, a no-nonsense New Yorker by the name of Zakkiyah Givens. As she watched the seconds tick by on the wall clock, her anxiety increased.

Hearing footsteps outside the door, Dionne straightened

in her chair and adjusted her tweed suit jacket. She could hear male voices, someone speaking in a hushed whisper, and rolled her eyes to the ceiling. Jules and his attorney, no doubt. They were standing in the hallway, plotting her demise, but Dionne wasn't fazed. She had a plan A, B *and* C in her arsenal, and she wasn't leaving the prestigious law firm without a divorce.

Her cell phone buzzed, and she took it out of her purse. Dionne punched in her password, read her newest text message and smiled for the first time that morning. It was from Immanuel. His words of encouragement made her feel supported, cared for. He called every night to check up on her, but Dionne hadn't seen him since he'd left her house earlier that week. It felt longer than four days, more like four months, but after the conversation they'd had about her marital status she knew it was important to give him space. She thought about him constantly, wondered how he was doing, and hoped he was thinking about her, too. Doubtful, since women threw themselves at him 24/7, but they had a strong connection, and Dionne felt fortunate to have Immanuel in her life. That's why she'd planned a special surprise for him. After her meeting, she was picking him up from Mastermind Operations and treating him to lunch. Thanks to Immanuel, the painters had done a great job repainting her deck, and all traces of the graffiti were gone. Unfortunately, she was still getting prank calls on her cell phone. Dionne was considering changing her number, but decided she would talk to Immanuel about the situation first. He'd know what to do; he always did.

"Dionne, let me do the talking this time—"

"Absolutely not," she said, adamantly shaking her head. "I can speak for myself."

"Yes, I know, but the last time we met you threw your water glass at Jules. I don't want things to get out of hand again."

"He called me a bitch. What did you expect me to do?"

Pride brightened her eyes, covered her face.

"Let me handle Jules this time, okay? I do this for a living, and I eat creeps like him for breakfast!"

The door opened and Jules, and his attorney, a lanky man named Mr. Munson, marched inside. Dionne wrinkled her nose. The stench of nicotine and cologne was so heavy in the air her stomach churned. *What are they trying to do? Kill me? Is that their strategy?*

"Good morning," she said with a polite nod. "Let's get down to business, shall we?"

Mr. Munson set his briefcase on the table and flipped it open. "Mr. Fontaine has revised his initial offer, and I think you'll both agree it's more than fair. Here is a copy for your review."

He slid the document across the table, and Dionne read it carefully, ensuring she didn't miss anything. It was a sham. It was the same settlement agreement he'd offered her back in August. The only thing he'd changed was her home address. "I'm not signing this."

"I knew you'd come to your senses," Jules said with a toothy smile. Standing, he scooped his iPhone off the table with one hand, and straightened his gray double-breasted suit jacket with the other. "I'm going back to work. See you at home, babe."

"Don't call me that," she snapped, annoyed with his smug, cocksure attitude. "I'm not your babe."

His eyes narrowed, and his face hardened like stone. "You're not coming home?"

"Not a chance in hell."

Silence fell across the room.

"My client doesn't want to go to court," Mr. Munson said, clasping his hands together. "So what do we have to do to resolve this situation in a peaceful, amicable manner?"

Zakkiyah spoke up, but Dionne interrupted her. She had to. This was her life, and she wanted to speak for herself. "I want sole ownership of the land I bought in Somalia last year," she said in a firm voice. "I bought it with my own money, as a gift to my parents, and—"

"Anything purchased during our marriage is joint property, babe. You know that."

"Mr. Fontaine is right. In order to keep the land, you'll have to offer him a financial settlement, or you can sell the property and split the proceeds evenly down the middle."

Jules sneered in triumph, as if he'd beat her at a game of chess. He draped an arm over the side of his chair. His eyes were filled with arrogance and hate.

Her temperature rose, and perspiration clung to her skin. Dionne could hear her heart beating, the loud, pulsing sound throbbing in her ears. She wanted to hurt Jules, imagined herself kicking him in the shin with her high-heeled shoes, but logic prevailed and she abandoned the thought. It was a challenge, but she remained calm and didn't lunge across the table to smack the grin off his face.

Glancing discreetly at her diamond Cartier watch, she watched the seconds tick by with nervous anticipation. Five...four...three...two...one...

Jules's cell phone rang at precisely ten o'clock, and he put it to his ear. "Talk to me," he chirped, drumming his fingers on the table. "I'm sorry, what did you say your name was?"

"Don't let Jules rattle you," Zakkiyah whispered. "Stick to the game plan..."

"No comment." Jules ended the call and rounded on Dionne, shouting and screaming insults. Sweat dripped down his face, and the veins in his forehead throbbed. "You're a real piece of work," he said, speaking through clenched teeth. "When were you going to tell me about your exclusive interview with *Atlanta Tribune* magazine at one o'clock today?"

Dionne made her eyes wide, pretended she was confused by the question. She hated his tone and his dark, malevolent stare. He looked like the villain in a horror movie, and seemed to transform right before her eyes. To win, she had to project confidence, not fear, so she held her head high and met his steely gaze. "I don't know what you're talking about."

"Yes, you do!" Jules gestured to his cell phone, raising it high in the air. "That was the editor of *Atlanta Tribune*. She asked if I wanted to be interviewed for the magazine as well."

Dionne remained quiet, crossed her legs, and pretended to study her manicured nails.

"This is how you repay me? After everything I've done for you?" Jules slammed his fist on the table and surged to his feet. He raged like a tropical storm crashing into dry land, yelling, cursing, screaming obscenities. "Dammit, Ross, don't just sit there! Do something!"

"There is nothing we can do," he answered with a shrug of his shoulders. "It's a free world. We can't stop her from doing interviews."

"Then I'll sue her ass for defamation of character." Eagerly nodding his head, he stuck out his chest and rested his hands on his hips. "You're not the self-made woman you claim to be. You're a fraud. Nothing but a low-down dirty gold digger who married up."

Dionne held a finger in the air. "Call me out of my name *one* more time and I'll spill the beans about your yearly sex trips to Thailand."

His jaw dropped, and the color drained from his face.

"That's right, Jules, I know all about your overseas 'business trips,'" she said, making air quotes with her hands. "I met with your former secretary last night, and she was most helpful."

"I can't believe this shit," he grumbled. "You stupid, conniving bitch."

"A bitch would have told *everyone* about your penchant for screwing underage girls, but I didn't say a word. I'm saving that juicy tidbit for my media tour."

His face crumpled like a sheet of paper. "You have no proof."

"Tune in to my weekly podcast tomorrow. It's going to be a fascinating hour, and I think you'll be impressed with how resourceful I am."

Jules dropped into his chair and tugged at the knot in his tie. "What do you want?"

He sounded defeated, looked it, too, but Dionne wasn't fooled by his woe-is-me act. He was trying to gain sympathy by playing the victim, tricking her so he could get the upper hand. He'd done it before, too many times to count, over the course of their tumultuous five-year marriage. If given the chance he would do it again.

"I want the land I bought in Somalia and a million dollars for my shares in Fontaine Enterprises, and the Pathways Center expansion project must be completed by March of next year."

He furrowed his eyebrow. "That's it? That's all you want?"

Zakkiyah clutched Dionne's arm. "Ask for spousal support and attorney fees," she whispered, dollar signs twinkling in her dark brown eyes. "That's another two million."

"This isn't about money."

"Of course it is! He's worth millions, and it's time to make him pay up."

"If I accept spousal support, Jules will hold it over my head for the rest of my life. Besides, I have my own money. I don't need his."

Mr. Munson cleared his throat. "Do we have a deal?"

Dionne wanted to jump for joy, but she remained in her seat. "Yes."

"Fine, I'll draft the papers and fax them to your attorney's office first thing tomorrow."

Zakkiyah opened her briefcase. "I have the revised divorce agreement right here."

Jules and Mr. Munson shared a bewildered look.

"Go ahead," she urged, pushing the document across the table. "Take a look."

"We'll need a few days to look it over."

Dionne shook her head. "You have an hour."

"An hour!" He was breathing heavily, huffing and puffing like a sprinter at the end of the hundred-yard dash. His eyes were wide with alarm. "We need more time."

"You've had almost a year. Enough is enough." Dionne rose to her feet, picked up her purse and put on her vintage-style sunglasses. "It's your choice. You can sign the divorce decree, or I can head to the *Tribune* for my one o'clock interview. What will it be?"

Dionne opened her car door and collapsed onto the driver's seat. It was over. Finally. After months of countless arguments and disagreements, she was a free woman. Free of Jules, his lies and his meddlesome family. Her plan had worked, gone off without a hitch, and she had Annabelle Clark to thank. She'd asked the novice life coach to call Jules posing as a magazine reporter, and she had given an award-winning performance.

Her thoughts turned to her family. Dionne wondered what they would say when she told them the news. Her parents were going to be upset—her sisters, too—but for once she wasn't concerned about their happiness. They didn't know what it was like living with Jules, had no idea how selfish and insensitive he could be, and Dionne knew in her heart she'd made the right decision. She'd done what was best for her, and that was all that mattered.

Starting the car, Dionne was surprised to see the time on the dashboard clock. It had taken Jules and Mr. Munson fifteen minutes to read the divorce decree, but they'd wasted another hour arguing with Zakkiyah about the confidentiality agreement. There was no media tour in the works, no interviews lined up with local magazines or reporters. But she'd signed the necessary papers and laughed to herself when Jules sauntered out of the room like a champion.

Dionne put on her seat belt and slowly backed out of her parking space. If she hurried, she could make it to Mastermind Operations by noon. Immanuel loved the food at the Italian bistro across the street from his office, and he'd treated her to lunch at the cozy family-owned restaurant on several occasions. *The last time we were there was the first time we almost kissed,* she thought with a dreamy sigh. Just the thought of it aroused her, made her giddy with excitement. Immanuel had been a great friend to her the past couple months, and if not for his great advice, she'd probably still be at Simmons & Sons Law Firm arguing with Jules. Dionne couldn't wait to share her good news with Immanuel and took off like a rocket down the block.

An hour later, Dionne pulled up in front of Mario's Italian Restaurant. She glanced at the front window to see if the restaurant was busy, and her lips parted in surprise. Dr. Pelayo was sitting at a round table, and she wasn't alone. Immanuel was her date. At the sight of him, her heart ached. He looked gorgeous in his casual business attire, more handsome than she remembered. *Is that even possible? I* just *saw him a few days ago!*

Dionne examined her competition, assessed the emergency room doctor with a critical eye. Her makeup was flawless, her dark brown hair was a mass of lush curls, and her crimson dress served up an eyeful of cleavage. More shocking still, she had love in her eyes. Dr. Pelayo was glowing, wearing a radiant smile. Her expression was the picture of happiness.

Dionne felt like a Peeping Tom and knew she should leave, but she couldn't stop staring at the attractive couple. Their attraction was evident, their chemistry so strong and intense she could feel the electricity pulsing between them from a hundred feet away. Dionne wanted to go inside and confront them, but struck the idea from her mind. Immanuel wasn't her boyfriend. Hell, they'd never even kissed. If she stormed into the restaurant, he'd think she was a nut. Her feelings were hurt, but she had to let him be. Had to back off. He was interested in someone else, and she had no choice but to accept it.

Sadness filled her, made her heart throb and ache. Immanuel was dating Dr. Pelayo. That was the real reason he'd rejected her the other night. Her marital status had nothing to do with it. *Why didn't he tell her the truth? Did he think she couldn't handle it? Or was that his way of letting her down easy?*

Dionne sat there thinking about the events of the past few weeks and the time she'd spent with Immanuel. They were some of the happiest moments of her life. Dining at premier restaurants, exploring museums and art galleries, hanging out with his family, spending hours on the phone confiding in each other. He'd come to mean a lot to her, and seeing him with another woman was a painful, crushing blow.

Dionne pressed her eyes shut and drew a deep breath to calm her nerves. She didn't have time to fret about Immanuel and his new girlfriend. She had work to do, lots of it, before Sharleen dropped her off at the airport. Nothing was worth missing her flight.

Taking one last look at the couple, Dionne stepped on the gas and pulled into traffic.

Chapter 15

The mood inside the grand ballroom at the Sheraton Seattle Hotel was lively and upbeat. Dionne couldn't wait to get on stage and deliver her speech to the sold-out crowd. Participants wearing smiles and name tags wandered around the room checking out the various booths and displays. Being among distinguished executives at the helm of profitable companies made Dionne realize this was the "big break" she'd been waiting for her whole life.

Boisterous laughter and conversation filled the bright, spacious room. As Dionne walked around, greeting people and shaking hands, thoughts of Immanuel filled her mind. *I wish he were here. We would have had fun together.*

Arriving in Seattle late last night, she'd headed straight to the hotel. Sophisticated and stylish, it was one of the city's flashiest, most popular hotels. It was a prime location for shopping and sightseeing, and its trendy restaurants were a hit among tourists and locals alike. The establishment had everything a traveler could want, and

Dionne planned to take full advantage of all the amenities the hotel had to offer.

Upon arriving at her suite, she'd collapsed onto the king-size bed. Instead of going to sleep, she'd turned on her laptop. She wanted her speech to be perfect, something that inspired and incited change, and had stayed up for hours working on it.

That morning, after a light breakfast, she'd enjoyed an in-suite massage, then a bubble bath. Immanuel had phoned while she was getting dressed, but she'd let his call go to voice mail. He didn't leave a message, and she didn't call him back. *What for? So he could gush about his new-found love?* Dionne didn't want to hear it. So instead of fretting about a man she wanted—but could never have—she enjoyed some retail therapy at her favorite department store. Feeling generous, she'd bought Chanel scarves for her mom and sisters, toys for her nieces and nephews, and a wool fedora for her dad to add to his enormous hat collection. Hopefully the gifts would help smooth things over with her family, and they'd forgive her for not being the perfect daughter and sister they wanted her to be.

"Dionne, how wonderful to see you again!" The program coordinator, a slender woman with bone-straight hair and wide hips, touched her forearm and led her to the stage.

Standing behind the lectern, Dionne watched as participants hurried to their seats. Sweat drenched her palms, and her mouth dried. To calm her nerves, she took a deep breath and allowed the fragrant scent in the air to relax her mind. Over the years, she'd spoken at workshops and career day events at prestigious universities, but this was her biggest stage yet, and Dionne didn't want to mess up.

"Please give a warm welcome to life coach and best-selling author Dionne Fontaine."

Polite applause filled the air, and cell phone cameras flashed.

Holding her head high, she straightened her shoulders and strode confidently across the stage. Dionne took her place behind the lectern, opened her leather-bound notebook and greeted the crowd with a wide smile. "I'm thrilled to be here, and I want to thank committee organizers for giving me the opportunity to speak to you about my personal journey to success."

The back door opened, and Dionne's gaze landed on the new arrival. Her eyebrows shot up, and her skin burned like fire. *Immanuel?* Feeling unsteady on her feet, as if her knees would buckle, she gripped the lectern stand to steady her balance. *What is he doing here? How did he know where to find me? Is he alone, or is his girlfriend with him?*

Her gaze zeroed in on his lips—the thick, juicy lips she was dying to kiss—then slid down his chest. Immanuel always looked amazingly cool, like a badass action hero in a Hollywood movie. Seeing him made her heart swoon. His camel-brown coat and black dress pants fit Immanuel perfectly, and his stare was intense, so laser-sharp she couldn't take her eyes off him. Dionne heard someone gasp, then watched as people turned around one by one to look at the back door. Eyes popped, jaws dropped, and women old enough to be his mother licked their lips and fanned their faces as if they were suffering from heatstroke.

Realizing she was ogling him, Dionne snapped to attention and glanced down at her notebook. Taking a moment to review her notes reminded her what was at stake. Dionne didn't have time to make eyes at Immanuel. She had forty-five minutes to deliver her message. She couldn't afford to squander a second of her time.

To capture the attention of everyone in the room, she raised her voice and spoke directly into the microphone. "As a woman of color, born to an immigrant couple from Somalia, I've experienced racism, sexism and discrimination, but I made a conscious decision to grab hold of my dreams. Through hard work and determination, I built a life that I'm proud of." Dionne waited until she had everyone's attention before she continued speaking. "I'm living the American dream, and it has nothing to do with where I live, how big my house is, or how much money I have in the bank…"

Dionne felt on top of the world, in complete control. She spoke openly, didn't hold back, and her transparency paid off. Everyone was staring at her, and the room was so quiet she could hear her pulse pounding in her ears.

"As employers and entrepreneurs, it's up to us to make things better for the next generation following in our footsteps. We—" Dionne emphasized the word as her gaze swept over the crowd "—we have to fight for fair treatment for all. I'm calling on each and every one of you to join the good fight, because equality doesn't just benefit women and visible minorities. It benefits *everyone*…"

Participants straightened in their seats, furiously taking notes, emphatically nodding their heads. Dionne spotted Immanuel snapping pictures of her with his iPhone and frowned. His baby blues were bright, filled with excitement, and he looked proud.

"Live your passion," she advised. "Do what brings you joy, whether that's teaching, photography or microbiology. Do it to the best of your ability."

Dionne didn't want to stop, wished she could spend the rest of the day imparting the words of wisdom her parents had shared with her over the years, but when she glimpsed her watch, she knew she had to wrap up her speech. "I hope your dreams are fully realized, and that you leave your mark on the world. Thank you for your time. It's been a pleasure speaking to you."

The crowd broke into applause, whistled and cheered with more zeal than baseball fans. Participants jumped to their feet, clapped so long and so loud, her heart swelled with happiness. Feeling like a rock star, Dionne took a seat on one of the padded chairs behind the lectern and expelled a deep breath. She spotted Immanuel watching her and returned his smile. Then she remembered his cozy lunch date with Dr. Pelayo yesterday and looked away.

The rest of the afternoon flew by. Each speaker was witty and entertaining, and by the time the conference wrapped up at three o'clock, Dionne was bursting with new ideas to build her brand and improve staff relations at Pathways Center.

Dionne stepped off the stage and shook hands with conference organizers. She was tired and her feet ached, but she signed copies of her latest life-coaching book, *90 Days to a Better You*, handed out business cards and posed for dozens of pictures.

Eager to speak to Immanuel, Dionne searched the room for him. She found him standing beside one of the food tables, and as usual he wasn't alone. Women were approaching him left, right and center, but when their eyes met he shouldered his way through the crowd and headed straight toward her.

Her heart jumped in her throat. To mask her inner turmoil, Dionne wore a blank expression on her face and arched her shoulders. His cologne fell over her, making it hard to think, but she forced her lips to move and greeted him warmly. "Hi. How are you?"

Immanuel wrapped his arms around her. "Baby, I'm so proud of you!"

Baby? The word reverberated around her mind, and when he kissed her cheeks and lovingly stroked her shoulders, Dionne thought her heart would burst with love. *Love?* The word scared her, conjured up painful memories, but she couldn't deny her feelings for Immanuel. He was every woman's dream, and she loved spending time with him. But that didn't mean she was willing to be his side chick. Pulling out of his arms, she swallowed hard and adjusted her cropped blazer and checkered dress.

"Dionne, your speech was outstanding! You killed it up there!"

"I did?" she asked, stunned by his praise. "You really think so?"

"Isn't it obvious? You got a standing ovation, and your fans mobbed you when you left the stage." He wore a broad smile. "I didn't think I'd ever get my turn with you."

"Immanuel, what are you doing here? You're supposed to be in Atlanta."

"You invited me, remember?"

Dionne frowned. "I did?"

"Yeah, when we were watching the game."

"I was joking. I didn't think you'd actually come."

"Do you want me to leave?" he asked in a solemn tone.

"Does your girlfriend know you're here with me?"

Wrinkles creased his forehead, and a scowl crimped his lips. "What girlfriend?"

"I saw you at Mario's with Dr. Pelayo yesterday, and it was obvious you guys were having a good time." Dionne searched his face for signs of deception, noting every move he made, but he seemed genuinely confused. Still, she asked the question weighing on her mind. "How long have you been a couple?"

"We're not."

"But she likes you."

Immanuel took Dionne's arm and led her to a quiet corner, away from the crowd. "Elena and I are not dating. I met with her yesterday to discuss a business matter, not to make a love connection. And besides, I'm interested in someone else."

Dionne arched an eyebrow, giving him a skeptical look.

She didn't know what to think. Was he feeding her a line or telling the truth? How could she know for sure?

"How did things go at the law firm yesterday?"

"We signed the divorce decree," she answered with a sad smile.

Immanuel rested a hand on her shoulders. "How do you feel?"

"Relieved, tired and anxious to get on with my life."

"If you don't have plans tonight I'd love to take you out for dinner."

"Can I take a rain check? I'm beat, and I want to turn in early tonight."

"Let's meet in the lobby at seven o'clock. That will give you plenty of time to rest."

"Are you *sure* you're not dating Dr. Pelayo?" she asked, unable to shake her doubts. In her experience, men like Immanuel didn't have one girlfriend, they had several, and Dionne didn't want to be his flavor of the week. "You guys have great chemistry and it's obvious she likes you—"

"Dammit, Dionne, I'm not attracted to her. I'm attracted to *you*."

Immanuel lowered his head and crushed his lips to her mouth. The kiss stole her breath and every lucid thought in her mind. She was stunned by his brazen behavior, but she didn't pull away. His kiss was exhilarating, and Dionne was hungry for more. She wanted him, craved him, and wasn't letting go of him until she had her fill. *Is this actually happening? Are we kissing or am I daydreaming?*

The kiss was definitely worth the wait. His lips were warm and tasted sweeter than chocolate. Dionne was under Immanuel's spell, caught in a sensuous, erotic trance she couldn't break free from. It was heaven. A perfect, incredible first kiss, and she didn't want it to ever end. Blocking out the noises around them, she linked her arms around his neck and caressed the back of his head with her hands.

"That was one hell of a kiss."

Dionne opened her eyes and met his piercing blue gaze. The ballroom was quiet, filled with only a handful of people, but to her surprise everyone was staring at them.

"Are we on for dinner tonight?"

"After *that* kiss?" she asked, making her eyes big and wide. "Absolutely!"

Releasing a hearty chuckle, he pulled her even closer to his chest. Immanuel nibbled on her bottom lip, then kissed her hard on the mouth with urgency. His behavior was reckless, nothing short of criminal, and she loved every minute of it. His passionate kiss, his caress, the naughty X-rated words he whispered in her ear. Immanuel was dreamy in every sense of the word, and feeling his hands on her body made her wish they were alone in her suite instead of in the grand ballroom. "You're gorgeous," he praised, nuzzling his chin against her neck. "And you smell delicious."

"I know, *and* I taste good, too."

"Let me be the judge of that."

He gave her another slow, sensuous kiss and she groaned into his mouth.

"I'll walk you back to your room," he said smoothly, caressing her hips.

Immanuel escorted Dionne out of the ballroom and through the hotel lobby.

I can't wait for dinner, she thought as they boarded the crowded elevator, hand in hand. He drew his hands down her arms, stroked her hips, and Dionne felt the urge to jump into his arms and kiss him all over. *Seven o'clock can't come soon enough!*

Chapter 16

Immanuel knocked on suite 1014 and waited patiently for Dionne to answer the door. Seconds passed with no sight of her. Where was she? Had she changed her mind about having dinner with him? Was she out with another man? One of the businessmen she'd met at the conference that afternoon? Immanuel rejected the thought. Dionne wouldn't stand him up. Not after that scorching, red-hot, goodbye-for-now kiss they'd shared outside her suite earlier. It was even better than their first, more passionate and intense. He'd never experienced anything like it before and was hungry for more. If not for a housekeeper interrupting them, they'd still be in the hallway making out.

Immanuel's cell phone rang, and he fished it out of his jacket pocket. His shoulders tensed, and his blood ran cold. He had nothing to say to Jules and wished the CFO would lose his phone number. *Doesn't he have a company to run?* Tired of Jules's incessant phone calls, he let the call go to voice mail.

Immanuel remembered their last conversation vividly. Last week, he'd had his report delivered to Jules via UPS, and the CFO had called him screaming bloody murder. Instead of taking responsibility for the mistakes he'd made in his marriage, he'd blamed Immanuel for "losing" his divorce, and threatened to ruin his security business. Jules was a sore loser, a bully who threw a fit whenever he didn't get his way, and Immanuel had no respect for him.

Immanuel wasn't fazed, didn't give a damn what Jules thought. He'd written a thorough report, and he was proud of the work he'd done. There was no proof of Dionne's infidelity, no evidence that she'd ever cheated, and he wasn't going to frame her to win favor with Jules. His grandmother had raised him to be honest and trustworthy, and he wasn't changing for anyone—not even one of the wealthiest men in the state. Now that his business relationship with Jules was over, he could pursue Dionne with a clear conscience. She was a beautiful soul with a big heart, and he'd do anything for her. To keep her safe, he'd commissioned his best employee to follow her 24/7, and although nothing else had happened since the graffiti incident, he'd implored his staff to stay on high alert.

His thoughts returned to their last time together. As Immanuel was running to Dionne's house, he'd spotted a black Cadillac idling at the end of the street and paused to read the license plate number. He'd asked Malcolm to help him track down the car and driver, and was confident the trail would lead straight to Jules Fontaine.

Immanuel didn't care what it took; he was going to keep Dionne safe. He worked long hours and looked forward to spending his downtime with her. They had a lot in common, and they never ran out of things to discuss. Immanuel wanted a life partner, someone he connected with on every level, and Dionne appealed to him in every way. She was the kind of woman he could bring home to his family, someone he'd be proud to have on his arm. Immanuel was scared of being hurt again, but he was ready to take a chance on love once more.

Immanuel knocked on the door again, longer and louder this time. A terrifying thought stabbed his heart with fear. Was Dionne in trouble? Was that why she wasn't answering the door? Because she was in danger? Taking a deep breath, he told himself to remain calm. He was overreacting. He'd only been waiting a couple of minutes. There was no need to panic.

He sent Dionne a text message, then knocked again. Hearing a noise behind him, he glanced over his shoulder and watched a group of housekeepers exit the elevator. Immanuel recognized one of the women from that afternoon and greeted her in Italian. He told her he'd locked himself out of his room, and asked if she'd be kind enough to open the door for him.

A frown darkened her face. "I'm sorry, sir, but that's against hotel policy."

To persuade her, Immanuel opened his wallet, took out a hundred-dollar bill, and put the money in her hands. "Please?" he asked, glancing at his watch. "I'm going to an important business dinner, and I don't want to be late."

Seconds later, Immanuel entered suite 1014 and flicked on the lights. "Dionne?" Sliding his cell phone into his pocket, he noticed everything was in its rightful place. Colorful cushions decorated ivory chairs, potted plants filled the air with a refreshing scent, pendant lights gave the suite a touch of class, and oversize windows revealed picture-perfect views of Seattle.

"Hello? Dionne? Are you here?" he called, walking into the master bedroom. Relief flooded his body, and released a deep sigh that fell from his lips. Dionne was sleeping. His eyes widened, as did his mouth. Her purple satin robe kissed her thighs, and her hair fell in curls around her shoulders. He stood in the doorway staring at her, thankful that she was safe and sound.

His gaze slipped down her curves, and his heart galloped. Immanuel recognized he was losing it and took a moment to regroup. Taking a deep breath didn't help. His heart continued to race, and he couldn't take his eyes off her juicy, sensuous mouth. God help him. Coming inside her suite was a bad idea, but his legs wouldn't move.

It amazed Immanuel how small she looked on the king-size bed. He was used to seeing her all dolled up, but preferred her simple, natural style. She didn't have any makeup on, and she smelled like tropical fruit, not a cosmetics counter.

His temperature soared. His inner voice told him to turn around and head for the door, but the urge to caress and stroke her smooth brown skin was overwhelming. Moved by the needs of his flesh, he took off his jacket, chucked it on the end of the bed, and kicked off his shoes. Immanuel knew he was tripping big-time, but his desires were all-consuming.

Stretching out on the bed beside her, he slid an arm around her waist. Their bodies were a perfect fit. Dionne didn't stir, but Immanuel was in heaven. He was holding Dionne, and it was a great feeling.

"This is a pleasant surprise." Dionne rolled onto her side and faced him. Opening her eyes, she fluttered her long, thick lashes. "I heard your voice, but I thought I was dreaming."

"I'm sorry. I didn't mean to wake you. I got worried when you didn't answer the door, so I asked one of the housekeepers to let me inside your room. I hope that was okay."

"Sorry about that. I called my mom, and after we got off the phone I dozed off."

"How is your mother doing?"

Sadness flickered across her face and seeped into her voice. "Miserable. I told her about the divorce, and she scolded me for being a disobedient daughter. Aside from that she's great," Dionne said, with false enthusiasm. "Thanksgiving is her favorite holiday, so she's busy getting ready for next week."

"Why are your parents so upset about the divorce? Couples split up every day," he pointed out. "Hell, my father's been divorced so many times I've lost count!"

"Divorce is shameful in the Somali culture, and the fact that I've been divorced twice is a huge embarrassment for my family. My failures cast a negative light on my parents, and I feel guilty for not living up to their expectations."

"Join the club. I was supposed to follow in my father's footsteps and become a championship race car driver, but I couldn't cut it."

"Was your dad disappointed in you?"

"That's the understatement of the year. He cut ties with me when I joined the Italian military, and said I tarnished the Morretti name and image by becoming a soldier."

"But the military is such an honorable and worthy profession."

"Tell that to my old man."

"What's your relationship like with your father today?"

"Strained. We rarely talk, but I make a point of seeing him whenever I'm in Italy. Even if I just stop by his villa to see my siblings for a short period of time. My stepsisters and -brothers are teenagers, and it's important to me to be a part of their lives."

Immanuel heard his cell ring, knew it was Malcolm calling from the distinctive ringtone, but he didn't move. His friends wanted him to meet up with them in Las Vegas to watch a boxing match at the MGM Grand tomorrow night, but he wasn't leaving Dionne.

"Your cell phone's ringing," she said, peering over his shoulder. "It's on the end table."

"What cell phone? I don't hear anything."

He reached out and touched her hair, curling a lock around his index finger.

"Do you still miss your fiancée?"

The question caught him off guard, but he answered truthfully, telling Dionne everything that was in his heart. "No, not anymore. I met a smart, captivating beauty with one hell of a right hook, and she's the total package," he said, his eyes glued to her face. "Seeing her is the best part of my day, and I hate when we're apart."

Her eyes smiled. "She sounds like an amazing woman. You should keep her."

"I plan to."

"This is nice. Lying in bed talking with you. We should do this more often."

Immanuel drew his hand across her cheek, and she purred in his ear. "Can I kiss you?"

A grin shaped her mouth. "Please do."

Immanuel nipped at her bottom lip, licking it with the tip of his tongue, and Dionne thought she'd die in anticipation. Desperate for him, she crushed her mouth to his. His lips were soft, the best thing she'd ever tasted. She wanted to be kissed, to be held and loved, and relished being in his arms. Her body ached for him, yearned for his touch.

Seizing his hands, she guided them to her hips, moved them down her thighs and over her bottom. That was all the encouragement Immanuel needed. He untied her robe, tossed it to the floor, and lowered his face to her breasts. He pushed them together, flicking his tongue against her erect nipples. He lavished them with kisses, sucked them into his mouth, stroking, massaging and caressing them. His touch fueled her desire. Immanuel grabbed her butt, squeezed it as if it were a Georgia peach and he was desperate for a bite.

"Your ass is amazing."

"Your *hands* are amazing," she gushed, her words falling from her lips in a breathless pant. She couldn't help thinking about her past relationships, and realized this was the first time she'd ever initiated sex with a lover. Immanuel excited her, made her experience feelings she'd never felt before, and Dionne wanted to show him how much he meant to her. She kissed him, parted his lips with her tongue, then flicked it against his. Pleasure filled her, coursed through her quivering body. "I could stay here with you, like this, for the rest of the night."

"That can be arranged. We can have room service in bed."

"*Or* we can feast on each other."

"I love how you think."

And I love you. Dionne held her tongue. To prevent herself from confessing her feelings, she slammed her mouth shut. "I want to make love tonight."

"To me?"

"No, to the hotel bellman," she teased, snuggling against him. "Yes, you. You're the only man I need."

"Making love is a big step."

"I know, but I'm ready. Aren't you?"

"Baby, I want you, but it's too soon."

Too soon? Are you kidding me? I've been dreaming about this moment for months!

"How would it look if I put the moves on you the day after your divorce is finalized?"

Rolling her eyes, she pulled out of his arms and swung her feet over the side of the bed. "Forget I said anything," she snapped, annoyed that he'd rejected her yet again. "I'm not in the mood to play games. I'm going to get dressed—"

"Come here. You're not going anywhere."

Immanuel grabbed her hand and dragged her down on top of him. He smothered her face with kisses, and she shrieked in laughter. "Do you have any idea how much I want you?"

"No. Show me."

Roughly cupping her breasts in his hands, he lowered his mouth and circled her nipple with his tongue. He sucked it, licked it, bit it softly with his teeth. He played in her hair, grabbing fistfuls, stroking her body as if his sole purpose in life were to please her. And she loved it. His kiss, his touch, the feel of his hard, muscled physique against hers. For weeks, she'd been lusting after him, and tonight she was going to have him—over and over and over again.

"I've been lying to myself for weeks," he whispered, his gaze as dreamy as his seductive tone. "I convinced myself you weren't my type, that we were all wrong for each other. But you're the only one for me, and I want you for more than one night."

His confession stunned her, and she fumbled with her words. "What are you saying?"

He answered with a deep, passionate kiss that gave her chills all over. He took off his clothes and chucked them on the floor. They lay naked in bed, exploring each other's bodies, kissing, laughing and talking dirty. Feeling his mouth on her neck, her breasts and her navel caused quivers to ripple across her skin. Dionne loved how broad and muscular his shoulders were, and couldn't resist kissing, squeezing and licking them.

Immanuel crushed his lips against hers. Dionne moaned into his mouth, took everything he gave, still wanting more, needing more. She loved kissing him, couldn't get enough, and wondered what the rest of his body tasted like. To find out, she licked from his ears to his chest and abs, then sucked his erection into her mouth.

Pleasure sparked in his eyes. Dionne twirled her tongue around his length and eagerly sucked, licked and kissed it. Having Immanuel inside her mouth made her feel strong, invincible and powerful. She'd never felt more comfortable in her skin and wanted to please Immanuel more than anything. Dionne couldn't get enough of him, and the more she stroked and caressed his hard, muscled body, the more she wanted him.

Immanuel opened his wallet, took out a condom and ripped open the packet. Watching him excited her, made her mouth wet with hunger. It was finally going to happen. After weeks of flirting and "accidentally" touching, she was finally going to experience the pleasure of having him inside her. Aroused and anxious, she felt blood rush to her core.

Immanuel brought her to his side, kissed her hard on the lips, and rolled the condom over his shaft. Dionne hungrily licked her lips. His erection doubled in size, right before her eyes, and she parted her legs to welcome him inside.

Immanuel slid his erection against her clit, slowly, as if he wanted to torture her. Tingles danced down her spine, erupting across her flesh. Dionne tried to keep it together, to hold her emotions in, but moans of satisfaction streamed from her lips. His movements were slow, deliberate, and each kiss increased her desire. She couldn't believe what he was doing to her, and he wasn't even inside her yet.

Immanuel gripped her hips, then eased his erection inside her. It was a snug fit, so damn tight she felt every inch of his length. Dionne couldn't stop shaking and lost complete control of her limbs. She was in her hotel suite, having the best sex of her life, but her mind was in the clouds, off in another stratosphere, no longer connected to her body.

"I love being with you, Dionne. You're perfect in every way…"

Soaking in his words, she reveled in his praise and admiration. It had never been like this before. They moved in perfect sync, holding each other tight. To stifle the wild, fevered noises streaming from her mouth, Dionne buried her face in the pillow. Immanuel picked it up and tossed it on the floor.

"Don't do that," he growled. "I want to hear every sound you make, every erotic moan."

Their lovemaking was fast and furious, an intense burst of adrenaline. It was the most thrilling hour of her life. He kissed her with a savage intensity, took everything she gave and more. Like his kiss, his stroke drove her wild. His erection swelled inside her, filling her sex. Immanuel was an incredible lover, the best she'd ever had, and she'd never forget their first time together.

Wrapping her legs around his waist, she grabbed his butt and pulled him even deeper inside her. Lightning struck Dionne's body. An orgasm stole her breath, made her wild with delirium. Immanuel gathered her in his arms and held her to his chest. He pumped his hips, moving at a fast, frenzied pace. His head fell back, and he groaned as he climaxed. Breathing heavily, he collapsed onto the bed and drew her to his side.

Seconds passed before her mind cleared and her feet touched the ground. Her skin was drenched in sweat, burning hot, but Dionne rested her head on his chest and closed her eyes. Immanuel pulled her closer to him and held her close. His arms were home, a warm, safe place. For the first time in years she felt an overwhelming sense of peace. *Wow, I can't believe that just happened. It was wonderful, amazing, beyond my wildest dreams!*

He stroked her hair, neck and shoulders, whispering sweet words into her ear. "I'm glad you invited me to Seattle," he said, pressing a kiss to her forehead. "I have an incredible weekend planned for us, and a big surprise for you on Monday morning."

"Immanuel, I'm leaving for Atlanta tomorrow."

"Change your flight and spend a few more days with me."

"I can't—"

"You can't, or you won't?" Immanuel cupped her chin in his hand and raised an eyebrow. "What's the point of being the boss if you can't break the rules sometimes?"

"I have a meeting on Monday morning with Channel 6 that I can't afford to miss."

"What's the meeting about?"

"The station did a story on me back in May, and I hit it off with the head producer," she explained, unable to contain her excitement. "He's developing a new reality show called *Celebrities Gone Wild*, and he wants me to be the resident life coach."

"Really? You'd agree to let cameras follow you around twenty-four/seven?"

"Absolutely. I want to help people in need of guidance and support, and television would be a great platform to show why life coaches are vital to society."

"When would you have time to do a TV show?" He stared down at her with a concerned expression on his face. "You already work eighty hours a week."

"I'll make time. This deal could catapult Pathways Center to the top, and I'll do anything to make my business more successful."

His frown deepened, but he spoke to her in a soft, soothing voice. "Since we only have twenty-four hours together, we better make the most of it."

"I agree. Seattle is one of my favorite cities in the world, and I'm up for anything."

"Do you want to order in, or go out? I made reservations at the best French restaurant in the city, but I'm cool with staying in if that's what you want—"

"I don't want food. I want to make love again."

His eyebrows shot up.

"I hope you're ready for round two, because I'm *starving*." Her gaze slid down his chest; her hands, too. Just as she had suspected, his erection was rock hard. *Lucky me!* she thought, rising from the bed. Feeling his eyes on her, she sashayed across the room, switched her hips to arouse and entice him. "I'm going to take a shower." Pausing in the doorway, she tossed a seductive look over her shoulder. "Are you coming?"

Chapter 17

Eagles soared in the clear blue sky, and the sun was the size of a beach ball—the most brilliant and radiant thing Dionne had ever seen. The 360-degree views of the city were spectacular, but nothing beat being with Immanuel. Standing on the observation deck of the Seattle Space Needle kissing him was the perfect way to end their romantic dream date. Seattle had lush landscapes, take-your-breath-away architecture and some of the best restaurants on the West Coast. Dionne loved everything about the charming, sophisticated city.

Snuggling against him, Dionne reflected on the past twenty-four hours. He'd loved her all night, made her body sing in every position imaginable, and now she had a permanent smile on her face. That morning, after making love in the shower, they'd dressed and enjoyed a hearty breakfast in the hotel restaurant. They'd spent the afternoon wandering around Pike Place Market, touring the Theo Chocolate Factory and admiring Italian Renaissance paintings at the Seattle Art Museum. As they strolled along the crowded streets, they'd snapped selfies at famous landmarks. The city had everything a traveler could want—culture, history, entertainment—and Immanuel had made sure she'd experienced a bit of everything. He'd promised to bring her back to Seattle for the Venetian ball, and Dionne was looking forward to returning for the black-tie event in February.

"You're addictive," he said, his words a hungry growl. "I can't get enough."

Dionne tightened her hold around his waist and sighed inwardly when he brushed his lips against her mouth for the second time in minutes. In his arms she felt safe, protected, and after everything that had happened the past few weeks his embrace was welcome.

"Do you want to grab a bite at Chico Madrid before we head to the airport?"

Dionne groaned and rested a hand on her stomach. "No way. I'm stuffed."

After a quick stop at the hotel to change, they'd taken a cab to SkyCity, the revolving restaurant in the Space Needle. It was the place to see and be seen in Seattle, and there was no shortage of bling in the dining room. Sitting cozy in their booth, they'd feasted on seafood, Peking duck and Italian wine. Feeding Immanuel chocolate cheesecake, Dionne had marveled at how much their relationship had changed since their first date. Six weeks ago, she was nervous about being alone with him, and now she wanted to spend all of her free time with him. Dionne was so comfortable with him, she confided in him about her problems. During dinner, she'd opened up to him about her struggles at work, her failed marriages, and her strained relationship with her parents and sisters.

Wrapped up in each other's arms, they boarded the elevator and got off in the lobby. Outside, locals streamed in and out of trendy restaurants, street performers sang and danced, and laughter spilled out of nearby bars and cafés. The air smelled of salt water, a clean, refreshing scent that made Dionne remember the romantic boat cruise Immanuel had taken her on last night. For hours they'd talked, danced and kissed. Their personalities complemented each other, but it was their differences that kept things exciting and interesting.

On Sixth Avenue, Dionne searched the streets for a taxi. "I don't see a cab anywhere."

"Let's walk. It stopped raining, and now it's a gorgeous autumn night."

Wrinkling her nose, she stared down at her designer outfit. Her gold ankle-tie pumps complemented her black leather dress perfectly, but they weren't made for an evening stroll. To please Immanuel, she'd straightened her hair and put on a sexy outfit and sultry makeup. He'd been complimenting her all night, and when he wasn't praising her look, he was stealing kisses and stroking her hips. "The hotel is six blocks away," she pointed out, glancing up and down the block for a yellow cab. "I don't know if I can walk that far in these heels."

"I'll carry you if you get tired."

"Save your energy for later." Dionne winked. "You're going to need it."

Strolling down the street, they chatted about their favorite places in Seattle, their plans for Thanksgiving and her upcoming trip to Italy. "I want you to be my date for Sharleen and Emilio's wedding." Dionne held her breath, waited anxiously for his response, but he didn't speak. "Please? I hate flying, and I need you to keep me company."

"No, you don't. You pop a sleeping pill and it knocks you out, remember?"

Dionne wanted to kick herself, wishing she hadn't told him about her fear of flying. She thought for a moment.

"It's a ten-hour flight. Imagine how much fun we'll have in first class."

"Baby, I'm sorry. I can't."

"But Italy's home. Don't you want to see your friends and family—"

"It's not home. Not anymore. I can never live in Venice again, and I don't want to."

"Never?" Her ears perked up, and her feet slowed. "Why not? What happened?"

"It's a long story."

"We have time." Dionne led him over to a wooden bench and sat down. "Our flight doesn't leave until six. That gives us plenty of time to talk."

He didn't move, so she patted the space beside her. "Please?"

Nodding his head, he took a seat and clasped his hands in front of him. He spoke in a whisper, as if each word was a struggle. "I left Venice because I was receiving death threats."

"Death threats!" Her pulse quickened, and her heart thumped in her ears. Dionne heard her cell phone ringing inside her purse, but she ignored it and blocked out the noises on the busy downtown street. She wanted to hear his story, so she leaned forward and moved closer to him on the bench. His scent aroused her, teasing her senses, but she kept her hands in her lap and off his chest. "Immanuel, what happened?"

"I provided security for the ambassador to the US for several years."

His voice was so low Dionne strained to hear what he was saying.

"It was an open secret that the ambassador had affairs, and one night while I was doing my rounds, his wife propositioned me to get even with her philandering husband."

"What did you do?"

"I turned her down, but she told her husband I approached her for sex. My colleague, a man I treated like a brother, corroborated her story." His eyes narrowed, and a dark shadow crossed his face. "I was arrested, charged, and spent a night in jail."

"That's ridiculous! You did nothing wrong, and there was no proof!"

"The charges were eventually dropped, but the damage had already been done. My business and reputation were tarnished. I had no choice but to leave town."

Resting a hand on his back, she slowly rubbed his neck and shoulders. It killed her to see him in pain, and Dionne wished there was something she could do to make things better. "Is that why you left Venice? Because of the stress of the investigation?"

Immanuel lowered his gaze to the ground. "I was receiving death threats, my office was vandalized numerous times, and I couldn't go anywhere without someone calling me a rapist."

"Baby, that's awful."

"Needless to say, the ordeal taught me a valuable lesson about life. The only person I trust is myself. Not my friends, not my family, and certainly not a girlfriend or colleague—"

"Immanuel, that's not true." Dionne touched his cheek and waited for him to look at her before she continued. "You can count on me. I'm not going anywhere. You have my word."

He nodded his head, but his frown remained.

"I'm glad you relocated to Atlanta, Immanuel. It was a *very* smart move."

"I agree. My business is taking off, I've reconnected with my relatives here in the States, and best of all I met you." Immanuel caressed her cheek, drew his thumb down her nose and across her lips. "You're an incredible woman, and I feel fortunate to know you."

"I'm the fortunate one." Dionne stood, sat down on his lap and draped her arms around his neck. She'd never felt more connected to anyone, and wondered if they could have a strong, lasting relationship. He protected her, cared for her, and she wanted Immanuel for more than just a night. "You saved my life, and I'm forever in your debt."

His expression softened, and his hold tightened around her waist. His baby blues were irresistible, and so was his smile. Dionne lowered her mouth and tasted his lips. Lust shot through her veins, ricocheted through her body. He caressed her arms and neck, playfully brushing his nose against hers. She didn't have the courage to tell Immanuel what was in her heart, so she communicated her feelings with her lips.

"I wanted to tell you sooner about my past, but I didn't know how," he confessed, breaking off the kiss. "I was embarrassed about what happened with the ambassador's wife, and I thought if I told you the truth you'd want nothing to do with me."

Dionne held his gaze. "You thought wrong."

"I'm glad I did."

A family of five with two rambunctious toddlers walked by, and Immanuel stared at them. Dionne saw the longing in his eyes, his sad smile, and wondered what was on his mind. "Would you like to have a family of your own one day?"

"If you had asked me that question five years ago, I would have laughed out loud, but I've had a change of heart. My cousins, Demetri, Nicco and Rafael, have all married beautiful, successful women, and I get jealous whenever I'm around them." Immanuel took her hands in his, holding them tight in his grasp. "What about you? Would you ever consider getting remarried?"

"Immanuel, I've been divorced twice."

"What does that have to do with anything? Your past doesn't dictate your future."

"I'm unlucky in love, and after two failed marriages I realize it's just not for me," she answered with a shrug. "That's why I'm going to focus on my business and building my brand."

"You're being too hard on yourself. You're an incredible woman and any man would be proud to call you his wife." Immanuel kissed the tip of her nose and ran his fingers through her hair. "I know I would."

Her skin prickled from his touch. He slid his tongue inside her mouth, swirled it around, and she pressed her body against his. Caught up in the moment, she yielded to the needs of her flesh, kissed him until she was hot, breathless and dizzy. "Think we have time for a quickie before our flight?" she asked, stroking the back of his neck.

Immanuel squeezed her thighs. "Baby, we'll *make* time."

Chapter 18

"I had a great time with you this weekend." Immanuel picked up Dionne's hand, raised it to his mouth and kissed her palm. "When you get back from Venice, I'm taking you to this quaint and cozy bed-and-breakfast in Savannah. It's ridiculously beautiful. Just like you."

His words made her feel sad and excited at the same time. *If you want to spend time with me, then come to Italy!* Sharleen and Emilio's wedding was in two weeks, but despite her best efforts, Immanuel was dead set against attending the three-day celebration. "I'd love that," she said, gazing into his deep blue eyes. "It sounds romantic."

"We're going to have the time of our lives," he promised.

They were standing in the airport parking garage, leaning against the hood of Immanuel's sports car, and Dionne couldn't wait until they got to her house so that they could make love. "Immanuel, I don't care where we go or what we do, as long as we are together."

He kissed her then with incredible tenderness, and she melted into his arms. His lips were her weakness, so potent her ears tingled and her thoughts scattered. He held her tight, as if he was desperate for her, and lovingly stroked her skin. Immanuel was confident, refined and sophisticated. And he wanted her. It was a heady feeling, one that filled her with pride and boosted her confidence. He was always teaching her things, treated her with warmth, kindness and respect. When they were together nothing else mattered.

A car horn beeped, breaking the spell, and Immanuel ended the kiss. He helped Dionne inside the car, jogged around to the driver's-side door, and got in. Immanuel put on his seat belt, and then started the engine. Stepping on the gas, he sped through the parking garage and exited Hartsfield-Jackson Atlanta airport.

Dionne had napped during the flight from Seattle, and now she was wide-awake and ready to hang out with her man. The words echoed in her mind. *My man! I love the sound of that*, she thought, admiring his handsome profile. *And I love the way he makes me feel. He is, without a doubt, the sweetest man I've ever met, and he'll always be my hero.*

"You're spending the night at my place."

His hand climbed up her thigh, tickled her skin, and Dionne giggled.

"I'll drive you to the TV station in the morning, and pick you up when you're done. We'll have lunch, then play hooky for the rest of the day. Sound like a plan?"

"You don't even have to ask. I'd love to."

Ten minutes later, they arrived in Brookhaven and stopped at the local grocery store. Immanuel bought snacks, wine and a movie, but Dionne doubted they'd end up watching the new romantic comedy. They'd had a quickie in her hotel suite before heading for the airport, but Dionne wasn't satisfied. If anything their lovemaking left her wanting more. Desperate for him, she couldn't wait to get him out of his clothes and into her bed. The thought aroused her, and a grin overwhelmed her mouth. "Can we stop at my place on the way to your house?" she asked, opening her Gucci handbag in search of her house keys. "I need to grab something to wear for tomorrow, but it won't take long."

"Of course, baby. Anything for you."

Immanuel flashed his trademark grin, a smile so dreamy it made her heart dance.

"Keep talking like *that* and I may never leave your house."

"Works for me. I love the idea of coming home to you every night."

Dionne was shocked, but she didn't let her feelings show. The thought of setting up house with Immanuel, a man she'd known for not even a couple months, should have terrified her, but it didn't. Last night, after making love, they'd had an emotional heart-to-heart talk. Immanuel made her feel so safe and secure, Dionne wanted to be with him forever.

Immanuel parked in the driveway and got out of the car. He opened the trunk, grabbed her overnight bag and wrapped an arm around her waist. Dionne loved that he was always kissing and touching her, and couldn't wait to get him inside her house.

"Your house in complete darkness," he said. "You should have left some lights on."

"Sorry, Dad, I forgot."

Immanuel slapped her bottom. "That's Big Daddy to you."

Dionne screamed in laughter. She liked their playful banter and enjoyed kidding around with him. Immanuel was protective of her and overreacted at times, but she didn't mind.

"I'll go inside and secure the property." Immanuel took the keys from her hands and pecked her cheek. "You wait here."

"Whatever you say, Big Daddy!"

His eyes twinkled, and his shoulders shook when he laughed. Immanuel unlocked the front door, flipped on the lights in the foyer, and slid inside the house. Dionne poked her head in the doorway, watched as he disabled the alarm and checked the living room windows. He told her to stay put, then jogged upstairs to the second floor.

Hearing tires screech on the road, Dionne glanced over her shoulder. Her eyes narrowed, and her body stiffened. The white Jaguar with the tinted windows parked at the curb belonged to Jules. She had to get rid of her ex before Immanuel returned. She didn't want him to ruin their night, and shuddered to think what would happen if the two men came face-to-face.

Jules jumped out of the driver's seat and slammed his door so hard Dionne was surprised the window didn't shatter into a million pieces. Her pulse pounded in her ears as she marched down the walkway. "Jules, you're not welcome here. Please leave."

"You must think I'm stupid—"

"You're right, I do," she mumbled, folding her arms across her chest. He smelled of whiskey and was slurring his words. Jules shouldn't be talking, let alone driving, and Dionne wondered if she should call the police to take him home.

"I heard about your interview at Channel 6 tomorrow morning," he said, shouting his words. "Cancel it, or I'll sue your ass for defamation."

Dionne glared at him. Jules liked to think he was the Almighty, but he wasn't, and she was sick of him telling her what to do. "The meeting has nothing to do with you."

"That's not what my sources tell me."

"They're wrong."

It was a struggle to keep her temper in check, but she didn't lash out at him. There was no telling who was watching. "If you don't leave right now I'll call the police and have you arrested for trespassing." Dionne took her cell phone out of her jacket pocket. "Don't tempt me—"

"Baby, is everything okay?"

Dionne heard Immanuel's voice behind her and summoned a smile. She glanced over her shoulder to reassure him everything was okay. Then all hell broke loose. Jules rushed past her, pushed Immanuel in the chest, and swung wild, frenzied punches that didn't connect.

"You no-good son of a bitch! I told you to trail her, not screw her!" Baring his teeth, he shouted insults and threats. "You're finished in this town. You hear me, Morretti? Done. I'm going to ruin you if it's the last thing I do."

Dionne couldn't catch her breath, fought to get oxygen into her lungs. It felt as if an orange was stuck in the back of her throat, and her temples throbbed in pain. *I told you to trail her, not screw her!* The words blared in her eardrum, piercing her heart and soul.

"Don't listen to him," Immanuel said, his tone filled with urgency and desperation. "He's trying to break us up, but I won't let that happen. Dionne, we belong together, and—"

"Is it true? Did he hire you to…" Dionne lost her voice and broke off speaking.

"Of course it's true," Jules snapped, his tone laced with hate. "I've paid him thousands of dollars since August, and I have the documentation to prove it."

"Jules hired me to trail you, but it's not as sinister as he's making it sound."

Her stomach heaved. The truth hit her hard, like a crippling blow to the chest. Dionne stared at Immanuel, noted his lowered gaze and bent shoulders, and knew he was lying to her. She couldn't believe this was the same man who'd promised to protect her, who had just made love to her hours earlier. He'd been conspiring with Jules for months, and his betrayal cut like a knife. Immanuel wasn't a hero; he was a fraud. His bitter betrayal broke her heart.

A sob rose in her throat, and it took everything in her not to burst into tears. Dionne willed herself not to cry. She was determined to keep it together in the presence of her adversaries. She felt dumb for trusting Immanuel—her ex-husband's hired hand—and her pain was so great her body ached. He'd played kickball with her heart, filled her head with empty lies and promises, and Dionne had no one to blame but herself.

"This isn't over, Morretti." Jules rounded on Dionne and spoke through clenched teeth. "No one messes with me and gets away with it. Cancel that interview at Channel 6 or else."

Immanuel stepped forward and jabbed a finger at Jules chest. "If you even *think* of hurting her I'll hunt you down and beat you like the dog you are."

"Don't touch me. This suit costs more than your entire wardrobe…"

Anger roared through Dionne's veins, and her hands balled into fists. She wanted to smack them both—especially Immanuel for deceiving her—but she kept a cool head.

"We'll see who gets the last laugh, Morretti."

Jules stalked over to his car, jumped inside and took off down the street.

"Baby, let's go inside."

"So, you can lie to me again? Hell no."

"We need to talk—"

Dionne cut him off. "About what? How you plotted with Jules to destroy me?"

"Don't say things like that."

"Why not? It's the truth." Something triggered in her brain, and she gave a bitter laugh. "Is Immanuel even your real name, or is that a lie, too? For all I know, you're married with kids. You're an accomplished liar, so I wouldn't put it past you."

"Dionne, don't talk like that. You know me—"

"No, I don't. You and Jules are cut from the same cloth. I wish I'd never met you."

"Don't let him come between us. He's not worth it."

"There is no us. We had sex a few times. That's all it was."

A cold wind whipped through the air, and Dionne hugged her arms to her chest. There was nothing left to say. They were over, and there was nothing he could say to change her mind. Dionne spun around, but Immanuel caught her arm.

"Don't touch me," she snapped breaking free of his grasp. "Don't you dare touch me!"

"Ma'am, is everything okay?" A jogger in an Adidas sweat suit and neon green sneakers stood on the sidewalk. "Is this guy bothering you? Do you want me to call the cops?"

Too choked up to speak, Dionne rushed inside the house and locked the front door behind her. There, in the privacy of her home, she curled up on the couch and let the tears flow from her eyes.

Chapter 19

Immanuel felt like the scum of the earth, and not just because he'd lied to Malcolm about being sick for the fourth consecutive day. He'd hurt Dionne—the only woman he'd ever truly loved and given his heart to. He was mad at himself for causing her such pain. It had been almost a week since their argument, but he still couldn't get her words out of his mind.

Hanging his head, he closed his eyes and raked his hands through his hair. *What was I thinking? Why didn't I tell her the truth when I had the chance?* He'd tried coming clean on numerous occasions, but he always lost the nerve. He didn't know what to say. It was never the right time. Or at least that's what he had told himself whenever guilt troubled his conscience. The truth was he didn't tell Dionne about his relationship with Jules because he didn't want to lose her. His wait-and-see approach had backfired, and now she wouldn't talk to him.

Immanuel walked into the living room, fell into his

favorite chair and reached for the bottle of vodka on the side table. *When did I finish it?* he wondered, scratching his head. *Last night? Two days ago? On Sunday when I was looking at pictures of Dionne on my cell phone?* He longed to see her, and would give anything to hold her one more time. He'd gone to Pathways Center so many times the receptionist had threatened to call the cops on him. Thankfully, Sharleen had come to his aid. She'd promised to talk to Dionne on his behalf and texted him words of encouragement every day. Not that it helped. Immanuel was miserable, sick over what he'd done. He had called her every single day and had gifts delivered to her office, but to no avail. His heart and mind were at war with each other, and for the first time in his life he didn't know what to do. Immanuel wanted a wife, not a playmate, and the only woman he wanted was Dionne. He craved her, longed to touch her and replayed the intimate moments they'd shared over and over again in his mind. In bed, she'd unleashed her wild side, given him the best sex of his life. A week later he could still hear her moans of pleasure in his ears.

His gaze drifted to the window. The dark, overcast sky mirrored his bleak mood. Living without Dionne was excruciating. Last night, after talking with Sharleen, he'd gone to Dionne's house to apologize. Her car was parked in the driveway and the lights were on in the kitchen, but she didn't answer the door. She was always on his mind, and he wanted her more than anything. He'd screwed things up, and now he had to fix them, but how?

Immanuel's cell phone rang, and he swiped it off the coffee table. Every time his phone rang he prayed it was Dionne, but it never was. Today was no different.

"Malcolm, what do you want?"

"I love you, too," he teased with a dry laugh. "I found Brad McClendon."

He gripped his cell, pressing it closer to his ear. Troubled about what Jules had told him weeks earlier, Immanuel had done extensive background checks on all of Dionne's past and present employees. There had been no red flags, nothing to raise alarms, but he'd been unable to locate her former right-hand man.

"After leaving Pathways Center, he reunited with his estranged wife, relocated to Augusta, and started his own life coaching business."

"If Brad didn't attack Dionne, then who did?" Pacing the length of the room, he voiced his frustrations. "Damn, after all these weeks of hard work, we're back to square one."

"Not so fast, Immanuel. There's more. I tracked down the guy who rented the Cadillac Escalade you saw parked on Dionne's street the night her house was vandalized."

"Good work, man. Where is he?"

"At Friendship House. It's a homeless shelter on Williams Street."

His ears perked up. In Seattle, he'd spent long hours talking with Dionne about her family, her career and her volunteer work. It was during that conversation at a downtown coffee shop that he'd learned about her charity work at Friendship House. The Fontaine Family had been involved with the organization for decades. Over the years Dionne had done everything including teaching cooking classes, tutoring students in math and feeding homeless youth.

"He's an ex-con with a lengthy rap sheet," Malcolm explained.

"I knew it. Jules paid him to attack Dionne, and now we finally have the evidence to prove it."

"You're wrong. It wasn't her ex."

Immanuel frowned. "Are you sure?"

"Positive. Jules doesn't know the guy, but someone in his family does, and you'll never believe who it is. I've

been a PI for two decades, but even I didn't see this coming…"

Stroking his chin, he listened closely to what his friend
had to say. Finally, after weeks of chasing leads and dead
ends, all the pieces of the puzzle fit. Anger burned inside
him, roared through his veins. He wanted to get even with
the person who'd orchestrated the attack on Dionne, but
he governed his temper.

"Do you know where Friendship House is?"

"No, but I'll find it. See you in twenty minutes."

Ending the call, he pocketed his cell and grabbed his
car keys off the kitchen counter. Ready to even the score,
he stalked through the living room and into the garage.
Immanuel knew who was after Dionne, and they were
going down.

"Get out or I'll throw you out!"

The velocity of Jules's tone made the windows in the
thirteenth-floor conference room shake, but Immanuel
didn't move. Tucking the manila envelope under his arm,
he locked the door and folded his arms across his chest.
Now he had everyone's attention. He was at Fontaine
Enterprises on official business, not to shoot the breeze
with the first family of Atlanta. He wasn't leaving until
he confronted the person who'd been terrorizing Dionne
for weeks.

His heart ached as an image of her flashed in his mind,
but he pushed past his pain and swallowed the lump in his
throat. After he left Fontaine Enterprises, he was going
to find Dionne, and this time he wasn't leaving Pathways
Center until they spoke. He didn't want to talk to her at
work with her staff listening in, but what choice did he
have? He'd given her space, but enough was enough. It
was time to bring his baby home. He wasn't going to lose

her, not after everything they'd been through, and he was desperate to reconcile with her.

"I'm calling security." Jules snatched the phone off the cradle and dialed.

"Good idea. They can arrest the person who's been terrorizing Dionne."

"Who are you?" Mrs. Fontaine asked, clutching her necklace. "What do you want?"

Seated around the glass table were Jules, his older sister, Adeline, and his parents, Francois and Helene Fontaine. They were all smartly dressed, and wore matching frowns.

"That's Immanuel Morretti, Dionne's new boy toy," Adeline said, her tone dripping with disgust. "You should be ashamed of yourself for carrying on with a married woman."

"And *you* should be ashamed of yourself for hiring a hit man."

The phone dropped from Jules's hand and fell to the table. "What?"

"Adeline, what is he talking about?" Mr. Fontaine asked. "What's going on?"

Immanuel stared at Adeline. Her eyes were dark, and her expression was blank. "Guess who I tracked down at Friendship House? Your old buddy Tyler Keaton. I wonder what your country club friends would think if they knew you socialized with hardened criminals."

The room sweltered with heat, and the air became thicker than fog.

"You have no proof," Adeline said with a dismissive shrug. "It's your word against mine, and who do you think the police are going to believe? A woman with a stellar reputation, or a lowly security guard with a chip on his shoulder?"

Immanuel opened the envelope, took out Malcolm's report, and dropped it on the table. "It's all right there. You were mad at Dionne for filing for divorce, so you hired Tyler to attack her. You rented him a car and gave him hundreds of dollars' worth of gifts and cash."

"Adeline! No!" yelled Mrs. Fontaine. "You didn't!"

"Ma, I had to do something. I couldn't let Dionne tarnish our image."

Jules spoke through clenched teeth. "I told you I could handle it."

"Jules, please. You talk a good game, but you're a spineless jellyfish."

Sweat dripped down Mr. Fontaine's face. "Are you going to tell the police what you know?" he asked, his eyes wide with fear. "Surely we can work something out that's beneficial for all parties involved."

"I bought your buddy Tyler a one-way ticket back to Detroit, and I personally put him on the bus." Immanuel addressed Adeline. "If Dionne so much as breaks a nail, I'll tell the police everything I know, so stay the hell away from her."

Adeline wouldn't meet his gaze, looking everywhere but at him.

Turning toward the door, he remembered a conversation he'd had with Dionne weeks earlier about her charity work and spun back around. "Adeline, since you like helping ex-cons, you're going to make a million-dollar donation to Re-entry Project Inc. on Dionne's behalf." He added, "And you're going to do it by four o'clock today."

"A million dollars!" Mrs. Fontaine shrieked. "That's blackmail!"

"No," he said in a firm tone of voice. "That's justice."

Immanuel stalked out of the room and marched down the hall.

"Morretti, wait up!"

Stopping, he faced Jules. He'd been wrong about the CFO. Jules had a vicious temper and an ego the size of

Texas, but he wasn't the one bent on revenge; his older sister was.

"I like the way you work, Morretti, and I could use someone with your insight and initiative at Fontaine Enterprises. Can we set up a time next week to talk?"

Immanuel didn't know if Jules was serious or pulling his leg, but it didn't matter. Dionne was his priority, not working with Fontaine Enterprises, and he didn't want to do anything to jeopardize their relationship. "No, thanks. I have my own business to run."

Jules released a deep sigh, shuffling and shifting his feet. "Tell Dionne I'm sorry. I had nothing to do with her attack. I feel horrible about what my sister did to her," he said in a low voice. He released a deep sigh. "If I could go back in time I would. Dionne's a good woman, but I took her for granted…"

I know, and if she takes me back I'll never, ever do the same.

"Take care of her, okay? She deserves happiness, and I hope she finds it in you."

Minutes later, Immanuel exited the elevator and marched through the sun-drenched lobby. He called Dionne's cell phone, and when her voice mail came on he left another message—his third one that day. Immanuel didn't know what else to do. He'd texted Sharleen and discovered Dionne had the day off work. At this rate, he wouldn't see her before she left for Italy on Friday. He had forty-eight hours to reconcile with her, but Immanuel feared he would run out of time. Feeling discouraged, he searched his contact list, found the number he was looking for and waited anxiously for the call to connect.

"Immanuel? What's up?"

He yanked open his car door and dropped into the driver's seat. "Emilio, I messed up."

"You sound like crap. What's going on?"

Immanuel vented, told his brother about his argument with Dionne and their bitter breakup last Sunday night. "I feel like I'm losing my mind," he confessed, staring aimlessly out the window. "Dionne won't speak to me, and I'm dying a slow death without her."

"You guys were a no-show for Thanksgiving, so I knew something was wrong," Emilio said quietly. "Dwelling on the past isn't going to help matters. We need a plan."

"We? You're going to help even though we have a strained relationship?"

"Had," he corrected, emphasizing the word. "Let's start over. What do you say?"

"I'd like that." A smile found his lips. "My baby was right. You *are* a good guy."

They laughed, and for the first time in days Immanuel felt hopeful about his future. He had Emilio back and a new, improved attitude. All he needed now was the woman he loved to make his life complete. "You're leaving for Venice on Friday, right?"

"Yeah, we have to arrive a few days before the wedding to finish up paperwork."

"Is Dionne traveling with the bridal party?"

"Yeah, she'll be on my private plane. Why?"

Immanuel shared his thoughts with his brother. Fired up, he felt his shoulders straighten and a rush of adrenaline that bolstered his confidence. He wanted Dionne back more than anything in the world, and wanted to prove his love in a big way. "What do you think?"

"That's your plan?" Emilio asked quizzically. "No offense, bro, but it stinks."

"Do you have a better one?"

"Yeah, I do. I don't mean to brag—"

"Then, don't. Just help me make things right with Dionne."

"To win her back, you'll have to fly to Italy."

Sweat clung to his shirt, made his palms damp and cold. Immanuel didn't know if he could. It was too soon. *What if the locals turned on him while he was out sightseeing with Dionne? What would she think of him? Would his past inevitably destroy their future?*

"Bro, the clock is ticking. What's it going to be? Do you want Dionne back, or not?"

Chapter 20

The words *Venice Skies* were painted on the side of the jet. The white custom-made airplane reeked of wealth and sophistication. It was a hotel in the sky, as luxurious as a penthouse suite, and filled with the best furnishings money could buy.

Stepping inside the bright, spacious cabin, Dionne noted the milk-white interior, plush seats and designer tables, and the state-of-the art electronics. R&B music played on the mounted speakers, and Dionne was surprised to see dozens of people chatting, eating and dancing as if they were at a nightclub. Stewards dressed in crisp navy blue uniforms served appetizers, poured champagne and walked around offering guests cashmere blankets.

"Good morning, Dionne. How are you?" Emilio kissed her on each cheek. "You look incredible. Is it just me or does she get more beautiful each day?"

Sharleen nodded her head and gave Dionne a one-armed hug. She looked adorable in her flashy bride-to-be getup, and her diamond tiara sparkled in the sunlight streaming through the cabin windows. "Girl, I love your outfit. You should be on an Italian runway!"

As if, she thought, rolling her eyes behind the protection of her sunglasses. *I haven't slept in days, and I have a killer headache. But you're my girl, and I want to support you on your big day.*

Waving at the members of the bridal party, Dionne strode through the cabin and found a seat at the rear of the plane, away from the raucous, inebriated group. She wanted to sleep, not socialize, and hoped Emilio and Sharleen's friends and family would keep their distance.

"Champagne?"

It was 9:00 a.m., far too early to have some bubbly, but Dionne could use something to quiet her mind and settle her nerves. Smiling her thanks, she accepted the flute and took a long drink. The liquid flowed down her throat, instantly calming her. A pleasant scent inundated the air, and her mouth watered at the aroma. Silver food trays filled with pastries, gourmet cheese and heart-shaped fruit covered the tables. Dionne didn't have the energy to get up. It had been a long, stressful week, and she was looking forward to resting during the ten-hour flight.

Kicking off her high heels, she rested back in her seat. Her thoughts returned to Thanksgiving. Upset with Immanuel, she'd decided to spend the holiday with her family, instead of at Emilio's Greensboro estate. After dinner, she'd had a frank talk with her parents and sisters, and they'd all promised to stop meddling in her life. Dionne didn't believe them, but she was glad everything was out in the open and they'd finally cleared the air. The highlight of the day had been playing flag football in the backyard with her nieces and nephews. Running around with the kids had helped take her mind off Immanuel.

Dionne opened her purse, took out her cell phone and

stared at the screen. The picture had been taken at Pike Place Market, and looking at the image of Immanuel made her miss him. Her nose twitched and her vision blurred, but she maintained her composure. Dropping her phone, she picked up her bottle of sleeping pills and flipped it open.

"Is everything okay? You seem upset, you're so quiet and withdrawn." Sharleen sat in the empty seat across from Dionne, put her purple feather boa over her shoulders and wore a sympathetic smile. "Talk to me, Dionne. I want to help."

"I'm great, fine, couldn't be better." It was a lie, one she'd been repeating for the past several days, but she'd suffer in silence rather than burden her friend with her problems. "Don't worry about me. Worry about memorizing your vows, because you're getting married in forty-eight hours!"

Sharleen pointed at the blue pill bottle. "What's that?"

"Sleeping pills. Can't fly without them."

"Sleeping pills!" Scowling, she plucked the bottle out of Dionne's hand and furiously shook her head. "You can't go to sleep. We're going to play party games, and I want you to mingle with our friends and family. It's a wedding celebration, remember?"

"I *knew* I should have flown commercial," Dionne grumbled, wondering if it was too late to de-board the plane. Peering down the aisle, she noticed the cabin door was locked and cursed under her breath. "I'll socialize *after* my nap."

"Why are you so tired? You were off yesterday and the day before."

Dionne swallowed a yawn. She hadn't had a good night's sleep since breaking up with Immanuel, and their argument had dominated her thoughts for weeks. He phoned constantly, sent her emails, text messages and dozens of red roses. Dionne wasn't impressed. Like most men, Immanuel thought flowers and expensive gifts could fix everything. He was fooling himself if he thought material things would win her over.

He'd shown up at her office, begging to see her, but Dionne couldn't bring herself to go to the reception area to talk to him. Not yet. Her emotions were still raw, her heart heavy with despair, and every time she remembered his bitter deception, tears filled her eyes.

"Let's compromise. I'll sleep for an hour, then join the festivities."

Sharleen leaned over and touched her leg. "Have you talked to Immanuel?"

"No. And I don't plan to. We're over." Her voice was quiet, filled with such anguish she didn't recognize it. Her eyes were moist, but she didn't cry. Dionne didn't want to ruin the festive mood inside the cabin or upset the glowing bride on the eve of her fairy-tale wedding. "Our relationship was built on lies and deception, and I have nothing to say to him."

"Dionne, don't say that. Immanuel loves you."

"No, he doesn't. He's been plotting behind my back from day one—"

"You have every right to be upset, but don't let your anger cloud your judgment."

Dionne took issue with what Sharleen said, but she didn't argue. *Was it true? Was she blinded by hurt and anger? Should she try to work things out with Immanuel?*

"Love is when your partner's happiness is more important than your own, and from day one Immanuel has done everything in his power to protect you. There's nothing he wouldn't do for you, and he's always had your best interests in heart."

"Then why did he deceive me? Why did he make me look like a fool in front of Jules?"

"I don't know. You'll have to ask him."

I can't. I'm emotional and upset, and every time I think about what he did I cry.

"The next time you see Immanuel, let him explain. Don't interrupt. Just listen."

Dionne nodded, realizing her friend had given her great advice. On Tuesday, when she returned from Italy, she'd meet with Immanuel. It was time. Time to move on and put the past behind her. She didn't know if their relationship could be salvaged, but she wanted to know the truth once and for all. "When did you get so wise?"

"When I met my Emilio." Her gaze fell across her husband-to-be, and her face lit up. "He redefined my definition of love, and because of him I'm a more understanding person."

"Good, then give me my sleeping pills!"

Laughing, Sharleen stood and dropped the bottle into Dionne's outstretched hands.

"Have a good nap."

"I will. See you in an hour." Dionne popped a pill into her mouth and washed it down with a glass of water. Yawning, she put on her earphones and slipped on her silk sleep mask. Reclining her seat, she closed her eyes and snuggled in her blanket. As Dionne fell asleep, images of Immanuel filled her mind, and his voice played in her ears like a love song.

Immanuel was dying to touch Dionne, wanting to reach out and caress her skin, but he exercised restraint. Dionne was sleeping peacefully, and he didn't want to disturb her. Remembering the last time he'd watched her sleep made his pulse hammer in his ears and an erection rise inside his boxer briefs. Her perfume was an intoxicating blend of fruits and flowers, and Immanuel liked the soft, soothing fragrance.

Dionne looked youthful and stylish in her off-the-shoulder blouse, gold accessories and jeans. Her makeup was simple; her hair was in a loose French braid. It had only been two weeks since their breakup, but it felt like months since he'd seen her, and his desire to kiss her was so strong his mouth watered at the sight of her glossy peach lips.

Immanuel tossed aside his business magazine. He wasn't reading it anyway. He'd been watching Dionne for hours, ever since he'd boarded his private plane that morning at ten o'clock, and was so eager to talk to her he couldn't sit still.

Stirring in her seat, she stretched and pulled off her sleep mask. The color drained from her face, and her eyes widened. He sensed her pain, her hurt. Immanuel didn't mean to hurt her, but he had. He wasn't going to lose her. Not today. Not ever. It wasn't too late. He'd fix things. Prove to her that he could be trusted with her heart. She had a beautiful spirit, an energetic, fun-loving personality, and despite the stress of the past few weeks she'd never lost her smile. Loving Dionne was easy, as natural as breathing, and he wanted to be her man.

"Immanuel, what are you doing here?"

"I came to see you. We need to talk."

Dionne glanced around the cabin, then at the side window. "Where is everyone?"

"En route to Venice in Emilio's private plane."

"I thought this *was* his plane."

"No, this is my plane," he said with pride. It was his guilty pleasure, a gift to himself when Mastermind Operations was named business of the year in *Italia Business* magazine. "Once you fell asleep everyone left and boarded Emilio's jet, *Lucca2009*, on runway three."

"You tricked me again! Why?"

"Because I wanted us to be alone."

"There is no us. You ruined *us* when you betrayed me."

His tongue froze inside his mouth. Immanuel didn't know where to start, but he spoke from the heart. Coming clean was therapeutic, the most freeing thing he'd ever done. He told her about his business relationship with Jules, what he'd written in his final report and who was responsible for her attack. Dionne didn't show any emotion when he told her Adeline had hired a man from Detroit to rough her up. "Ask me anything," he implored. "I want to make things right, and I want you to trust me again."

"I appreciate everything you and Malcolm have done for me."

"Adeline won't be bothering you anymore, and if she does she'll be arrested."

"Thank you for telling me the truth, but it doesn't change anything between us," she said, her voice a solemn whisper. "I was married to someone who lied and kept secrets from me for years, and I won't be a fool for love again."

"I was a jerk. Is that what you want to hear?" His palms itched and were damp with sweat. If he could just touch her, kiss her, she'd see what was in his heart and forgive him. He got up, crouched in front of her seat and placed his hands on top of hers. "I was scared of losing you, so I held back. I'm sorry that I hurt you, and I'll never do it again. Going forward, I'll be honest and up-front about everything."

"You should have been honest and up-front from the beginning."

Silence fell across the cabin.

Dionne was staring off into space, acting as if he weren't there, but Immanuel wasn't discouraged. They had plenty of time to work out their problems, and he was confident they'd be a couple again by the time the plane landed in Venice. "Baby, talk to me. What's on your mind?"

"I'm not your baby."

"Yes, you are. You were made for me, and no one else will do." Immanuel studied her, sensing that he was finally making progress, and moved closer to her. "Dionne, I can't live without you. I won't. You're my everything, and I'm nothing without you."

To his relief, her eyes brightened, and a small smile curled her lips.

"No one else compares to you." He took her hands in his and held them to his chest.

"You're a strong, self-made woman who carries herself with poise and grace—"

"That's a lie. I'm not."

Immanuel furrowed his eyebrows. "You're not what? I don't understand."

"I'm not a self-made woman." Hanging her head, she fiddled with the gold ring on her left hand. "I didn't build my business through blood, sweat and tears. My publisher put that in my bio to sell more books, but it isn't true. I used the alimony settlement from my first divorce to buy my office at Peachtree Plaza."

He cupped her chin in his hands, forcing her to meet his gaze. "Why are you ashamed? You've done nothing wrong."

"I feel like a fraud. I'm not a rags-to-riches success story, and I feel guilty for profiting off a lie. "

"You're not, so stop thinking that way. You used your alimony settlement to better yourself and help others, and that's nothing to be ashamed of." He paused. "In my opinion you *are* a self-made woman at the top of her game. And you're hot, too!"

Dionne burst out laughing, and his chest inflated with pride.

"Do you still need a tour guide in Italy?" he asked.

"Yes, Mr. Morretti, as a matter of fact I do. When are you available?"

Chuckling, he cupped her cheeks in his hands and showered her lips with kisses. They were sweeter and more addictive than red wine, and he couldn't get enough. "You've made me the happiest man alive!"

Dionne tossed her head back and shrieked with laughter. "You're *so* dramatic!"

"I'm not dramatic. I'm just a man desperately in love."

Surprise splashed across her face.

"How do you say 'I love you' in Somali?"

"Waan ku ieclahav."

"Wow, that's a mouthful," he said good-naturedly. "*Waan ku ieclahav*, Dionne. I love you with all my heart, and I always will, even when I'm old, gray and senile!"

Laughing through her tears, she asked, "How do you say 'I love you' in Italian?"

"Ti amo."

"*Ti amo*, baby. You're the best thing that's ever happened to me, and all the man I need."

They held each other tight, kissed with an intoxicating blend of tenderness, passion and hunger. Immanuel knew in his heart they'd be together forever. He had everything he'd ever wanted in life—a rewarding career, his family and most important the love of a good woman—and he'd never take his blessings for granted again.

Chapter 21

Palazzo Grassi, the seventeenth-century palace along the Grand Canal in Venice, Italy, was a striking piece of architecture. It was filled with glass chandeliers, contemporary art and paintings, gleaming marble, and wide, Gothic-style windows that offered breathtaking views of the canal. There was something romantic and mysterious about the palace, and the moment she'd entered it she'd fallen under its seductive spell.

Seated inside the ballroom, at the table to the left of the swan ice sculpture, Dionne sipped her red wine. The weekend had been one nonstop party, filled with one surprise after another, and she was having the time of her life with Immanuel and his loud, irreverent family.

Dionne swept her gaze around the room, admiring the striking gold-and-red decor. Soaring floral arrangements were packed with roses and wisteria, and the heady scent inundated the air. Candelabras bathed the room in a soft light, and satin-draped tables were covered with fine china, designer linens and menu cards adorned with Swarovski crystals.

A server in a black couture gown refilled her glass and quickly departed. There was no end to the glamour and grandeur of Sharleen and Emilio's wedding, and as Dionne ate her strawberry soufflé, she reflected on the events of the day. The wedding had been held in the main hall of the palace. The forty-five-minute ceremony was so touching Dionne—and every other female guest—had wept tears of joy. The bride wowed in a tulle mermaid gown with quarter sleeves, and the groom looked dapper in his crisp white tuxedo. Watching the happy couple feeding each other cake at the head table warmed Dionne's heart. Emilio had given Sharleen the wedding of her dreams, and she was thrilled her favorite couple were now husband and wife.

Laughter rang out, and Dionne glanced up from her plate. All across the room, guests decked out in jewels and couture fashion danced, mingled and sipped champagne. Peering around the chocolate fondue tower, she searched the room for Immanuel. Dionne couldn't find him anywhere. Ten minutes earlier, his cousins, Demetri, Nicco and Rafael, had pulled him aside, and she hadn't seen him since. Dionne didn't mind, though. She was having fun visiting with his grandmother, and wondered if all the stories the little old lady had told her about Immanuel's wild teenage years were true.

"Tell us the story again. I just *love* hearing it, especially the part when Immanuel took you in his arms, whisked you away to safety and saved the day..."

Dionne turned to Angela. The TV reporter wasn't the only one with stars in her eyes. Sisters-in-law Jariah and Paris Morretti were sitting on the edge of their seats, too. Since arriving in Venice three days earlier, she'd told the story numerous times, and every time she did Immanuel's grandmother broke down and cried. Being around Gianna made Dionne miss her own grandparents. *Who knows?* she thought, eating the last bite of her dessert. *Maybe Immanuel will come with me to visit them next year.*

Dionne caught herself. She had to introduce Immanuel to her parents before she took him halfway around the world to Somalia. In many ways, he reminded her of her father, and she was confident her two favorite men would hit it off. "I was walking to my car, talking to my cousin on my cell, when I felt someone grab me from behind..."

Eyes wide, her expression filled with terror, Gianna clutched Dionne's hand in a fierce grip.

Dionne finished the story and laughed when the women clapped and cheered.

"Immanuel's such a great guy," Jariah gushed.

"I agree," Dionne said, her heart overcome with love. "Thank God he uncovered the truth, or my ex-sister-in-law would probably still be terrorizing me."

"I think you're great for my grandson, and it's wonderful that you and I are a lot alike."

"We are, Gianna? Really? In what ways?"

"Isn't it obvious?" She winked and fluffed her curls. "We're both smart and sexy!"

Laughing, the women clinked glasses.

Spotting Immanuel at the bar, she put down her fork and dabbed at her lips with her napkin. She wanted to explore the palace, and hoped her handsome boyfriend would take her for a tour of the grounds. Excusing herself from the table, she walked confidently across the room. Dionne felt like a goddess in her beaded floor-length gown and sultry, exotic makeup. Her hair was in a braided bun, adorned with crystals, and Immanuel had been praising her look all night.

"I don't think we've met."

An attractive man with striking eyes and chiseled features appeared at her side. "I'm Dante, the young, wickedly handsome brother of the groom," he said smoothly, his voice carrying the hint of a West Coast accent. "And you are?"

These Morretti men sure have a way with words, she thought, giving him the once-over. *And they're all hot, hot, hot!* She took the hand he offered and smiled when he kissed her on each cheek. "I'm Dionne. It's a pleasure to meet you, Dante."

"A beautiful name for a beautiful woman." Wearing a pensive expression on his face, he stroked his square, chiseled jaw. "*Dante and Dionne* has a nice ring to it, don't you think? We could be the hot new 'it' couple!"

"You're going to have a ring around your *eye* if you don't get away from my girl."

Giggling, Dionne watched as the brothers embraced. All weekend, Immanuel had been introducing her to his relatives, and her head throbbed just thinking about all the people she'd met. Dante was a gregarious, life-of-the-party type, and Dionne liked him immediately.

"Holy crap! *You're* Dionne?"

Taken aback by his reaction, she said, "Yes, I am. Is that a problem?"

"No, it's fine. *You're* fine. In fact, too beautiful for him." Dante gave Immanuel a shot in the ribs with his elbow. "You know she's way out of your league, right?"

"Hater!" Immanuel winked at Dionne, then offered his arm. "May I have this dance?"

Nodding, she clasped his forearm and followed him to the dance floor. It was crowded with hundreds of guests, but they found a spot and wrapped their arms around each other. The song playing was in Italian. Dionne didn't know what it was about, but she loved the way it made her feel. Excited, aroused, in the mood for passionate, sensuous lovemaking.

"I'm going to ravish you from head to toe when we get back to my hotel suite."

Dionne fluttered her eyelashes and wore an innocent smile. "Why wait?"

"You're such a naughty girl," he said with a grin. "Whatever shall I do with you?"

"I'm sure you'll think of something. You always do."

"What's next?"

Glancing at the head table, Dionne remembered the conversation she'd had with Sharleen earlier in the powder room, and said, "The garter toss, the bouquet toss and…"

"No, not tonight. What's next for us?"

"Isn't this conversation a little premature? We've only been dating a few weeks."

"No, not to me. I'm turning forty in June, and all I want for my birthday is you," Immanuel said. "How does a summer wedding in Venice sound?"

Dionne took a moment to sort her thoughts and consider her words. They were having a great time together, and she didn't want to do anything to hurt his feelings, but they were moving too fast. "I've had two failed marriages, and if I get married again I want it to be forever."

"Not *if* you get married again, *when*." His gaze met hers, held her in its strong, seductive grip. "You know what they say. Third time's the charm."

"I have a history of plunging headfirst into relationships, and I think that's why I've never had success with the opposite sex. This time around, I want to take things slow."

"How slow are we talking? As my grandmother so kindly pointed out this morning at breakfast, I'm not getting any younger," he joked, stroking her shoulders. "If I proposed to you on Valentine's Day, what would you say?"

"That's less than two months away."

"You didn't answer the question."

Dionne was conflicted, unsure of what to say, and struggled to put her feelings into words. "Baby, I love you, but I'm scared of being a three-time loser in the game of love. What if we get married and things don't work out? What if we fall out of love, and—"

"That's impossible. We're destined to be together, and I'll never, *ever* leave you."

"I want us to date for a year before we get engaged."

"A year? That's a long time."

Dionne laughed and shook her head at him. "Paris told me Morretti men waste no time putting a ring on it, and she was right!"

They laughed together, then shared a soft, sweet kiss on the lips.

"I'm glad you turned down that TV deal," he confessed, openly sharing his feelings. "Now I don't have to compete with celebrities for your time."

Dionne nodded her head in understanding. Yesterday, while reclining by the hotel pool, the TV producer had called and offered her a job on his reality show, and she'd surprised herself and Immanuel by turning him down. Dionne wanted to grow her business, but she didn't want to work twelve-hour days or travel four days a week; she wanted to spend her free time with Immanuel and no one else. "To be honest, it was an easy decision to make."

"If you want to take things slow, then that's what we'll do." Immanuel held her close to his chest. "Baby, you're my everything, and I'll do anything to make you happy."

Love shone in his eyes, warmed his face with happiness. Peace filled her, silencing her fears and doubts. Dionne knew then, as Immanuel kissed her, she'd finally found her soul mate, a strong, sensitive hero who'd love and protect her until the end of time.

* * * * *

PRINCE'S VIRGIN
IN VENICE

TRISH MOREY

To magical Venezia,
floating city of love and romance.

CHAPTER ONE

PRINCE VITTORIO D'MARBURG of Andachstein was fed up. Bored. Even in Venice at the height of carnival season, even on his way to the most exclusive party of the festival, still the Playboy Prince couldn't ignore the overwhelming sense of frustration that permeated his skin and drilled straight down into his bones.

Or maybe it was just the icy pricks from the February pea soup fog needling his skin that were turning his thoughts from carnival to cynical. It was a fog that turned the magical city invisible, precisely when the *calles* and narrow bridges were more crowded than ever with waves of costumed partygoers surging to and fro, competing for the available space—brightly garbed men and women for whom the fog failed to dampen the air of excitement and the energy that accompanied Carnevale.

It was if the floating city had been let off a leash and, fog or no, it was going to party.

Vittorio cut a swathe through the endless tide of carnival-goers, his cloak swirling in his wake, his mood blackening with every step.

The thronging crowds somehow parted and made way for him. He didn't think too much about it. Maybe it was his warrior costume—a coat of mail and blue leather dressed with chain and gold braid—or maybe it was his battle-ready demeanour. Either way, it was as if they could read the hostility in his eyes as he headed towards the most exclusive party of the night.

And they could all see his eyes. Vittorio had given up playing with disguises when he was a child. There'd been no point. Everyone had always known it was him behind the mask.

Before the ancient well in the square that housed the Palazzo de Marigaldi, Vittorio's long strides slowed. Ordinarily he would have been relieved to reach his destination and escape the exuberant crowds—*should* have been relieved—except for the fact that his father had all too gleefully shared the news in his latest call, just minutes earlier, that the Contessa Sirena Della Corte, daughter of one of his oldest friends, was opportunely going to be in attendance.

Vittorio snorted—just as he'd done when his father had told him.

Opportunely.

He doubted it.

Opportunistically would no doubt be a better word. The woman was a human viper draped in designer artistry, lying in wait for a royal title—which marriage to him would bestow upon her. And his father, despite Vittorio's blanket protests, had encouraged her to pursue her desperate ambition.

Little wonder Vittorio was in no hurry to get there.

Little wonder that, despite the assurances he'd made to his old friend Marcello that nothing would stop him attending his party tonight, Vittorio's enthusiasm had been on the wane ever since his father's call had come through.

Dio.

He'd come to Venice thinking the famous carnival would offer an escape from the stultifying atmosphere of the palace and the endless demands of the aging Prince Guglielmo, but it seemed they had stalked him here—along with the Contessa Sirena.

His father's choice for his next bride.

But after the experience of his first doomed marriage Vittorio wasn't about to be dictated to again—not when it came to the woman who would share his marriage bed.

The crowds were thickening, party deadlines were calling, and their excitement was at odds with his own dark thoughts. He was a man out of place, out of time. He was a man who had the world at his feet, and destiny snapping at his heels. He was a man who wanted to be able to make his own choices, but he was cursed with the heritage of his birth and his need to satisfy others before he could entertain his own needs.

He all but turned to walk away—from his destiny as much as from the party. He wasn't in the mood for going another few rounds with Sirena—wasn't in the mood for her blatant attempts at seduction, the pouting, and the affected hurt when her all too obvious charms went ignored.

Except there was no question of his not going. Marcello was his oldest friend and Vittorio had promised him he would be there. Sirena would just have to keep on pouting.

But curse his father for encouraging the woman.

Something caught his eye. A flash of colour amongst the crowd, a static burst of vermilion amidst the moving parade of costumes and finery, a glimpse of a knee, down low, and a hint of an upturned angular jaw up high—like snatches of a portrait in oils when all around were hazy watercolours.

His eyes narrowed as he willed the surging crowd to part. Catching a glance of a dark waterfall of wavy hair over one shoulder when the crowd obliged, he saw the woman turn her masked face up to the bridge, moving her head frantically with every passing costume, scanning, searching through the short veil of black lace that masked the top half of her face.

She looked lost. Alone. A tourist, most likely, fallen victim to Venice's tangle of streets and canals.

He looked away. It wasn't his problem. He had somewhere to be, after all. And yet still his eyes scoured the square. Nobody looked as if they had lost someone and were searching for her. Nobody looked anywhere close to claiming her.

He glanced back, seeking her between richly decorated masks topped with elaborate wigs and feathers, their wearers resplendent in costumes that spoke of centuries long past, when men wore fitted breeches and women wore gowns with tight bodices spilling their plump white breasts. For a moment he couldn't find her, and thought her gone, until a group of Harlequins with jester hats ringing with bells passed. And then he saw her raise one hand to her painted mouth before seeming to sag before him.

He watched as she thumbed off the mask and shook her hair back on a sigh—the long hair that curled over one shoulder. She swept it back with one hand, and her cloak slipped down to reveal one bare shoulder and a satin gown riding low over one breast, before she shivered and hurriedly tucked herself back under the cover of the cloak.

She was lost.

Alone.

With the kind of innocent beauty and vulnerability that tugged at him.

And suddenly Vittorio didn't feel so bored any more.

CHAPTER TWO

LOST IN VENICE. Panic pumped loud and hard through Rosa Ciavarro's veins as she squeezed herself out of the flow of costumed crowds pouring over the bridge and found a rare patch of space by the side of the canal, trying to catch her breath and calm her racing heart. But nothing could calm her desperate eyes.

She peered through the lace of her veil, searching for a sign that would tell her where she was, but when she managed to make out the name of the square it meant nothing and offered no clue as to where she was. Scanning the passing crowds for any hint of recognition proved just as useless. It was pointless. Impossible to tell who was who when everyone was in costume.

Meanwhile the crowds continued to surge over the bridge: Harlequins and Columbinas, vampires and zombies. And why not zombies, when in the space of a few minutes her highly anticipated night had teetered over the edge from magical into nightmarish?

Panic settled into glum resignation as she turned her head up to the inky sky swirling with fog and clutched her own arms, sighing out a long breath of frustration that merely added more mist to the swirling fog. It was futile, and it was time she gave up searching and faced the truth.

She'd crossed too many bridges and turned too many corners in a vain attempt to catch up with her friends, and there was no chance they'd ever find each other now.

It was the last night of Carnevale, and the only party she'd been able to afford to go to, and instead she was lost and alone at the base of a fog-bound bridge somewhere in Venice.

Pointless!

Rosa pulled her thin cloak more tightly around her shoulders. *Dio*, it was cold. She stamped her feet against the stones of the pavement to warm her legs, wishing she'd had the sense to make herself something warmer than this flimsy gown with its bare shoulders and high-low hem. Something that better suited the season. Preferably something worn over thermals and lined with fur.

'You'll be dancing all night,' Chiara had protested when Rosa had suggested she dress for the winter weather. 'Take it from me, you'll roast if you wear anything more.'

But Rosa wasn't roasting now. The damp air wound cold fingers around her ankles and up her shins, seeking and sucking out what body warmth it could find. She was so very cold! And for the first time in too many years to remember she felt tears prick at the corners of her eyes.

She sniffed. She wasn't the type to cry. She'd grown up with three older brothers who would mercilessly tease her if she did. As a child, she'd stoically endured any number of bumps and scratches, skinned knees and grazed elbows when she'd insisted on accompanying them on their adventures.

She hadn't cried when her brothers had taught her to ride a bike that was too large for her, letting her go fast on a rocky road until she'd crashed into an ancient fig tree. She hadn't cried when they'd helped her climb that same tree and then all clambered down and run away, leaving her to pick her own tentative way down. She'd fallen the last few feet to the dusty ground, collecting more scratches and bumps. All wounds she'd endured without a whimper.

But she'd never before been separated from her friends

and lost in the labyrinthine *calles* of Venice on the biggest party night of the year, without her ticket or any way to contact them. Surely even her brothers would understand if she shed a tear or two of frustration now?

Especially if they knew the hideous amount she'd spent on her ticket!

She closed her eyes and pulled her cloak tighter around her, feeling the icy bite of winter working its way into her bones as resignation gave way to remorse. She'd had such high hopes for tonight. A rare night off in the midst of Carnevale. A chance to pretend she *wasn't* just another hotel worker, cleaning up after the holidaymakers who poured into the city. A chance to be part of the celebrations instead of merely watching from the sidelines.

But so much money!

Such a waste!

Laughter rang out from the bridge, echoing in the foggy air above the lapping canal—laughter that could well be directed at her. Because there was nobody to blame for being in this predicament but herself.

It had seemed such a good idea when Chiara had offered to carry her phone and her ticket. After all, they were going to the same party. And it *had* been a good idea—right up until a host of angels sprouting ridiculously fat white wings had surged towards them across a narrow bridge and she'd been separated from her friends and forced backwards. By the time she'd managed to shoulder her way between the feathered wings and get back to the bridge Chiara and her friends had been swallowed up in the fog and the crowds and were nowhere in sight.

She'd raced across the bridge and along the crowded paths as best she could, trying to catch up, colliding with people wearing headdresses constructed from shells, or jester hats strung with bells, or ball gowns nearly the width of the narrow streets. But she was relatively new to Venice,

and unsure of the way, and she'd crossed so many bridges—
too many—that even if Chiara turned back how would she
even know where to find her? She could have taken any
number of wrong turns.

Useless.

She might as well go home to the tiny basement apartment she shared with Chiara—wherever that was. Surely
even if it took her all night she would stumble across it
eventually. With a final sigh, she reefed the mask from her
face. She didn't need a lace veil over her eyes to make her
job any more difficult. She didn't need a mask tonight, period. There would be no party for her tonight.

Her cloak slipped as she pushed her hair back, inadver-
tently exposing one shoulder to the frigid air. She shivered
as she grappled with the slippery cloth and tucked herself
back under what flimsy protection it offered against the
cold.

She was bracing herself to fight her way back over the
bridge and retrace her steps when she saw him. A man
standing by the well in the centre of the square. A man in
a costume of blue trimmed with gold. A tall man, broad-
shouldered, with the bearing of a warrior.

A man who was staring right at her.

Electricity zapped a jagged line down her spine.

No. Not possible. She darted a look over her shoulder—
because why should he be looking at *her*? But there was
nothing behind her but the canal and a crumbling wall beyond.

She swallowed as she turned back, raising her eyes just
enough to see that he was now walking purposefully towards her, and the crowd was almost scattering around him.
Even across the gloom of the lamp-lit square the intent in
his eyes sent adrenaline spiking in her blood.

Fight versus flight? There was no question of her response. She knew that whoever he was, and whatever he

was thinking, she'd stayed there too long. And he was still moving, long strides bridging the distance between them, and still her feet refused to budge. She was anchored to the spot, when instead she should be pushing bodily into the bottleneck of people at the bridge and letting the crowd swallow her up and carry her away.

Much too soon he was before her, a man mountain of leather tunic and braid and chain, his shoulder-length hair loose around a face that spoke of power. A high brow above a broad nose and a jawline framed with steel and rendered in concrete, all hard lines and planes. And eyes of the most startling blue. Cobalt. No, he was no mere warrior. He must be a warlord. A god. He could be either.

Her mouth went dry as she looked up at him, but maybe that was just the heat that seemed to radiate from his body on this cold, foggy evening.

'Can I help you?' he said, in a voice as deep as he was tall.

He spoke in English, although with an accent that suggested he was not. Her heart was hammering in her chest, and her tongue seemed to have lost the ability to form words in any language.

He angled his head, his dark eyes narrowing. *'Vous-êtes perdu?'* he tried, speaking in French this time.

Her French was patchier than her English, so she didn't bother trying to respond in either. *'No parlo Francese,'* she said, sounding breathless even to her own ears—but how could she not sound breathless, standing before a man whose very presence seemed to suck the oxygen out of the misty air?

'You're Italian?' he said, in her own language this time.

'Si.' She swallowed, the action kicking up her chin. She tried to pretend it was a show of confidence, just like the challenge she did her best to infuse into her voice. 'Why were you watching me?'

'I was curious.'

She swallowed. She'd seen those women standing alone and waiting on the side of the road, and she had one idea why he might be curious about a woman standing by herself in a square.

She looked down at her gown, at the stockinged legs visible beneath the hem of her skirt. She knew she was supposed to look like a courtesan, but… 'This is a costume. I'm not—you know.'

One side of his mouth lifted—the slightest rearrangement of the hard angles and planes of his face that turned his lips into an almost-smile, a change so dramatic that it took her completely by surprise.

'This is Carnevale. Nobody is who they seem tonight.'

'And who are you?'

'My name is Vittorio. And you are…?'

'Rosa.'

'Rosa,' he said, with the slightest inclination of his head.

It was all she could do not to sway at the way her name sounded in his rich, deep voice. It was the cold, she told herself, the slap of water against the side of the canal and the whisper of the fog against her skin, nothing more.

'It is a pleasure to meet you.'

He held out one hand and she regarded it warily. It was a big hand, with buckles cuffing sleeves that looked as if they would burst open if he clenched so much as a muscle.

'I promise it doesn't bite,' he said.

She looked up to see that the curve of his lips had moved up a notch and there was a glimmer of warmth in his impossibly blue eyes. And she didn't mind that he seemed to be laughing at her, because the action had worked some kind of miracle on his face, giving a glimpse of the man beneath the warrior. So he was mortal after all…not some god conjured up by the shifting fog.

Almost reluctantly she put her hand in his, then felt his

fingers curl around her hers and heat bloom in her hand. It was a delicious heat that curled seductively into her bloodstream and stirred a response low down in her belly, a feeling so unexpected, so unfamiliar, that it sent alarm bells clanging in her brain.

'I have to go,' she said, pulling her hand from his, feeling the loss of his body heat as if it had been suctioned from her flesh.

'Where do you have to go?'

She looked over her shoulder at the bridge. The crowds were thinning now, most people having arrived at their destinations, and only latecomers were still rushing. If she set off now, at least she'd have a chance of getting herself warm.

'I'm supposed to be somewhere. A party.'

'Do you know where this party is?'

'I'll find it,' she said, with a conviction she didn't feel.

Because she had no idea where she was or where the party was, and because even if she did by some miracle manage to find the party there was the slight matter of an entry ticket no longer in her possession.

'You haven't a clue where it is or how to get there.'

She looked back at him, ready to snap a denial, but his eyes had joined with his lips and there was no mistaking that he'd know she was lying.

She pulled her cloak tighter around her and kicked up her chin. 'What's it to you?'

'Nothing. It's not a crime. Some would say that in Venice getting lost is compulsory.'

She bit her tongue as she shivered under her cloak.

Maybe if you hadn't dropped more money than you could spare on a ticket, and maybe if you had a phone with working GPS, you wouldn't mind getting lost in Venice.

'You're cold,' he said, and before she could deny it or

protest he had undone the chain at his neck and swung his cloak around her shoulders.

Her first instinct was to protest. New to city life she might be, but in spite of what he'd said she wasn't naïve enough to believe that this man's offer of help came without strings. But his cloak was heavy and deliciously warm, the leather supple and infused with a masculine scent. The scent of *him*. She breathed it in, relishing the blend of leather and man, rich and spiced, and her protest died on her lips. It was so good to feel snug.

'*Grazie,*' she said, warmth enveloping her, spreading to legs that felt as if they'd been chilled for ever. Just for a minute she would take this warmth, use it to defrost her blood and re-energise her deflated body and soul, and then she'd insist she was fine, give his cloak back and try to find her way home.

'Is there someone you can call?'

'I don't have my phone.' She looked down at the mask in her hands, feeling stupid.

'Can I call someone for you?' he asked, pulling a phone from a pouch on his belt.

For a moment Rosa felt a glimmer of hope. But only for a moment. Because Chiara's phone number was logged in her phone's memory, but not in her own. She shook her head, the tiny faint hope snuffed out. Her Carnevale was over before it had even begun.

'I don't know the number. It's programmed into my phone, but…'

He dropped the phone back in its pouch. 'You don't know where this party is?'

Suddenly she was tired. Worn out by the rollercoaster of emotions, weary of questions that exposed how unprepared and foolish she'd been. This stranger might be trying to help, and he might be right when he assumed she didn't know where the party was—he *was* right—but she didn't need a post-mortem. She just wanted to go back to her apartment and her bed, pull the covers over her head and forget this night had ever happened.

'Look, thanks for your help. But don't you have somewhere to be?'

'I do.'

She cocked an eyebrow at him in challenge. 'Well, then?'

A gondola slipped almost silently along the canal behind her. Fog swirled around and between them. The woman must be freezing, the way she was so inadequately dressed. Her arms tightly bunched the paper-thin wrap around her quaking shoulders, but still she wanted to pretend that everything was all right and that she didn't need help.

'Come with me,' he said.

It was impulse that had him uttering the words, but once they were out he realised they made all kinds of sense. She was lost, all alone in Venice, and she was beautiful—even more beautiful than he'd first thought when she'd peeled off her mask. Her brandy-coloured eyes were large and cat-like in her high-cheekboned face, her painted curved lips like an invitation. He remembered the sight of her naked shoulder under the cloak, the cheap satin of the bodice cupping her breast, and a random thought amused him.

Sirena would hate her.

And wasn't that sufficient reason by itself?

Those cat-like eyes opened wide. *'Scusa?'*

'Come with me,' he said again. The seeds of a plan were already germinating—a plan that would benefit them both.

'You don't have to say that. You've already been too kind.'

'It's not about being kind. You would be doing me a favour.'

'How is that possible? We'd never met until a few moments ago. How can I possibly do you any favour?'

He held out his forearm to her, the leather of his sleeve creaking. 'Call it serendipity, if you prefer. Because I too have a costume ball to attend and I don't have a partner for the evening. So if you would do me the honour of accompanying me?'

She laughed a little, then shook her head. 'I've already told you—this is a costume. I wasn't waiting to be picked up.'

'I'm not trying to pick you up. I'm asking you to be my guest for the evening. But it is up to you, Rosa. Clearly you planned on going to a party tonight.'

He eased the mask from where she held it between the fingers clutching his cloak over her breasts and turned it slowly in his hands. She had no choice but to let it go. It was either let him take it or let go of the cloak.

'Why should you miss out on the biggest night of Carnevale,' he said, watching the way her eyes followed his hands as he thumbed the lace of her veil, 'just because you became separated from your friends?'

He could tell she was tempted—could all but taste her excitement at being handed a lifeline to an evening she'd all but given up on, even while questions and misgivings swirled in the depths of her eyes.

He smiled. He might have started this evening in a foul mood, and he knew that would have been reflected in his features, but he knew how to smile when it got him something he wanted. Knew how to turn on the charm when the need arose—whether he was involved in negotiations with an antagonistic foreign diplomat or romancing a woman he desired in his bed.

'Serendipity,' he repeated. 'A happy chance—for both of us. And the bonus is you'll get to wear my cloak a while longer.'

Her eyes lifted to meet his—long-lashed eyes, shy eyes, filled with uncertainty and nerves. Again, he was struck by her air of vulnerability. She was a very different animal from the women he usually met. An image of Sirena floated unbidden into his mind's eye—self-assured, self-centred Sirena, who wouldn't look vulnerable if she was alone in six feet of water and staring down a hungry shark. A very different animal indeed.

'It is very warm,' she said, 'thank you.'

'Is that a yes?'

She took a deep breath, her teeth troubling her bottom lip while a battle went on inside her, then gave a decisive nod, adding her own tentative smile in response. 'Why not?'

'Why not indeed?'

He didn't waste any time ushering her across the bridge and through the twisted *calles* towards the private entrance of the *palazzo* gardens, his mood considerably lighter than it had been earlier in the evening.

Because suddenly a night he hadn't been looking forward to had taken on an entirely different sheen. Not just because he was going to give Sirena a surprise and pay her back for the one she had orchestrated for him. But because he had a beautiful woman on his arm in one of the most beautiful cities in the world and the night was young.

And who knew where it would end?

CHAPTER THREE

ROSA'S HEART WAS tripping over itself as the gorgeous man placed her hand around the leather of his sleeve and cut a path through the crowds, and her feet struggled to keep up with his long strides.

Vittorio, he'd told her his name was, but that didn't make him any less a stranger. And he was leading her to a costume ball somewhere, or so he'd said. But she had no more detail than that. And she had nobody and nothing to blame for being here but a spark of impulse that had made her abandon every cautionary lesson she'd grown up with and provoked her into doing something so far out of her comfort zone she wondered if she'd ever find a way back.

'Why not?' she'd said in response to his invitation, in spite of the fact she could think of any number of reasons.

She'd never in her twenty-four years done anything as impetuous—or as reckless. Her brothers would no doubt add *stupid* to the description.

And yet, uncertainty and even stupidity aside, her night had turned another corner. One that had tiny bubbles of excitement fizzing in her blood.

Anticipation.

'It's not far,' he said, 'Are you still cold?'

'No.'

Quite the contrary. His cloak was like a shield against the weather, and his arm under hers felt solid and real. If anything, she was exhilarated, as though she'd embarked upon a mystery tour, or an adventure with an unknown destination. So many unknowns, and this man was at the top of the list.

She glanced up at him as he forged on with long strides through the narrow *calle*. He seemed eager to get where he was going now, almost as if he'd wasted too much time talking to her in the square and was making up for lost time. They passed a lamp that cast light and shadow on his profile, turning it into a moving feast of features—the strong lines of his jaw and nose, his high brow and dark eyes, and all surrounded by a thick mane of black hair.

'It's not far now,' he said, looking down at her.

For a moment—a second—his cobalt eyes met hers and snagged, and the bubbles in her blood spun and fizzed some more, and a warm glow stirred deep in her belly.

She stumbled and he caught her, not letting her fall, and the moment was gone, but even as she whispered her breathless thanks she resolved not to spend too much time staring into this man's eyes. At least not while she was walking.

'This way,' he said, steering her left down a narrow path away from the busy *calle*. Here, the ancient wall of a *palazzo* disappeared into the fog on one side, a high brick wall on the other, and with each step deeper along the dark path the sounds of the city behind became more and more muffled by the fog, until every cautionary tale she'd ever heard came back to mock her and the only sound she could hear was her own thudding heartbeat.

No, not the only sound, because their footsteps echoed in the narrow side alley and there also came the slap of water, the reflection of pale light on the shifting surface of the path ahead. But, no, that would mean—

And that was when she realised that the path ended in a dark recess with only the canal beyond.

A dead end.

Adrenaline spiked in her blood as anticipation morphed into fear. She'd come down this dark path willingly, with a man of whom she knew nothing apart from his name. If it even *was* his name.

'Vittorio,' she said, her steps dragging as she tried to pull her hand from where he had tucked it into his elbow. 'I think maybe I've changed my mind…'

'*Scusi?*'

He stopped and spun towards her, and in the gloomy light his shadowed face and flashing eyes took on a frightening dimension. In this moment he could be a demon. A monster.

Her mouth went dry. She didn't want to stay to find out which. 'I should go home.'

She was struggling with the fastening of his cloak, even as she backed away, her fingers tangling with the clasp to free herself and give it back before she fled.

Already she could hear her brothers berating her, asking her why she'd agreed to go with someone she didn't know in the first place, telling her what a fool she'd been—and they'd be right. She would never live down the shame. She would regret for ever her one attempt at impetuosity.

'Rosa?'

A door swung open in the recess behind Vittorio, opening up to a fantasy world beyond. Lights twinkled in trees. A doorman looked to see who was outside and bowed his head when he spotted them waiting.

'Rosa?' Vittorio said again. 'We're here—at the *palazzo*.'

She blinked. Beyond the doorman there was a path between some trees and at the end of it a fountain, where water rose and fell to some unseen beat. 'At the ball?'

'Yes,' he said, and in the low light she could see the curve of his lips, as if he'd worked out why she'd suddenly felt the urge to flee. 'Or do you feel the need to remind me once again that you are just wearing a costume?'

Rosa had never been more grateful for the fog as she swallowed back a tide of embarrassment.

Dio, *what must he think of me? First he finds me lost and helpless, and then I panic like I'm expecting him to attack me.*

Chiara was right—she needed to toughen up. She wasn't in the village any more. She didn't have her father or her brothers to protect her. She needed to wise up and look after herself.

She attempted a smile in return. 'No. I'm so sorry—'

'No,' he said, offering her his arm again. '*I'm* sorry. Most people take a motorboat to the front entrance. I needed the exercise but walking made me late, so I was rushing. I should have warned you that we would be taking the side entrance.'

Her latest burst of adrenaline leeched out of her and she found an answering smile as she took his arm and let him lead her into a garden lit with tiny lights that magically turned a line of trees into carriages pulled by horses towards the *palazzo* beyond.

And as they entered this magical world she wondered... She'd been told to expect heavy security and bag searches at the ball, but this doorman had ushered them in without so much as blinking.

'What kind of ball is this?' she asked. 'Why are there no tickets and no bag searches?'

'A private function, by invitation only.'

She looked up at him. 'Are you sure it's all right for me to come, in that case?'

'I invited you, didn't I?'

They stopped just shy of the fountain, halfway across the garden by the soaring side wall of the *palazzo*, so she could take in the gardens and their magical lighting. To the left, a low wall topped with an ornate railing bordered the garden. The canal lay beyond, she guessed, though it was near impossible to make out anything through the fog, and the buildings opposite were no more than shifting apparitions in the mist.

The mist blurred the tops of the trees and turned the lights of those distant buildings into mere smudges, giving the garden a mystical air. To Rosa, it was almost as if Venice had shrunk to this one fairy-tale garden. The damp air was cold against her face, but she was deliciously warm under Vittorio's cloak and in no hurry to go inside. For inside there would be more guests—more strangers—and doubtless there would be friendships and connections between them and she would be the outsider. For now it was enough to deal with this one stranger.

More than enough when she thought about the way he looked at her—as if he was seeing inside her, reaching into a place where lurked her deepest fears and desires. For they both existed with this man. He seemed to scrape the surface of her nerve-endings away so everything she felt was raw. Primal. Exciting.

'What is this place?' she asked, watching the play of water spouting from the fat fish at the base of the three-tiered fountain. 'Who owns it?'

'It belongs to a friend of mine. Marcello's ancestors were *doges* of Venice and very rich. The *palazzo* dates back to the sixteenth century.'

'His family were rulers of Venice?'

'Some. Yes.'

'How do you even *know* someone like that?'

He paused, gave a shrug of his shoulders. 'My father and his go back a long way.'

'Why? Did your father work for him?'

He took a little time before he dipped his head to the side. 'Something like that.'

She nodded, understanding. 'I get that. My father services the mayor's cars in Zecce—the village in Puglia where I come from. He gets invited to the Christmas party every year. We used to get invited too, when we were children.'

'We?'

'My three older brothers and me. They're all married now, with their own families.'

She looked around at the gardens strung with lights and thought about the new nephew or niece who would be welcomed into the world in the next few weeks, and the money she'd wasted on her ticket for the ball tonight—money she could have used to pay for a visit home, along with a special gift for the new baby, and still have had change left over. She sighed at the waste.

'I paid one hundred euros for my ticket to the ball. That's one hundred euros down the drain.'

One eyebrow arched. 'That much?'

'I know. It's ridiculously expensive, and ours was one of the cheapest balls, so you're lucky to get invited to parties in a place like this for free. You can pay a lot more than I did, though. Hundreds more.'

She swallowed. She was babbling. She knew she was babbling. But something about this man's looming presence in the fog made her want to put more of herself into it and even up the score. He was so tall, so broad across the shoulders, his features so powerful. Everything about him spoke of power.

Because he hadn't said a word in the space she'd left, she felt compelled to continue. 'And then you have to have a costume, of course.'

'Of course.'

'Although I made my costume myself, I still had to buy the material.'

'Is that what you do, Rosa?' he asked as they resumed their walk towards the *palazzo*. 'Are you a designer?'

She laughed. 'Hardly. I'm not even a proper seamstress.

I clean rooms at the Palazzo d'Velatte, a small hotel in the Dorsoduro *sestiere*. Do you know it?'

He shook his head.

'It's much smaller than this, but very grand.'

Steps led up to a pair of ancient wooden doors that swung open before them, as if whoever was inside had been anticipating their arrival.

She looked up at him. 'Do you ever get used to visiting your friend in such a grand place?'

He just smiled and said, 'Venice is quite special. It takes a little getting used to.'

Rosa looked up at the massive doors, at the light spilling from the interior, and took a deep breath. 'It's taking me a *lot* of getting used to.'

And then they entered the *palazzo*'s reception room and Rosa's eyes really popped. She'd thought the hotel where she worked was grand! Marketed as a one-time *palazzo*, and now a so-called boutique hotel, she'd thought it the epitome of style, capturing the faded elegance of times gone by.

It was true that the rooms were more spacious than she'd ever encountered, and the ceilings impossibly high—not to mention a pain to clean. But the building seemed to have an air of neglect about it, as if it was sinking in on itself. The doors caught and snagged on the tiled floors, never quite fitting into the doorframes, and there were complaints from guests every other day that things didn't quite work right.

Elegant decay, she'd put it down to—until the day she'd taken out the rubbish to the waiting boat and witnessed a chunk of wall falling into the canal. She figured there was not much that was elegant about a wall crumbling piece by piece into the canal.

But here, in this place, she was confronted by a real *palazzo*—lavishly decorated from floor to soaring ceiling with rich frescoes and gilded reliefs, and impeccably furnished with what must be priceless antiques. From somewhere high above came the sounds of a string quartet, drifting down the spectacular staircase. And now she could see the hotel where she worked for what it really was. Faded…tired. A mere whisper of what it had been trying to emulate.

Another doorman stepped forward with a nod, and relieved Rosa of both Vittorio's leather cloak and her own wrap underneath.

'It's so beautiful,' she said, wide-eyed as she took it all in, rubbing her bare arms under the light of a Murano glass chandelier high above that was lit with at least one hundred globes.

'Are you cold?' he asked, watching her, his eyes raking over her, taking in her fitted bodice and the skirt with the weather-inappropriate hem.

'No.'

Not cold. Her goosebumps had nothing to do with the temperature. Rather, without her cloak and the gloom outside to keep her hidden from his gaze, she felt suddenly exposed. Crazy. She'd been so delighted with the way the design of the gown had turned out, so proud of her efforts after all the late nights she'd spent sewing, and she'd been eager to wear it tonight.

'You look so sexy,' Chiara had said, clapping her hands as Rosa performed a twirl for her. 'You'll have every man at the ball lining up to dance with you.'

She had *felt* sexy, and a little bit more wicked than she was used to—or at least she had felt that way then. But right now she had to resist the urge to tug up the bodice of her gown, where it hugged the curve of her breasts, and tug down the front of the skirt.

In a place such as this, where elegance and class oozed from the frescoes and antique glass chandeliers, bouncing light off myriad marble and gilded surfaces, she felt like a cheap bauble. Tacky. Like the fake glass trinkets that some of the shops passed off as Venetian glass when it had been made in some rip-off factory half a world away.

She wondered if Vittorio was suddenly regretting his rash impulse to invite her. Could he see how out of place she was?

Yes, she was supposed to be dressed as a courtesan, but she wished right now that she'd chosen a more expensive fabric or a subtler colour. Something with class that wasn't so brash and obvious. Something that contained at least a modicum of decency. Surely he had to see that she didn't belong here in the midst of all this luxury and opulence?

Except he wasn't looking at her with derision. Didn't look at her as if she was out of place. Instead she saw something else in his eyes. A spark. A flame. *Heat.*

And whatever it was low down in her belly that had flickered into life this night suddenly squeezed tight.

'You say you made your costume yourself?' he asked. If she wasn't wrong, his voice had gone down an octave.

'Yes.'

'Very talented. There is just one thing missing.'

'What do you mean?'

But he already had his hands at her head. Her mask, she realised. She'd forgotten all about it. And now he smoothed it down over her hair, adjusting the crown so that it was centred before straightening the lace of her veil over her eyes.

She didn't move a muscle to try to stop him and do it herself. She didn't want to stop him. Because all the while the gentle brush of his fingers against her skin and the smoothing of his hands on her hair set off a chain reaction of tingles under her scalp and skin, hypnotising her into inaction.

'There,' he said, removing his hands from her head. She had to stop herself from swaying after them. 'Perfection.'

'Vittorio!'

A masculine voice rang out from the top of the stairs, saving her from having to find a response when she had none.

'You're here!'

'Marcello!' Vittorio answered, his voice booming in the space. 'I promised you I'd be here, did I not?'

'With you,' the man said, jogging down the wide marble steps two by two, 'who can tell?'

He was dressed as a Harlequin, in colours of black and gold, and the leather of his shoes slapped on the marble stairs as he descended. He and Vittorio embraced—a man hug, a back-slap—before drawing apart.

'Vittorio,' the Harlequin said, 'it is good to see you.'

'And you,' Vittorio replied.

'And you've brought someone, I see,' he said, whipping off the mask over his eyes, his mouth curving into a smile as he held out one hand and bowed generously. 'Welcome, fair stranger. My name is Marcello Donato.'

The man was impossibly handsome. *Impossibly.* Olive-skinned, with dark eyes and brows, a sexy slash of a mouth and high cheekbones over which any number of supermodels would go to war with each other. But it was the warmth of his smile that made Rosa instinctively like the man.

'My name is Rosa.'

She took his hand and he drew her close and kissed both her cheeks.

'I'm right in thinking we've never met, aren't I?' he said as he released her. 'I'd be sure to remember if we had.'

'I've only just met Rosa myself,' Vittorio said, before she could answer. 'She lost her party in the fog. I thought it unfair that she missed out on the biggest night of Carnevale.'

Marcello nodded. 'That would be an injustice of massive proportions. Welcome, Rosa, I'm glad you found Vittorio.' He stepped back and regarded them critically. 'You make a good couple—the mad warrior protecting the runaway Princess.'

Vittorio snorted beside her.

'What's so funny?' she said.

'Marcello is known for his flights of fancy.'

'What can I say?' He beamed. 'I'm a romantic. Unlike this hard-hearted creature beside me, whom you managed to stumble upon.'

She filed the information away for future reference. The words had been said in jest, but she wondered if there wasn't an element of truth in them. 'So, tell me,' she said, 'what is this Princess hiding from?'

'That's easy,' he said. 'An evil serpent. But don't worry. Vittorio will protect you. There's not a serpent in the land that's a match for Vittorio.'

Something passed between the two men's eyes. A look. An understanding.

'What am I missing?' she asked, her eyes darting from one to the other.

'The fun,' Marcello said, pulling his mask back on. 'Everyone is upstairs on the second *piano nobile*. Come.'

Marcello was warm and welcoming, and nobody seemed to have any issues with the way she was dressed. Rosa began to relax. She'd been worrying about nothing.

Together they ascended the staircase to the *piano nobile*, where the principal reception rooms of the *palazzo* were housed one level above the waters of the canal. With its soaring ceilings, and rock crystal chandelier, Rosa could see that this level was even more breath-taking, more opulent, than the last. And the *pièce de résistance* was the impossibly ornate windows that spread generously across one wall.

'Is there a view?' she asked, tempted to look anyway. 'I mean, when it isn't foggy?'

'You'll have to come back,' Marcello said, ignoring the crowded reception rooms either side, filled with partygoers, and the music of Vivaldi coming from the string quartet, and walking to the windows before them. 'On a clear day you can see the Rialto Bridge to the right.'

Rosa peered through the fog, trying to make sense of the smudges of light. But if the Rialto Bridge was to the right... 'You're on the Grand Canal!'

Marcello shrugged and smiled. 'Not that you can tell today. But Venice wearing its shroud of fog is still a sight to behold, so enjoy. And now please excuse me while I find you some drinks.'

'We're in San Polo,' she said to Vittorio.

The hotel where she worked was in the Dorsoduro *sestiere*, the ball she was supposed to be attending was in the northern district of Cannaregio. Somehow she'd ended up lost between them and within a whisker of the sinuous Grand Canal, which would have hinted at her location if only she'd found it.

A smudge of light passed slowly by—a *vaporetto* or a motorboat carefully navigating the fog-shrouded waterway—and Rosa's thoughts chugged with it. Vittorio had been kind, asking her to accompany him, but strictly speaking she wasn't lost any more.

She turned to him. 'I know where I am now.'

'Does that matter?'

'I mean, I'm not lost. At least, I can find my way home from here.'

He turned to her, putting his big hands on her shoulders as he looked down at her. 'Are you looking for yet another reason to escape?'

A wry smile kicked up one side of his mouth. He was laughing at her again, and she found she didn't mind—not when seeing his smile made her feel as if she was capturing something rare and true.

'I'm not—'

He cocked an eyebrow. 'Why are you so desperate to run away from me?'

He was wrong. She wasn't desperate to run away from him. Oh, sure, there'd been that moment when she'd panicked, at the end of the path outside the side gate, but she knew better now. Vittorio was no warrior or warlord, no demon or monster. He was a man, warm and real and powerful…a man who made her blood zing.

Except the warm weight of his hands on her shoulders and the probing questions in his eyes vanquished reasoned argument. There was only strength and heat and fear that it would be Vittorio who might change his mind. And then he'd take his hands away. And then she'd miss that contact and the heat and the zing and the pure exhilaration of being in his company.

A tiny worm of a thought squeezed its way through the connections in her brain. *Wasn't that reason enough to run?*

She was out of her depth with a man like him—a man who was clearly older and more worldly-wise, who moved in circles with people who owned entire *palazzos* and whose ancestors were amongst the *doges* of Venice. A man who made her feel stirrings in her belly, fizzing in her blood—things she wasn't used to feeling.

Nothing in the village—not a teenage crush on her maths teacher nor a dalliance with Antonio from the next village, who'd worked a few months in her father's workshop, had prepared her for meeting someone like Vittorio. She felt inadequate. Underdone.

She was dressed as a courtesan, a seductress, a temptress. But that was such a lie. She swallowed. She could hardly admit that, though.

'You invited me to this party tonight because I was lost and you felt sorry for me, because I was upset and was going to miss my own party.'

He snorted. 'I don't do things because I feel sorry for

people. I do things because I want to. I invited you to this party because I wanted to. And because I wanted you to be with me.' His hands squeezed her shoulders. 'So now, instead of trying to find all the reasons you shouldn't be here, how about you enjoy all the reasons you should?'

What could she say to that? 'In that case, it very much seems that I am stuck with you.'

'You are,' he said, with a smile that warmed her to her bones. 'At least for as long as this night lasts.'

'A toast.' Marcello said, arriving back with three glasses of Aperol spritz. He handed them each a glass. 'To Carnevale,' he said, raising his glass in a toast.

'To Carnevale,' said Rosa.

'To Carnevale,' echoed Vittorio, lifting his glass in Rosa's direction, 'And to the Venetian fog that delivered us Rosa.'

And if the words he uttered in his deep voice were not enough, the way Vittorio's piercing blue eyes looked at her above his glass made her blush all the way down to her toes. In that moment Rosa knew that this night would never last long enough, and that whatever else happened she would remember this night for ever.

She was skittish—so skittish. She was like a colt, untrained and unrehearsed, or a kitten, jumping at shadows and imaginary enemies. And it wasn't an act. He was good at spotting an ingénue, a pretender. He was used to women who played games and who made themselves out to be something they were not.

Just for a moment Vittorio wondered if he was doing the right thing, pitting her against Sirena. Maybe he should release her from her obvious unease and awkwardness and let her go back to her own world, if that was what she really wanted, back to what was, no doubt, the drudgery of her work and the worry of losing the paltry sum of one hundred euros.

Except Vittorio was selfish enough not to want to let her go.

He saw the way her eyes widened at every new discovery, at every exquisite Murano glass lamp, every frescoed wall or gilded mirror that stretched almost to the ceiling.

She was like a breath of fresh air in Vittorio's life. Unsophisticated and not pretending otherwise. She was a refreshing change when he had been feeling so jaded.

And she was a beautiful woman in a gown that fitted like a glove and make him ache to peel it off.

Why should he let her go?

CHAPTER FOUR

IT WASN'T A party or even a ball. It was like being part of a fairy-tale.

Rosa ascended the wide staircase to the second level above the water—yet another floor with soaring ceilings and exquisite antiques and furnishings. The music from the string quartet was louder here, richer, its sweet notes filling the gaps between the sound of laughter and high-spirited conversation coming from the party rooms either side of the staircase.

And the costumes! A brightly coloured peacock strutted by as they reached the top, all feathers and flashes of brilliant colour, and Rosa couldn't help but laugh in sheer wonderment as a couple with ice-white masks wearing elaborate gowns and suits of the deepest purple nodded regally as they strolled past arm in arm.

Rosa felt herself swept away into a different world of riches and costumes—a sumptuous world of fantasy—and only half wished that the man who had rescued her from the foggy *calles* wasn't quite so popular, because then she could keep him all to herself.

Everyone seemed to recognise Vittorio and to want to throw out an exchange or a greeting. He was like a magnet to both men and women alike, but he always introduced her to them, including her in the conversation.

And, while her presence at his side wasn't questioned, she wondered what she might see if everyone wasn't wearing masks. Would the women's eyes be following Vittorio's every move because he was so compelling? Would they be looking at her in envy?

If she were in their place she would.

And suddenly the music and the costumes and the amazing sumptuousness of the *palazzo* bled into a heady mix that made her head spin. She was part of a Venice she'd never seen and had only ever imagined.

Suddenly there was a shriek of delight from the other wing, and a commotion as someone made their way through the crowds into the room.

'Vittorio!' a woman cried, bursting through the party-goers. 'I just heard you were here. Where have you been hiding all this time?'

But not just any woman.

Cleopatra.

Her sleek black bob was adorned with golden beads, the circlet at her forehead topped with an asp. Like Vittorio, she hadn't bothered with a mask. Her eyes were kohled, their lids painted turquoise-blue, and her dress was simply amazing. Cut low—*really* low—over the smooth globes of her breasts, it was constructed entirely of beads in gold and bronze and silver, its short skirt just strings of the shiny beads that shifted and flashed skin with her every movement.

It wasn't so much a dress, Rosa thought as she took a step back to make room for the woman to reach up and kiss Vittorio on both cheeks, as an invitation. It showed the wearer's body off to perfection.

Cleopatra left her face close to his. 'Everyone has been waiting hours for you,' she chided, before she stood back to take in what he was wearing.

Or maybe to give him another chance to see her spectacular costume.

She held her hands out wide. 'But must you always look so dramatic? It's supposed to be a costume party.'

'I'm wearing a costume.'

'If you say so—but can't you for once dress out of character?'

'Sirena,' he said, ignoring her question as he reached for Rosa's hand, pulling her back into his orbit. 'I'd like you to meet a friend of mine. Rosa, this is Sirena, the daughter of one of my father's oldest friends.'

'Oh,' she said, with a knowing laugh, 'I'm *far* more than that.'

And then, for the first time, Sirena seemed to notice that there was someone standing next to Vittorio. She turned her head and looked Rosa up and down, letting her eyes tell Rosa what she thought about his 'friend'.

'Ciao,' she said, her voice deadpan, and Rosa couldn't be certain that she was saying hello as opposed to giving her a dismissal.

She immediately turned back to Vittorio, angling her back towards Rosa.

Definitely a dismissal.

'Vittorio, come with me—all our friends are in the other room.'

'I'm here with Rosa.'

'With who? Oh…'

She gave Rosa another look up and down, her eyes evaluating her as if she was a rival for Vittorio's affections. Ridiculous. She'd only just met the man tonight. But she wasn't mistaken. There was clear animosity in the woman's eyes.

'And what do you think of Vittorio's outfit…? What was your name again?'

'Rosa,' Vittorio growled. 'Her name is Rosa. It's not that difficult.'

'Of course it's not.' Sirena gave a lilting laugh as she

turned to the woman whose name she couldn't remember and smiled. 'What do you think of Vittorio's outfit? Don't you think it's a bit over the top?'

'I like it,' she said. 'I like the blue of the leather. It matches his eyes.'

'It's not just blue, though, is it?' Sirena said dismissively. 'It's more like *royal* blue—isn't it, Vittorio?'

'That's enough, Sirena.'

'Well, I would have said it was *royal* blue.'

'Enough, I said.'

The woman pouted and stretched herself catlike along the brocade chaise longue behind her, the beads of her skirt falling in a liquid slide to reveal the tops of her long, slender legs—legs that ended in sandals with straps that wound their way enticingly around her ankles.

The woman made an exquisite Cleopatra. But then, she was so exquisitely beautiful the real Cleopatra would no doubt have wanted to scratch out her eyes.

'It's all right, Vittorio, despite our difference in opinion Rosa and I are going to be good friends.' She smiled regally at Rosa. 'I like *your* costume,' she said.

For the space of one millisecond Rosa thought the woman was warming to her, wanted so much to believe she meant what she'd said. Rosa had spent many midnight hours perched over her mother's old sewing machine, battling with the slippery material and trying to get the seams and the fit just right. But then she saw the snigger barely contained beneath the smile and realised the woman hadn't been handing out a compliment.

'Rosa made it herself—didn't you, Rosa?'

'I did.'

Cleopatra's perfectly threaded eyebrows shot up. 'How... *enterprising.*'

Vittorio's presence beside her lent Rosa a strength she hadn't known she had, reminding her of what her brothers had always told her—not to be cowed by bullies but to stand up to them.

Her brothers were right, but it was a lot easier to take their advice when she had a man like Vittorio standing beside her.

Rosa simply smiled, not wanting to show what she really thought. 'Thank you. Your costume is lovely too. Did you make it yourself?'

The other woman stared at her as if she had three heads. 'Of course I didn't make it myself.'

'A shame,' Rosa said. 'If you had you might have noticed that there's a loose thread...'

She reached a hand out to the imaginary thread and the woman bolted upright and onto her sandalled feet, a whole lot less elegantly than she had reclined, no doubt imagining one tug of Rosa's hand unleashing a waterfall of glass beads across the Persian carpet.

'This gown is an Emilio Ferraro creation. Of *course* there's no loose thread.'

'Oh, I'm sorry. I must have been mistaken.'

Sirena sniffed, jerked her eyes from Rosa's and placed a possessive hand on Vittorio's chest. 'Come and see our friends when you're free. You won't *believe* what they're wearing. I'll be waiting for you.'

And with a swish of her beaded hair and skirt she was gone.

'That,' said Vittorio, 'was Sirena.'

'Cyclone Sirena, you mean,' Rosa said, watching the woman spinning out of the room as quickly as she'd come in, leaving a trail of devastation in her wake.

She heard a snort and looked up to see Vittorio smiling down at her. It was a real smile that warmed her bone-deep, so different from one of Sirena's ice-cold glares.

'You handled that very well.'

'And you thought I wouldn't?' she said. 'My brothers

taught me to stand up to bullies.' She didn't mention that it was Vittorio's presence that had given her the courage to heed her brothers' advice.

'Good advice,' he said, nodding. 'If she finds that thread you saw she'll bust the balls of her precious Emilio.'

Rosa returned his smile with one of her own. 'There was no thread.'

And Vittorio laughed—a rich bellow that was laced with approval and that made a tide of happiness well up inside her.

'Thank you,' he said, his arm going around her shoulders as he leaned down to kiss her cheek. 'For the best belly laugh I've had in a long time.'

It wasn't really a kiss. Mouth to cheek…a brush of a whiskered jaw…a momentary meeting of lips and skin—probably the same kind of kiss he might bestow upon a great-aunt. Even his arm was gone from her shoulder in an instant. Yet to Rosa it felt far more momentous.

It was the single most exciting moment in her life since she'd arrived in Venice.

Chiara had told her that magical things could happen at Carnevale. She'd told her a whole lot of things and Rosa hadn't believed her. She'd suspected it was just part of Chiara's sales technique, in order to persuade Rosa to part with so much money and go along to the ball with her.

But maybe her friend had been right. Rosa had been kissed by a man. She couldn't wait to tell her friend.

'You're blushing,' said Vittorio, his head at an angle as he looked down at her.

She felt her blush deepen and dropped her head. 'Yes, it's silly, I know.'

He put his hand to her chin and lifted her face to his. 'No,' he said. 'It's delightful. It's been a long time since I saw a woman blush.'

She blinked up at him, her skin tingling where his fingers lingered.

Oh, boy.

Talk about a distraction… She'd wanted to ask him more about Sirena, but the woman had faded into insignificance. Now all she could think about was Vittorio and the way he made her feel.

'Come, come!' said Marcello, clapping his hands as he walked into the room to gather everyone. 'The entertainment downstairs is about to begin. You don't want to miss it.'

Downstairs, the entire level of the *piano nobile* had been divided into performance areas, with stages and dramatic velvet drapes, and they spent the next hour wandering between the rooms to see the spectacle of gymnasts and jugglers and opera singers, and aerobatic performers who spun on ropes in the air. Then it was the turn of the clowns, and Rosa was soon almost doubled up with laughter at their antics.

She found herself thinking about Chiara and wondering how her night was going. They'd treated themselves to the cheapest tickets to the cheapest Carnevale ball they could find—and that only gave admission to the dancing segment of the evening. They hadn't been able to afford the price for the dinner and entertainment that came first. But surely even that entertainment would be no match for this.

And then Vittorio took her hand in his and she stopped thinking about Chiara, because her heart gave a little lurch that switched off her brain.

She looked sideways up at him to find him watching her, the cobalt of his eyes a shade deeper, his sensual slash of mouth curled up at the ends.

He gave the slightest squeeze of her hand before he let her go, and she turned her eyes back to the entertainment. But suddenly she wasn't laughing any more. Her chest felt too tight, her blood was buzzing, and she was imagining all kinds of impossible things.

Unimaginable things.

Chiara had said that magical things could happen at Carnevale.

Rosa had been a fool not to believe her.

She could *feel* the magic. It was in the air all around her. It was in the gilded frames and lush silks and crystal chandeliers. It was in the exquisite *trompe l'oeils* that adorned the walls with views of gardens that had only ever existed in the artist's eyes. And magic was pulsing alongside her, in leather of blue and gold, in a man with a presence she couldn't ignore—a man who had the ability to shake the very foundations of her world with just one look from his cobalt blue eyes.

Chiara had said she might meet the man of her dreams tonight. A man who had the power to tempt her to give up her most cherished possession.

She hadn't believed that either.

It would have to be a special kind of man for her to want to take such a momentous step. A *very* special kind of man.

Vittorio?

Her heart squeezed so tightly that she had to suck in a breath to ease the constriction.

Impossible. Life didn't work that way.

But what if Chiara had been right?

And what if Vittorio was the one?

She glanced up to sneak another look at him and found him already gazing down at her, his midnight hair framing the quizzical expression on his strong face.

His heart-stoppingly beautiful, strong face.

And she thought it would be madness not to find out.

Sirena either had spies everywhere, or she had a knack for knowing when Rosa had left his side for five minutes. The entertainment was finished but, while the party wouldn't wind down until dawn, Vittorio had other plans. Plans that didn't include Sirena, no matter how hard she tried to join in.

'This is supposed to be a *party*,' Sirena sulked conspiratorially to Marcello when she cornered him standing at the top of the stairs, where Vittorio was waiting for Rosa so they could say their goodbyes. 'A party for *friends*. An *exclusive* party. But did you see that woman Vittorio dragged along?'

'Her name is Rosa.'

Sirena took no notice. 'Did you see what she was wearing, Marcello? It was appalling.'

'Nobody's listening, Sirena,' Vittorio said dismissively.

'Rosa seems very nice,' said Marcello. 'And I like her costume.'

Vittorio nodded. 'She *is* nice. *Very* nice.' He thought about the way she'd pulled that ruse with the loose thread and smiled. 'Clever, too.'

Sirena pouted, her hand on Marcello's arm, pleading. 'She wasn't even invited.'

'*I* invited her.'

'You know what I mean. Someone like her wouldn't normally be allowed anywhere near here.'

'Sirena, give it up.' Vittorio turned away, searching for Rosa. The sooner he got her away from here—away from Sirena—the better.

'That's our Vittorio for you,' Marcello said, trying to hose down the antagonism between his guests, playing his life-long role of peacemaker to perfection. 'Always bringing home the strays. Birds fallen from their nests. Abandoned puppies. It made no difference. Vittorio, do you remember that bag of kittens we found snagged on the side of the river that day? *Dio*, how long ago was that? Twenty years?'

Vittorio grunted, hoping that Rosa was nowhere within earshot, because he didn't want her overhearing any of this.

He did remember that day. Marcello had been visiting. They'd wandered far and wide beyond the castle walls that day—much further than Vittorio had been permitted to roam. They'd both been about ten years old, and filled with the curiosity and compulsion of young boys to explore their world.

They'd been wading in the stream, chasing the silvery flashes of fish in the shallows, when they'd heard the pitiful cries. By the time they'd found the bag and pulled it from the stream all but one of the kittens had perished, and the plaintive mewls of the lone survivor had been heartrending. Vittorio had tucked the tiny shivering creature into his shirt and hurried back to the castle.

'So now you're saving sweet young things who get themselves lost in the streets of Venice? Quite the hero you've turned out to be,' said Sirena.

'It's lucky Vittorio was in the right place at the right time,' Marcello said, still doing his utmost to pour oil on troubled waters. 'Rosa would have had a dreary night by herself otherwise.'

Sirena bristled, ignoring Marcello's peacekeeping efforts. 'And does your father know you've found another stray?'

Vittorio sighed. *Where the hell was Rosa?* 'What's who I bring to a party got to do with my father?'

'Only that the three of us might finally settle our differences and work out a timeline for uniting our two families. That's what was supposed to happen tonight. That's what was intended.'

'Intended by whom? By your father and mine? By you? Because it certainly wasn't intended by me—tonight or any other night.'

He turned away. Where *was* she?

'Oh, Vittorio…' he heard Sirena say behind his back, and he recognised the change in her voice as she switched on the charm offensive. He heard the slither of beads and when he turned back he saw that she'd dropped Marcello's arm and edged herself closer to him. She placed one hand on his chest and snaked it around his neck. 'Do you *have* to play so hard to get? You know we're made for each other. And while I admit it's been fun at times, playing this game of cat and mouse, it gets so tiring…always keeping up the charade.'

Vittorio put his hand over her forearm and sighed. 'You're right, Sirena. It *is* tiring,' he said. 'I think it has gone on long enough.'

'You see?' she said, her smile widening. 'I knew you'd think it was time we worked this out. We have to start making plans. Marcello will be your best man, surely?'

She didn't let her eyes shift from her target as Marcello, knowing it should be the groom who asked him, muttered an anxious, 'I'd be honoured, of course.'

'We'll have to have the wedding in the cathedral in Andachstein, of course,' Sirena said, as if Marcello hadn't uttered a word, 'and in spring. It's so beautiful in Andachstein in spring. But where should we honeymoon? We *have* to start planning, Vittorio. It's so exciting.'

Her nails were raking the skin at the back of his neck, but if the woman thought she was stroking his senses into compliance she was very much mistaken.

He put his hand over her forearm, pulling her hand away before he dropped it unceremoniously into what little space there was between them.

'No, Sirena. What I meant was that this farce has gone on long enough. Can you for once accept that whatever our fathers might have schemed, whatever they promised you, and whatever fantasy you've been nurturing in your mind, it's never going to happen. That is my promise to you.'

'But Vittorio,' she said, once again reaching out for him, with a note of hysteria in her voice this time. 'You can't be serious. You can't mean that.'

'How many times do I have to tell you before you accept the truth?'

'The truth is you're a playboy—everyone knows that. But you have to settle down some time.'

'Maybe I do,' he conceded, and it was the only concession he was prepared to make. 'But when I settle down it won't be with you.'

She spun away in a clatter of beads. 'You bastard!' She turned her regal chin over one shoulder and glared at him, the rage in her eyes all hellfire and ice. 'Go back and slum it with your little village slut, then. See if I care.'

Finally the real Sirena had emerged. He sighed. What kind of man would want to hitch himself to *that*, no matter the packaging? 'What you care or don't care about is not my concern, Sirena. But, for the record, that's exactly what I plan to do.'

Watching Sirena storm off, her sandalled feet slapping hard on the marble floor, was one of the most satisfying yet exhausting moments of Vittorio's life. Maybe she had finally got it through her head that there was never going to be a marriage between them. *Dio*, he was sick of this world of arranged marriages and false emotions.

But right now he had more pressing needs. He needed to find Rosa. He'd been wrong to bring her here. He'd exposed her to the best and the worst aspects of his life. And he'd exposed her to the worst of himself, using her as cannon fodder to make a point to a woman he had no intention of marrying.

What had he been thinking, inviting her here tonight? She deserved to be treated better than the way he had treated her. She'd been out of her depth—he'd known that from the start. She'd been overawed by the wealth and sumptuousness of this world she'd been given a glimpse of and yet she had handled herself supremely well, dealing with Sirena's antagonism with a courage he hadn't anticipated.

He slapped Marcello on the back in acknowledgement of what he'd attempted and told him he'd be back soon.

He didn't want to contemplate the carnage if Sirena found Rosa before he did. He'd never forgive himself. He was already feeling ill at ease for taking advantage of Rosa's circumstances the way he had. Serendipity, he'd called it. *Serendipity nothing.* He'd been out-and-out opportunistic. He'd charged Sirena with that same crime, and yet he was guilty of the charge himself. When he'd found Rosa he'd seen a decoy—a buffer for Sirena's insistent attention.

He should just take Rosa home, back to her dingy hotel and her humdrum life. Maybe she would be relieved to be back in her own world. Maybe she would see it as an escape. She should.

He wandered from room to room, brushing aside the calls to him to stop and talk.

He knew he should take her home. Except part of him didn't want to let her go—not just yet. His final words to Sirena hadn't been all bluff. Not when he thought about Rosa's upturned face looking into his. He remembered the change in her expression, her laughter drying up, her lips slightly parted. He remembered the hitch in her breath and the sudden rise of her chest.

He'd seen the way she'd gazed up into his eyes.

Rosa had been the best part of his evening.

He hated it that it had to end. And he had enough experience of the female to know that she didn't want it to end just yet either.

Eventually he found Rosa, surrounded by a group of guests he recognised—members of Sirena's retinue, simpering men and women who were her 'rent-a-court', always sitting around waiting on her every word, waiting for a rare treat to be dispensed. Now they were formed around Rosa like some kind of Praetorian Guard, looking at Rosa as if *she* was the treat.

Sirena's work, no doubt. It had her fingerprints all over it.

'Here you are,' he said, barely able to keep the snarl from his voice as he surveyed the smug-looking group. 'I've been looking everywhere for you.'

She didn't look pleased to see him. Her eyes didn't meet his with relief, or with the delight he would have preferred. The brandy in her eyes was un-warmed. Non-committal. Even her body language had changed, her movements stiff and formal.

'I've been making some new friends,' she said.

He glanced around at the six of them, all dressed the same—or rather, *un*dressed the same. The men were bare-chested, wearing white kilts, blue and white striped head-dresses and wide gold armbands. The women had the addition of a golden bralette.

Cleopatra's so-called friends. More like a guard of honour. And he knew that, like Sirena, they were capable of tearing an unsuspecting person to pieces. He wasn't the only one who would be able to see her lack of sophistication and absence of guile. Rosa was like the first bright flare of a matchstick in a darkened room. She was all vulnerability in a world of weary cynicism.

'I'm sorry to disappoint your new *friends*,' he lied, eye-balling each and every one of their heavily kohled eyes, 'but we're leaving. I'm taking you home.'

Rosa's chin kicked up. 'What if I'm not ready to go home? I know where I am now. I can find my own way.'

'We can take you,' one of her new friends offered, with a lean and hungry smile.

'Yes,' said another, his lips drawing hyena-like over his

teeth as he took one of her hands. 'Stay a little longer, Rosa. We'll see that you get home.'

'It's up to you,' Vittorio told her.

There was no hiding the growl in his voice even as he had to force himself to back off—because if she didn't want him he could hardly drag her out of here, no matter that his inner caveman was insisting he simply throw her over his shoulder and leave. She was a grown-up, with a mind of her own, and if she was foolish enough to choose them over her it would be on her own head.

But still the idea sat uneasily with him.

She looked from the group to Vittorio and he saw the indecision in her eyes, the brittle wall of resistance she'd erected around herself waver. And, like that moment by the bridge, when he'd seen her shoulders slump as she recognised the hopelessness of her situation, he could tell the moment she made a decision.

'No,' she said to the group with a smile of apology. 'Thank you for your kind offer. But it's late and I have to work tomorrow.'

Vittorio grunted his approval while they pleaded with her to reconsider. So she'd witnessed what was in their eyes and decided he was the lesser of two evils? At least she had *that* much sense.

But it occurred to him that he might have to rethink his plans for the evening. Things had changed in the balance between them. He'd thought she was learning to trust him, losing her skittishness, but something had happened in the time she'd been out of his sight. Something that had fractured the tentative bond that had been developing between them.

It was too bad, but it was hardly the end of the world.

Tomorrow he would return to Andachstein, a tiny coastal principality nestled between Italy and Slovenia. He had duties there. There was a film festival gala to attend and a new hospital wing to be opened, along with school visits to make—all part of his royal duties as heir. So he'd see Rosa safely home now, and then he'd head back to the family *palazzo*—the legacy of a match between the daughter of a Venetian aristocrat and one of Andachstein's ancestral princes.

No doubt his father would be waiting for the news he'd been wanting to hear for years. He was not going to be happy to hear there was none.

'I'll be fine now,' she said, once they were out of the room. 'I'll find my own way home.'

'I don't think so.'

'Listen, Vittorio—'

'No. *You* listen. If you think I'm going to let you loose in the fog-bound *calles* at this time of the morning, after half the city's been partying all night, you've got another think coming. That lot upstairs aren't the only ones who'd take advantage of a lone woman feeling her way home in the fog.'

She swallowed, and he saw the kick of her throat even as her eyes flashed defiantly. He could tell she saw the sense in his words, even if she didn't want to.

'So I'm still stuck with you, then,' she said.

'So it would seem.'

She turned her head away in resignation and they descended the staircase in silence, together but apart, the earlier warmth they'd shared having dissipated.

His mood blackened with every step, returning him to that dark place he'd been earlier in the evening. It didn't help that Rosa had lost the air of wonderment she'd arrived with. It didn't help that she couldn't find him a smile and that he had been relegated to mere chaperone—one that she was only putting up with under sufferance. It raised his hackles.

'I'm sorry,' he said, maybe a little more brusquely than

he'd have preferred, but then, he wasn't in the mood for pleasantries. 'Perhaps I shouldn't have brought you here. I shouldn't have invited you.'

'Why shouldn't you have invited me?' she asked. 'Because I don't belong? Because I'm no better than a little village slut for you to slum it with?'

'You heard. How much did you hear?'

'I heard enough.'

Vittorio wanted to slam his head against the nearest wall. As if it wasn't enough that Sirena had subjected her to those poisoned barbs face to face, Rosa had heard what Sirena had said behind her back.

'I didn't call you that.'

'I didn't hear you deny it,' she said, but she didn't sound angry, as she had every right to. She sounded...disappointed.

He could have explained that there would have been no point, that it wasn't what *he* thought of her and that Sirena would have taken no notice, but she was right. He hadn't made any attempt to deny or correct it.

Dio. What a mess.

They collected their cloaks in silence, and only three words were playing over and over in Rosa's mind.

Little village slut.

Stone-faced, Vittorio covered her shoulders with first her own cloak and then his cursed scented leather cloak. She hated the fact that it smelt so good now, and tried to slip away from beneath it.

'I don't need that.'

But he persisted, like a father whose patience with his recalcitrant toddler was all but used up. 'Yes, you do,' he insisted, and he turned her towards him and did up the fancy clasp she'd had trouble undoing before.

She looked everywhere but at him. And the moment he

released her she turned away from his touch and his stony features, wishing she could so easily turn away from the warmth of his cloak and the promise it had given her.

Instead, the evening had finished up a huge disappointment. It had been a rollercoaster of emotions from the start, from excitement to panic to despair to hope. Or a kind of hope. But now she could see that that hope had been like those strings of beads in the glamorous Sirena's skirt, and that one pulled thread would have seen it fall apart and skitter away into a million irreconcilable parts.

And now there was just the end to be negotiated.

She took a deep breath. She'd had a night out. A fantasy night such as she could never have expected or afforded. She'd had an experience with which to reassure Chiara, when her friend apologised profusely about losing her in the crowds without her phone or ticket, as she expected she would.

And she'd had a glimmer of something special. Of a man who looked like a warrior, a man who'd been chivalrous and generous enough to include her in his world, a man who simultaneously excited and frightened her, a man who made her insides curl when he looked at her as if she was something special.

At least she imagined that was what he'd been thinking.

She sighed. Soon she would be back home in the tiny basement apartment she shared with Chiara and this night would be just a memory.

Little village slut.

The words kept on circling in Rosa's mind. It was true, she did come from a small village in the heel of Italy. A dot of a town, to be sure. But that was where the truth ended. And it was so unfair.

'They're only words,' her brothers had told her when she'd been bullied at school. *'Words can't wound you.'*

She'd wanted to believe her brothers. Maybe she had

for a time—except perhaps now, because the man she'd thought he was, the man she'd built up in her mind, had turned out to be somebody else. The man who had been a stranger to her, the man she'd thought was something else entirely, was a stranger still.

'Where are we going?' she asked, when Vittorio led her down the steps into the garden.

'We're going home by motorboat,' he said, as he steered her to the big wooden doors that were opened for them onto the Grand Canal.

Rosa shivered as the damp air surged in. She'd forgotten how very cold the fog was—although that didn't make her want to be any more grateful for Vittorio's cloak or want to tell him that he'd been right. She wouldn't give him the satisfaction.

A few steps below them a motorboat sat rocking on the lapping waters of the canal. Fog still clung low, swirling in the air and rendering the glow of lights to ghostly smudges.

'Palazzo D'Marburg,' he told the driver, handing her into the boat before bundling her into the covered interior.

The motor chugged into life once they were seated, and the boat pulled away slowly into the canal, still moving slowly when it cleared the dock. It was so painfully slow that Rosa wished they had walked after all. The journey home would take for ever at this rate, and the interior of the cabin was already too small for the both of them. Too intimate. Vittorio took up too much of the space and sucked up the remaining oxygen in the cabin. Was it any wonder she was breathless?

And meanwhile the man opposite her had turned to stone, his expression grim, his body language saying he was a man whose patience had worn thin and who was stoically waiting to be rid of her. Or a man who was sulking because she wasn't falling victim to his charms any more.

Well, she was waiting too—to be free of this warrior whose charms had long since expired.

Maybe she should have stayed at the party. She'd been meeting people and having fun, hadn't she? Okay, so she hadn't liked the way a couple of them had looked at her enough to want them to take her home, but at least she'd been able to breathe there, and her heart hadn't tripped over itself like it did every time this man so much as looked at her.

She would have been perfectly all right if she'd stayed. And Marcello would have looked after her if he'd thought she was in any danger. Vittorio was such a drama queen.

He chose that moment to shift in his seat, his big knee brushing against her leg, and she bristled in response. What *was* it about the man? He couldn't move without making her notice. He took up so much space. He had such presence. He made her feel small. Insignificant.

She sucked in air and, and as if it wasn't bad enough that she had to put up with the scent of him, even the air now tasted of him.

Suddenly it was all too much—the fog and the rocking and the cursed muffled silence. It was like being entombed with one of those Chinese stone warriors from the Terracotta Army she'd seen on display at a museum in Rome on a school visit. And she wasn't ready to be entombed.

She launched herself at the door that led to the small rear deck.

'It's too cold out there,' he growled.

'I don't care!' she flung back at him, shoving her way through the door.

She had no choice. She had to get outside. She had to escape.

The cold air hit her skin like a slap in the face, but at least the air outside didn't taste of Vittorio and smell like Vittorio, and it wasn't filled with the bulk of him. Finally she could breathe again. She gulped in great lungsful of it, letting it cleanse her senses even as she huddled her arms around her chest.

Of course he followed her, as she'd known he would, standing beside her silently like a sentinel. She didn't have to turn her head to know he was there. She could sense his presence. Feel his heat. Cursed man.

The motorboat chugged and rocked its way slowly along the canal. It was other-worldly. The sounds and sights of the city had vanished. Items appeared suddenly out of the fog—a lamp on a post, another motorboat edging its way cautiously by—and then just as quickly were swallowed up again.

And he was the most other worldly part of it all.

A fantasy gone wrong.

She searched through the fog, suddenly frantic, trying to find a reference point so that she could tell how long this trip would last. But there was nothing. Not a hint of where they were. No clue to how long she would be forced to endure this torture.

Nothing but silence. Tension. And her utter disappointment with how this evening had ended when it had started out with such excitement. Such promise.

Like a rubber band stretched too far, she snapped. 'Why did you ask me to come with you tonight?'

Slowly, almost as slowly as the boat they were travelling on, he turned his head towards her. His expression told her nothing and his face was a mask of stone.

'Because you were lost and alone. Because I thought I could help.'

She scoffed. 'I think we both know that's not true, Vittorio. I don't want that line you spun me about chivalry and concern for my happiness and well-being and not wanting me to miss out on the last night of Carnevale. I want the real reason.'

He was silent for a few seconds, but Rosa wasn't going to give him time to make something else up.

She gathered the strength to ask the question that had been plaguing her ever since that woman dressed as Cleopatra had burst onto the scene. 'Who is Sirena to you?' she demanded. 'What claim does she hold over you?'

'None. Sirena is nothing to me.'

Rosa gave a very unladylike snort, and if it made her sound like the country girl she was, instead of some pampered city girl with polished manners, she didn't give a damn. 'You expect me to believe that when I witnessed her draped all over you like a limpet.'

'That meant nothing,' he said. 'Whatever Sirena likes to think.'

She shook her head. 'She thinks you're going to marry her!'

He looked shocked.

'I was there,' she said. 'I heard what she said.'

He took a deep breath and sighed, long and hard. 'My father wants me married. It would suit him if I married his friend's daughter. That is all.'

'That's *all*?' She laughed into the mist, her breath turning to fog. 'What I don't understand is why I had to get dragged into your mess. Did you know she'd be at the ball tonight?'

'I'd had word.'

Finally something that made sense. She gave a long sigh of her own. 'So there we have it,' she said, nodding her head as she looked out into the mist and the pieces of the puzzle fell into place. 'You invited me to come with you to make her jealous.'

'No! It was never to make her jealous.'

'Then what? To run interference? To make a point? Was it sport you had in mind? Is *that* what asking me to go with you was all about?'

He said nothing—which told her everything she needed to know.

She heard his deep breath in, felt him shift as he ran his hand through his untamed hair.

'You were lost.'

'One of your strays?'

He sniffed. 'Maybe. And I thought I could help you—and you could help me—at the same time.'

She shook her head 'Bottom line, Vittorio, you used me.' Even as she said the words tiny tears squeezed from her eyes. She'd had such high hopes for this night. He'd made her think all kinds of things. That she mattered. That he cared. That she wanted...

'Rosa...'

'No,' she said, turning further away, because he didn't care, and the disappointment of the evening was weighing heavily down on her, crushing her.

'Rosa.' His hands were on her shoulders. 'I'm sorry.'

'And that's supposed to make it better? That's supposed to make it all right?'

She hated it that her voice sounded so quaky, that she sounded so needy, when she'd thought that growing up with three brothers had toughened her up for anything. She hated it that she could feel the warm puff of his breath on her hair. She hated it that his hands were on her shoulders and it wasn't enough. She hated herself because she wanted more.

'No, it's not all right. I hurt you.'

She sniffed as he turned her with his big hands, but she didn't resist. Didn't resist when he drew her against his body and wrapped his arms around her. Didn't object when she felt him dip his head and kiss her hair.

'Can you forgive me?'

It felt so warm, being cradled against his big body. So firm. So hard. And the drumbeat of his heart added another note to the lullaby chugging of the engine, made the movement of the boat beneath their feet like the rocking of a cradle.

'I'm sorry that I hurt you,' he said. 'I knew Sirena would be angry. The only reason I said I should never have invited you was because I'd anticipated Sirena's reaction. I knew she'd be furious and she didn't disappoint. To subject you to that was unthinkable. You didn't deserve that.'

She should pull away. Her tears had passed and she should put distance between them, she knew. He'd treated her shamefully and she should want nothing more to do with him, apology or no. Why should she forgive him?

But she remembered the way he'd looked at her during the entertainment. She remembered the warmth of his hand, that shared moment when it had seemed the world was made of magic. His body felt so good next to hers. So very warm. And that was a kind of magic too. Was it wrong to want the magic to last just a little bit longer?

He stroked her back and she felt the crushing disappointment of the evening ebb slowly away. 'It was a good party,' she said. It was a concession of sorts. Because it *had* been an experience. She had so much to tell Chiara in the morning. 'I enjoyed it. Most of it.'

He squeezed his arms and she felt the press of his lips to her hair again, and she knew she wasn't drawing away from him any time soon.

'That's good. I'm sorry that Sirena had to spoil it for you.' A moment later he added, 'No, I'm sorry *I* had to spoil it for you.'

Rosa thought about how the woman had looked in her costume, her limbs so long, her skin so smooth and perfect. The woman had made Rosa feel so ordinary. So drab and inconsequential. The woman would have made the real Cleopatra feel inconsequential.

'She's very beautiful, isn't she?'

He sighed and placed his chin on her head. 'Beauty is an empty vessel,' he said, his deep voice a bare whisper over the chug of the motor. 'It needs something to fill it. Something meaningful and worthwhile to flesh it out and make it whole.'

She was struck by his whispered words. 'Where did you hear that?'

'Something my mother once said.'

'She sounds very wise.'

'She could be, at times.' A pause. A sigh. 'She's dead now.'

'I'm sorry.'

'Thank you, but it's not your fault.'

'I understand. But my mother is gone too. She was diagnosed with leukaemia. She died three years ago. There's not a day goes by that I don't think about her…that I don't miss her.'

He shook his head. 'And now it's my turn to say I'm sorry, and your turn to say it's not my fault.'

She laughed a little at his words, then stopped. The sound was so unexpected when her thoughts had been tuned to disappointment. 'The language of death. It's so complicated.'

He loosened one arm and lifted his hand to her face, touching her gently with the knuckle of one finger. He was so gentle that she barely felt the brush of his skin against hers, and yet his touch sent bone-deep tremors through her. Made her want to lean into his hand.

Then he took her chin and lifted her face to his. 'Maybe instead we should talk the language of the living.'

Her breath hitched in her throat. His hand was warm against her skin, his face filling her vision. She swallowed. 'I think I'd prefer that.'

His eyes were dark blue against the foggy night and the force of them pulled her towards him.

Or maybe it was just the motion of the boat drawing their

faces together. Or perhaps the fog muted every word, rendering every breath more intimate than it would otherwise have been. Because suddenly his mouth was hovering mere millimetres over hers, then even closer, his warm breath mingling with her pale puffs of air, and then his lips met hers and her world tilted on its axis.

He had soft lips. In a face that looked as if it had been chiselled from stone she hadn't expected that. Nor tenderness, surprising in its sweetness. But there was warmth and heat and the feel of his long-fingered hands through her hair. The combination was lethal.

Time stood still. The chugging of the engine disappeared under the *whump-whump* of her own heartbeat in her ears. The world was reduced to this boat, to this one man and one woman and the magic swirling like the fog around them. She sighed into him, melting as his mouth moved over hers, parting her lips so that she could taste him, and his kiss deepened, his tongue tracing the line of her teeth, duelling with hers.

He tasted of coffee and liqueur, leather and man, and underneath was another layer which was heat and strength and desire, and she wanted more.

This was a kiss—not a mere peck on the cheek like he'd given her earlier. This was a kiss that spun her senses out of control, a kiss that melted her bones and short-circuited her brain.

When finally they drew apart her knees were trembling and her breathing was ragged, as though she'd run a sprint.

'Rosa…' he whispered in her hair. His breathing was coming fast too, and she could see that he had also been affected by their kiss. 'I'm so sorry.'

'You're sorry that you kissed me?'

He made a sound, like a laugh. 'Oh, no. I'm not sorry for that. Not sorry at all.'

'That's good,' she said, still clinging to him, afraid that

if she let go he might take his arms away and her legs wouldn't have the strength to hold her up. 'I think...' she started. 'I think that I forgive you.'

'You do?'

'But only on one condition.'

'Name it.'

'Only if you kiss me again.'

He growled.

To Rosa it sounded like a cry of triumph, of victory, as he swept her up in his arms and twirled her around so that her feet left the deck. At any other time she would have been fearful of falling out of the vessel, but not now. With Vittorio's strong arms around her she felt that nothing could go wrong. And when he put her down his big hands were cupping her face.

'I dreamed about this,' he said.

She was breathless all over again. 'You dreamed about kissing me?'

'More. I dreamed about spending the rest of the night with you.'

She gasped. There was no way she could prevent it. It was as involuntary as the flip of her stomach and the sudden clench of muscles between her thighs she'd never realised existed.

'But that's up to you. Let's see about my earning your forgiveness first.'

His mouth descended once more. She felt the tickle of his falling hair around her face, the graze of his whiskered cheeks and the exquisite, unexpected softness of his lips as his mouth met hers.

He took it slowly. He nibbled and suckled at her lips, teased her tongue with his and beckoned hers into the heated cavern of his mouth; he reassured the rest of her body that it wasn't missing out by sending his hands underneath the cloaks and sweeping them in arcs from her shoulders to the curve of her behind, and if forgiveness could truly be earned in a kiss he was earning a lifetime's worth.

But the kiss didn't end there. He changed gear, ratcheting up from gentle and considerate to plundering. Demanding. And she gave herself up to passion and to a heat such as she'd never known. She was burning up from the inside out.

Tiny details assumed major status. The precise angle of his mouth over hers, the puff of his breath on her cheek, the creak of leather as his arms moved around her. Tiny things, insignificant in themselves, and yet all part of something major, something momentous. Her breasts were straining tight inside her bodice, her nipples ached, and all she knew, with the tiny part of her brain that was still functioning, was that she never wanted these feelings to end.

Was it magic? Or merely lust?

She didn't care.

What did it matter when it felt this good?

By the time his head drew back she was lost to it. They could have fallen into the dark and frigid waters of the canal and she would have noticed nothing—not even the steam that would have come from their union.

'Make love to me, Rosa.' His breathing was rushed and ragged, his voice no more than a rasp on the night air. 'Spend the night with me.'

A spike of fear made its presence known—an age-old fear that she'd carried with her all her womanly life—and despite her earlier fantasies about the magic of the night that fear reared its head.

Sure, she wasn't completely naïve. She knew how things were supposed to work. But what did she really know of the intimacy of the bedroom? What if she couldn't? What if she did something wrong? What if it hurt? What if she made a fool of herself?

But those fears were no match for the arousal that spiralled up from within and surrounded her. Like a suit of armour, it protected her from her fears. There were still curling tendrils of doubt, but they were all but blunted, making room for anticipation and heady excitement, because this night would be a night like no other.

And somehow she knew she couldn't be in better hands.

She sucked in a breath while he waited for her answer, needing the cold night air to cool her while it could. 'I'd like that,' she said, and he gave a low growl of approval in his throat.

He took a moment to yell instructions to the driver and she had a sense of the boat changing direction as he turned her face up to his for another kiss.

Maybe it was just lust, Rosa thought as he pulled her against his mouth.

But there was magic happening tonight too.

Pure magic.

CHAPTER FIVE

FROM THE FIRST moment their eyes had met Rosa had recognised that there was something about this man, something magnetic that had drawn her towards him, something commanding. But something that scared her, too. There was an edge to him, as though if she ventured too close she might fall.

And yet she'd agreed to spend the night with him.

But now, stepping from the deck of the motorboat and into a building, she felt a further sense of unease. Because it wasn't any ordinary building.

'What is this place?' she asked as he led her by the hand towards a flight of stairs. It was not a hotel, as she'd been expecting. And it was no humble apartment. 'Is this your home?'

'What? Here in Venice? No,' he said dismissively. 'It's a private residence. I just get to stay here occasionally.'

He shrugged, as if having access in any capacity to a *palazzo* on the Grand Canal was nothing special.

Rosa looked around. Maybe this *palazzo* didn't quite rival Marcello's in grandeur, but it was still very definitely a *palazzo*, and it was filled with treasures of Murano glass, sculptures, chandeliers and gilt everything.

'So where *do* you live?' she asked, her heels tapping on the marble staircase.

'North of here. Near the border with Slovenia.'

'Near Trieste?'

He turned to her and smiled. 'Do you always ask this many questions when you're nervous.'

'I'm not nervous,' she lied on a lilting laugh.

But a few moments later he opened the door to a bedroom and her heart all but jumped out of her chest with nerves.

He dimmed the lights, but there was no dimming the vision that met her eyes, because across the room was a wide bed—impossibly wide. She swallowed. There was only one place this could end, and she wanted it, but still...

'Would you like something to drink?' he offered, already stripping away her armour of cloaks, peeling away her courage at the same time. 'Prosecco or another spritz?'

She shook her head. She didn't need more alcohol, or anything with bubbles. There was already too much fizzing going on in her blood.

'Then water.'

He pulled a bottle of water from a cabinet and poured them both a glass. She accepted it, more to give herself something to do with her hands rather than because her throat was suddenly desert-dry.

She was still contemplating that bed. She knew what the act entailed, but why was there no guidebook for the prelude? *Dio*, she really hoped she didn't mess this up.

She heard the soft tap of his glass being put down on a cabinet behind her, and then a sound that could only be the unbuckling of his leather trousers and a long zipper being undone. She clutched her glass with both hands.

Help!

'Rosa...' he said as he gently took her arm and turned her towards him.

He was bare-chested, dressed only in the leather of his costume pants. Her hungry eyes could not help but drink in the muscular perfection of his shoulders, his chest and his sculpted abdomen. She'd thought him perfect wrapped in leather of blue and gold, but now, dressed only in a pair of leather trousers slung low over his hips, he looked even more magnificent.

Breathtaking. Heart stopping.

Terrifying.

He smiled, then eased the glass from her tangled fingers and put it aside. 'Now,' he said, as he put his hands to her neck and eased her hair back over her shoulders. 'Where were we?'

Her mind was a blank. She had no idea what he was talking about, let alone how to answer.

But his warm hands answered his question for her, meeting at the nape of her neck and drawing her closer to him. Closer to his intense blue eyes. Closer to his parted, waiting lips.

She felt the heat of his mouth, the warmth of his hands at the back of her head, holding her to him. She felt the heat of his body even before he drew her still closer and her breasts met the hard wall of his chest as he deepened the kiss.

Her breasts ached for release. Her nipples were pressing hard against a suddenly too tight bodice as her blood swirled drunkenly around her veins. Her legs felt boneless and she had to put her hands to his chest to steady herself. But once they were there steadying herself against his body was the lesser priority. She needed to feel him, to drink in the texture of his sculpted body, to see if he felt as good as he looked.

And he did. He was magnificent, his body a landscape of contrasts. Hard muscles. Smooth skin. Wiry tangle of chest hair. Firm nub of nipples. But the realisation only ramped up both her desire and her nervousness.

'You're trembling...' He breathed rather than said the words as his lips worked the soft folds and ridges of her ears, his breath fanning like a musical breeze against her skin. 'Are you cold?'

Anything but. She was alight with fire, flames were burning her up from within, breathing life into the coals that already glowed hot deep down in the pit of her belly.

'No...' she whispered on a gasp of oxygen, and that tiny, one-syllable word was all she was capable of before his mouth once against captured hers and she was sucked back into the vortex of his kiss.

Was it possible to spin any more out of control?

Yes, she realised when she felt his fingers tug on the pull of her zip. Clever fingers to find such a well-disguised invisible zip, but even the knowledge that he was a man used to finding his way into women's clothing couldn't stop another rushing tide of heat as her dress loosened around her and threatened to fall away.

And, then like the burst of cool air that swirled into the exposed space at her back, a surge of panic saw her hands fold over her breasts. She wasn't wearing a bra and there would be nothing between them...

It was too late, and she realised how unsophisticated it must make her look, but all she could do was clutch her dress to her all the harder.

'So shy,' he said with a smile. 'Anyone would think...'

She turned her head away, but not before he'd seen the truth she tried to hide skittering across her eyes and the heated blush flooding her skin.

'No...' he said, and when she dared look back she saw disbelief mixed with something that looked like horror in his eyes. 'But you *can't* be a virgin. How old are you?'

'I'm sorry,' she said, wanting to run away. 'I didn't realise virginity came with a use-by date.'

He let her go and stepped away. Ran a hand through his hair. A *virgin*! Why the hell hadn't he picked up on it? She'd been like a startled doe trapped in the headlights from the start—flighty and nervous and blushing like a schoolgirl.

And desperate to point out that she was no courtesan. All the clues had been there and yet he'd been too blind to see what had been staring him in the face.

He turned and she was still standing there, holding her dress to her breasts like a shield. 'Rosa,' he said, 'why didn't you tell me? You should have told me.'

'When should I have done that, exactly? When you found me lost in the square and you asked my name? Or when you were kissing me on the motorboat and asked me to make love to you? When would have been the best time to slip my lack of sexual expertise casually into the conversation?'

She had a point. But a *virgin*?

He shook his head. Virgins were trouble. They had expectations. It wasn't a sacrifice most made lightly—parting with the known and the safe for the unknown. They took the act of love as an act of sharing and a promise of commitment. They had hopes and dreams he had no way of fulfilling.

'Look—' he said, shaking his head.

'I'm sorry,' she said cutting him off. 'You asked me to spend the night with you.' The end of her tongue found her lips. 'I said yes. So why should this make a difference?'

'It's your first time,' he replied. 'You don't want to waste it on a one-night stand. And that's all it will be, Rosa. That's all it can ever be—one night. I can't offer you any more than that.'

'I just want to finish what you started. I don't want any more than that.'

No? That was what they all said, and then afterwards would come the tears.

'Rosa—'

'Please,' she said. 'I really want to. I'm just a bit nervous, that's all.'

She took a deep breath, then took her hands away from

her dress and let it crumple to the floor, standing naked before him but for her panties.

Breath hissed through his teeth. *Dio*, but she was beautiful. Curvy, with dark-tipped breasts and a narrow waist that begged a man to run his hands down the sides, to drink them in, to feel for himself the exquisite flare of her hips.

An erection he thought had been banished by her revelation kicked back into life with a vengeance.

'Are you sure about this?' he asked, taking a step closer. Because she needed to be certain.

'I'm sure,' she said. 'What do you want me to do?'

'Oh, Rosa,' he said as he swung her into his arms, 'Your first time—all I want you to do is feel and enjoy.'

He laid her on the bed and sat beside her, held her face in his hands and kissed her gently on the mouth.

She was so nervous, her skin alive to sensation and his every touch like a brand, but he stilled her with his kiss. Soothed her.

'Don't be afraid,' he said, as if he could see inside her.

She smiled tremulously up at him and he kissed her again before dipping his mouth lower, kissing her throat, her collarbones, her shoulders, then kissing first one peaked nipple and then the other.

'So beautiful,' he said, and returned to her mouth, his kiss deeper, giving and taking more.

Her hands moved of their own volition, wanting to feel, to explore. His muscles bunched and shifted under her hands, and every touch, every texture, fed into her need, adding to the mix bubbling in the cauldron inside her.

She'd thought it would be quick, that it would be over soon. But he took his time exploring her body with his hot mouth and his clever fingers, until every nerve-ending in her body felt as if it was about to explode. When he drew down her underwear and touched a hand to her mound, one finger sliding between her slick folds, she almost did. Then and only then he stood and peeled down his leather trousers.

His erection sprang free and she gasped, feeling a momentary spike of panic. He was too big…there was no way… But then he was back, kissing her, and she could feel him hard against her belly, and she knew she wanted him inside her—whatever it took.

Still he didn't rush. Her body was burning up with need. She was panting with it, desperate, searching for relief, when he reached for a packet on the bedside table. He ripped it open and knelt above her, sliding protection down his long length. So long…

And then he was there, nudging at her entrance and sending those acutely sensitive nerve-endings into a frenzy. He kissed her deeply, opening her to him, his tongue plundering as he raised one of her legs over his hip and plunged into her.

Stars exploded behind her eyes. Stars that sent shimmering fragments whirling around the delicious feeling of fullness at her core.

He held himself still, his words coming in heady gasps. 'Are you all right?'

She remembered how to breathe, drawing in a ragged breath. 'I'm good,' she managed.

He started to move, to withdraw, and she missed him already. Newly found muscles clamped down, trying to hold on to him, and just when she thought he was lost to her he was back, and she was better than good.

He picked up the rhythm and in the friction he generated she found her stars again, this time strewn on the surface of the sea, wave after wave of shimmering sensation building inside her with every thrust. She was tossed higher and higher, faster and faster, until with one final plunge the star-filled waves crashed over her and washed her bonelessly to the shore.

She came back from the delicious place he'd sent her to slowly. Reluctantly. She wondered why the world in front of her eyes seemed so much the same as it had been before when everything had irrevocably shifted.

She'd expected to feel different. Regretful. Maybe even a little sad.

Instead, she felt...*good.*

Vittorio lay breathing hard next to her, his body hot, his skin slick with sweat. He lifted his head and kissed her cheek. 'Did I hurt you? Are you okay?'

She smiled and shook her head. There'd been a momentary flash of pain, but it had been lost in a shower storm of stars.

She kissed him back. 'Thank you. That was nice.'

His eyebrows shot up. *'Nice?'* he growled as he rolled out of bed to pad to the bathroom.

She grinned and scooted up the bed, slipping under the covers to hide her naked body. It was insane, after what they'd just done, but with him gone she felt exposed again.

'Very nice?'

She heard him chuckle and then he returned, sliding into the bed alongside her.

'Oh,' she said, unsure of the protocol. 'Should I go home now?'

'I promised you one night,' he said, settling her into the crook of his shoulder so he could dip his head to kiss her again. 'We might as well make the most of it.'

It was later, much later, and Vittorio's body was humming its way down from another crescendo. Rosa's fingernails were idly stroking his chest, and she asked, 'What happened to the kitten you rescued?'

He'd been so lulled by the rhythmic strokes of her fingernails, making swirls in the hair on his chest, that he almost missed the question.

'What?'

'The one you pulled from the bag in the stream.'

'You heard that?'

'I was nearly at the stairs when I saw Sirena was talking to you and Marcello. What happened to it? Did you keep it?'

'I took it to the housekeeper.'

He thought back. There would have been no point taking it to his father. His father would have told him that he was his mother's son and therefore weak—too weak to be the heir to the throne.

'My father would have told me to show some backbone for once in my life and throw the wretched thing back where I'd found it.'

But Maria had cried when she'd heard his story and she'd taken it and cuddled it before setting about finding it some bread to soak in milk.

'She kept it in the kitchen to keep down the mice.'

The thick medieval castle walls had shifted so often over the centuries, and been renovated so many times, it was impossible to plug all the tiny hidey holes. He'd often arrived in the kitchen to find Maria breathless as she chased after another mouse with her straw broom across the flagstones.

'You had your own housekeeper?'

'Que?' Too late he realised he'd almost given too much away, but this woman had a way of breaking down his defences. Of disarming him. 'Oh. After my mother died…'

'Of course,' she said, filling in the blanks as she understood them, relieving him of the need to finish while the circles of her fingers grew larger, sweeping lower over his abs. 'Somebody had to look after you both.'

'Somebody had to,' he agreed, lulled by the caress of her nails on his skin.

Maria had looked after them, along with a *castello* full of staff and courtiers and advisers. For a moment he felt guilty that he couldn't tell her, and that once again he was keeping secrets from her. But it wouldn't be the same if she knew. It would change things. It always did. It was better to leave it the way she understood it to be—that he was a friend of someone whose family had once been something important in Venice.

'Your father sounds very controlling. I mean, not just the kitten, but expecting you to marry who he chooses.'

He gave a low snort. 'That's one word for it. But I've been married. It ended badly.'

'Oh, I didn't know. I'm sorry.'

'It's not your fault,' he said, and she chuckled as both of them remembered their earlier conversation.

'Some families are like that, though, aren't they?' she said. 'Expecting to stage-manage their children's lives, maybe even wanting them to live the life they couldn't.'

He nodded, feeling the caress of her fingertips like a balm to his soul. 'What about your family, Rosa?' He smiled apologetically. 'Your *papà*, I mean. What's he like?'

'Wonderful. He's the one who urged me to leave home and find work somewhere else. I was happy at home— it was nice taking care of the house for everyone after Mamma died—but one by one my brothers married and left home, and eventually there was just my *papà* and me. He told me that if I didn't leave home and the village I'd never see anything of the world, and I'd be stuck looking after him when he got old.'

Her hand stopped and her head lifted.

'I don't think I should be talking about my father right now.'

He patted her shoulder. 'My fault,' he said, wondering why he had asked. He didn't need to know anything more about Rosa than what she'd brought to this bed. He didn't need to know about her family. He didn't want to hear it. 'Let's talk about something else.'

'Talk?' she said, her fingertips back in action and growing bolder, her nails raking circles around his navel, swooping in and out. Teasing. Taunting.

His loins stirred. 'You've got a better idea?' he asked, his voice laced with a gravel edge.

Her fingertips edged lower, gliding over his tip. Her courage was growing by the minute. She'd always been a quick learner.

'Could we, do you think...? Just once more?'

Could we? He was suddenly harder than the question was to answer. But he had to remember she was new at this. Brave, curious, but inexperienced.

'You're not too sore?'

She shook her head, her fingers encircling him. Stroking him.

'Right now I'd like you to make love to me again,' she said. 'I can be sore tomorrow.'

CHAPTER SIX

VITTORIO WOKE TO watery sunlight slipping through the gaps in the heavy brocade drapes, a supreme sense of satisfaction and a goodly measure of anticipation. But sunlight…? So the fog had lifted.

He rolled over on his back and reached out an arm, searching for the source of his satisfaction and the reason for his anticipation, only to find the other side of the bed empty and the sheets cold.

What the…?

He rose up on his elbows. 'Rosa?' he called into the gloom, his eyes scanning the room, searching for any evidence of her.

But the chair where he'd flung her dress after he'd peeled it off was empty and the rug where he'd placed her shoes after he'd slipped them off was bare. There was only his rapidly discarded leather trousers littering the floor.

'Rosa!' he called, louder this time, swiping back the covers to pad barefoot across the carpet to the bathroom. But that room was dark and empty too.

She was gone.

He headed back to the bedroom, sat on the side of the bed and picked up his watch from the side table. Almost noon. *Dio*, what time had they got to sleep? The last thing he could remember thinking was that he would shut his eyes for ten minutes to recover—and then he didn't remember thinking anything at all.

He put his head in his hands and thought back. She'd said something about working today. He'd wondered at the time if it had just been an excuse to escape the party, but she'd told him she was a cleaner in a three-star hotel. Maybe she *did* have to work. Which meant... What godawful time must she have left?

He stood up on a sigh and headed back to the bathroom, swiping open the nearest curtains on the way. Milky light spilled into the room, banishing the gloom, while outside, if Venice had a hangover it didn't show.

Venice was getting on with being Venice. *Vaporettos* and gondolas alike were ferrying tourists backwards and forwards, rubbish barges filled with last night's garbage were skulking out of the way as a water ambulance screamed along the canal.

He had to get back to Andachstein.

Even so, he thought as he looked at his face in the bathroom mirror, his hands stroking his rough jaw, it was disappointing that she'd cut and run before he could make love to her one last time.

He stepped under the rain-shower spray, sighing in approval as he turned his face into the hot water and felt it cascade down his body. Just because he was in a fifteenth-century *palazzo* it didn't mean he had to go without modern plumbing.

He smiled to himself. A virgin. Rosa had started out so shy and timid and then turned to liquid mercury in his arms, as sinuous as the canal that weaved its way outside his windows. One spark and she'd sizzled with sensuality, turning an otherwise dark night into a blaze of heat and passion.

He'd been honest—at least as far as commitment went. He'd laid all his cards on the table. One night and one night only, and definitely no chance of for ever. So it was probably for the best that she'd already gone. It avoided any of those awkward post-coital conversations when last night's warnings tended to get somehow twisted by the act of intercourse, when words took on a different meaning from how they'd been intended and first understood.

How many times had he heard the same old arguments? *'But that was before you made love to me...'* and *'I thought you cared about me...'*

At least she'd saved them both that anguish.

He roughly towelled himself off and dropped his towel on the floor as he headed for the dressing room. A virgin. How about that? It had been a long time since he'd encountered a virgin. He didn't tend to move in the same circles as teenagers or gauche twenty-somethings.

She'd made him laugh. And she'd been perfectly right. It wasn't as if virginity self-destructed if you didn't use it up. It was just that most people he knew seemed to have found a way to dispense with it before they'd abandoned their teens.

He had his underwear and trousers on, and had just pulled a white shirt from a hanger, was reefing it over his shoulders, when he saw it. A glint of something gold amidst the tangle of linen and coverlets on the bed. His eyes narrowed. A trick of the watery light?

He moved closer as he buttoned his shirt. No. There was definitely something there. Something small.

He reached down and picked it up and realised what it was as the pearl swung free on the ring that attached it to a golden stud. One of Rosa's earrings.

She'd left it here.

On purpose?

The moment the thought popped into his mind he discarded it. He was far too world-weary. While plenty of women he'd met would, Rosa wouldn't play games like that. She wasn't the type.

It looked old. She would be sure to miss it.

He should return it. There were no excuses. He knew where she worked.

He should give it to the housekeeper and have it delivered. Rosa would have it back in a matter of hours.

He should return it.

He twirled the delicate earring in his fingers, held it to his nose as if by doing so he could conjure up her scent.

He should return it.

His fingers closed around it where it lay in his palm and he slipped it into his trouser pocket.

He would return it.

Later.

CHAPTER SEVEN

'WHERE DID YOU get to?' Chiara cried, bolting upright in bed and turning on her bedside lamp the second Rosa walked into the tiny basement flat the girls shared. 'I've been worried sick about you.'

'I got lost,' Rosa said, checking the time on the alarm clock glowing red. Four-thirty a.m.

She unzipped her gown and let it slip down her body for the second time that night, shivering at the memory of the first. She would have time for an hour's sleep if she put her head down on her pillow right now.

Sleep? After what she'd experienced tonight? She might be kidding herself about that. But at least she'd have an hour to savour the memories.

'I'm really sorry I suggested carrying your phone for you,' Chiara said, watching her prepare for bed. 'I feel so bad for ruining your night.'

'Don't worry about it. How was the ball?'

'So much fun,' she said, and her face lit up before she could think better of it. 'I tried to find you. We searched and searched and I called the hotel in case you'd come back, but nobody had seen you. I didn't expect to be home before you.'

'It's okay. Forget it.'

'So where were you?'

'I met someone,' Rosa said, sliding between the sheets. 'He invited me to a party he was going to.'

'He? A man? You went to a party with a stranger?' Chiara was all agog. She swung her legs out of bed and sat up. *'You?'*

Rosa didn't take offence at her friend's surprise. She knew what she meant.

'What was he like?'

'Oh, Chiara…' Rosa sighed, propping herself up on her elbow, head resting on her hand. 'You should have seen him. He was tall, and strong, and… I wouldn't call him really handsome—but powerful-looking. With the most amazing blue eyes I've ever seen.'

'What was his name?'

'Vittorio.' Even now the sound of it on her tongue was delicious.

'And he asked you to go to a party with him?'

She smiled. *'Si.'*

'Why?'

Rosa shrugged. This part could do with a bit of airbrushing of the truth. She plucked at some imaginary fluff on her sheet. 'He felt sorry for me that I was missing my costume ball after I'd spent so much money on a ticket.'

'And there *was* a party, I hope?'

'Oh, yes. In this amazing *palazzo* right on the Grand Canal. It even had a second *piano nobile*—can you imagine? The party was on the second level and the first level was set up with the entertainment. They had music and jugglers and opera singers, and even gymnasts performing on ropes. It was amazing. And you should have seen the costumes, Chiara! *Amazing.*' Rosa punched her pillow and settled down. 'Can you turn off the light? We have to get up soon.'

'And you were at this party all night, then?'

'Uh-huh. Turn off the light.'

'And then you came home?'

'I'm tired,' Rosa said, hugging her precious secret to

her, not willing to share just yet. She might tell Chiara one day about what had really happened. Maybe. 'And we've got to be up in less than an hour.'

Chiara sniffed and extinguished the light, clearly recognising the sense in Rosa's words and the fact she was not going to hear any more tonight.

'All right, have it your way. But I want all the details tomorrow!'

'Goodnight,' said Rosa noncommittally, snuggling into her pillow, and only then noticing the press of her earring stud into her flesh. In her rush to get to bed she'd forgotten to take her earrings off. She removed the offending article and reached for the one on the other side—only to find it gone.

She sat up, switching on the lamp.

'What now?' said Chiara grumpily. 'I thought you wanted to go to sleep?'

'I can't find one of my earrings.' Her eyes searched the floor around the bed. She got out and shook her dress, in case she'd dislodged it when she'd pulled the gown over her head. But of course it wasn't there, because she hadn't done that at all.

'Go to bed.'

'They were my grandmother's,' she said. 'A gift from my grandfather on their wedding day.' And, apart from her mother's sewing machine, they were the only thing of real value she had.

'Go to bed!' Chiara repeated grumpily. 'Look for it tomorrow.'

'But—'

'Turn off the light!'

Rosa did a quick sweep with her hands of her bedding and her pillow before she complied and climbed back into bed. She switched off the light and settled back down.

Where could it be? She'd been wearing them both at Vit-

torio's. She remembered seeing them when she'd looked
in the mirror in the bathroom. But that had been before…

Dio. But at least if it was there someone might find it—a
cleaner or a housekeeper—and she might be able to get it
back. Better that than thinking it had fallen out on her way
home somewhere along the twisty *calles*.

Either way, if she couldn't find it here she'd go looking
after her shift tomorrow—*today*.

One night only.

She thought about Vittorio's warning that one night was
all there would be, that it wasn't an affair and he didn't do
for ever. If he was at home she wouldn't pester him. She
wouldn't ask for him. She just wanted her earring back, if
it had been found. And if he learned she had visited he'd
understand why she'd had to come back. She was sure he
would.

So she'd retrace her steps to his *palazzo*, and if she didn't
find it on the way she'd knock on the door. There was no
harm in asking, surely?

Rosa was almost overcome with exhaustion by the time
she finished her shift. She'd been exhausted before she'd
started, though for an entirely different reason, but by the
end of the shift it was pure drudgery weighing her down.
It seemed every visitor had hung around until the end of
Carnevale and then checked out today, which had meant
changeovers in almost every room.

By the time she was finished all she wanted to do was
collapse in a heap in her bed. Except that wouldn't get her
pearl earring back, so she changed into jeans and a jacket
and headed out into the tortuous *calles* of Venice once
again, trying to retrace her steps.

It was no wonder she took a wrong turn once or twice—
she was so busy looking at the ground in front of her—but
eventually she found it: the gate where she'd made her es-

cape that morning from Vittorio's *palazzo*. She rang the buzzer and waited. And waited.

She rang the buzzer again.

Eventually the door opened to reveal a stern-looking middle-aged woman. 'This is a private residence. We're not open to visitors.'

'No,' Rosa said, before the woman could shut the door as abruptly as she'd opened it. 'I was here last night. I lost an earring.'

The woman shook her head. 'I think you have the wrong residence.' She started closing the gate again.

'I was with Vittorio,' Rosa said. 'I don't want to bother him, but it was my grandmother's earring, given to her on her wedding day. I think I may have lost it here, and if I could get it back…'

The woman sniffed as she opened the gate a fraction more, looking Rosa up and down as if finding her story hard to believe and yet not impossible. 'Vittorio is no longer here. I don't know when he'll be back. He's not in Venice very often.'

'I didn't come to see Vittorio,' said Rosa. 'It's my grandmother's earring I'm looking for. That's all. I promise.'

The woman sighed. 'Then I'm sorry. I can't help you, I'm afraid. I cleaned that room myself. Nothing was found.'

And she eased the door shut in Rosa's face.

It could have been worse, Rosa thought, heading home, still checking the ground in case her earring had come loose during the evening and fallen out on the way home. The housekeeper might have practically slammed the door in her face but at least she'd listened to her. At least she knew she hadn't lost it there.

'I'm sorry, Nonna,' she said as she got closer to home and there was still no sight of the missing earring. 'I'm sorry I didn't take better care of it for you.'

The streets had no answer.

It was gone.

She'd thought she'd got off scot-free, but maybe this was the price she had to pay, Rosa rationalised as she dragged herself back to the hotel and her tiny basement flat and home to bed. For nothing came without a cost. She knew that.

Maybe one lost earring was the price she had to pay for one night of sin.

And the worst part of it was her night with Vittorio had been so special, so once-in-a-lifetime, she almost felt the loss of one of her grandmother's earrings was worth it.

CHAPTER EIGHT

THE SUMMONS FROM his father's secretary came within five minutes of Vittorio's arrival back at the *castello*. Vittorio snorted as he settled back into his rooms. Some things never changed. His father had never once come to *him*, let alone met him at the castle doors when he'd returned from being away. Not when he'd come home as a child on holiday from boarding school in Switzerland. Not when he'd come home after three years of college in Boston.

Although there was something to be said for knowing how a person worked. You knew exactly how to press their hot buttons.

'At last,' his father said when Vittorio arrived thirty minutes after the summons.

On the Guglielmo Richter Scale, as Vittorio had termed it as a boy, his father seemed to be in good spirits, and he wondered if he shouldn't have taken longer to accede to his father's request.

'I've been waiting for news. I thought you might have had the decency to let me know before now, but now that you're finally here tell me everything.' Prince Guglielmo clearly enunciated his demands as he wandered from one side of his office to the other. In his blue double-breasted jacket, and with one hand tucked behind his back, he looked as if he was inspecting the guard.

Through the vast windows behind him Vittorio could see down to the glorious sweep of Andachstein coast that separated Italy from Slovenia, and the swarm of white yachts that lay at anchor in the protected harbour while their occupants entertained themselves in the casinos, clubs and restaurants that lined the white sand beaches. Even at the tail end of winter they came in their droves—the rich and famous, the billionaires and their mistresses, the actors and actresses. The only difference was that in summertime it would be a sea of white and there wouldn't be a spare berth anywhere.

His father stopped pacing.

'Well? Have you set a date?' the older Prince prompted. 'Can we alert the press, the public? I need to get Enrico on to it immediately, before the news leaks from other sources.'

Other sources. Clearly his father didn't trust Sirena to keep a secret. If there had been one to keep. But he didn't say that. Instead he frowned and said, 'Have I set a date…?' He was being deliberately obtuse, playing the game.

His father snorted, impatience winning over civility, edging him higher up the Guglielmo Richter Scale. 'You and the Contessa Sirena, of course. Who else?' He fixed his son with a gimlet stare. 'Have you agreed a date?'

Vittorio picked up a paperweight from his father's desk—a crystal dragon, symbol of the principality—and tossed it casually from one hand to the other. He saw his father's eyes follow the object that he'd been forbidden to touch as a child. He half expected him to snap now, tell him to put it down in case he dropped it, as he had then. But his father said nothing and Vittorio sighed. It was time to put his father out of his misery.

He put the paperweight down and leant with both hands against the desk, wanting no distractions when he delivered his message. 'There is no date. There will be no marriage. At least not between Sirena and me.'

'What?'

His father's voice boomed so loud in the cavernous room that Vittorio swore the windows rattled.

'When are you going to take your responsibilities seriously?'

'There's no rush.'

'There *is* a rush! It was all supposed to be organised. You two were supposed to come to an agreement. All you had to do was set a date and it seems you can't even be trusted to do that.'

'Actually, I have an idea,' Vittorio suggested. 'If you're so desperate to welcome Sirena into the family business, why don't you marry her yourself?'

His father spluttered and banged his fist on the desk. 'You damned well know this isn't about the Contessa. This is about providing Andachstein with an heir. Without a prince there can be no principality. Andachstein will be swallowed up into the realm of Italy.' He looked his son up and down with disdain. 'You might like to think you're invincible, my son, but you won't last for ever, you know.'

'Look, Father,' he said with a sigh. 'It will happen. I will marry again. But don't expect that I'm going to fall in with your plans just because it's what you want. And don't make such a big deal out of it.'

'I'm *dying*!' Guglielmo blurted, his face beetroot-red.

The son who had grown up with a father who had always used drama to bend the people around him to his will said, 'We're all dying, Father.'

'Insolence!'

'I'm thirty-two years old. I'm not a child, even if I am your son. So if you've got something to tell me then simply tell me.'

'Heart problems.' His father spat out the words.

Heart problems? But that would mean... Vittorio bit back on the obvious retort while his father waved his hands around, looking for words.

'Something to do with the valves,' his father said, 'I forget the name. So fix it, I told the doctors. Replace them. And they told me that while one of them was operable the other was more problematic. They say it is fifty-fifty that I would survive the operation. Without it they say I most likely have less than a year to live.'

Guglielmo collapsed into the chair behind his desk, suddenly weary, and Vittorio noticed that he looked more like an eighty-year-old, rather than the sixty he was supposed to be.

'I've decided to take my chance on life,' he said, 'rather than on some cold operating table.' He turned to his son. 'But I want you married before I die, whatever happens.'

'Dio,' Vittorio said, with the shock of realisation reverberating through his body. 'You're actually serious.'

'Of course I'm serious!' he said. 'And I have a son who won't face up to his responsibilities and do what his duty demands of him.'

Vittorio's hands fisted at his sides. Dying or no, his father was not getting away with that one. 'I faced up to my responsibilities once before. Don't you remember? And look how that turned out!'

His father waved his arguments aside. 'Valentina was weak. She was a bad choice.'

'She was *your* choice,' Vittorio snarled.

His father had decided on the match before the two had even been introduced. The first time they'd met Vittorio had been smitten. She'd seemed like a bright and beautiful butterfly and he'd fallen instantly and irrevocably in love with her. And he'd believed her when she told him that she loved him.

But she had been young and impressionable, and he'd been too foolish to see what was in front of his face. That the family helicopter pilot she'd insisted move with her to the *castello* at Andachstein, so that she could continue her flying lessons, was teaching her a whole lot more than how to handle a helicopter...

He would never forgive himself for not talking her out of leaving with her lover after he'd confronted her with the knowledge that they'd been seen together. He'd been too gutted. Too devastated. He'd loved her so much and she'd betrayed him, and so he'd let her run distraught to her pilot and escape, tears streaming down her face.

He'd never been sure who had been at the controls when they'd hit the powerlines that had ended their lives.

'*Dio*, Father, don't you understand why I don't want you to have anything to do with choosing another bride for me?'

It was as much about getting out from under his father's thumb as it was about the fact that he'd sworn never to be such a fool again. Never to trust a woman's lies. Never to let his heart control his decisions.

His father mumbled something under his breath. Something mostly incoherent. But Vittorio was sure he heard the word *ungrateful* in the mix.

'Well,' he said, 'something has to be done and I don't have long to wait. I'm giving you three months.'

'What?'

'Three months should be perfectly adequate. Find your own bride, if you must, but you're getting married in the Andachstein Cathedral in three months and that's my final word. I'll have Enrico make a list of the best candidates.'

His father couldn't be serious. But then, Vittorio had thought he was joking about dying. *Heart problems. A year to live.* If it were true, Vittorio would be the new Prince of Andachstein, not just the heir apparent.

The ground shifted under his feet. Longevity ran through the line of Andachstein Princes—the last had died at ninety-seven. The youngest ever to die had been seventy-eight. He'd imagined his father, in these modern medicine times, had at least another twenty years to run down on his body clock.

'No,' Vittorio said, and his father's head jerked up, as if Vittorio was rejecting his demand out of hand. 'Not Enrico,' he said. His father's secretary had just as poor judgement for who would make a good wife as his father did. 'I'll get Marcello to help me.'

His father cocked one wiry eyebrow. 'She needs to be the right kind of woman,' he said. 'With the right family connections.'

'Of course.'

'Not to mention good breeding stock.'

Vittorio almost raised a smile. He wasn't entirely sure how he was supposed to assess that, but he simply said, 'Next you'll be insisting she's a virgin.'

The older man looked over at him. 'I may be dying, but I'm not stupid. The search will be difficult enough without making it impossible.'

This time Vittorio did smile. There was no way he wasn't trying before buying.

His father nodded, taking his son's smile as agreement, seemingly satisfied with how the meeting had gone. 'You have three months. Don't let me down. I would very much like to meet the next Princess of Andachstein before I die.' His voice cracked on the final word and he put his head down and gave a dismissive wave of his hand. 'Now, leave me.'

Vittorio nodded, and left his father at his desk, and as he walked down the long corridor that led from his father's official rooms to his own apartment he wondered about the glint that he'd seen in his father's eyes.

Tears?

It hardly seemed possible. He'd never seen his father cry. Not when they'd been sitting at the bedside of his wife of thirty years and she'd given up her last breath and slipped silently away. Not even when they'd interred her in the family crypt and the hound she had loved for twelve years had howled uncontrollably and mournfully at their feet, as if he knew he'd just lost his best friend. Every other mourner except his father had lost it right then.

But tears would mean that his father was almost human.

Was that what knowing you were going to die—having an end date rather than a vague statistic—did to you? Made you confront your own mortality? Made you human?

His father.

Dying.

It was an impossible concept to grasp.

He'd always been closer to his mother. She'd never been warm, exactly—he'd felt far more welcome in the kitchen than in his mother's salon—but she'd been the one who'd held the two men in her life together, and when she'd died the yawning chasm between father and son had widened. And that had been before Valentina had died and the gulf and the resentment between them had grown still wider.

Vittorio was in no hurry to get married again. His experience of marriage was no fond memory. And his parents...? They were hardly shining lights for the institution. No, he was in no hurry.

But he *was* heir to the throne of Andachstein. A position he might be forced to take up long before he had ever imagined. And it *was* his duty to sire an heir.

And, when it all came down to it, Guglielmo was still his father—the only father he'd ever had. So, despite their differences over the years, didn't he owe him something?

Vittorio's footsteps echoed in the old stone stairwell that led up to his apartments the back way. There was a flashier terrazzo-tiled staircase that went the front way, but he preferred the feel of the stone under his feet, the stone steps that held the grooves of the feet of his ancestors and their servants. Ever since he was a child he'd liked stepping into those grooves and wondering how many footsteps it would take to make a dent in the stone. He liked to think he was doing his bit by contributing his own footfall.

Every few steps there was a long narrow window that offered glimpses of the tree-covered hills behind the coast and the city. Once used by archers against marauding invaders, now they were glassed in against the weather. He stopped at one near the top and gazed out over the countryside, not really seeing, just thinking.

Maybe it was time. He was thirty-two and he was tired. Tired of the Sirenas of this world hunting for a title. Tired of the life he was leading.

There had to be something else.

Something more.

It couldn't be too hard to find himself a wife once he set his mind to it, surely? It shouldn't take long to vet the candidates. It wasn't as if he had to go through the motions of falling in love with the woman first.

He'd been in love with Valentina and what a disaster that had turned out to be. But then, was it any wonder? Look at his role models. He wasn't sure his father had ever loved his mother. They'd had separate suites as far back as Vittorio could remember. He'd never once witnessed a display of affection between them.

When it came down to it, it was a miracle he even existed…

CHAPTER NINE

HE CAME OUT of the fog in blue leather trimmed with gold, his long cape swirling in his wake. He emerged tall and broad and powerful, his cobalt eyes zeroing in on her, as if he'd sensed her presence through the mist.

He strode purposefully towards her, stopping bare inches away, so close that she could feel the heat of his body coming at her in waves…so close that she was sure his intense eyes would bore into hers and see inside her very soul.

'Rosa…' he said, in a deep voice that threatened to melt her bones.

'Vittorio,' she said, breathless and trembling, 'you came for me.'

'I had no choice,' he said, and he opened his arms for her.

She stepped into the space he had created just for her and felt his arms ensnare her in his heat and strength as he dipped his head to hers.

Her lips met his. She sighed into his mouth and gave herself up to the delicious heat of his mouth. His tongue. His taste. She felt herself swung into his arms, as if she were weightless, and then time slipped and they were in bed, and he was poised over her, and his name was on her lips as he drove into her…

'Rosa!'

The voice was wrong. It didn't fit. It was in the way.

She tried to ignore it. Tried desperately to hang on to what was happening even as the vision wobbled at the edges.

'Stop mooning,' someone said.

Someone who sounded like Chiara.

But what would she be doing at Vittorio's *palazzo*?

'It's time to get up!'

Rosa blinked into wakefulness, feeling a soul-crushing devastation. Feeling cheated. She'd thought Vittorio had come back for her, but it had been nothing but yet another pointless and cruel dream.

'All right,' she said, blinking, getting herself out of bed. 'I'm coming.'

'Forget about him,' Chiara said, brushing her hair.

'Forget about who?'

'Vittorio, of course. He must have been something special for you to dream about him all the time.'

'Who says I was dreaming about him?'

Chiara raised her eyebrows. 'Why else would you call out his name? You've really got it bad.'

Rosa kicked up her chin as she headed for the bathroom. 'I don't know what you're talking about. It was a dream, that's all.'

'When are you going to tell me what happened that night?'

'I told you what happened.'

Chiara just laughed. 'Hurry up,' she said. 'Or you'll be late for work.'

Rosa stepped under the shower spray. How could she share the events of that night with Chiara and convey the magic of the evening without cheapening it? No. She held the secret of what had happened that night like a precious jewel, still too new and too special to share with anyone.

She didn't have stars in her eyes. She wasn't stupid. She knew that despite the dreams that plagued her nights she'd never see Vittorio again. Not that the knowledge stopped her looking out for him every time she ventured anywhere near the Grand Canal. She'd hear a deep voice or see a broad pair of shoulders up ahead and for a split second she'd be hurtled back to that night and think she'd found him again. But the voice always belonged to someone else, and the man with broad shoulders would turn and the likeness would end there.

She didn't mind. He'd told her how it would be. She didn't expect to see him ever again.

He'd just been so wonderful that night. So tender and gentle, so generous in his willingness and desire to ensure her pleasure, so generous in the knowledge he'd shared.

She knew about lovemaking now. She knew what she liked in bed and how to pleasure a man. She had Vittorio to thank for introducing her to the ways of the bedroom.

She didn't really mind that she would never see him again.

She just had a horrible feeling he had ruined her for any other man.

'So this is the list Enrico gave you?'

Marcello looked up and down the three-page printout listing the eligible noblewomen his father's secretary had assembled who might just be persuaded to take on Vittorio and the title of Princess of Andachstein. There was a photograph of each woman alongside her name, together with a sketchy bio giving height, age and weight.

Vittorio snorted. 'I see Enrico's covered all the important details.'

'A veritable smorgasbord of aristocratic talent,' Marcello said drily 'But one thing worries me.'

'What's that?'

'You've only got three months until the date of the wedding. Does that give you enough time to sleep with them all?'

The would-be groom crossed his legs at the ankles and smirked. Now that he'd made up his mind to fall in with his father's crazy plan and find himself a wife—a princess for Andachstein—he found he liked the idea more and more. An arranged marriage, a convenient marriage—but this time without foolishly falling in love. All he had to do was produce an heir. If the marriage itself floundered after that, so be it. It would be nobody's fault. Nobody would be hurt. It was perfect. Failsafe.

Besides, he was growing tired of his lifestyle. Tired of fighting his destiny. But he wasn't interested in searching for a wife by any other means. So he'd had Enrico clear the appointments that could be cleared, undertaken those that couldn't be avoided, and now, within the space of a week, was sitting in one of the reception rooms in Marcello's *palazzo*.

'Did you see who's at the top of the list?'

Marcello cocked an eyebrow. 'I did notice that. Maybe your father ascribes to the view that it's better the devil you know?'

Vittorio laughed. '*He* might. But I'm not that much of a masochist.' He sat up, forearms on knees, hands clasped. 'So what do you think?'

Marcello flicked between the pages, exhaling long and loud as he shook his head. 'Well, it's not the list *I* would have given you.'

'In what way?'

'Doormats, one and all.'

Vittorio leaned forward and snatched the pages out of his friend's hands. 'They can't all be doormats?'

Marcello nodded. 'Every last one of them.'

'Apart from Sirena, you mean.'

'Well, apart from her, clearly. Otherwise that's a carefully curated list of "women who won't."'

Vittorio frowned. 'Won't what?'

Marcello shrugged. 'Argue. Object. Have an opinion on anything or speak their own mind.'

Vittorio gazed at the list more enthusiastically. 'Sounds exactly like what I want!'

'Ah, Vittorio,' Marcello said, shaking his head. 'Some of us know that you're not entirely the bad boy Prince that you like to make out. But you're no walkover either. You'd be bored with any one of these before she'd made it halfway down the aisle. By the time she did you would have plucked a woman from the choir who showed a bit more spirit.'

'All right,' said Vittorio, thrusting the papers onto the nearby coffee table. 'What have *you* got for me?'

'Ah,' said Marcello, a man in his moment. 'Three of the best.' He pushed a folder across the table and flipped open the cover to reveal candidate number one. 'Katerina Volvosky. Former ice-skating supremo, now an international rights lawyer working with the UN. She comes with good, if not royal lineage. Her father is a former ambassador to the USA. Her mother is a doctor—a burns specialist.'

Vittorio nodded. She was attractive, and looked intelligent. 'She definitely looks like she wouldn't be afraid to voice an opinion. What makes you think she'd want to get married?'

'She's just been dumped by her long-term boyfriend, she's thirty-five, and her body clock's ticking. She'd have time for an heir and a spare at the very least. I think, given the right inducement, she could be persuaded to marry you.'

'Huh. As if anyone would need an inducement to marry me.'

Marcello snorted. 'You just go right on believing that, Vittorio.' He turned the page. 'Potential bride number two—Emilija Kozciesko, former animal activist turned environmentalist, a woman with a passion for protecting the Mediterranean in particular. Her mother was president of Ursubilia for ten years, her father is a concert pianist who put his career aside to support his wife's political aspirations. And—get this—she speaks eight languages.'

Vittorio looked at the picture. She was beautiful too, but with a feistiness in her features that said she would fight tooth and nail for what she believed in. No doormat there. She was standing on the bow of a boat, looking out to sea, with the wind catching her long hair. Dark hair that reminded him of something. *Someone*. He dug his hand deeper into his pocket.

'And her body clock?'

'No issues. She's twenty-eight, but she's a rebel who recognises that it's easier to agitate when you're attached to a title.'

Vittorio held out one hand. 'Pass me that list of doormats again.'

'Hah!' Marcello said, sweeping them out of reach. 'Be serious. Now, option number three…' He flipped the page to a photograph of a stunning blonde with Nordic good looks. 'Inga Svenson. Shipping heiress whose family has fallen on hard times. Former model, B-grade actress and now children's ambassador. She's also fluent in French, Italian, English…along with all the Scandinavian languages, of course.'

Vittorio was impressed. 'And she hasn't found a husband yet because…?'

'She was engaged to be married when the family business imploded. She got unceremoniously dumped and the fiancé promptly found himself another heiress.' Marcello eyed his friend. 'She's vulnerable, and I know how you like to rescue vulnerable things.'

Vittorio's fingers squeezed tight.

'What's that in your hand?' asked Marcello.

'What?' Vittorio looked down to see Rosa's earring in his fingers. He hadn't even realised he'd been playing with it. 'Oh, just a trinket,' he said, putting it back in his trouser pocket.

Marcello looked at him levelly. 'A trinket that you keep

in your pocket? Have you taken to collecting souvenirs, Vittorio? Because if you have that could be a precursor to something entirely more sinister.'

Vittorio snorted and leaned forward in his chair. 'You make me laugh, my friend.'

He lined up the three photographs next to each other and pushed away the middle one—Emilija, with the dark hair that reminded him of someone.

'Right, how do you propose we do this?'

CHAPTER TEN

'ROSA!' CHIARA YELLED, thumping her roommate on the chest with a pillow. 'Get out of bed. You'll be late.'

'Ow, that stung,' Rosa said, rubbing her sore chest as she struggled to come to. Her head felt full, as if it had somehow absorbed her pillow in the night. But Chiara was right—she needed to get up. Rosa was usually the first of the two to get ready, but lately that was changing, and Chiara was already dressed in her uniform and tying her hair back.

Rosa swung her legs over the side of the bed and pushed herself upright—and immediately wished she hadn't. She put her hand to her mouth. Whatever had been on that pizza last night must have disagreed with her.

'God, you look awful,' Chiara said, watching her. 'What's wrong with you?'

'I don't feel—'

She didn't get any further. A wave of heat welled up inside her and Rosa bolted for their tiny bathroom, where she collapsed boneless while her stomach rebelled against the world.

'You really are sick,' said Chiara, handing her a wet hand towel once the heaving spasms had passed, leaving Rosa breathless and almost too weak to wipe her heated face.

'Must have been the pizza,' Rosa said, gasping, pressing her face into the towel.

'We shared the pizza. It can't be that.'

'You feel okay?'

'I'm fine. And I had all the wine, because you said you didn't like how it smelt, so if anyone should feel sick it's me.'

'So if it wasn't that pizza, and it couldn't have been the wine, what else can it be?' Rosa struggled to her feet and splashed more cold water on the towel, wiped her neck and throat. 'Please let it not be the flu. I can't afford to take time off.'

She put her hands on the sink and leaned against them, waiting for her body to calm. She took a breath and looked up, and caught sight of her roommate's scowling expression in the mirror over the sink.

'What?'

'You felt queasy yesterday at breakfast too.'

She shook her head, pushing herself away from the sink. She really needed to get moving. 'The coffee was too strong. I felt fine all day after that.'

'You love your coffee.'

Not yesterday, Rosa hadn't. One whiff and she'd turned her head away.

She threw off her nightgown and pulled her uniform from the hanger on the single clothes rail the girls shared. 'An aberration,' she said.

Chiara watched her clamber into the button-up dress. 'Only…if you think about it…it's about six weeks since Carnevale.'

'So?' Rosa looked around. 'Where are my shoes? Have you seen my shoes?' she asked, only to see the heels poking out from under her bed, where she always left them.

'Six weeks since you got lost and said you met someone. A man…' She let that sink in before she asked, 'When was your last period, Rosa?'

Rosa lifted her head, her expression deadpan as she

thought back, counting the weeks, finding they didn't add up. 'Come on, Chiara. Now you're frightening me.'

'Aha!' Chiara said. 'And why would you be frightened? Unless there's something you're not telling me.'

'Stop it,' she said, pushing past her to go back into the bathroom.

She looked at her face in the mirror. She needed to slap on some make-up and do something to fix the weird pallor of her skin...hide the dark shadows under her eyes. She couldn't be pregnant. She just couldn't.

'You had sex with him, didn't you?' Chiara said. 'This stranger who took you to a party.'

'You make it sound shabby,' Rosa protested. 'It wasn't like that.'

'Aha! Then you *did* sleep with him!'

'Okay, so I did. What of it?'

Chiara clapped her hands, her eyes alight at the admission. 'And you never said a word.'

'I don't know why you're so excited,' Rosa said.

'Sorry,' Chiara said, looking suitably penitent. 'I'm just happy for you. Was it good?'

'Chiara!'

'All right. All right. But you could be pregnant, then?'

'I can't be pregnant.' She fiddled in her make-up bag, searching. She was absolutely ruling out being pregnant. 'He used contraception.'

'Condoms aren't one hundred per cent reliable,' Chiara said. 'And you're not on the pill, are you?'

'Of course I'm not!'

Chiara rolled her eyes, but had the good sense not to say anything about that. 'Do your breasts feel tender?'

Rosa's hand stalled on the mascara wand that she'd just started wielding over her lashes. She flicked her eyes to Chiara's, remembering the pillow she'd been walloped in the chest with. *How did she know?*

'Maybe it's just a twenty-four-hour bug? I don't know. But until I know for sure I'm not going to panic about it.'

Like hell. Just the thought of being pregnant made her feel sick with fear.

'I'll get a test from the pharmacy at lunch,' Chiara offered. 'You need to do it as soon as you can.'

Rosa shook her head. 'Don't waste your money.' *Please, God, let it be a waste of money.* 'Anyway, if anyone is going to be buying a test it should be me.'

'No. You'll put it off because you don't want to know, just in case you are. But you need to know one way or the other, and the sooner the better. Because if you are pregnant you need to start thinking about your options.' Then her roommate smiled and gave her a quick hug. 'Now, are you sure you're feeling well enough to go to work?'

The only good thing about that morning was that an entire tour group had checked out and the hotel was down two cleaners who had the flu. She didn't have time to panic, she told herself, exhausted after the third room-clean and changeover. She operated on autopilot, not letting herself think about anything beyond linen and towels and scooping away all the used bottles of cheap toiletries and replenishing them with new.

Because if she didn't think, she couldn't panic. And if she didn't panic, then she wouldn't work herself up over something that was probably nothing.

Though why would her period be late...?

Stress. Overwork. Money worries. That would probably do it. It wasn't as if she was in denial...she was just considering the other options. Making sense of it.

By the time her lunch break rolled around Rosa wanted to tell Chiara to forget it. She was feeling much better than she had in the morning. But Chiara had already slipped away to the *farmacia* and was having none of it.

She tugged Rosa into their tiny basement flat and then their tiny bathroom, passed her the box, and said, 'Do it.'

Rosa looked at the packet, read the instructions. 'It says to do it first thing in the morning.'

'Rosa,' her friend growled, pointing at the toilet behind her shoulder. 'Go.'

She did as she was ordered this time, but she grumbled all the way from the opening of the box, through the peeing on the stick to the waiting.

There was no point. She couldn't be pregnant. It was a waste of money and she'd be delighted to tell Chiara when the test showed up as negative.

Except it didn't.

She swallowed. Looked at the instructions again in case she'd read them wrongly. Looked back at the stick. She had never been more grateful that she was sitting down.

Chiara banged on the door. 'Well, what's happening? What does it say?'

Rosa washed her hands, splashing a little water on her face for good measure. She lifted her heated face to the mirror. She didn't look any different. A little paler than usual, maybe, and her eyes a little wide with shell shock.

She didn't *feel* any different. Shouldn't she feel different? Shouldn't she know? But pregnant... A baby... She was going to be a mother.

Rosa swallowed and looked down at the hand she'd curled low over her abdomen. And she realised the price for one night of sin wasn't just the loss of one of her grandmother's earrings.

The price was much, much higher.

'Come on!' cried Chiara impatiently from outside the door. 'What's going on?'

Rosa took a deep breath and opened the door, holding up the stick. 'Apparently I'm pregnant.'

And she let Chiara's arms enfold her.

***

'But if I'm pregnant,' Rosa said, sitting on her bed and nursing the cup of sweet tea that Chiara had made for her. 'Doesn't Vittorio have a right to know? Don't I have a responsibility to tell him?'

'There's no "if" about it. You're pregnant,' Chiara said. 'And why do you think he'd want to know?'

'Because he's the father?'

'Have you seen this man since?'

'No. Not since that night.'

'Did he give you his phone number? Anything else so you could contact him?'

'No. Only his first name.' Rosa shook her head. 'He said it was only for one night.'

Chiara sat back and slapped her hands on her legs. 'That says it all, right there. He's married.'

'No!'

'Face it, Rosa. A man picks you up and makes love to you and tells you that it's one night only—what do you *think* that means? His wife is probably about to give birth to their fourth *bambino* and didn't feel like going out that night. Do you really think he'll want to know he's got another one on the way?'

'No. He's not like that!'

'How do you know? You knew him for all of ten minutes, and that was most likely spent with him working out the fastest way to get inside your pants.'

'Stop it! It wasn't like that!'

'All right. But seeing as you haven't told me what it *was* like, what am I supposed to think?'

Rosa flicked her eyes up to her friend. 'Vittorio said his father wants him to get married.' Hadn't that been why Sirena was pursuing him? So that she would be the next Mrs… Mrs… She didn't know what. He'd never told her what his surname was.

She swallowed. So that she couldn't find him?

'Right. And he does what his father tells him, does he? How old was he? Twelve?'

'Chiara!'

'Well, who does what their father demands when they're all grown up?'

'So he has a demanding father? I don't know.'

Chiara gave an exasperated sigh. 'Clearly.' Then she sat down next to Rosa on the bed and put an arm around her shoulders. 'But you know, you might as well forget about him. You've got more pressing things to worry about now.' She gave her shoulders a squeeze. 'Like what you're going to do about this pregnancy.'

'What do you mean, what I'm going to do about it? I'm pregnant, aren't I? What *can* I do?'

'Oh, *cara*,' her roommate said softly. 'You must know it's not the only way you have to go. There are things you can do. You don't need a child now—how are you going to provide for it?'

'But it's a *baby*, Chiara. I'm having a baby.'

'It's not *technically* a baby yet, though, is it?'

'But it will grow.'

'I'm not saying you shouldn't do it, all I'm saying is having the child is not your only option. You need to think about all your options, Rosa, and what is best for you.'

'And the baby?' Rosa sniffed, her hand already wrapped protectively over the belly under which it lay. 'What about what's best for the baby?'

'I can't answer that,' said Chiara, 'but I can honestly say that there are plenty of children living in dreadful circumstances who would probably have preferred not to have been born at all.' She smoothed the hair from Rosa's brow. 'All I'm saying is think about it, okay? Don't assume that you're trapped and that you have no choices. You have choices. They might not be easy, but they're there.'

CHAPTER ELEVEN

'WHAT THE HELL'S wrong with you, Vittorio?' Marcello said. 'You're not taking this seriously. How do you expect to find yourself a bride to marry by the date your father decreed if you won't ask one?'

Vittorio sighed, hands in pockets, and turned away from the big windows overlooking the Grand Canal. More than halfway through the three months his father had decreed and he was back in Venice—although the intention had been to bring either Katerina or Inga to Venice with him and formally propose.

It was a business decision first and foremost, sure, but Marcello had suggested that no woman was going to say no in such a romantic setting, even if the wedding itself would have to take place in the cathedral in Andachstein.

The worst of it was that he didn't understand it himself. He'd decided to comply with his father's demands. He'd decided to follow his destiny. He'd decided it was a good thing. Perfect. Failsafe. And yet…

'For God's sake Vittorio, what are you thinking?'

'Nothing.'

Marcello sighed theatrically. 'Tell me something I don't know. Now, let's take this from the top. Katerina Volvosky. What do you think of her?'

'She seems nice,' he conceded. They'd been twice to the opera, and had flown to Paris in the royal jet for dinner one night.

'Nice,' said Marcello, deadpan. 'Right. How about Inga?'

Vittorio nodded. Together they'd gone ballooning in Turkey, with a side visit to Petra in Jordan. 'Yes, she's nice too.'

'And you can't decide between these two...' he made apostrophes in the air with his fingers '..."*nice*" women?'

'No,' Vittorio said on a shrug. And they *were* nice women. Lovely women, both. 'There's nothing wrong with either of them,' Vittorio said. 'They'd both be fine.' They were intelligent, passionate about their interests and attractive. 'They'd both be an asset to Andachstein.'

'So let's take it back to basics, shall we? Let's make it really, really easy for you.'

Vittorio turned back to look out at the shifting traffic on the canal, his fingers toying with the earring in his trouser pocket. 'I wish you would.'

Because he wasn't finding any of it easy as his eyes sought out the direction of the hotel where Rosa worked. What would she be doing right now? Would she be on her lunch break? Did she even *get* a lunch break?

'Which woman is better in bed?'

'What?' Vittorio spun around.

'Which one—Katerina or Inga—do you like better in bed?'

Vittorio's eyebrows shot up, answering the question with another. He shrugged. 'I don't know.'

'They're both as good as each other?'

Vittorio turned back to the view. 'I haven't slept with them.'

Marcello blinked. Slowly. 'You haven't slept with them? *You?*' He pressed the knuckle of one finger into the bridge of his nose. 'Vittorio,' he said, looking up, 'don't mind me asking this, but are you all right? Health-wise, I mean? Is there something you're not telling me?'

Vittorio shook his head. 'Never better.'

Marcello looked as if he didn't believe him. What was his problem? The women were nice enough, certainly, and they'd given him enough cues to let him know that they wouldn't say no if he did ask. It was just that when it came down to it he hadn't felt like taking them to bed.

'Okay,' said a weary-sounding Marcello. 'Then all I can suggest to sort this out is to flip a coin.' He held out his hand. 'Have you got one on you?'

'No,' he said, turning back to the canal and looking in the direction of the Dorsodura *sestiere*, where her hotel was situated. But he did have an earring.

'Is there something out there?' asked Marcello, coming closer to see for himself. 'Something that I'm missing?'

'No,' Vittorio said.

Not something. Someone. He'd always intended to return Rosa's earring and, given that he was back in Venice, there was no time like the present.

Serendipity.

'I have to go,' he said, already heading for the stairs.

'But, Vittorio, you need to make a decision—'

'Later,' he said. *'Ciao.'*

Vittorio strode purposefully through the narrow streets of Venice. He wasn't wearing leather today, nor even a swirling cloak, and yet people still moved out of his way when they saw him coming, flattening themselves against the walls of the *calles* or ducking into shop and café doorways.

He barely noticed. He was a man on a mission and he was too busy working out how long it had been since he'd seen her to care. Carnevale... Six weeks ago? Seven? Did she still work at the same hotel? Was she still in Venice or had she moved on? Or gone home to her tiny village in Puglia?

The sooner he got to the hotel, the sooner he'd find out. Eventually he found it—a shabby-looking hotel, tucked away in the corner of a square with a tiny canal running down one side. The entire side of the wall looked as if it was leaning into it.

He marched through the entry doors that announced it as Palazzo d'Velatte into a tiny foyer and saw heads swivel towards him. He marched towards a thin man sporting a backwards horseshoe of hair and standing behind a tiny counter. He wouldn't swear on a stack of bibles, but he was sure he saw the man swallow.

'Are you checking in?' he asked, craning his neck so high there was no missing the Adam's apple in his throat, bobbing up and down.

'No. I'm looking for someone who works here. A woman.'

'Erm…' The man offered a simpering smile. 'We don't offer that kind of service.'

'She's a cleaner. Her name is Rosa. Does she still work here?'

'I'm not sure I can divulge that—'

Vittorio leaned over the reception desk. 'Does. She. Still. Work. Here?'

The man's eyes bugged. 'Well, yes, but…' His eyes darted to his watch. 'She won't finish her shift for another two hours.'

'So she's working today? In this hotel?'

'Well, yes…'

Vittorio smiled—although it was probably more of a baring of his teeth, because he noticed he didn't get one in return. 'Then I'll find her myself.'

He looked around the tiny foyer, spied a likely set of stairs and set off.

'Wait!' the man called. 'You can't do that.'

'Watch me,' he said, taking the steps three at a time.

There were only three levels. It shouldn't take long.

On the first level he found nothing.

On the second level he found a cleaner backing out of a room and towing a vacuum cleaner behind her.

'Rosa?' he asked.

The woman looked up. She was a pretty woman, with bright eyes and dark curly hair tied back in a ponytail behind her head, but definitely not Rosa.

Her eyes narrowed when she saw him. She straightened, looking him up and down, frankly assessing. 'You're looking for Rosa?'

'Do you know where I can find her?'

'Your name wouldn't be Vittorio, by any chance?'

'What if it is?' he said.

Her eyes widened in appreciation before they flicked upwards. 'In that case, she's working the floor above.'

It was the worst day of her life. She'd started the morning throwing up and now, after confronting the room of some guests who had clearly thought last night was party night, only to lose the 'party' they'd consumed all over the bathroom, she kept right on heaving while she cleaned up the mess and cleared away the soiled towels. They were empty retches, because there was nothing in her stomach to bring up, but that didn't stop her retching all the same.

But she could hardly beg off work, because she needed this job and she didn't need anyone knowing she was pregnant. Not until she'd worked out what to do.

Dio, she felt so drained.

She replaced all the towels in the now clean bathroom with fresh ones and then caught sight of her reflection in the bathroom mirror as she swung around. She was shocked at what she saw. She looked like a ghost of herself. Her dull, lifeless eyes were too big for her head, and her hair stuck together in tendrils around her face after her temperature had spiked during each pointless yet violent round of dry heaving.

She needed to take a moment to get herself straightened up before anyone saw her like this.

'Rosa!' someone called in a booming deep voice, and a shudder went down her spine and sent the muscles clenching between her thighs.

She knew that voice. She'd heard it in her dreams at night. She'd imagined hearing it a hundred times a day in the crowded *calles* and the market stalls along the busy canals. She'd looked around, searching for the source, but it had never been him, of course.

'Rosa!' she heard—even closer.

Her heart thudded loudly in her chest. She wasn't imagining it this time. She peeked out of the bathroom to see a bear of a man entering the room. So tall and broad, with his mane of hair brushed back from his face, his carved features fixed into a frown.

'Vittorio…' she whispered, before her insides twisted on a rush of heat and sent her lurching once more for the pan.

There was nothing to lose. Nothing to give up but the strength in her bones and any shred of self-respect she'd ever had as she gagged where she'd flopped, huddled on the floor. But for him to see her this way was beyond cruel.

And yet he was by her side in an instant, pressing a damp towel to her heated forehead, his big hand on her back, as if lending her strength. As if he were saying, *I'm here*.

Gradually the churning eased, the spasms passed. She had the strength to lean back, to take the dampened towel from his hands and press it to her face. *Dio*, how could she let him see her ghastly face?

'What are you doing here?' she said, between gasps.

'What's wrong with you?' he replied, ignoring her question. 'You're ill.'

'No,' she said, trying to struggle to her feet.

She was confused. She still had rooms to clean, and Vittorio was here, and she didn't understand any of it.

When she turned, Chiara was there at the door to the room, silently watching.

'Are you going to tell him?' she said.

'Tell me what?' he said, looking from one woman to the other, but she could see by the dawning realisation on his face that he was already working it out for himself.

She looked up into a face that spoke of power and strength and everything she lacked in this moment, and told him. 'I'm so sorry, Vittorio, but I'm pregnant.'

He roared. A cry of anguish or triumph she couldn't be sure. But before she could decide she was swept up into his strong arms and cradled against his chest. She could have protested. She was hardly an invalid. She could walk. But instead of protesting she simply breathed him in, The scent was as she remembered. Masculine. Evocative. It was all she could do not to melt into the *whump-thump* of his heart in his chest.

'Where is her room?' she heard him say.

Followed by Chiara's voice. 'I'll show you.'

'I have to finish my shift,' she said weakly.

'No, you don't.'

He laid her down on her bed. Reverently. Gently. As if she were a fragile piece of glass blown by a master craftsman rather than made of flesh and blood.

'Leave us,' he told Chiara, and the usually bossy but now boggle-eyed Chiara didn't bother trying to argue with him and meekly withdrew.

He sat down beside her and smoothed the damp hair from Rosa's brow. 'It's mine?' he asked.

'What do you think?' she snapped, through a throat that felt raw from throwing up.

He smiled at that, although she didn't understand why. There was nothing funny that she could see about any of this.

He looked around at the tiny windowless room that contained two beds—cots, really—a small chest of drawers that doubled as a bedside table with a lamp between them, and a hanging rack filled with an assortment of clothes.

'This is where you live?'

She nodded, her strength returning enough that she could scoot herself upright with her back to the wall. 'With Chiara.'

'The two of you?' he asked, clearly aghast. 'Here? Barely above the water level?'

'It's not that bad. It's cheap for Venice. Chiara said it only floods at king tides, and not very often.'

He shook his head and swore softly under his breath. 'Have you seen a doctor?'

'Not yet,' she said. 'I was still—'

'Working out what to do about it?'

He'd stiffened as he said it and she noticed an edge to his voice. A harsh edge. Judgmental?

She swallowed. 'I was still coming to terms with it. I only found out a couple of days ago.'

He pulled out his phone, thumbing through it. 'When were you going to tell me?'

Rosa closed her eyes. Maybe this was another of her dreams. Maybe the hormones running through her bloodstream had turned her a little bit mad and she'd conjured Vittorio up—a combination of thin air and wishful thinking.

'Well?'

She opened her eyes, half surprised that he was still there. 'Chiara said you wouldn't want to know. That you probably had a wife and four *bambini* tucked away somewhere.'

'Why would you believe that when you were there that night? You heard what Sirena said. You knew my father wanted me to marry her. Why listen to Chiara?'

'Because you told me "one night and one night only." That you didn't do for ever. It made as much sense as your father wanting you to marry his friend's daughter.'

This time he swore out loud.

'You mean you *don't* have a wife and children somewhere?'

He smiled down at her, and then whoever he was calling picked up. 'Elena, I need some help,' he said, and issued a list of demands. 'We're going to get you seen to,' he said. 'My housekeeper is organising it. She knows everyone in Venice. And meanwhile we're going out.'

She shook her head. 'I should get back to work. I've been away too long already.'

'You're not going back to work today. If I have anything to do with it you're never going to clean another room in your life.'

'What?'

'Are you all right to walk now?'

She nodded. She felt a million times stronger than she had before, but she was still confused. Nothing he said made sense. The fact he was even here made no sense.

'Good. Then get changed,' he said, gently pressing his lips to her forehead. 'I'm taking you out.'

'Where to?'

'First of all I'm taking you somewhere you can get a decent meal. You need feeding up. And then we're going to sit down for a talk.'

He took her to a restaurant tucked away in an alleyway behind the Rialto Bridge, where the tables were dressed in red and white checked tablecloths. Clearly they were off the tourist trail, in a restaurant that catered to locals, because instead of the multitude of languages she was used to hearing in the hotel and the *calles* the predominant language was Italian.

There they lunched on the best *spaghetti alle vongole* Rosa had ever tasted—but then, she wasn't just hungry by then, she was ravenous. The pasta with tiny clams filled a void inside her, and her once rebellious stomach welcomed every mouthful. Relished it.

Not even the presence of this man opposite could stop her. He seemed to heighten her appetite along with her senses. Maybe it was because he was content just to eat his own pasta as he watched her eat hers, watching approvingly every mouthful she consumed.

But there was something going on behind those cobalt blue eyes, she could see. Something that went beyond ensuring that she ate well. Something calculating. Unnerving.

'What have you been doing the last few weeks?' she asked between mouthfuls, wanting to break the tension, to see if she could encourage him to say what was on his mind.

'This and that,' he said, giving nothing away. 'What about you?'

'Same. Work, mostly. I was planning to take a few days off and go home. Rudi, one of my brothers, and his wife Estella are due to welcome their second child soon. But that was before I found out—well, you know.'

'Why wouldn't you still go home?'

She shook her head, halting her loaded fork halfway between bowl and mouth. 'I don't know that I can face my father or my family right now. I don't think my head's in the right place.'

'Will they even be able to tell so early?'

'It's not that. It's because I feel like I've let them down. Papà wanted me to live and see the world—he wouldn't have encouraged me to leave the village otherwise. But I don't think he was expecting this to happen. Not to me. Not so soon.'

'Would he be angry?'

'No. Not exactly. Probably just—disappointed.' She put her fork down and looked up at him. 'And isn't that worse?'

Vittorio didn't know. He had a father who specialised in anger. He'd got so used to disappointing his father over the years it was no longer a deterrent. If it ever had been. It had become more like a blood sport between them rather than a familial relationship.

Rosa finished off the last of her pasta and leaned back in her seat. 'That was amazing. Thank you.'

'Good,' he said. 'And now we need to talk.'

'I'm ready,' she said.

But he shook his head, looking at the tables full of diners clustered around them—tables full of diners who all spoke Italian and who might overhear. 'Not here.'

She had to hand it to Vittorio—if you had to sit down to have a talk you could find a worse venue than floating down the Grand Canal. She'd raised her eyebrows when he'd stopped at the gondola stand, but he'd merely shrugged and said, 'When in Venice...' and handed her into the gently rocking vessel.

He was doing it again—sweeping her out of her world and into his—but this time there was no panic. No fear. Because it was broad daylight and she knew enough about him to trust him. Besides, it was his child that she carried in her womb. His seed that had taken root.

Once they were seated on the golden bench the gondolier set off, sweeping his oar rhythmically behind them in the time-honoured way, sending the long, sleek vessel effortlessly skimming over the surface of the canal.

All these months she'd been in Venice and never once had she taken a gondola ride. It was something for the tourists, and hideously expensive in her eyes, but here on the water you gained a different perspective. It was seeing

Venice as it was meant to be seen, from the watery streets
that made up its roadmap.

For a while they were content to take in the views and
point out the sights as they slid under the magnificent white
Rialto Bridge, with its eleven arches, crowded with tourists looking down at the passing traffic, looking down at
them with envy.

And if Venice in the fog had been atmospheric and mystical, under the pale blue skies of spring it turned magical.
It was as if the city had been reborn and emerged fresh and
renewed from under its winter coat.

The colours of the buildings popped. Red brickwork
stained with salt, pastel pink and terracotta, Tuscan yellows
and even shades of blue trimmed with white competed for
attention as they stood shoulder to shoulder above the slick
green-grey waters of the canal.

And at its heart were the waterways they traversed, the
canals alive with *vaporetto* and motorboats and gondolas
all fighting for space. For a few minutes they were just two
more tourists, enjoying the sights and sounds.

And there, with Vittorio smiling at her, she couldn't
imagine a place she'd rather be—not even at home in her
village, with her *papà* and her brothers and their families
nearby. It was magical. And the most magical thing about
it was that Vittorio was actually here, bursting into her
life as suddenly as he had on that cold, fog-bound night
of Carnevale.

It was no wonder that she'd missed him. No wonder that
she'd dreamed of him. He was tall and broad and powerful.
He was larger than life. He was—*more*. More than anything she'd ever experienced before. And he made her feel
more alive than she'd ever felt.

At one stage she was smiling up at the bridge they were
about to pass under when she turned and saw the he was
taking a photograph of her. She tried to protest. 'I would

have made more of an effort,' she said, pulling her hair away from her face.

'You look beautiful,' he said, and her heart felt as if it would bursting.

And still the question that he had not yet answered hung between them.

'Why did you come today?' she asked. 'I never expected to see you again.'

'I came with one purpose. But now you have given me another.'

Her brow furrowed with confusion. 'I don't understand...'

He took her hand in his. 'I wanted to see you, even if briefly. And seeing you again has reminded me. We were good together, Rosa.'

Sensation skittered down her spine. She blinked. She hadn't known what to expect, but certainly not that. 'It's good to see you.'

More than good. She'd dreamed about him. Had replayed every moment of their lovemaking until she could run it on a loop in her head, and the experience was still as exciting as it had been the first time.

He smiled as he pressed her hand to his lips. 'What are you going to do?'

Back to that. She looked at the buildings, glorious relics of centuries gone by and still defying the logic that said buildings must be built on solid ground.

She turned back to him. 'What can I do? I have so few options. But I want to do what's best for the baby.'

He nodded and squeezed the hand he still held.

'Marry me.'

The words were gone before she could grasp and process them, lost on the lapping waters and the hustle and bustle and sounds of the busy canal. She couldn't have heard right.

'Scuzi?'

'Marry me. Our child will have a mother and a father and you'll have no need to feel ashamed when you go home. And you'll never have to clean another hotel bathroom in your life.'

She laughed. 'Don't be ridiculous, Vittorio. I don't expect a proposal. That's crazy.'

'Rosa, I mean it.'

She looked up into his face and the fervent look in his blue, blue eyes stopped her in her tracks. 'You're actually serious?'

'Of course I'm serious.'

'But it's so sudden. You can't make a decision like that so quickly.'

'I already have.'

'But *I* can't!'

The idea was ridiculous. There were all kinds of reasons why it made no sense. They barely knew each other. And it was so early in her pregnancy—anything could happen, and then they'd be stuck together, and one or both of them would resent it for ever.

The gondola slipped slowly down the sinuous canal and the richly decorated *palazzos* drifted by, at odds with the turmoil going on in Rosa's mind.

She'd always wanted to marry for love. She wanted what her mother and father had shared before her mother had been cruelly wrenched from them by her disease: a deep, abiding love, the kind of love that took death to break it apart.

She knew that it was no idle dream, no fantasy that she aspired to, that she wished for herself. She'd witnessed it first-hand, initially with her grandparents and then with her parents, and she wanted it for herself. More than that, she believed she deserved it.

So this—Vittorio's bizarre offer—wasn't how it was supposed to be. This was all wrong. She was pregnant by a man she'd met only once before and now he was asking her to marry him because of the baby she was carrying.

It was so not how she'd imagined a proposal to be.

It would be crazy to say yes.

Even if a part of her was tempted.

She gasped in a breath as she numbly watched the passing parade. How many nights had she lain awake, when all was silent aside from Chiara's soft breathing, and thought about that night? Replaying the events, the emotions, the heart-stopping pleasures of the flesh he'd revealed to her? He'd taught her so much. Had given her so much.

For how many nights had she dreamed he would come for her?

And here he was.

And if a city could defy logic and be built atop the sea then maybe what he said could make some kind of sense too. He'd come for her today. Despite saying they'd never see each other again.

He'd tilted her world off its axis in just one night. If he could do that, then maybe it wasn't so impossible. Maybe they had what it took to make a marriage work?

She turned back to him. 'Did you come here today to ask me to marry you?' she asked.

'No,' he said, slipping his hand into his trouser pocket. 'Otherwise I would have come prepared with a ring to offer you. But I do have this…'

And there, in the palm of his hand, lay her grandmother's gold and pearl earring.

Her hand went to her mouth as her heart skipped a beat. She could scarcely believe it. She reached down to touch it, still not believing it was real, curling her fingers around the precious item, still warm from being tucked away next to Vittorio's body.

'This is the reason I came today. I found it nestled on your pillow after you had gone.'

She looked up at him. 'But I went to your *palazzo*. Your housekeeper said nothing had been found.'

'She didn't know. I intended to return it before now.'

'I thought I'd lost it for ever.'

'I meant to have Elena package it up and send it to you. But then, if I had…'

She looked up at him as electricity zipped down her spine. 'You might never have found out about the baby.'

He smiled down at her. 'Serendipity,' he said.

And she curled the hand holding the earring close to her chest, tears of gratitude, of relief, of joy, pricking at her eyes.

'Or maybe fate, or even destiny.'

Or magic, she thought as he pulled her into his kiss. *Don't forget magic.*

It was like coming home, her lips meeting his, their warm breath intermingling, the taste of him in her mouth. And she wondered if a day that had started so badly, so desolate and without hope, could get any better.

He drew back as the gondolier drew his vessel into a private dock outside a *palazzo*. And even though it had been foggy the one night he'd brought her here she would have recognised it in a heartbeat.

Vittorio's *palazzo*.

He was on his feet and had leapt onto the deck like a natural before he handed her out of the vessel. He slipped the gondolier some notes and then collected her arm to lead her inside.

'There's one more thing I need to tell you. One more reason you need to agree to marry me.'

CHAPTER TWELVE

'Now I *KNOW* this is some kind of joke.' Rosa burst from the chair she'd been settled in, needing to pace the room in long, frantic strides. 'You can't do this to me, Vittorio. You can't ask me to marry you—can't try to convince me to marry you with your kisses and your sweet talking about destiny and fate—and then drop a bombshell by telling me you're a prince. The Prince of Andachstein, no less!'

'Rosa, calm down.'

'How do you expect me to calm down? How did you think I'd react? That I would bow and scrape and be grateful that I've been offered this royal condescension? Am I supposed to be humbled? Or intimidated? Or both?'

'Rosa, listen!'

'No. I don't want to listen. I'm going home.'

She turned towards the doors—gilt-framed doors, elaborately carved with tigers and elephants, just one more treasure in a *palazzo* dripping with treasures of Murano glass and crystal chandeliers and rich velvet-upholstered antiques.

And it wasn't as if she hadn't noticed the insane luxury of this *palazzo* before. How had she accepted his explanation that it was simply somewhere he stayed without realising that he must have connections to the rich and famous—or that he must be one of them? Had she been so blinded by lust at that stage that she hadn't cared to notice? That she hadn't been able to see what was in front of her face?

She sniffed. 'Don't bother showing me out. I found the way myself once before. I can find my way home.'

'What? Home to your squalid basement apartment and your hand-to-mouth cleaning job? Home to throwing up every morning while you clean up somebody else's mess? Why would you want to go back to that life when I can offer you so much more?'

She spun on her heel. 'Because it's *my* life, Vittorio,' she said, her hands over her chest. 'It might be hard, and it might involve cleaning up the filth and garbage of other peoples' lives, but it's the life I choose to lead because that's the life I know. That's the world I belong to—not yours.'

'And you think, therefore, that that's the only life you deserve? You sell yourself short, Rosa. I would never have expected that.'

'I thought you belonged to my world too. At least that you were closer to my world. When you took me to the party that night you made me think that you were on the fringes of Marcello's world. "He's descended from the *doges* of Venice," you told me. I asked you how you knew such people. "Friends," you said. Your father and his were friends. Just friends. You let me think your father worked for him, and yet your father sits on the throne of Andachstein. Were you laughing at me when I told you I understood? When I told you about my father working for the mayor of our small village? Because you should have been. You sure made a fool out of me.'

'No! You constructed your own story. You believed what you wanted to believe.'

'You could have told me then how wrong I was. But you didn't make one effort to correct me.'

'How was I supposed to tell you? If I'd told you I was a

prince in that square would you have believed me? Would you have come with me?'

'Of course not!'

'You see?'

'No! You could have told me you were a prince when we were in the garden before the party.'

'And would you have believed me then?'

She wavered. *Probably not*. But still… 'Look, we slept together. But you can't be serious. You can't expect me to marry you.'

'Rosa,' he said, 'what are afraid of?'

'I'm not afraid.'

'Aren't you? Weren't you ready to say yes to me before, when you thought I was just a man?'

'Well, maybe…'

'Then what's changed? Unless you're afraid that you're not good enough to be a princess? Is that what you're telling me? That you don't deserve it?'

'You should have told me.'

'Did you tell me you were a virgin? Before you were in my bedroom, having already agreed to make love?'

'Maybe not—but it's not like that puts us on an even footing. After all, you're *still* a prince.'

He didn't need her to spell it out. What he needed was for her to agree to marry him.

'Why are you so angry with me? You wanted me to make love to you that night.'

'Yes. I wanted you to make love to me. *You*. Vittorio. The man I met that night. Not the Prince of some random principality I've barely heard of. I wasn't there for *him*.'

'Does it matter? I'm still the same person.'

'Of course it matters! You're next in line to the throne of Andachstein. Royalty. I'm a girl from a tiny village in the heel of Italy. Don't you think there's something of a power imbalance there?'

'I do. But there's another one that we have to deal with. Because you're the one who holds all the cards.'

'I don't see how. Like I said, you're still a prince, whatever I decide.'

'But you're the one carrying the heir.'

She blinked. 'But if we don't—if I don't—'

'There's no escaping it,' he said. 'You can't just sidestep being the mother to the heir of a throne.'

She kicked up her chin. 'It might be a girl. Surely a girl can't be the heir to the throne in a principality steeped in antiquity? Surely the throne can't go to an accidental princess?'

'That's why I'm taking you to a clinic, so that we can find out.' He looked at his watch. 'It's time we were leaving.'

'I didn't say I was going to marry you even if it is a boy.'

'And you didn't rule it out. Let's go.'

'But it's too early to tell,' she said.

'No,' he said. 'It's not.

Rosa could scarcely believe it—that a blood test that took only a few moments could deliver them the sex of their unborn child at such an early stage. But the doctor taking the sample of her blood had assured her it was correct.

'This test is not commercially available yet, but it is accurate in determining the sex of an unborn baby with up to ninety-five percent certainty.'

'What if it's one of the five per cent?' she said while they sat quietly together afterwards. 'What if it is a girl?'

'I'll take that risk. Meanwhile, you carry my son and the heir to the throne of Andachstein. You can say no to marrying me. You can walk away from this marriage if you choose. But in doing so, know that you are denying our child his rightful destiny.'

'You would put that load on my shoulders?'

'The load is already there. It is up to you what you decide to do with it.'

She turned away, her mind reeling. The pregnancy. The arrival of Vittorio. Finding out he was a prince. A proposal of marriage.

It was like being bombarded from every side with no respite. There was no time to take anything in. No time to process anything. And yet she had to make a decision that would impact her entire life—and that of their unborn child.

She swallowed. 'And if I agree to marry you?'

'Then our son will be brought up to assume his rightful place in Andachstein, with all the rights, privileges and responsibilities that go with it.'

She thought about the tiny basement flat that would never do to bring up a child in. She thought about her home in Zecce, a tiny dot of a dusty village in Puglia, where their child would grow up happy—she would make sure of that—but in no way in wealth or the lap of luxury. And she thought about this *palazzo* that would be part of his heritage, and no doubt much more besides.

Would it be fair to deprive their son of all that because his father had neglected to inform her that he was a prince?

And the biggest question of them all. What about love? Where did love factor in? He'd said nothing of love.

'What about love?' she asked, her throat so dry she had to force the words out.

'We'll both love our son,' he said.

She squeezed her eyes shut. So that was how it was. She'd read far too much into his sudden arrival, his kind attention, his comfort and his care. She'd read far too much into a romantic gondola ride and the fact that he'd wanted to see her again to return her grandmother's earring, as if it meant something.

But it had been an accident that he'd turned up. A twist of fate. He hadn't come for her at all—he was simply returning a piece of jewellery. And now the only reason he wanted her to stay was because she was having his baby. The child of a prince.

'You're using me,' she said.

'No.'

'Yes! You used me before and now you're using me again. But this time because I'm carrying your child.'

'It's not like that.'

'Isn't it? Then what would you call it? Blackmail? A world of spun gold for my child if I agree to marry you? Otherwise he lives the life of a peasant?'

'Think of the child. It's the best thing for the child. The fair thing.'

She spun away. She didn't want to hear it. Because part of her knew he was right. How could she say no and deprive their child of its birthright?

But this was not how her dreams had looked. Vittorio had come for her, yes, but not the way she'd imagined. Not for love. And now her dreams were turned to dust, and her hopes of love with them.

She couldn't help but wonder whether he had loved his first wife. A stab of jealousy pierced her heart. Or perhaps this was just how royal families did things—even in the twenty-first century—cold, loveless, contractual marriages.

How could she live without love? It was the foundation stone of her very existence. But then, how could she live without Vittorio? Without his touch? With just her dreams to sustain her, to mock her, when she could have the real thing even in the absence of love.

How could she wake up from those dreams to a sense of devastating loss and know that things could have been different if only she hadn't been so headstrong? So proud?

Think of the child,' he'd said.

And she was. But she was thinking about herself too. Thinking about parting from this man one last time after he'd found her again, and how much harder this time would be when it didn't have to be this way.

In the end, when it came down to it, he wasn't offering her a choice at all.

'All right,' she whispered, feeling her life spiralling out of control. 'I'll marry you.'

But not without conditions.

CHAPTER THIRTEEN

MARCELLO ANSWERED VITTORIO'S call on the third ring. 'I was wondering when I was going to hear from you again,' Marcello said. 'Have you come to your senses and made a decision yet?'

'You'll be delighted to know I have.'

'So who's the lucky lady? Katerina or Inga?'

'Neither.'

'What kind of game are you playing now?' Marcello sounded as if he was at the end of his tether. 'You know—'

'I know. I have to marry someone. So I am. I'm marrying Rosa.'

There was a pause at the end of the line. 'You don't mean—the woman from that night at Carnevale? The one you brought to the party?'

'The very same.'

Marcello snorted. 'Well, it's good you've made a decision, but how is your father going to react to that news?'

'It's other news that might just swing it. She's pregnant, Marcello, and—get this—she's having a boy.'

'You sly dog. You've been seeing her, then. That explains why your heart wasn't seriously in the hunt for a bride.'

'No, I haven't seen her since Carnevale. Not until today.'

'Ah,' said Marcello. 'She must have made quite an impression on you, in that case. I'm beginning to see why you might have been off your game. If you'd told me you were besotted with the woman it would have saved everyone a lot of time and effort.'

Vittorio growled. 'Stop talking rubbish, Marcello!'

'When are you going to tell your father?'

'As soon as Rosa's father agrees to the marriage.'

There was a pause at the end of the line. 'You—Prince Vittorio of Andachstein—are going to ask a woman's father for permission to marry her? After you've already taken certain liberties with his daughter, evidenced by the fact that she's pregnant with your child?'

Vittorio wished his friend wouldn't make such a big deal out of every single thing. 'Rosa's giving up a lot. She wants to do at least this part the old-fashioned way. We're travelling to Puglia this weekend.'

'And you have agreed?'

'Rosa insisted I meet her family and ask his permission or no wedding.'

'I like this woman more and more,' Marcello declared, chuckling down the phone line. 'I'm so glad to know you're not getting yourself a doormat. But, Vittorio, have you thought about what you're going to do if her father says no?'

'Ciao,' Vittorio said, putting his phone down on the coffee table.

Rosa's father wasn't going to say no. He couldn't.

As for not getting a doormat—he was well aware of that. He'd seen the way she'd stood up to Sirena that night, refusing to be cowed. He'd seen the way she'd stood up to him, insisting that she wasn't going to give up her job and move into the *palazzo* until such time as her father had given permission and the wedding was confirmed to proceed.

He shook his head as he looked around him at the luxurious fittings and furniture of the *palazzo*, all with a view of the Grand Canal. Why she would want to stay in that job and live in her dingy room when she could have all this, he didn't know. But it seemed important to her, and he figured she might as well enjoy what freedom she had now.

Soon enough she would be married to him and she'd find herself bound up in palace protocol and demands that she had no say in. She might as well enjoy her independence now.

He shook his head. No doormat there. With Rosa he was getting the whole package. A woman who could light up his nights, to please him—and who had already proved herself a breeder, to please his father.

What could be better than that?

Unless it was the child. A son.

His son.

It was something he'd yearned for once. Something he'd waited for with every passing month of his marriage. He'd expected it to happen quickly. After all, nothing else had been a problem. He'd been served up a bride he'd fallen madly in love with. All he'd needed was the news that he would become a father and the royal line of Andachstein would live on, his destiny fulfilled.

It had all seemed so easy in those bright, halcyon days. Except his wait had been fruitless. And then he'd discovered the reason why, and his world had turned sour and rancid, with bitterness usurping hope.

This child was like a reclaimed dream. A second chance. But he wouldn't make the same mistake again. He was taking no chances if this marriage didn't work out. He wasn't about to risk losing himself in the process.

There were some places he wouldn't go again.

Love was one of them.

CHAPTER FOURTEEN

IT WAS A two-hour drive from Bari Airport to Zucca. First along the straight highway that crossed the ankle of Italy, before turning on to narrower and yet narrower roads that meandered past stone walls and olive groves through the undulating countryside.

The sprinkle of towns and villages here seemed mostly deserted, except for the odd herd of goats and the brightly coloured pots of geraniums and the bougainvillea clambering over crumbling walls. Here and there an old man in a chair outside his house would lift a lazy hand as they passed.

Summer felt closer here, in this far southern region of Italy. The sky was clear blue, the air was clean and warm, and the late April sun held the promise of hot, airless summer days.

Along the route Rosa told Vittorio about her family. There was her father, Roberto, her three brothers, Rudi, Guido and Fabio, and their wives, Estella, Luna and Gabriella. There were three *bambini* between them now, with the addition of Rudi and Estella's second child, born just a week ago. The first granddaughter had been a cause of much excitement, and had been named Maria Rosa after her late grandmother and her aunt.

Vittorio tried to pay attention and take it all in, but it was hard when his gut was roiling. Oddly, he was never afraid to meet his own father, to put up with his disappointment and even his anger, but he was nervous about meeting Roberto. Rosa's father was an unknown quantity, and he suspected that the man wasn't about to be dazzled by his title.

'They're all going to be so excited to learn there's going to be another cousin soon.'

'You don't think it's too early to tell them about the baby?' Vittorio asked.

Rosa wasn't showing yet—not in a way anybody else would notice. Surely only he would appreciate the extra fullness to her breasts and what it meant.

'If we're going to get married because I'm having your baby,' she said, 'why should we pretend otherwise?'

He looked across at her in the passenger seat. There was a strange note to her voice, as if it was fraying around the edges and she was straining to hold it together.

'Are you tired?' he said. They had made an early start to make it to Zucca by lunchtime, and with the flight and then the undulating road he wouldn't be surprised if she was feeling a little motion sick.

'I'm fine,' she said, looking out of her window.

'Is everything all right?'

She sighed, still keeping her head turned away. 'Everything's fine.'

He grunted. Clearly something was wrong, but he wasn't about to argue the point. He'd given her plenty of opportunity to say if anything was bothering her.

They didn't speak for the final ten minutes of their journey, and when they pulled up outside the stone walls of her family home they didn't have to announce their arrival. Their vehicle had obviously been heard, because a swarm of people piled out of the house, their faces beaming, their arms outstretched.

Rosa just about bounded from the car, casting off her strange glumness like a cloak, laughing and squealing as she was gathered into the warm embrace of her family. The realisation that he was somehow the cause of her mood ratcheted up his own grumpiness.

He leaned against the car, his arms crossed, watching the reunion. Such a foreign, unknown thing—like an object he had to study to work out the very shape and texture of it.

So this was family?

Everyone seemed to be speaking at once, voices piling up one over another, men and women, and the two older babies were being passed around so that Rosa could hug them and cluck over them and remark on how much they'd grown. And there was Rosa, in the midst of the celebrations, hugging and laughing and happy. Everyone was happy.

In the background, with his hands on his hips as he watched on, stood the man who had to be her father. He wasn't as tall as his three sons, but he stood broad-shouldered and rosy-cheeked and proud as he waited for a chance to welcome his daughter home.

'Papà!' he heard her squeal when she saw him, and then they were in each other's arms and everyone was crying and whooping and back-slapping some more.

And then, as if Vittorio were an afterthought, Rosa said something and all heads swivelled towards him. In their gazes he saw interest and suspicion, curiosity and mistrust—until Rosa came back and claimed his hand and pulled him into the fray, introducing him to them all.

It was because he was with her that they welcomed him, he had no doubt. And even if they didn't trust him they welcomed him as Rosa's friend, and not as the heir to the throne of a tiny principality that had been irrelevant to their family until now. He knew who mattered here and it wasn't him, and he felt the power imbalance that she'd pointed out as existing between them tilt markedly the other way.

In Venice she was alone. Vulnerable.

But here she was surrounded by her family, like a guard all around her, and *he* was the outsider, the one who had to prove himself.

They sat down under a vine-covered pergola at a table already spread with platters of antipasto and cheeses and crusty loaves of bread, all sprinkled with dappled light. Rosa handed out gifts for the babies. Gifts she'd made. Sailor suits for the boys and a lacy gown she'd made for the tiny Maria Rosa. Everyone praised Rosa's needlework—gifts she'd made herself on her mother's beloved old sewing machine and all the more special for it.

'Tell us about Andachstein,' Rudi said, pouring ruby-red Puglia wine into glasses.

And Vittorio found himself telling them all about the principality—a gift of the far corner of his lands by an ancient monarch, bestowed upon a knight in return for faithful service. He told them about the *castello*, set high on the hilltop above the sparkling harbour far below. He told them of the landscape, of the rugged wooded hills and the pathways lined with thyme and rosemary that scented the air.

They all listened with rapt attention while they ate and drank wine. Rosa's beautiful eyes were the widest, and she looked both excited and afraid. He realised he'd never spoken to her of the place where she would one day live.

He squeezed her hand to reassure her and the conversation moved on.

The three wives were about to prepare the next course when the sound of a baby crying came from inside the house.

'I'll come and help with lunch,' said Rosa.

'No, you stay,' said Estella, 'I need you here. Wait.'

She was back a few minutes later, dropping a bundle on Rosa's lap. 'Say hello to your auntie Rosa, Maria.'

Rosa's eyes lit up as she took the tiny bundle. 'Oh, Estella, she's beautiful. Look at those big eyes…and such long hair!' The child blinked up at her, her rosebud mouth still moving, tiny hands crossed over her chest.

Vittorio watched as Rosa cradled the child in her arms. Not a two-year-old this time, and not an eleven-month-old like he'd seen her hold before, already halfway to childhood. This was practically a newborn.

And he was struck by the beauty of the tableau.

Something shifted inside him at that moment. It shifted the tiniest of fractions, and yet it was so momentous that for a few moments his throat choked shut.

In a few months Rosa would be holding their child. And if she could look so beautiful, so beatific, holding somebody else's child, how much more rapturous would she look when she was holding theirs?

Everything she did told him that he was doing the right thing. She would be the perfect mother.

'You are so lucky to go to the city and meet your handsome man,' said Luna, generously ladling pasta into bowls that got passed from hand to hand around the table. 'You would never have found anyone as good-looking as Vittorio in the village.'

'Hey,' said Guido, looking aggrieved. 'What's that supposed to mean?'

'Exactly what it sounds like,' said Fabio, rolling his eyes. 'Apparently all the hot guys are in the cities.'

'No,' Rudi said, the voice of authority. 'Luna means all the good men are already taken, don't you, Luna?'

'Is that what you meant, Luna?' laughed Gabriella, clearly not convinced.

Estella laughed too. 'I could have sworn you meant something else entirely.'

'These women,' Rudi said, shaking his head. 'They are something else.' He pointed a finger at their guest in warning. 'Vittorio,' he said, 'don't expect Rosa is going to be any different. And don't, whatever you do, think that she's going to be a pushover. These women, they have a mind of their own.'

'Rudi!' Rosa scolded.

Vittorio just looked sideways at Rosa and smiled. 'I'll keep that in mind.'

Rosa's father wasn't old—not in years anyway—but the creases in his leathered face and the oil stains on his hands spoke of a man who had not just worked but rather had laboured his entire life. A man who had suffered the devastating loss of his wife but who had carried on, welcoming the new generation of Ciavarros one by one.

'Come,' he said to Vittorio after the family had sated themselves on the feast the women had prepared. 'We need to have a talk, man to man.'

Rosa squeezed Vittorio's hand as he rose to follow Roberto. He was inordinately grateful for the gesture. It was ridiculous, but he hadn't felt this nervous since he was a child, starting boarding school in Switzerland as a seven-year-old, when he'd felt as if he'd gone to a different world, with new languages to grapple with and comprehend, and older boys who'd seen a man-child and decided to take him down a peg or two before he was too big and he got the upper hand.

They left the family under the vine-covered pergola and Roberto led him to a patio on the other side of the house via the big kitchen, where he pulled a bottle and two shot glasses from a shelf.

Both men settled themselves down and Roberto poured a hefty slug into each glass, handing Vittorio one.

'To Rosa,' he said, and the pair clinked glasses.

The older man threw his down his gullet. Vittorio followed suit, and felt the liquor set fire to his throat and burn all the way down.

He set his glass on the table without feeling he'd disgraced himself, only to see Rosa's father top the glasses up.

'And to you, Vittorio,' he said, and downed the second glass.

Vittorio swallowed the fiery liquor down, feeling it burst into flames in his belly.

'It's good, no?' said Roberto. 'I make it myself.'

'Very good,' Vittorio agreed, thankful that his voice box still worked.

He was even more thankful to see the stopper placed back in the bottle.

'I hear you want to marry my daughter.'

'I've asked her, it's true.'

'She also tells me that she is carrying your child.'

Vittorio was catapulted right back to school again—to a summons to the headmaster's office for punching a boy who had been picking on a junior grader. He'd got the *don't think just because you're a prince* speech then, and he half expected to hear it again now.

'Also true.'

The other man nodded and sighed. 'Maria—my wife—was very beautiful. Rosa has her eyes.'

'They're beautiful eyes. The colour of warmed cognac,' Vittorio said.

'Yes,' said Roberto with a wide smile that smacked of approval. 'That's it. I used to tell Maria that I could get drunk just by looking into her eyes.' His eyes brightened. 'She would tell me, "Go and drink your grappa if you want to get drunk. I have work to do."' He laughed a little, then sniffed, ending on a sigh. 'There is a lot of Maria in Rosa. I can promise you, you will never be bored.'

'I know that.'

'But Rosa says that while she wants what's best for the *bambino*, she is not sure.'

His words were like a wet slap about the face.

'It's so sudden,' Vittorio said, 'and there's a lot Rosa will need to take on. It's not a normal marriage, in many respects.'

Roberto nodded. 'True. But then, what *is* a normal marriage? When it comes down to it, every marriage is a game of give and take, of compromise and of bending when one least wants to bend.'

And breaking, Vittorio thought. Sometimes marriages just broke you into pieces.

'Did Rosa tell you I was married once before?'

'*Si,*' he said, with a nod of his head. 'She says you are a widower.'

'It wasn't a good marriage and it didn't end well,' Vittorio said, studying his feet.

'You see,' Roberto said. 'We are not so different. You might be a prince, but we are both widowers, after all. We both know loss.'

'I guess we do,' he said.

'You know,' Roberto said, leaning back in his chair, 'when a man marries a woman for life, and he has a good marriage, and he only gets thirty years, that is nowhere near enough.' He shook his head. 'I am sorry that you haven't found this satisfaction—yet.'

He leaned forward, removing the stopper from the bottle again. He poured two more slugs before he put the stopper back, raised his glass.

'Here is to the marriage of you and Rosa,' he said. 'May it be a good one from the very beginning. And may it be a long one, filled with love.' He nodded, and said, 'I give you my blessing,' before downing the shot.

The liquor stuck in Vittorio's throat and burned. Or maybe it was her father's words as he'd blessed the union.
Love...

All Vittorio wanted from this marriage was the heir Rosa

was carrying. A spare would guarantee the principality's survival. Having Rosa in his bed would be a bonus.

But love?

Surely her father could see that this was a convenient marriage? That love didn't factor into it? Surely he wasn't that unworldly?

But what was he to say in the face of the man's reminiscences about his own loving marriage and his wishes for them to be happy? He could hardly tell Roberto that he would never let himself love his daughter, not when he had been embraced so warmly into the family. That was between him and Rosa.

The man had given his approval. Vittorio swallowed down on the burning in his throat. It didn't feel altogether comfortable, but wasn't Roberto's blessing the thing he'd come for?

The announcement was made. Roberto had given his blessing and the entire family would go to Andachstein for the wedding. Cheers ensued, but a ruddy-cheeked Roberto quelled them, because he had even more news to share— the secret Rosa had shared with him—that in a few months they would be welcoming a new baby into the family, his new grandson.

Bottles of Prosecco appeared from nowhere and corks popped. Toasts were made, backs were slapped, cheeks were kissed, and Vittorio found himself hugged by everybody, men and women, multiple times. His acceptance into the family was now beyond dispute.

The one person who didn't seem to want to hug him was the one he wanted to the most. Rosa had let him quickly kiss her on the lips as everyone had toasted the couple, before she'd swooped upon one of her nephews and sat down, hiding herself beneath him. She knew what she was doing.

She was using the child as a human shield. What he didn't understand was why.

He stood in a circle of men and watched her with the child, making a fuss of it, talking with her sisters-in-law and avoiding his eye. It was killing him. It had been so many weeks since he'd taken her to bed that magical night, and having her back in his life, being so close, was an exercise in frustration.

He burned for her. He wanted nothing more than to bury himself in her sweet depths.

But she'd refused to move into the *palazzo* with him. She'd refused to sleep with him. Not until everything was settled, she'd said.

He watched her laughing. Her hair was down today, curling over her shoulders, dancing in the light spring breeze, and her eyes were warm like cognac heated by a flame.

Well, everything was settled. Her father had given his approval of their marriage. The wedding would go ahead. Andachstein would have its heir.

And tonight he would hold Rosa and make love to her again.

The celebrations were on the wane by late afternoon, and one by one the brothers drifted off to their own homes with their families and sleepy babies. Roberto was sitting in an armchair, quietly snoring, when Rosa said she was tired and was going to turn in.

At last, thought Vittorio.

They collected their overnight bags from the car, and Vittorio felt his anticipation rising with every step back into the house. Rosa was wearing a dress splashed with big bright flowers today, with a full skirt, and a cardigan over her shoulders. He wasn't sure whether he was going to be able to wait to get the dress off before he rucked up her skirt and took her.

'I hope my family wasn't too much for you today,' she said.

'No,' he said as he followed her through the house, his hands itching to hold her, to glide over her skin, smooth as satin. 'You have a good family. Noisy, but good.'

She laughed a little over her shoulder. 'Definitely noisy.' And then she opened a door. 'Here's where you're sleeping tonight.'

He stepped into the room, confused. He looked around. There was one single bed surrounded by girlie things. A basket of dolls in one corner. Pictures of Rosa growing up. Artwork that she must have done as a child on the walls and a poster of a boy band she must have once followed.

'This is your old room?'

'It's the most comfortable single bed there is. It's yours tonight.'

He tried to pull her into his arms. 'But where are *you* sleeping? I thought that tonight we could celebrate our engagement.'

She laughed again and slipped out of his reach.

'Won't you stay with me?' he invited.

She shook her head. Her beautiful face was lit by a sliver of moonlight through the curtain, and he was reminded of liquid mercury and silver, fluid and impossible to contain.

'I can't make love to you under my father's roof.'

'He's asleep. He won't know.'

'*I'll* know,' she said, shaking her head, smiling softly.

He reached for her again, knowing he could change her mind if only she would let him kiss her. He knew she would melt in his arms. But she backed off to the door, all quick-silver and evasion.

'Then when?' he said, a cold bucket of resignation pouring down over him. 'When can we make love again?'

'Our wedding night, of course,' she said.

'What? But that's weeks away.' Three or four. Too many to contemplate.

'Then it will be all the more special for waiting.'

'Rosa,' he said, pleading now, raking one hand through his hair.

'No,' she said. 'You're getting what you want. Let me have this.'

'But do you know how long it's been?'

She smiled a sad, soft smile. 'I know how long it's been for me.' She blew him a kiss. 'Goodnight.'

Vittorio was alone. All alone in a single bed dressed with her sheets and her pillows and surrounded by her childhood things. All of which made it impossible to sleep. Impossible to relax.

It was like being tortured. Being so close to her, surrounded by her, but unable to touch her. It would be better to be sleeping under a tree somewhere far away.

With a groan, he gave up on sleep and got out of bed, snapping on the light. He moved to a big old chest of drawers and looked at the photos on top—photos of Rosa growing up.

There was one of her with a gap-toothed smile and pigtails at school. Even then her eyes had been beyond beautiful. Another showed her flanked by her brothers, all on bikes. Rosa had been a young teenager then, wearing shorts and a checked shirt, and there was a view of coastal cliffs and sea behind her. A family holiday by the sea. Another one had been taken of her between her mother and father.

Vittorio picked it up. Roberto was right. Rosa looked like a younger version of Maria. He touched a finger to her cheek and growled softly in the night. Soon she would be his. Soon there would be no more room for playing this game of look-but-don't-touch. Soon they would share a bed and much, much more.

And he thought of what Rosa's father had said to him, *'You will never be bored.'*

He believed him.

But, *Dio*, meanwhile he burned.

CHAPTER FIFTEEN

VITTORIO DIDN'T HAVE time to visit Andachstein and deliver the news to his father personally, but he was selfish enough not to want to miss his reaction when he heard the details of his marriage. He had Enrico set his father up to expect a video call the evening they returned to Venice.

At the appointed time Vittorio called, and a few moments later his father appeared on his screen, waving away his secretary. 'Yes, yes, I can manage this now, Enrico.'

Vittorio smiled. 'I've got news, Father.'

Guglielmo grunted as he turned his attention to the screen, and Vittorio could see his patience was already wearing thin.

'There's only one piece of news I'm interested in hearing, so this had better be good.'

'Then you're in luck. I'm getting married.'

'Huh,' he snorted. 'About time. I was hoping I might finally hear something once I had Enrico draw up that list. Who is it, then? Or have you finally managed to sort out your differences with the Contessa.'

'I'm not marrying Sirena.' The words were more satisfying than he'd expected. Far more satisfying.

'No?' The old Prince rubbed his jaw. 'I'm not sure how Sebastiano is going to take that.'

His father's surprise quickly turned to resignation, as Vittorio had suspected it would. Prince Guglielmo's friend's disappointment was not his most pressing concern. Getting his son married and producing heirs was. Just who provided those heirs was incidental.

'Then who is the lucky woman?'

'Her name is Rosa Ciavarro.'

His father frowned. 'I don't recall seeing anyone on Enrico's list by the name of Ciavarro.'

'She wasn't on Enrico's list. Her family come from the village of Zecce in the south of Italy.'

'A village, you say? Then who is her father?'

'Roberto Ciavarro.'

His father shook his head and looked even more perplexed. Vittorio smiled. He could enjoy letting his father fruitlessly search for connections, but then again there would also be a great deal of satisfaction in revealing the truth.

'I believe he runs the local gas station and motor vehicle repair shop. I hear his speciality is servicing Piaggio Apes.'

Colour flooded his father's cheeks, but to his credit he didn't blow. He was used to being baited by his son.

Vittorio let the news sink in for a second, before he offered, 'Apes are those three-wheel trucks that zip down the narrow laneways carrying produce to market.'

'I know what they are!' his father growled, and his son could almost feel the old man's temperature escalate. 'Don't treat me like an idiot.'

The old man looked upwards to the ceiling, almost as if he was hoping for divine intervention. When that didn't come, he sighed. 'So tell me,' he said, with the air of someone who couldn't be shocked any more than he already had been, 'what does this Rosa do?'

'She works in a hotel in Venice.'

His father swallowed, looking pained. 'Dare I ask in what capacity?'

'She's a maid. A cleaner.'

Closed eyes met that response, along with lips pressed

together tightly before they parted enough to say, 'A peasant. You want to marry a peasant. Is this some kind of joke?'

Vittorio knew that he'd well and truly blown that part of his brief. His bride was supposed to be the right kind of woman—someone eligible, from their own social strata, and preferably from the list Enrico had drawn up.

'Because I can tell you it's not funny from where I'm sitting. Can't you for once be serious about your responsibilities?'

Vittorio bristled. 'I've never been more serious about anything, Father. I'm going to marry Rosa.'

His father threw up his hands. 'What on earth for? I suppose you're going to get stars in your eyes and tell me you love the girl.'

'Of course I don't love her. When did this family ever marry for love?'

Guglielmo snorted. It was an agreement of sorts. An acknowledgement of the root cause of all that had been wrong with Vittorio's family. The age-old resentment that lay festering in Vittorio's gut sent up curling tendrils of bitterness. When had love ever come into anything this family did?

'Then why?'

'Because she's pregnant.'

His father shrugged, waving one hand in the air. 'Is that all? It happens. One might say with someone of your ilk it's an occupational hazard. You have the morals of a common alley cat, after all.'

'Perhaps, given my title, not quite so common.'

'Might as well be.' The aging Prince sniffed. 'Anyway, a mere pregnancy still doesn't mean you have to marry the wench. An heir is no good to us if it turns out to be a g—'

'She's having a boy.'

For the first time Vittorio saw his father pause and show just the slightest modicum of interest. The older man's eyes narrowed as he wheeled back, his gimlet eyes focused hard on his screen as he stroked his beard again. 'You're sure of that?'

'That's what the blood test results said.'

His father sighed and rested his head on his hand. 'But still…a commoner. A peasant, no less.'

'This is the twenty-first century, Father—think about it. The press will lap it up. It's a fairy-tale romance: the Prince and the maid…the ordinary girl who becomes a princess. And a royal baby as the icing on the cake. It's got newspapers and women's magazines across the world written all over it. And when has Andachstein ever had such good press coverage? Think what it will do for our economy. Our hotels and casinos will be filled to overflowing.'

'They're already filled in summer.'

'We'll build more, and those will be full in winter too.'

His father continued to trouble his neat white triangle of a beard, his expression conflicted, before his chin suddenly went up, jerking his beard out of his fingers. 'Do you have a picture of this girl?'

Vittorio pulled out his phone, finding the picture of Rosa he hadn't been able to resist taking that day on the gondola—the one with her dark eyes lit up and her cupid's-bow lips smiling, the wind scattering tendrils of her dark hair across her face. It was a picture that showed Rosa in all her unguarded beauty, raw and innocent—though he knew that she wasn't as innocent as she appeared.

He'd seen to that.

He held it to the screen, saw his father's eyes narrowing as he surveyed the photo, his fingers now more contemplative on his neat beard, and breathed a sigh of relief, knowing that she'd just passed one almighty test. Clearly his father agreed that Rosa would at least pass muster as a princess.

'She'll need instruction,' his father decreed. 'In grooming and, no doubt, in deportment. And she'll need education on the history of the principality and her future role and duties within it.'

Vittorio nodded as he pocketed the phone. 'She'll get it.'

'She's got a lot to catch up on before she can be let loose in public.'

'I said, she'll get it.'

'See that she does. I mean...' his father sighed before continuing '...a simple girl, plucked from a village...'

'Did I *say* she was simple?'

His father paused. 'You're right. She managed to get herself pregnant by a prince, didn't she?'

It was Vittorio's turn to shake his head. 'Father, for the record, she had no idea I was a prince. And she didn't get herself pregnant. *I* got her pregnant.'

Guglielmo waved his hand in the air dismissively. 'Yes, yes, a technicality. But it happened, and it proves she's a breeder. At least that takes care of who you're going to marry.'

Vittorio couldn't prevent the smile that followed his dinosaur of a father's words. 'Was that congratulations, Father? Because I can almost believe you consented to this marriage.'

The old Prince sniffed as he looked away from the screen and started shuffling his papers.

'I agree to this marriage,' he said, without looking up. 'Given that it is the only option I am apparently going to be presented with. But that does not mean I have to celebrate it.' He looked back at the screen, a look of confusion on his face, and then he yelled over his shoulder. 'Enrico! How do I turn this cursed contraption off?'

CHAPTER SIXTEEN

ROSA WAS ALMOST looking forward to the next few weeks
of wedding planning. She'd called Chiara while Vittorio
was speaking with his father and given her the news, asking her to be her bridesmaid. She imagined they'd spend
evenings together in their apartment, poring over bridal designs. She even entertained tentative plans to sew her own
gown. There was enough time, if she could settle on a design and find the right fabric. And if her mother couldn't
be there in person, Rosa felt, then at least her sewing machine could provide the magical means of sewing Rosa's
wedding gown together.

But it seemed things didn't operate that way when you
were going to marry a prince.

Vittorio returned from his call, looking smug and well
satisfied, and announced that her time was up. He was moving her into the *palazzo* the very next day, in preparation
for the wedding and her move to Andachstein.

Rosa dug her heels in. 'I don't see why.'

'There's every reason why. Because you're now my fiancée, and I can't guarantee your safety while you stay in
that basement hovel you call a home.'

'Safety?' she said, really wishing her voice hadn't
squeaked.

'You're going to be a princess, Rosa. As soon as the official announcement is made you're going to have people

lining up wanting a piece of you. Reporters, the paparazzi, even conmen. All sorts of hangers-on.'

Maybe he was laying it on thick, but he hadn't been in a very good mood lately, and she had a lot to do with that.

'I've tolerated your obstinacy long enough. I can't protect you while you live in the basement of a hotel, where anyone and everyone can just walk in unchallenged. You'll be safer here.'

'I don't call it obstinacy. I call it independence.'

'Call it what you like. It's coming to an end. You're moving into the *palazzo*.'

'What about Chiara?' Rosa said, because there was no way she wanted to be in the sprawling *palazzo* alone with Vittorio but for a sprinkling of staff. It wasn't as if she had super powers. There was no way she was going to be able to stick to her guns and resist him until the wedding without help.

'If it means you'll do what I ask,' he conceded grumpily, 'then Chiara can come too.'

'I didn't think you were *asking*.' She sniffed. 'It sounded more like an order to me.'

He cursed under his breath. *Dio*, a man needed the patience of Job. But then, hadn't her father and brothers warned him?

'Okay,' he said, 'that's the first thing.'

'There's more?'

'I've organised sketches from some of the best designers to be delivered, so you can work out who you'd like to design and create your gown.'

'What if I want to make it myself?'

'Come on, Chiara—this isn't some cheap knock-off you'll be wearing when you walk down the aisle. This is going to be televised all over Europe and possibly the world. Do you want that kind of pressure?'

'I don't make cheap knock-offs.'

He held up his hands. 'Fine. Only I don't think you're going to have much free time in the next few weeks anyway.'

'Why?' she asked, her arms crossed against her chest. 'When you've already made me give up my job?'

'Because Enrico—my father's secretary—is preparing several volumes for you to study on the history, constitution and governance of Andachstein.'

'That sounds like bags of fun.'

'You'll need to be familiar with it all by the time you're required to attend and speak at official functions.'

'What functions?' She hadn't spoken in public since she'd been at school, and even in front of her school friends she'd been a bundle of nerves.

'Lots of them. The people have missed having a princess. My mother was patron of the children's hospital and at least a dozen other charitable organisations besides. You'll be expected to fill that role.'

She kicked up her chin. 'So I agree to marry you and I lose my life.'

'It's not all bad, Rosa,' he said, gritting his teeth. 'You gain me.'

'Huh,' she said, and turned away.

It wasn't an easy thing to do. She'd fallen a little bit in love with him that magical night of Carnevale and nothing had changed that. Not the fact that he'd disappeared for six weeks, because he'd been honest about that. And not the fact that he'd quietly neglected to inform her that he was a prince until it was too late and she'd already discovered she was pregnant.

Because she hadn't fallen a little bit in love with a prince. She'd fallen for the man. Vittorio. And lately he reminded her more and more of how he'd been that night. There was an edge to him, magnetic and powerful, bordering on dangerous, and the knowledge that she'd put it there by defying him was exciting. Intoxicating.

She didn't need an aphrodisiac. She still dreamed of him at night, still replayed their love scenes, every touch and every sound. She still longed to make love to him again and again.

But she wanted all of him this time. She didn't just want his lust. She wanted his affection. More than that, she yearned for his love.

Come the wedding, she would be bound to him. They would be man and wife under the sight of God and she would take her place in the marital bed. And she would enjoy it.

But for now the only thing she had control of, the only ace she had up her sleeve, was her resolve to keep Vittorio at arm's length. So he might look beyond the sex and see the woman she was.

If Vittorio had thought having Rosa residing in the *palazzo* might weaken her resolve and make her more accessible and more amenable to his affections, and if he'd thought he might pay her a little nocturnal visit, he had another think coming.

Rosa and Chiara were moving in amidst a whirl of excitement—mostly on Chiara's part. She was running up and down the stairs, shrieking at just about everything. But that wasn't the worst of it. He'd thought the move was taking longer than he'd expected, and he'd gone to see what was happening, and found his staff carrying beds around.

'What the hell is going on?' he bellowed as he watched them grappling with an ancient four-poster bed.

'Calm down,' snapped Rosa. 'There's no need to shout.'

'Just answer my question.'

She shrugged on a grin. 'We're simply moving this bed into my room.'

'You've already got a bed in your room.'

'But there isn't a bed for Chiara.'

'She has an entire bedroom at her disposal.'

'Oh, but Vittorio,' she said, 'we *like* sharing a room. How else are we going to talk late into the night?'

'You could always phone each other,' he said.

She laughed. 'That would be silly when we're in the same building.' She smiled up at him. 'Don't worry,' she said. 'It's only until the wedding.'

And she leaned up to press the lightest of kisses to his lips. A touch. A tease. A peck. And nowhere near enough. He tried to catch her and pull her close, but she'd whirled away, quicksilver in motion, before he could get hold of her.

He grumped back to his suite.

Only until the wedding.

He wanted her. He burned with wanting her. But what irked him more was that he could not help but admire her.

'Not a doormat,' Marcello had said.

Not a chance.

She was like a wily negotiator, the way she made her quiet demands. And there was no budging her. She would not be swayed. But she was definitely tempted. Otherwise why would she move Chiara into her room? She didn't trust herself and Chiara was her wall.

It was infuriating. She was defending the terms of their agreement like a tigress defending its cub.

He smiled a little at that. Whatever kind of father he turned out to be, he knew Rosa would make a good mother. He'd seen her holding her tiny niece and nephews. He'd seen the way she doted on them. And maybe, just maybe, she would help him be the kind of father he wished he'd had.

He sighed as he went to his room and rummaged through his closet for gym clothes. He could last. It seemed he had no choice but to burn off some energy in more conventional ways. But, hell, a man could burst with wanting her.

CHAPTER SEVENTEEN

ROSA RUBBED THE bridge of her nose and sighed as she studied the dusty tome in the library.

'What's wrong?' asked Chiara, who was lying on a chaise longue nearby and reading a bridal magazine.

'The constitution of Andachstein. It's the most boring thing I've ever read in my life. I'm never going to get through all these volumes. No wonder Vittorio said I wouldn't have enough time to make my own gown.'

'Hey,' Chiara said, flicking through the pages, 'Vittorio wants you to have a designer gown, and I say go for it. There's only a few weeks until the wedding. You'd be crazy to try and rush it yourself when a designer would have an entire team of seamstresses at their disposal. You can always make something else for the wedding. A garter for your leg, or Vittorio's bow tie.' She looked up suddenly. 'Do princes even wear bow ties to their own weddings?'

'Who knows?' said Rosa, turning back to her tome. 'Don't they usually wear medals or a sash?'

Chiara shrugged next to her, and for a while there was silence but for the flicking of pages—Chiara's magazine pages, because it was taking for ever for Rosa to make her way through even one of the pages in her turgid tome. She sighed again.

Chiara looked up. 'Tell you what. How about we take a look at some of those sketches from the designers Vittorio organised? You've barely looked at them and you don't have long to make a decision.'

'Yeah…' Rosa said, rubbing her forehead with her hand. She had barely looked at them because she'd had her heart set on designing and making her own gown, but time was slipping by and there was so much to do. So much to read. 'Maybe you're right.'

'Great,' said Chiara, jumping up. 'You could do with a break. I'll go get them. Be right back.'

Rosa sat back in her chair and closed her eyes. Her head ached with the effort of trying to make sense of the medieval mumbo jumbo she was reading. How was she ever supposed to get a handle on it all?

'Rosa?'

She opened her eyes with a start to see Vittorio standing in the wide doorway.

'Are you all right?'

Her heart skipped in her chest as he strode towards her purposefully, like a powerful cat, all grace and barely leashed power. In a soft winter-white sweater that hugged his sculpted chest and fitted black trousers he looked amazing, and her hands ached to reach out and trace the skinscape of his body through the luxurious wool.

'I'm fine,' she said.

But her skin was tingling, and she was feeling strangely vulnerable. It was the first time they'd been alone together since she'd moved into the *palazzo*. The first time she hadn't had Chiara's presence to shield her and give her the confidence to pretend to be unmoved and light-hearted.

There was no pretending to be unmoved now. Her mouth had gone dry.

'Then what is the problem?'

You, she wanted to say. She looked around him. *Where was Chiara?*

'These damned books,' she said. 'They're so boring. I can't be expected to read them all.'

'You don't like the history of Andachstein?'

'I don't see a lot to interest me so far, no.'

He smiled and looked around too, and she knew he was checking for Chiara. His smile widened when he didn't find her.

'Then maybe you are starting in the wrong place. Andachstein has a rich and fascinating history.' He rounded the desk. 'Perhaps I can show you.'

'It's okay,' she said, even as he leaned over her and examined the volumes on the desk. She felt his heat wrap around her, caress her like a breeze stirring a crop of grain, sparking her sensitive nerve-endings, coaxing her nipples into hard peaks.

'Have you read about the lace industry? That would interest you, surely?'

'Andachstein has a lace industry?'

He nodded and plucked one volume from the collection on the desk and opened it to a particular page. 'Here,' he said, pointing to where there were some photographs of various patterns of lace, some delicately shell-like, others resembling flowers. 'The then Princess Rienna wanted to open schools to girls. She invited a group of nuns to move from Bruges to Andachstein and start a school. They brought with them their lace-making skills and passed them on to the girls and women of the principality.'

Rosa tried to ignore his presence at her shoulder and concentrate on his words, but she could feel the puff of his breath in her hair and against her skin and it was all she could do not to turn her face to his.

'She sounds,' she said, trying to stop her voice sounding tremulous, 'very forward-thinking.'

'She was. She wanted to do something to repay Andachstein for saving her life and she saw this as a way.'

This time her head did turn to his—just a little. Her gaze caught the strength of his jaw, the curve of his lips and strong nose, and she looked away again, feeling dizzy. Breathless. She hadn't been this close to Vittorio for so long, and the masculine scent of him was like a drug.

Her eyes were fixed on the pages in front of her, her hands flat on the desk lest they move of their own volition towards him. *Where the hell was Chiara?*

'How was she saved by Andachstein?'

'Rienna was a Celtic princess, taken prisoner on a pirate ship bound for Constantinople. Various accounts say she had eyes the colour of sapphires. She'd been kidnapped from her home and intended as a gift for the Sultan, destined to join his harem as one of his concubines. There was a storm and the pirate ship got blown off course into Andachstein waters, where a naval vessel attacked the ship and freed the Princess. The girl's father was so grateful he offered her to the then Prince, whose own wife had died in childbirth, along with their stillborn son, one year earlier. Princess Rienna went on to bear him eight children, and her intensely blue eyes have been passed down through the generations ever since.'

This time Rosa did turn her head—all the way. She looked up at his cobalt eyes, entranced by the story of pirates and Celtic princesses and times long gone. 'Will our son have those same eyes?'

He turned those eyes down at her, and she felt her insides quiver.

'If he is my son.'

'You know he is your son.'

'I do,' he said, and his eyes were so intense that her breath hitched and she wasn't sure for a moment whether he was answering the same question. She knew that if he asked her in this moment if she wanted to make love to him she would utter those same two words.

His lips were closer. How had that happened when she hadn't taken her eyes from him? His lips were only a breath from hers now, the time that separated them no more than a heartbeat.

She was going to kiss him. There was nothing surer, no matter the bargain they'd made or the terms he'd agreed to. *Her* terms—except they didn't seem to matter now.

All that mattered was that Vittorio was here now.

'I found them!' Chiara breezed into the room and stopped dead.

Beside her Rosa was almost certain she heard Vittorio growl.

'Sorry, am I interrupting something?'

Rosa sprang up from her chair. 'No. Vittorio was just filling me in on some of Andachstein's history. Weren't you, Vittorio?'

'Something like that,' he said, pushing himself upright.

'Chiara and I are going to look at those sketches and choose a designer,' Rosa said, talking too fast but unable to stop herself. 'You were right, of course, I will never have time to make something myself.'

'In that case,' said Vittorio, looking from one woman to the other, 'I will leave you to it.'

And he departed.

'What was that about?' asked Chiara.

'Nothing,' said Rosa, both grateful and annoyed at Chiara's sudden reappearance. 'Show me the designs.'

Chiara looked as if she didn't believe her, but then her excitement returned. 'I think I've found the perfect gown. There are others too, but what do you think?'

Rosa took the sketch. It was an off-the-shoulder gown with a fitted bodice, three-quarter sleeves and a back finished with a row of tiny pearl buttons that dropped much lower. There was a long train and a cathedral veil trimmed in lace. Swatches of the suggested fabric—a white Shantung silk—and a sample of the veil were attached.

There were no embellishments apart from the row of tiny buttons at the back. Nothing fancy. Nothing fussy. Just sleek, unfettered design.

Rosa felt a zing of excitement. 'It's beautiful.'

Chiara grinned. 'It would look magic on you. You'll only be three months pregnant by then, and you shouldn't be showing, but even if you are it will be hidden by the cut of the skirt.'

Rosa quickly flipped through the pages to see the other designs. She stopped at one—a gown made entirely of lace. Andachstein lace. Her thumb fingered the swatches while she was thinking.

'You'd rather have a gown made in lace?' Chiara said.

Rosa smiled. 'No, but it's given me an idea.'

CHAPTER EIGHTEEN

ANDACHSTEIN'S CATHEDRAL WAS a grand affair on the headland overlooking the harbour, with origins that harked back to Roman times. The cathedral had been built and ruined and rebuilt over the ages, until the existing building had been erected from the ruins some time in the fourteenth century and extended half a dozen times since.

A testament to the architect's love and knowledge of arches, the cathedral boasted a long central aisle and a Gothic rose window at one end, with a golden domed nave at the other. Stained-glass windows had been added over the centuries.

Rosa knew all this as she stood at the entrance, her father by her side and Chiara behind her, to straighten her train and stop her veil blowing away. Vittorio had brought her here for a rehearsal, and she'd been stunned then by the magnificence and history of the place. The tiny chapel in the village where she'd grown up, where they'd said goodbye to her mother, seemed like a dot in a dusty landscape in comparison.

And now, with the music from the pipe organ sweeping out of the interior, rising to the moment where she would have to enter the cathedral, Rosa had a moment of self-doubt.

What was she doing here?

She'd been thrust into this position because of one passionate night that had been meant to be the end. She was marrying a man whose child she carried. They were about to exchange vows declaring that they would love and cherish each other, that they would forsake all others.

But did Vittorio love her? Would he ever love her enough to forsake all others? She wanted so much what her mother and father had shared. She wanted it all. Marriage, family, and love at the heart of it.

What if it never happened?

What if Vittorio never loved her?

She wouldn't be able to bear it.

She'd wither slowly from the inside out.

Her father must have noticed her shallow breathing. He patted the hand tucked under his arm.

'All right?' he asked, his forehead creased into a frown, concern lining his eyes.

She took a deep breath and found a weak smile to reassure him. Of course she was. She had to be. She thought of her unborn child, of the things she would be denying him if she turned her back on all this now, and she couldn't do it. Not just to satisfy her own personal needs and longings.

She smiled up at her father again. 'Bridal jitters,' she said. 'I'm fine.'

He kissed her then, and told her, 'You look beautiful today. No father could be prouder.'

Rosa gave a tremulous smile. How could she not look beautiful today? Her gown was divine. She'd decided on a simple sleek design, similar to the one in the sketch Chiara had shown her, and together with the designer had decided on a champagne-coloured silk. A long veil edged with Andachstein lace was held in place with a tiara that had belonged to Vittorio's mother and boasted a magnificent Brazilian topaz.

The whole ensemble was so utterly perfect she was glad she'd been talked out of trying to make a dress herself. Besides, it had given her time to tackle some other projects.

'My only regret is that your mother isn't here to witness this moment.' Her father gave a sad, soft smile, his eyes glazed. 'She would be so proud, and I know she is smiling down on you like the sun is today.'

'Don't make me cry,' Rosa pleaded, dabbing at her eyes.

And then there was no time for tears as the music shifted up a notch.

'There's our cue,' her father said as a footman gave him a signal. 'Are you ready?'

Rosa sucked in a breath, smiled weakly and nodded. 'Ready,' she said.

The sun through the stained-glass windows drenched the waiting congregation in puddles of coloured light. Dust motes glowed like sparks of gold in the vast space above. Either side of her were wall-to-wall smiles. But she didn't have eyes for any of it.

For there at the front, waiting for her, stood Vittorio, tall and proud. Her breath caught in her throat. Because, outfitted in the black dress uniform of the Andachstein Guard, trimmed with gold braid and buttons, once again he looked just as he had that first night—more like a warrior, or a warlord, or even a god, than any mere mortal.

He watched her approach…didn't take his eyes off her as she took every slow step down the aisle. He was smiling a little, she noticed as they grew closer, just enough to soften the hard angles and planes of his warrior face, and in his eyes she saw approval and satisfaction, desire and maybe even a little wonderment.

But was there room in them for a little love? She wanted with all her heart to see love there.

At the last moment she noticed her family, all smiles as they passed, and there was Prince Guglielmo watching too, wearing his perpetual frown and as beady-eyed as ever.

She drew level with her groom and he offered her his arm, his amazing blue eyes searching her face.

Beautiful, he mouthed, and her heart gave a little kick that had her trembling.

Tonight she would lie with this man in the marital bed. Tonight they would consummate this unlikely marriage and be as one. All this time Vittorio had thought *he* was the one missing out, the one hard done by, but he had no idea of the sacrifice she'd made in not giving in to her desires. She wanted to be back in his arms more than he knew. She'd longed for this night, this intimacy, this connection. But she was afraid of it too, and of what it might mean.

She'd told Vittorio that she was worried that this marriage would mean losing her independence. But tonight she knew she was in danger of losing herself.

The ceremony began. The priest spoke his solemn words, music soared at intervals, and a choir filled with what sounded like angels turned hymns into the sweetest sounds she had ever heard.

Rosa felt as if she was standing outside herself, watching on. How could it be her, Rosa Ciavarro, from a tiny village in the south of Italy, standing there marrying a prince? It was unbelievable. Surreal.

When they exchanged their vows it was Vittorio who sounded confident and assured in the soaring space, whose voice didn't waver. It was Vittorio who looked her in the eye and made her want to believe that some part of this was not just an act of convenience, going through the motions, that some part of it was real.

And then they were pronounced husband and wife, and their lips met in a kiss that had her doubting again. Because it was more businesslike than affectionate. Sealing the deal.

He walked her down the aisle a married woman—a princess—and she felt numb. Shell-shocked.

In a touch of unexpected informality the guests spilled out of the cathedral behind them, full of congratulations and good wishes for the newlyweds. She found herself separated from Vittorio as they were tugged in different directions, but even that didn't matter because everyone was so happy.

Until a woman latched on to her arm. 'I suppose I should congratulate you,' she said.

Rosa turned. There was no mistaking the vampish woman, even though Cleopatra had turned honey-blonde since she'd last seen her. 'Thank you, Contessa.'

'I'll let you into a little secret, though,' the woman whispered as she air-kissed Rosa's cheeks. 'He'll never love you. His lot are incapable of it.' She smiled as she stepped back. 'So you might as well lose those stars in your eyes right now.'

Rosa gasped, too stunned to speak. Was she that obvious? Was she so transparent that everyone could see the longing to be loved written plain on her face?

And then her brothers and their wives and children were swarming around her and she was surrounded by joy and love in abundance, and she almost felt greedy that she wanted more when she already had more than some people had in a lifetime.

'Where's my wife?' she heard a booming voice say over the crowd.

My wife.

A zing of electricity sent shockwaves down her spine. Possession. It was there in his words, there in his tone.

Nothing to do with love. It was all about lust, and anticipation for the evening ahead. She knew because the time had come and she felt it too.

And then the crowd parted and Vittorio was there, larger than life. His jewel-coloured eyes lit up when he saw her. 'Ah, there you are, my Princess. We have a state reception to get to,' he said. 'But first—'

He swept her up in his arms and kissed her, to the cheers of the crowd. Not like the kiss he'd given her in the cathedral—that one had been warm but brief. Sweet. Official, even. This was a kiss that spoke of barely restrained passion, of desire that was about to be taken off the leash. A kiss that left her breathless and weak-kneed and pulsing in places that knew how Vittorio could make them feel and wanted it as much as she did.

Maybe tonight she should just let herself be possessed. Maybe tonight should be all about desire. About slaking mutual need and lust.

And tomorrow, and all the tomorrows to come, maybe then she could worry about love.

The party was still raging, the orchestra still playing and wedding guests still dancing, when Vittorio approached Rosa and growled softly in her ear, 'It's time.'

Rosa had been enjoying herself, having found ten minutes to be with her family. She'd smiled when Chiara had taken to the dance floor yet again with Marcello. Marvelled when Prince Guglielmo had accompanied Sirena to the floor for a waltz. But mostly she'd just enjoyed being in the company of her family again. Soon they'd have to return to Zecce and she'd miss them.

But now Vittorio was telling her it was time. She trembled. His breath was warm against her skin, his own scent flavoured with the cognac he'd had with coffee. It was a powerful combination. Addictive.

Her heart was thumping in her chest as they made their exit and he walked her down the long passageway, their footsteps ringing out on the stone floor, the sounds of the reception given up to silence.

She didn't talk.

There were no words. And even if there had been, her throat was too tight.

He didn't talk.

He didn't rush. His steps were measured. Unhurried.

It was nerve-racking.

Excruciating.

A flight of stairs took them to the next level and then into his apartments. By the time he opened the door to his softly lit suite her nerves were stretched to breaking point. She knew her things had been moved into his suite while the formalities took place today, but this was the first time she'd seen his room. As she took it in, the dark wood furniture, the big leather sofas and the wide expanse of the massive four-poster bed, one word immediately sprang to mind.

Masculine.

He closed the solid door behind them with an equally solid *thunk*. She jumped at the sound.

'Nervous, my Princess?' he said, close behind her.

She'd dispensed with her veil before the reception, and now there was nothing between the puff of his breath and the nape of her neck. So close that she could feel his heat.

'It's been a long day,' she said.

She would have taken a step away, but his hands were already at her shoulders, and his lips—she gasped—his lips were pressed to that place where his breath had touched. Warmth suffused her flesh and threatened to turn her bones to jelly.

'Did I tell you,' he whispered, his thumbs stroking the bare skin of her back, 'how beautiful you look today?'

She nodded. He had—though not in so many words. And he'd made her believe it.

She'd expected he'd turn her then, and pull her into his kiss, but instead his thumbs traced a line down the V at her back, his touch sparking fires under her skin.

'And I love this dress,' he said, his fingers reaching the point where the row of tiny buttons began. 'But now it's time to do something I've been itching to do all evening.'

She felt his fingers settle on the top button. His long fingers on his big hands. She wanted to protest—he would never manage to undo the tiny buttons, she would have to call for a maid to help.

But she felt the first button give. His lips pressed to the other side of her neck and she felt the brush of his hair against her skin and breathed him in. She would have turned herself then, to kiss him, to replay that wondrous deep kiss he'd given her after they were married, but he wouldn't let her, and his surprisingly nimble fingers were still working away at the buttons.

But, as with his measured steps, he didn't rush. He took his own sweet time, pressing his lips to the skin of her exposed back as his fingers moved still lower, until he reached the small of her back, where the touch of his fingers tripped a secret cord that pulled tight inside her so that her muscles clenched. His hands were nowhere near her breasts, but she felt them swell, her nipples turning to bullets.

The gown was loosening around her. 'You don't have to do them all,' she said, surprised to hear how husky her voice sounded.

He chuckled softly against her skin and the sensation reverberated through her flesh and down to her bones.

'You sound impatient, my Princess.'

If she wasn't mistaken, his voice had gone down an octave.

'Surely you don't want me to hurry the most special night of your life?'

She was, and she did,—but she wasn't about to admit that.

She was at fever pitch when she felt the last button give. She felt his hands slide down inside her dress to cup her cheeks, and then sweep up her sides to cup her breasts. Breath caught in her throat. *At last!*

Then, and only then, he turned her and lifted her face to meet his. Lips met lips. Mouth slanted across mouth. Breath intermingled. And it was like returning to a fantasy place where her every dream came true.

She groaned, protesting into their kiss as he angled her away, but only to ease her arms from the sleeves and let the gown fall in a pool at her feet.

'*Dio...*' he said, looking down at her, taking in the tiny scraps of delicate lace that barely covered her breasts and the tiny triangle that concealed the V at the apex of her thighs. Thigh-high lace-topped stockings completed her underwear. 'What are you doing to me? All day long and you were as good as naked under that gown.'

Rosa felt empowered. 'Do you like them? I made them myself.' She could see by the flare and the heat in his eyes what his answer would be before she asked the question.

'Like them?' he said, his fingers tracing the intricate gold patterns in the lace.

'It's lace made by the Andachstein Lace-Makers' Guild. I ordered it especially.'

He lifted his eyes to hers. 'Did they have any idea what you planned to do with their lace?'

He sounded as if he had a lump in his throat that it was difficult to talk past. She smiled. 'Do you think they'd mind?'

'I'm not sure, but I've got a pretty good idea you've just committed an offence against the moral fabric of Andachstein society.'

'You'd charge me?'

'No, but only on one condition.'

'Which is?'

'You let me take them off.'

She smiled, hope creeping into her heart. 'I thought you'd never ask.'

He gave a roar of triumph and swept her into his arms, placing her reverently on the bed before shedding his dress uniform. Shoes and other garments were going everywhere, until he stood naked before her, proud and erect. She gasped. Her memories had failed her. Her dreams hadn't done him justice. The man was magnificent.

And now he leaned over her, kissing her lips, his big hands in her hair, cupping her cheek, following the curve of her shoulders and seeking the clasp for her bra, finding it.

He slid the fabric away and drew back. Air hissed through his teeth before he dipped his head again and drew one nipple into his hot mouth. So hot. Her back arched as he suckled, sending spears of pleasure straight to her core, and then again when he turned his attentions to her other breast.

'So beautiful,' he said, before he scooped his hands lower, over the curve of her abdomen and the flare of her hips.

She was panting when he dipped his head and pressed his lips over the place where their unborn child lay. So gentle. So tender. She wanted more. Needed more.

But he bypassed the heated place that screamed out for his attention, and moved straight to her ankles, sliding off first one high-heeled shoe and then the other, before kissing his way up her calf and then her inner thigh, until she was molten and pulsing with need.

'Vittorio!' she cried.

'I know,' he said, his hands curled into the sides of the scrap of lace that was all that separated them. 'I feel it too,' he said, and slowly drew them down her legs.

She was burning up before he slipped a hand between her thighs and coaxed them apart. She was on fire before he slipped one finger between her lips and brushed past that tight nub of nerve-endings, inciting it to fever-pitch.

'So hot,' he said on a groan.

'Vittorio!'

'I know,' he said again, soothing her as he knelt between her legs, his big hands palming her body, her breasts, her arms, her belly, her legs, as if he couldn't get enough of the feel of her. He poised himself over her, kissed her deep and hard, devouring her like a starving man who had been served up a feast.

She welcomed him at her entrance. Cried out with the contact, with the agony and the ecstasy of it, with the frustration and the promise. Cried out again when he surged into her, filling her, pausing before he withdrew and surged in again. This was skin against skin, his skin against hers in the most intimate of contacts, and it was pure magic.

She was already on the brink, already close, when he dipped his mouth and tugged on one peaked nipple. A shooting star flashed behind her eyes, one star that became two, and then another, until her world hurtled through the path of a meteor shower and everything was light and fire and the brilliance of feeling.

She was still spinning back down to earth, still finding her place back in the world and feeling warm and delicious when she said it.

It wasn't her fault—not entirely—but she was lulled by Vittorio's big body next to hers, his strong arms still around her, their legs interwoven, and they seemed the most natural words in the world to well up inside her at that moment.

She pressed her lips to his magnificent chest, felt the squeeze of his arm at her shoulders. *'I love you.'*

She felt him stiffen. Felt every muscle in his body tense. Felt him pull away.

'Vittorio…?'

'No,' he said, his body stiff as he rolled away. 'Don't say that. I didn't ask you to say that.'

Only then did she realise that she'd spoken out loud the words branding her heart.

'Why? What's wrong? I know it's too soon. But it's how I feel.' She reached out a hand to his shoulder, feeling as if she was losing him. 'I can't help how I feel.'

He sprang from the bed. 'Did I ask you to love me?

Don't love me,' he said. 'Never love me. Because I can't love you back.'

'Vittorio—'

'Don't you remember? I was a bastard to you at Carnevale. I used you.'

'What? That's all in the past. We're beyond that. Why are you dragging it out now?'

'Because you need to remember the kind of person I am. I don't love people, Rosa.'

'But now... Surely now that we're married—'

'You *know* why I married you. If you hadn't been pregnant we wouldn't be married now. It's got nothing to do with love.'

His words stung. So what if he was speaking the truth? It was his attitude that slashed at her soul. 'But it could. What is to stop me loving you and you loving me? It's normal. It's natural.'

'Not in my world!' he yelled. 'Do you think I can simply flick a switch? So don't love me. Don't ever tell me you love me. And don't expect anything of me. It's not going to happen.'

'You just made love to me—'

'It was *sex*, Rosa. Just sex! That's all it was. It's time you understood that. That's all it can ever be.'

He stormed out of the room through a side door that slammed heavily in his wake. She heard water running. A shower. And she sensed he wouldn't be back to share her bed tonight.

She sat shell-shocked in the bed, perilously close to tears, her wedding night reduced to ashes, her hopes and dreams in tatters. But she refused to let loose the tears. She took great gulps of air until the urge to cry was suppressed, even as Sirena's words came back to haunt her.

'He'll never love you. His lot aren't capable of it.'

What was Vittorio so afraid of? He'd acted as if it was

a curse. A horrid affliction for which there was no cure and death the only release. But there was nothing to fear from love.

And he was wrong, she knew it. He *could* love. A man who had grown up from a boy who would rescue a drowning kitten. A man who rescued strays and the vulnerable. This was not a man devoid of love.

He just didn't know how to show it.

Or maybe he just didn't know how to show it to *her*. Maybe he'd loved his first wife so much that he'd never got over her death.

Rosa was too afraid to ask. That wasn't a conversation she wanted to have on their wedding night.

The new bride sniffed, a new resolution forming in her mind. She knew how to sew. She was good at stitching pieces of fabric together and making something good, something worthwhile. So she would take the tattered shreds of her hopes and dreams and stitch them back together.

Because, despite what Vittorio had told her to do, there was no way she was giving up on her hopes and dreams just yet.

CHAPTER NINETEEN

THE NEW PRINCESS of Andachstein threw herself into her role. She visited the local primary schools and read the children storybooks and every child was entranced. She gave speeches at colleges into which she incorporated her newfound knowledge of the history and the proud heritage of Andachstein.

Wherever she appeared with Vittorio they were mobbed by cheering crowds waving the Andachstein flag. And when the first pictures of her baby bump were snapped and flashed to the world by the media, satisfaction levels regarding the principality went through the roof.

And if Vittorio himself wasn't entirely happy with how things were proceeding, Prince Guglielmo was beside himself. 'You got yourself a gem there, Vittorio,' he said during their weekly meeting. 'An absolute gem.'

Vittorio couldn't disagree. Rosa was proving perfect in the role. She was proving perfect in his bed. This night of their wedding had been an aberration. She'd made no unwanted transgressions since. But then, how could she when she said nothing at all? Sure, she was passionate enough, but they made love without a word from her. It was as if she was there in body, but not in soul.

But wasn't that what he wanted?

'What is the Princess up to today?' his father asked, dragging him out of his misery.

For the first time Vittorio noticed that his father looked a little better. A little younger than he had before. It couldn't all be down to the recent haircut he'd clearly had.

Vittorio leaned one hip against the desk and tossed the crystal paperweight from one hand to the other. It spoke volumes for his father's lighter mood that he barely blinked at Vittorio's audacity. He sighed.

'She's at a meeting of the Lace-Makers Guild. She's asked to become their patron. Apparently the women were delighted to have a patron who is herself a seamstress.'

The old man nodded his approval. 'Her first solo appointment? Impressive. We're not working her too hard, are we?'

'I don't think so.'

But maybe that was the problem, Vittorio mused, looking out of the window at the harbour below. Maybe she was just tired.

He shook his head and turned back to his father. 'Rosa seems to be loving it. And the baby is growing well. Rosa just had her twenty-week scan. All is looking good.'

'Good! So we're still expecting a boy?'

Vittorio smiled. 'That is now beyond doubt.' He'd seen the unmistakable evidence on the screen himself.

The old Prince grunted. 'Excellent.' And then he sighed and walked to stand in front of one of the big picture windows, his hands clasped behind his back. 'Late November, then...' he said, his voice reflective.

'That's what they say.'

'My doctors say there is a new technique. Still risky, but less so.'

For a moment Vittorio searched for this thread in the conversation, and then his father spun around and said, 'I'm thinking I would like to see my grandson growing up. I'm thinking I should tell the doctors to go ahead with my surgery.'

'But still risky?' Vittorio queried.

'Eighty per cent chance of success, they tell me. That sounds better than one hundred per cent chance of death if I don't have it, wouldn't you say?'

Vittorio left his father in unusually high spirits. The chance offered by surgery, he guessed. That would do it.

But then he saw Sirena walking towards him. 'Contessa,' he said.

She smiled. She was dressed in what he'd heard was called a 'tea dress', all big floral skirts and a tribute to the fifties, right down to the gloves, hat and strappy shoes.

'*Buongiorno*, Vittorio,' she said, stopping to kiss him on both cheeks. 'I hope married life agrees with you.'

'What are you doing here, Contessa?' he asked, sidestepping the question. He'd hoped that now he was married she would set her sights on some other target.

'I have an appointment with Guglielmo.'

'With my father?'

'Well, not really an appointment, as such. We're having a picnic down by the lake. It's such a beautiful day for a picnic, don't you think?' She raised her eyebrows and gave a flutter of her gloved hand. 'I'd better go. He's waiting for me.'

And with a click-clack of her heels she was gone, and Vittorio was left thinking, maybe she already had.

Rosa had enjoyed her first solo appointment. She'd been right to tell Vittorio she could handle this one herself.

The women of the Lace-Makers' Guild had made her so welcome. They'd given her an amazing display of their craft—flashing hands shifting threaded bobbins and pins— and she'd been dazzled by their skills. They'd even given her a lesson in lace-making, and watched patiently while she'd attempted to follow the pattern before declaring that she was much better at using their lace in her sewing projects than creating it. Then they'd all laughed and shared late-morning tea together.

Then they'd presented her with two gifts. One a lace shawl for their baby. So fine and beautiful, with a pattern of doves cleverly tatted through it. And the second a pair of pillowcases for the royal bed. Exquisitely made, they must have taken weeks and weeks to create.

She'd promised them that they would be cherished, even if she couldn't think about her marriage bed without a tinge of sadness. It had been weeks since their marriage—weeks during which she'd said not a word during their lovemaking. Weeks during which she wasn't even sure Vittorio had noticed.

A group of children were waiting with their teachers outside the Lace-Makers' Guild, pre-schoolers from the nearby kindergarten, huddled under a shady tree, out of the hot July sun. All she wanted to do was be out of the hot sun too, and inside the air-conditioned comfort of her waiting car, being whisked back to the cool confines of the *castello* high above the town, where the summer heat didn't seem to penetrate.

But the children were waiting for her, and she wasn't about to disappoint them. She knelt down to their level just as a delivery van trundled slowly past, pulling to a stop a few houses up the street. Rosa took no notice of the man who jumped out with a parcel under his arm—she was already talking to the children.

A little boy presented her with a posy of flowers.

A little girl in a wheelchair was wheeled forward to ask a question.

'Can I be a princess when I grow up?' she asked shyly.

Rosa took her small hand in hers, and said, 'You can be anything you want.'

The little girl threw her arms around Rosa's neck and hugged her tight. And Rosa thought that it wasn't so bad, being a princess, even if your husband didn't think he could love you.

Someone shouted something up the road. There was a murmur of concerned voices, and then more shouting, but she was still disentangling herself from the girl's arms when she heard her driver call, 'Your Highness! Watch out!'

Children started shrieking. 'Run this way!' she heard one teacher call.

She turned her head to see her driver lunging for her. But there was something that would beat him. The delivery truck, bearing down on them, with a man futilely chasing after it.

Fight or flight? There was no question.

She pushed the wheelchair as hard as she could and flung herself after it.

CHAPTER TWENTY

VITTORIO WAS FURIOUS by the time he got to the hospital. Furious with himself. He should never have agreed to let Rosa go by herself today. And he was furious with everyone who might have had a part in this.

But most of all he was furious because of all the things he could have said to her and never had. All the things he *should* have said to her. And all the cruel things he'd said to her because he had been so desperate to protect himself.

'What happened?' he demanded of her driver as he marched along the disinfectant-smelling corridor in the hospital. 'I want to know everything that happened and in detail. And then I want to know *how* it happened.'

It was all the chauffeur could do to keep up with him, let alone give him a detailed account of all that had transpired.

'The delivery vehicle is being checked over now,' the man said. 'But it looks like brake failure.'

'On a damned hill, of all places,' Vittorio said, seething, 'and right above where Rosa was standing.'

'The Princess was kneeling down,' said the driver, 'talking to a child in a wheelchair. The child was hugging her. The Princess didn't know what was happening until too late.'

A doctor strode towards them. 'Prince Vittorio, I'm Dr Belosci. I'm looking after the Princess. I'll take you to her. We're prepping her for Theatre now.'

Fear slid down Vittorio's spine.

He dismissed the driver, waiting for him to be out of earshot. 'Is it the baby?' Nobody had told him there was a problem with the baby—but then nobody had mentioned Theatre either.

'No. Didn't they tell you? The baby's fine. It's Her Highness's ankle. A tree took the brunt of the crash, but a tyre snapped free with the force of the collision and caught her on the ankle.'

Breath whooshed out of Vittorio's lungs. 'She's going to be all right, then?'

'They're both going to be fine. Just as soon as we can get that ankle set. Come and see her, and then I'll show you the X-rays.'

The baby was all right, his heartbeat sound and strong. Someone had come and told her that the little girl in the wheelchair had got a bump on the head but was fine. It couldn't be better.

Rosa hugged her baby bump while she drifted in and out of dreamland. She'd told them she didn't want a fuss, that she would be just as happy back in her own bed in the *castello*, but they'd insisted, telling her she was to be attached to a drip and that she needed an operation on her ankle.

And then she'd remembered the pain as she'd waited for the ambulance and thought maybe it was better to be here in hospital after all. At least it was quiet here.

She heard voices coming down the corridor. Loud voices. No—one loud voice and one quieter. No guessing which one was Vittorio's.

She put one hand to her head. *Dio*, why had they had to tell him? Couldn't they have waited until after the operation? The baby was fine. It wasn't as if he wanted to see *her*.

The door to her room creaked open. 'Rosa?' he said.

She turned her head away. 'The baby's fine, Vittorio. Didn't they tell you?'

'Yes, they told me.'

'So, thanks for coming, but don't feel you need to stay. I'm in good hands here.'

'Rosa, I came to see *you*.'

She laughed. Maybe it was the drugs in her drip, or maybe she was just fed up with being silent, but she wasn't going to stay silent any more. 'Nice one, Vittorio, but I don't think so.'

'Rosa—'

She snapped her head around. 'What are you still doing here? Staying long enough to convince the staff we're madly in love, like you pretended to be at our wedding? Well, I don't read the tabloids—and even if I did that fantasy died a death on our wedding night, thanks to you. So I don't need you to stay, Vittorio. I don't *want* you to stay.'

But he didn't leave. Infuriatingly, he sat down in the visitor's chair beside the bed.

'For once and for all, the baby is fine. I'm sure someone here will let you know the moment that changes. Can you please go?'

She heard him sigh, and was about to snap at him again when he said, 'I didn't come here because of the baby.'

'Liar,' she said, but she was curious enough to hear what else he had to say.

'All right. I was worried about the baby. But I came because you'd been hurt and I was worried about you. Because today I realised something that has been staring me in the face for almost as long as we've been together.'

Her heart slammed into her chest wall. She barely dared to breathe waiting for him to continue. 'What did you realise?' she said when he wouldn't tell her.

'That I care for you, Rosa. I just didn't want to admit it because I was afraid you might leave me. When I heard about the accident today I thought I might lose you without ever telling you…'

'But why were you afraid I'd leave you?'

'Because my first wife did. Because she told me she loved me and she lied. Because she betrayed me, and I was scared it might happen again.'

'You thought I might *betray* you?'

He laughed. 'I know. It seems ridiculous. But I had to protect myself somehow. Not loving you—not admitting it—seemed the best way.'

She blinked up at him, wondering if he was really there, wondering if the drugs were giving her hallucinations and spinning stories that she wanted to hear. 'So what are you admitting?'

He took her free hand. 'I love you, Rosa. I'm sorry I made you sad. I'm sorry I ruined our wedding night. If I could make it up to you I would, a thousand times over.'

Tears pricked Rosa's eyes. 'Only one thousand?'

He smiled down at her and pressed his lips to hers before he said. 'Every night of our marriage. How does that sound instead?'

She smiled tremulously up at him. 'Much better. I love you so much, Vittorio.'

He gave a smile of wonderment then, as if he was exploring the new territory of these words and finding it to be everything he wanted and more. 'I love you, Rosa.'

They kissed just as the doctor bustled in.

'I'm so sorry to interrupt,' he said. 'Theatre is ready.'

'Don't be,' Vittorio said, smiling down at Rosa. 'We've got the rest of our lives to finish this.'

EPILOGUE

PRINCE GUGLIELMO ROBERTO D'MARBURG of Andachstein was born late one November morning, with a shock of black hair, a healthy set of lungs and weighing in at a very healthy four kilograms.

Measurements had been taken, paperwork completed, and the nursing staff had left now that the formalities were complete. Finally it was time for the new family to be left alone to bond.

Rosa relaxed into the pillows on the bed, her baby cradled in her arms, and leaned down to drink in his new baby breaths. 'He's so beautiful,' she said, her heart already swollen in size to accommodate this new love.

The baby yawned then, cracking open his eyes. 'Look,' she said. 'Blue eyes like sapphires. He's like a mini you.'

Vittorio sat by her side, one hand stroking his wife's still damp hair, the other under the arm holding their child, totally entranced.

'You were amazing,' he said to her. 'So strong.'

She shrugged, the pain of childbirth gone now that she was holding her reward. 'That's what women do. All around the world every day. It's not that special.'

'It's a miracle,' he said. 'Today I witnessed a miracle, performed by the woman I love.'

She smiled over at him. Things had been so different since her accident. Something had shifted in her warrior's hard and cynical heart, and the word he'd been most afraid to use and to hear was now a word she heard several times a day. And it would never grow old.

'Thank you,' she said. 'I love you, Vittorio.'

He lifted the closest of her hands and kissed it gently. 'And I love *you*. For this child you have given me. For just being you. But most of all I love you for loving me.'

Tears sprang from her eyes. Tears of joy.

'I made you cry,' he said, touching the pads of his forefingers to her eyes to wipe away the dampness.'

'Only because I'm so happy.'

'Then never stop crying,' he said, smiling. 'Thank you for rescuing me, Rosa. That day I found you lost by the bridge in Venice… I look back at that moment and I see…'

'Serendipity?' she offered.

'No,' he said. 'It was magic. Pure magic.'

And he leaned over and kissed the woman he loved.

* * * * *

THE VENETIAN
ONE-NIGHT BABY

MELANIE MILBURNE

To Mallory (Mal) and Mike Tuffy.
It was so lovely to meet you on the European
river cruise a few years ago—it must be time
for another one! It's been wonderful to continue
our friendship since. We always look forward to
seeing you in Tasmania. Xxx

CHAPTER ONE

SABRINA WAS HOPING she wouldn't run into Max Firbank again after The Kiss. He wasn't an easy man to avoid since he was her parents' favourite godson and was invited to just about every Midhurst family gathering. Birthdays, Christmas, New Year's Eve, parties and anniversaries he would spend on the fringes of the room, a twenty-first-century reincarnation of Jane Austen's taciturn Mr Darcy. He'd look down his aristocratic nose at everyone else having fun.

Sabrina made sure she had extra fun just to annoy him. She danced with everyone who asked her, chatting and working the room like she was the star student from Social Butterfly School. Max occasionally wouldn't show, and then she would spend the whole evening wondering why the energy in the room wasn't the same. But she refused to acknowledge it had anything to do with his absence.

This weekend she was in Venice to exhibit two of her designs at her first wedding expo. She felt safe from running into him—or she would have if the hotel receptionist could find her booking.

Sabrina leaned closer to the hotel reception counter. 'I can assure you the reservation was made weeks ago.'

'What name did you say it was booked under?' the young male receptionist asked.

'Midhurst, Sabrina Jane. My assistant booked it for me.'

'Do you have any documentation with you? The confirmation email?'

Had her new assistant Harriet forwarded it to her? Sabrina remembered printing out the wedding expo programme but had she printed out the accommodation details? She searched for it in her tote bag, sweat beading between her breasts, her stomach pitching with panic. She couldn't turn up flustered to her first wedding expo as an exhibitor. That's why she'd recently employed an assistant to help her with this sort of stuff. Booking flights and accommodation, sorting out her diary, making sure she didn't double book or miss appointments.

Sabrina put her lipgloss, paper diary, passport and phone on the counter, plus three pens, a small packet of tissues, some breath mints and her brand-new business cards. She left her tampons in the side pocket of her bag—there was only so much embarrassment she could handle at any one time. The only bits of paper she found were a shopping list and a receipt from her favourite shoe store.

She began to put all the items back in her bag, but her lipgloss fell off the counter, dropped to the floor, rolled across the lobby and was stopped by a large Italian-leather-clad foot.

Sabrina's gaze travelled up the long length of the expertly tailored charcoal-grey trousers and finally came to rest on Max Firbank's smoky grey-blue gaze.

'Sabrina.' His tone was less of a greeting and more of a grim *not you again*.

Sabrina gave him a tight, no-teeth-showing smile. 'Fancy seeing you here. I wouldn't have thought wedding expos were your thing.'

His eyes glanced at her mouth and something in her stomach dropped like a book tumbling off a shelf. *Kerplunk*. He blinked as if to clear his vision and bent down to pick up her lipgloss. He handed it to her, his expression as unreadable as cryptic code. 'I'm seeing a client about a project. I always stay at this hotel when I come to Venice.'

Sabrina took the lipgloss and slipped it into her bag, trying to ignore the tingling in her fingers where his had touched hers. She could feel the heat storming into her cheeks in a hot crimson tide. What sort of weird coincidence was *this*? Of all the hotels in Venice why did he have to be at *this* one? And on *this* weekend? She narrowed her gaze to the size of buttonholes. 'Did my parents tell you I was going to be here this weekend?'

Nothing on his face changed except for a brief elevation of one of his dark eyebrows. 'No. Did mine tell you I was going to be in Venice?'

Sabrina raised her chin. 'Oh, didn't you know? I zone out when your parents tell me things about you. I mentally plug my ears and sing *la-de-da* in my head until they change the subject of how amazingly brilliant you are.'

There was a flicker of movement across his lips that

could have been loosely described as a smile. 'I'll have to remember to do that next time your parents bang on about you to me.'

Sabrina flicked a wayward strand of hair out of her face. Why did she always have to look like she'd been through a wind tunnel whenever she saw him? She dared not look at his mouth but kept her eyes trained on his inscrutable gaze. Was he thinking about The Kiss? The clashing of mouths that had morphed into a passionate explosion that had made a mockery of every other kiss she'd ever received? Could he still recall the taste and texture of her mouth? Did he lie in bed at night and fantasise about kissing her again?

And not just kissing, but...

'*Signorina?*' The hotel receptionist jolted Sabrina out of her reverie. 'We have no booking under the name Midhurst. Could it have been another hotel you selected online?'

Sabrina suppressed a frustrated sigh. 'No. I asked my assistant to book me into this one. This is where the fashion show is being held. I have to stay here.'

'What's the problem?' Max asked in a calm, *leave it to me* tone.

Sabrina turned to face him. 'I've got a new assistant and somehow she must've got the booking wrong or it didn't process or something.' She bit her lip, trying to stem the panic punching against her heart. *Poomf. Poomf. Poomf.*

'I can put you on the cancellation list, but we're busy at this time of year so I can't guarantee anything,' the receptionist said.

Sabrina's hand crept up to her mouth and she started nibbling on her thumbnail. Too bad about her new manicure. A bit of nail chewing was all she had to soothe her rising dread. She wanted to be settled into her hotel, not left waiting on stand-by. What if no other hotel could take her? She needed to be close to the convention venue because she had two dresses in the fashion parade. This was her big break to get her designs on the international stage.

She. Could. Not. Fail.

'Miss Midhurst will be joining me,' Max said. 'Have the concierge bring her luggage to my room. Thank you.'

Sabrina's gaze flew to his. 'What?'

Max handed her a card key, his expression still as inscrutable as that of an MI5 spy. 'I checked in this morning. There are two beds in my suite. I only need one.'

She did *not* want to think about him and a bed in the same sentence. She'd spent the last three weeks thinking about him in a bed with her in a tangle of sweaty sexsated limbs. Which was frankly kind of weird because she'd spent most of her life deliberately *not* thinking about him. Max was her parents' godson and almost from the moment when she'd been born six years later and become his parents' adored goddaughter, both sets of parents had decided how perfect they were for each other. It was the long-wished-for dream of both families that Max and Sabrina would fall in love, get married and have gorgeous babies together.

As if. In spite of both families' hopes, Sabrina had never got on with Max. She found him brooding and distant and arrogant. And he made it no secret he found her equally annoying…which kind of made her wonder why he'd kissed her…

But she was *not* going to think about The Kiss.

She glanced at the clock over Reception, another fist of panic pummelling her heart. She needed to shower and change and do her hair and makeup. She needed to get her head in order. It wouldn't do to turn up flustered and nervous. What sort of impression would she make?

Sabrina took the key from him but her fingers brushed his and a tingle travelled from her fingers to her armpit. 'Maybe I should try and see if I can get in somewhere else…'

'What time does your convention start?'

'There's a cocktail party at six-thirty.'

Max led the way to the bank of lifts. 'I'll take you up to settle you in before I meet my client for a drink.'

Sabrina entered the brass embossed lift with him and the doors whispered shut behind them. The mirrored interior reflected Max's features from every angle. His tall and lean and athletic build. The well-cut dark brown hair with a hint of a wave. The generously lashed eyes the colour of storm clouds. The faint hollow below the cheekbones that gave him a chiselled-from-marble look that was far more attractive than it had any right to be. The aristocratic cut of nostril and upper lip, the small cleft in his chin, the square jaw that hinted at arrogance and a tendency to insist on his own way.

'Is your client female?' The question was out before Sabrina could monitor her wayward tongue.

'Yes.' His brusque one-word answer was a verbal Keep Out sign.

Sabrina had always been a little intrigued by his love life. He had been jilted by his fiancée Lydia a few days before their wedding six years ago. He had never spoken of why his fiancée had called off the wedding but Sabrina had heard a whisper that it had been because Lydia had wanted children and he didn't. Max wasn't one to brandish his subsequent lovers about in public but she knew he had them from time to time. Now thirty-four, he was a virile man in his sexual prime. And she had tasted a hint of that potency when his mouth had come down on hers and sent her senses into a tailspin from which they had not yet recovered—if they ever would.

The lift stopped on Max's floor and he indicated for her to alight before him. She moved past him and breathed in the sharp citrus scent of his aftershave—lemon and lime and something else that was as mysterious and unknowable as his personality.

He led the way along the carpeted corridor and came to a suite that overlooked the Grand Canal. Sabrina stepped over the threshold and, pointedly ignoring the twin king-sized beds, went straight to the windows to check out the magnificent view. Even if her booking had been processed correctly, she would never have been able to afford a room such as this.

'Wow…' She breathed out a sigh of wonder. 'Venice never fails to take my breath away. The light. The colours. The history.' She turned to face him, doing her best to not glance at the beds that dominated the room.

He still had his spy face on but she could sense an inner tension in the way he held himself. 'Erm… I'd appreciate it if you didn't tell anyone about this…'

The mocking arch of his eyebrow made her cheeks burn. 'This?'

At this rate, she'd have to ramp up the air-conditioning to counter the heat she was giving off from her burning cheeks. 'Me…sharing your room.'

'I wouldn't dream of it.'

'I mean, it could get really embarrassing if either of our parents thought we were—'

'We're not.' The blunt edge to his voice was a slap down to her ego.

There was a knock at the door.

Max opened the door and stepped aside as the hotel employee brought in Sabrina's luggage. Max gave the young man a tip and closed the door, locking his gaze on hers. 'Don't even think about it.'

Sabrina raised her eyebrows so high she thought they would fly off her face. 'You think I'm attracted to *you*? Dream on, buddy.'

The edge of his mouth lifted—the closest he got to a smile, or at least one he'd ever sent her way. 'I could have had you that night three weeks ago and you damn well know it.'

'*Had* me?' She glared at him. 'That kiss was…was a knee-jerk thing. It just…erm…happened. And you gave me stubble rash. I had to put on cover-up for a week.'

His eyes went to her mouth as if he was remembering the explosive passion they'd shared. He drew in an uneven breath and sent a hand through the thick pelt of his hair, a frown pulling at his forehead. 'I'm sorry. It wasn't my intention to hurt you.' His voice had a deep gravelly edge she'd never heard in it before.

Sabrina folded her arms. She wasn't ready to forgive him. She wasn't ready to forgive herself for responding to him. She wasn't ready to admit how much she'd enjoyed that kiss and how she had encouraged it by grabbing the front of his shirt and pulling his head down. Argh. Why had she done that? Neither was she ready to admit how much she wanted him to kiss her again. 'I can think of no one I would less like to "have me".'

Even repeating the coarse words he'd used turned her on. Damn him. She couldn't stop thinking about what it would be like to be *had by him*. Her sex life was practically non-existent. The only sex she'd had in the last few years had been with herself and even that hadn't been all that spectacular. She kept hoping she'd find the perfect partner to help her with her issues with physical intimacy but so far no such luck. She rarely dated anyone more than two or three times before she decided having sex with them was out of the question. Her first and only experience of sex at the age of eighteen—*had it really been ten years ago?*—had been an ego-smashing disappointment, one she was in no hurry to repeat.

'Good. Because we're not going there,' Max said.

Sabrina inched up her chin. 'You were the one who kissed me first that night. I might have returned the kiss but only because I got caught off guard.' It was big fat lie but no way was she going to admit it. Every non-verbal signal in her repertoire had been on duty that night all but begging him to kiss her. And when he finally had, she even recalled moaning at one point. Yes, moaning with pleasure as his lips and tongue had worked their magic. *Geez.* How was she going to live *that* down?

His eyes pulsed with something she couldn't quite identify. Suppressed anger or locked-down lust or both? 'You were spoiling for a fight all through that dinner party and during the trip when I gave you a lift home.'

'So? We always argue. It doesn't mean I want you to kiss me.'

His eyes held hers in a smouldering lock that made the backs of her knees fizz. 'Are we arguing now?' His tone had a silky edge that played havoc with her senses.

Sabrina took a step back, one of her hands coming up her neck where her heart was beating like a panicked pigeon stuck in a pipe. 'I need to get ready for the c-cocktail party...' Why, oh, why did she have to sound so breathless?

He gave a soft rumble of a laugh. 'Your virtue is safe, Sabrina.' He walked to the door of the suite and turned to look at her again. 'Don't wait up. I'll be late.'

Sabrina gave him a haughty look that would have done a Regency spinster proud. 'Going to *have* your client, are you?'

He left without another word, which, annoyingly, left her with the painful echo of hers.

Max closed the door of his suite and let out a breath. Why had he done the knight in shining armour thing? Why should he care if she couldn't get herself organised enough to book a damn hotel? She would have found somewhere to stay, surely. But no. He had to do the decent thing. Nothing about how he felt about Sabrina was decent—especially after that kiss. He'd lost count of how many women he'd kissed. He wasn't a man whore, but he enjoyed sex for the physical release it gave.

But he couldn't get *that* kiss out of his mind.

Max had always avoided Sabrina in the past. He hadn't wanted to encourage his and her parents from their sick little fantasy of them getting it on. He got it on with women he chose and he made sure his choices were simple and straightforward—sex without strings.

Sabrina was off limits because she was the poster girl for the happily-ever-after fairytale. She was looking for Mr Right to sweep her off her feet and park her behind a white picket fence with a double pram with a couple of chubby-cheeked progeny tucked inside.

Max had nothing against marriage, but he no longer wanted it for himself. Six years ago, his fiancée had called off their wedding, informing him she had fallen in love with someone else, with someone who wanted children—the children Max refused to give her. Prior to that, Lydia had been adamant she was fine with his decision not to have kids. He'd thought everything was ticking along well enough in their relationship. He'd been more annoyed than upset at Lydia calling off their relationship. It had irritated him that he hadn't seen it coming.

But it had taught him a valuable lesson. A lesson he was determined he would never have to learn again. He wasn't cut out for long-term relationships. He didn't have what it took to handle commitment and all its responsibilities.

He knew marriage worked for some people—his parents and Sabrina's had solid relationships that had been tried and tested and triumphed over tragedy, especially his parents. The loss of his baby brother Daniel at the age of four months had devastated them, of course.

Max had been seven years old and while his parents had done all they could to shield him from the tragedy, he still carried his share of guilt. In spite of the coroner's verdict of Sudden Infant Death Syndrome, Max could never get it out of his mind that he had been the last person to see his baby brother alive. There wasn't a day that went by when he didn't think of his brother, of all the years Daniel had missed out on. The milestones he would never meet.

Max walked out of his hotel and followed the Grand Canal, almost oblivious to the crowds of tourists that flocked to Venice at this time of year. Whenever he thought of Daniel, a tiny worm of guilt burrowed its way into his mind. Was there something he could have done to save his brother? Why hadn't he noticed something? Why hadn't he checked him more thoroughly? The lingering guilt he felt about Daniel was something he was almost used to now. He was almost used to feeling the lurch of dread in his gut whenever he saw a small baby. Almost.

Max stepped out of the way of a laughing couple that were walking arm in arm, carrying the colourful Venetian masks they'd bought from one of the many vendors along the canal. Why hadn't he thought to book a room at another hotel for Sabrina? It wasn't as if he couldn't afford it. He'd made plenty of money as a world-acclaimed architect, and he knew things were a little tight with her financially as she was still building up her wedding-dress design business and stubbornly refusing any help from her doctor parents, who had made it no secret that they would have preferred her to study medicine like them and Sabrina's two older brothers.

Had he *wanted* her in his room? Had he instinctively seized at the chance to have her to himself so he could kiss her again?

Maybe do more than kiss her?

Max pulled away from the thought like he was stepping back from a too-hot fire. But that's exactly what Sabrina was—hot. Too hot. She made him hot and bothered and horny as hell. The way she picked fights with him just to get under his skin never failed to get his blood pumping. Her cornflower-blue eyes would flash and sparkle, and her soft and supple mouth would fling cutting retorts his way, and it would make him feel alive in a way he hadn't in years.

Alive and energised.

But no. No. No. No. No.

He must *not* think about Sabrina like that. He had to keep his distance. He had to. She wasn't the sex without strings type. She wasn't a fling girl; she was a fairytale girl. And she was his parents' idea of his ideal match—his soul mate or something. Nothing against his parents, but they were wrong. Dead wrong. Sabrina was spontaneous and creative and disorganised. He was logical, responsible and organised to the point of pedantic. How could anyone think they were an ideal couple? It was crazy. He only had to spend a few minutes with her and she drove him nuts.

How was he going to get through a whole weekend with her?

CHAPTER TWO

Sabrina was a little late getting to the cocktail party, which was being held in a private room at the hotel. Only the designers and models and their agents and select members of the press were invited. She entered the party room with her stomach in a squirming nest of nibbling and nipping nerves. Everyone looked glamorous and sophisticated. She was wearing a velvet dress she'd made herself the same shade of blue as her eyes and had scooped her hair up into a bun and paid extra attention to her makeup—hence why she was late to the party.

A waiter came past with a tray of drinks and Sabrina took a glass of champagne and took a generous sip to settle her nerves. She wasn't good at networking…well, not unless she was showing off in front of Max. She always worried she might say the wrong thing or make a social faux pas that would make everyone snigger at her.

Large gatherings reminded her of the school formal the day after she'd slept with her boyfriend for the first time. The rumourmongers had been at work, fuelled by the soul-destroying text messages her boyfriend had sent to all his mates. Sabrina had heard each cruelly taunting comment, seen every mocking look cast in her direction from people she had thought were her friends.

She had stood behind a column in the venue to try and escape the shameful whispers and had heard her boyfriend tell a couple of his mates what a frigid lay she had been. The overwhelming sense of shame had been crippling. Crucifying.

Sabrina sipped some more champagne and fixed a smile on her face. She had to keep her head and not time-travel. She wasn't eighteen any more. She was twenty-eight and ran her own business, for pity's sake. She. Could. Do. This.

'You're Sabrina Midhurst, aren't you?' a female member of the press said, smiling. 'I recognised you from the expo programme photo. You did a friend's wedding dress. It was stunning.'

'Yes, that's me,' Sabrina said, smiling back. 'And I'm glad you liked your friend's dress.'

'I'd like to do a feature article on you.' The woman handed Sabrina a card with her name and contact details on it. 'I'm Naomi Nettleton, I'm a freelancer but I've done articles for some big-name fashion magazines. There's a lot of interest in your work. Would you be interested in giving me an interview? Maybe we could grab a few minutes after this?'

Sabrina could barely believe her ears. An interview in a glossy magazine? That sort of exposure was gold dust. Her Love Is in the Care boutique in London was small and she'd always dreamed of expanding. She and her best friend Holly Frost, who was a wedding florist, hoped to set up their shops side by side in Bloomsbury in order to boost each other's trade. At the moment, they were blocks away from each other but Sabrina knew it would be a brilliant business move if they could pull it off.

She wanted to prove to her doctor parents the creative path she'd chosen to follow wasn't just a whim but a viable business venture. She came from a long line of medicos. Her parents, her grandparents and both her brothers were all in the medical profession. But she had never wanted that for herself. She would much rather have a tape measure around her neck than a stethoscope.

She had been drawing wedding gowns since she was five years old. All through her childhood she had made dresses out of scraps of fabric. She had dressed every doll and teddy bear or soft toy she'd possessed in wedding finery. All through her teens she had collected scrapbooks with hundreds of sketches and cuttings from magazines. She'd had to withstand considerable family pressure in order to pursue her dream and success was her way of proving she had made the right choice.

Sabrina arranged to meet the journalist in the bar downstairs after the party. She continued to circulate, speaking with the models who had been chosen to wear her designs and also with the fashion parade manager who had personally invited her to the event after her daughter had bought one of Sabrina's designs.

She took another glass of champagne off a passing waiter.

Who said word of mouth didn't still work?

Max came back to the hotel after the dinner with his client had gone on much later than he'd originally planned.

He hadn't intended having more than a drink with Loretta Barossi but had ended up lingering over a meal with her because he hadn't wanted to come back to his room before Sabrina was safely tucked up and, hopefully, asleep in bed. Unfortunately, he'd somehow given the thirty-six-year-old recently divorced woman the impression he'd been enjoying her company far more than he had, and then had to find a way to politely reject her broadly hinted invitation to spend the night with her. But that was another line he never crossed—mixing business with pleasure.

He was walking past the bar situated off the lobby when he saw Sabrina sitting on one of the plush sofas talking to a woman and a man who was holding a camera in his lap. As if she sensed his presence, Sabrina turned her glossy honey-brown head and saw him looking at her. She raised her hand and gave him a surreptitious fingertip wave and the woman with her glanced to see to whom she was waving. The woman leaned forward to say something to Sabrina, and even from this distance Max could see the rush of a blush flooding Sabrina's creamy cheeks.

He figured the less people who saw him with Sabrina the better, but somehow he found himself walking towards her before he could stop himself. What had the other woman said to make Sabrina colour up like that?

Sabrina's eyes widened when he approached their little party and she reached for her glass of champagne and promptly knocked it over. 'Oops. Sorry. I—'

'You're Max Firbank, the award-winning architect,' the young woman said, rising to offer her hand. 'I've seen an article about your work in one of the magazines I worked for a couple of years ago. When Sabrina said she was sharing a room with a friend, I didn't realise she was referring to you.' Her eyebrows suggestively rose over the word *friend.*

Sabrina had stopped trying to mop up her drink with a paper napkin and stood, clutching the wet and screwed-up napkin in her hand. 'Oh, he's not *that* sort of friend,' she said with a choked little laugh. 'I had a problem with my booking and Max offered me his bed, I mean *a* bed. He has two. Two big ones—they look bigger than king-sized, you could fit a dozen people in each. It's a huge room, so much space we hardly know the other is there, isn't that right, Max?' She turned her head to look at him and he almost had to call for a fire extinguisher because her cheeks were so fiery red.

Max wasn't sure why he slipped his arm around her slim waist and drew her to his body. Maybe it was because she was kind of cute when she got flustered and he liked being able to get under her skin for a change, the way she got under his. Besides, he didn't know any other woman he could make blush more than her. And, yes, he got a kick out of touching her, especially after That Kiss, which she enjoyed as much as he had, even though she was intent on denying it. 'You don't have to be shy about our relationship, baby.' He flashed one of his rare smiles. 'We're both consenting adults.'

'Aw, don't you make a gorgeous couple?' the woman said. 'Tim, get a photo of them,' she said to the man holding the camera. 'I'll include it in the article about

Sabrina's designs. That is, if you don't have any objection?'

Hell, yeah. He had one big objection. He didn't mind teasing a blush or two out of Sabrina but if his family got a whiff of him sharing a room with her in Venice they would be measuring him for a morning suit and booking the church. Max held up his hand like a stop sign. 'Sorry. I don't make a habit of broadcasting my private life in the press.'

The woman sighed and handed him a business card. 'Here are my details if you change your mind.'

'I won't.' He gave both the journalist and the photographer a polite nod and added, 'It was nice meeting you. If you'll excuse us? It's been a big day for Sabrina. She needs her beauty sleep.'

Sabrina followed Max to the lift but there were other people waiting to use it as well so she wasn't able to vent her spleen. What was he thinking? She'd been trying to play down her relationship with Max to the journalist, but he'd given Naomi Nettleton the impression they were an item. She stood beside him in the lift as it stopped and started as it delivered guests to their floors.

Max stood calmly beside her with his expression in its customary inscrutable lines, although she sensed there was a mocking smile lurking behind the screen of his gaze. She moved closer to him to allow another guest into the lift on level ten and placed her high heel on Max's foot and pressed down with all her weight. He made a grunting sound that sounded far sexier than she'd expected and he placed the iron band of his arm around her middle and drew her back against him so her back was flush against his pelvis.

Her mind swam with images of them locked together in a tangle of sweaty limbs, his body driving into hers. Even now she could feel the swell of his body, the rush of blood that told her he was as aroused as she was. Her breathing quickened, her legs weakened, her heart rate rocketed. The steely strength of his arm lying across her stomach was burning a brand into her flesh. Her inner core tensed, the electric heat of awakened desire coursing through her in pulses and flickers.

The mirrors surrounding them reflected their intimate clinch from a thousand angles but Sabrina wasn't prepared to make a scene in front of the other guests, one of whom she had seen at the cocktail party. After all, she had a professional image to uphold and slapping Max's face—if indeed she was the sort of person to inflict violence on another person—was not the best way to maintain it.

But, oh, how she longed to slap both his cheeks until they were as red as hers. Then she would elbow him in the ribs and stomp on his toes. Then she would rip the clothes from his body, score her fingernails down his chest and down his back until he begged for mercy. But wait...why was she thinking of ripping his clothes off his body? No. No. No. She must not think about Max without clothes. She must not think about him naked.

She. Must. Not.

Max unlocked the door and she brushed past him and almost before he had time to close it she let fly. 'What the hell were you playing at down there? You gave the impression we were sleeping together. What's *wrong* with you? You know how much I hate you. Why did you—?'

'You don't hate me.' His voice was so calm it made hers sound all the more irrational and childish.

'If I didn't before, I do now.' Sabrina poked him in the chest. 'What was all that about in the lift?'

He captured her by the waist and brought her closer, hip to hip, his eyes more blue than grey and glinting with something that made her belly turn over. 'You know exactly what it was about. And just like that kiss, you enjoyed every second of it. Deny it if you dare.'

Sabrina intended to push away from him but somehow her hands grabbed the front of his jacket instead. He smelt like sun-warmed lemons and her senses were as intoxicated as if she had breathed in a potent aroma. An aroma that made her forget how much she hated him and instead made her want him with every throbbing traitorous cell of her body. Or maybe she was tipsy from all the champagne she'd had downstairs at the party and in the bar. It was making her drop her inhibitions. Sabotaging her already flagging self-control. Her head was spinning a little but didn't it always when he looked at her like that?

His mouth was tilted in a cynical slant, the dark stubble around his nose and mouth more obvious now than earlier that evening. It gave him a rakish air that was strangely attractive. Dangerously, deliciously attractive. She was acutely aware of every point of contact with his body: her hips, her breasts and her belly where his belt buckle was pressing.

And not just his belt buckle, but the proud surge of his male flesh—a heady reminder of the lust that simmered and boiled and blistered between them.

The floor began to shift beneath her feet and Sabrina's hands tightened on his jacket. The room was moving, pitching like a boat tossed about on a turbulent ocean. Her head felt woolly, her thoughts trying to push through the fog like a hand fumbling for a light switch in the dark. But then a sudden wave of nausea assailed her and she swayed and would have toppled backwards if Max hadn't countered it with a firm hand at her back.

'Are you okay?' His voice had a note of concern but it came from a long way off as if he was speaking to her through a long vacuum.

She was vaguely aware of his other hand coming to grasp her by the shoulder to stabilise her, but then her vision blurred and her stomach contents threatened mutiny. She made a choking sound and pushed Max back and stumbled towards the bathroom.

To her mortifying shame, Max witnessed the whole of the undignified episode. But she was beyond caring. And besides, it had been quite comforting to have her hair held back from her face and to have the soft press of a cool facecloth on the back of her neck.

Sabrina sat back on her heels when the worst of it was over. Her head was pounding and her stomach felt as it if had been scraped with a sharp-edged spoon and then rinsed out with hydrochloric acid.

He handed her a fresh facecloth, his expression wry. 'Clearly I need some work on my seduction routine.'

Sabrina managed a fleeting smile. 'Funny ha-ha.'

She dragged herself up from the floor with considerable help from him, his hands warm and steady and impossibly strong. 'Argh. I should never drink on an empty stomach.'

'Wasn't there any food at the cocktail party?'

'I got there late.' She turned to inspect her reflection in the bathroom mirror and then wished she hadn't. Could she look any worse? She could almost guarantee none of the super-sophisticated women he dated ever disgraced themselves by heaving over the toilet bowl. She turned back around. 'Sorry you had to witness that.'

'You need to drink some water. Lots of it, otherwise you're going to have one hell of a hangover in the morning.' His frown and stern tone reminded her of a parent lecturing a binge-drinking teenager.

'I don't normally drink much but I was nervous.'

His frown deepened and he reached for a glass on the bathroom counter and filled it from the tap and then handed it to her. 'Is this a big deal for you? This wedding expo?'

Sabrina took the glass from him and took a couple of sips to see how her stomach coped. 'It's the first time I've been invited to exhibit some of my designs. It's huge for me. It can take new designers years to get noticed but luckily the fashion show floor manager's daughter bought one of my dresses and she liked it so much she invited me along. And then Naomi, the journalist in the bar, asked for an interview for a feature article. It's a big opportunity for me to get my name out there, especially in Europe.' She drained the glass of water and handed it back to him.

He dutifully refilled it and handed it back, his frown still carving a trench between his brows. 'What did you tell her about us?'

'Nothing. I didn't even mention your name. I just said I was sharing a room with a friend.'

'Are you sure you didn't mention me?'

Sabrina frowned. 'Why would I link my name with yours? Do you think I want anyone back home to know we're sharing a room? Give me a break. I'm not *that* stupid. If I let that become common knowledge our parents will have wedding invitations in the post before you can blink.' She took a breath and continued, 'Anyway, you were the one who made it look like we were having a dirty weekend. You called me "baby", for God's sake.'

'Drink your water,' he said as if she hadn't spoken. 'You need to get some rest if you want to look your best for tomorrow.'

Sabrina scowled at him over the top of her glass. 'Do you have to remind me I look a frightful mess?'

He released a slow breath. 'I'll see you in the morning. Goodnight.'

When Sabrina came out of the bathroom after a shower there was no sign of him in the suite. She wondered if he'd left to give her some privacy or whether he had other plans. Why should she care if he hooked up with someone for a night of unbridled passion? She pulled down the covers on one of the beds and slipped between the cool and silky sheets and closed her eyes...

Max went for a long walk through the streets and alleys of Venice to clear his head. He could still feel the imprint of Sabrina's body pressing against him in the lift. He'd been hard within seconds. His fault for holding her like that, but the temptation had caught him off guard. Had it been his imagination or had she leaned back into him?

He wanted her.

He hated admitting it. Loathed admitting it but there it was. He was in lust with her. He couldn't remember when he'd started noticing her in that way. It had crept up on him over the last few months. The way his body responded when she looked at him in a certain way. The way his blood surged when she stood up to him and flashed her blue eyes at him in defiance. The way she moved her dancer-slim body making him fantasise about how she would look naked.

He had to get over it. Ignore it or something. Having a fling with Sabrina would hurt too many people. Hadn't he hurt his parents enough? If he started a fling with her everyone would get their hopes up that it would become permanent.

He didn't do permanent.

He would get his self-control back in line and get through the weekend without touching her. He opened and closed his hands, trying to rid himself of the feeling of her soft skin. Trying to remove the sensation of her touch. What was wrong with him? Why couldn't he just ignore her the way he had for most of his adult life? He'd always kept his distance. Always. He avoided speaking with her. He had watched from the sidelines as she'd spoken to everyone at the various gatherings they'd both attended.

There was no way a relationship between them would work. Not even a short-term one. She had fairytale written all over her. She came from a family of doctors and yet she had resisted following the tradition and become a wedding-dress designer instead. Didn't that prove how obsessed with the fairytale she was?

His mistake had been kissing her three weeks ago. He didn't understand how he had gone from arguing with her over something to finding her pulling his head down and then his mouth coming down on hers and... He let out a shuddering breath. Why was he *still* thinking about that damn kiss? The heat of their mouths connecting had tilted the world on its axis, or at least it had felt like it at the time. He could have sworn the floor had shifted beneath his feet. If he closed his eyes he could still taste her sweetness, could still feel the soft pliable texture of her lips moving against his, could still feel the sexy dart of her tongue.

The worst of it was he had lost control. Desire had swept through him and he still didn't know how he'd stopped himself from taking her then and there. And *that* scared the hell of out him.

It would not—*could* not—happen again.

When Max entered the suite in the early hours of the morning, Sabrina was sound asleep, curled up like a kitten, her brown hair spilling over the pillow. One of her hands was tucked under the cheek; the other was lying on the top of the covers. She was wearing a cream satin nightie for he could see the delicate lace trim across her décolletage peeking out from where the sheet was lying across her chest.

The desire to slip into that bed and pull her into his arms was so strong he had to clench his hands into fists. He clearly had to do something about his sex life if he was ogling the one woman he wanted to avoid. When was the last time he'd been with someone? A month? Two…or was it three? He'd been busy working on multiple projects, which hadn't left much time for a social life. Not that he had a much of a social life. He preferred his own company so he could get on with his work.

Work. That's what he needed to concentrate on. He moved past the bed to go to the desk where he had set up his laptop the day before. He opened one of the accounts he was working on and started tinkering.

There was a rustle from the bed behind him and Sabrina's drowsy voice said, 'Do you have to do that now?'

Max turned around to look at her in the muted light coming off his laptop screen. Her hair was a cloud of tangles and one of her cheeks had a linen crease and one spaghetti-thin strap of her nightie had slipped off her shoulder, revealing the upper curve of her left breast. She looked sleepy, sexy and sensual and lust hit him like a sucker punch. 'Sorry. Did I wake you?'

She pushed back some of her hair with her hand. 'Don't you *ever* sleep?'

I would if there wasn't a gorgeously sexy woman lying in the bed next to mine.

Max kept his features neutral but his body was thrumming, hardening, aching. 'How's your head? Have the construction workers started yet?'

Her mouth flickered with a sheepish smile. 'Not yet. The water helped.'

He pushed a hand through his hair and suppressed a yawn. 'Can I get you anything?'

'You don't have to wait on me, Max.' She peeled back the bed covers and swung her slim legs over the edge of the bed. She padded over to the bar fridge and opened it, the light spilling from inside a golden shaft against her long shapely legs.

'Hair of the dog?' Max injected a cautionary note in his tone.

She closed the fridge and held up a chocolate bar. 'Nope. Chocolate is the best hangover cure.'

He shrugged and turned back to his laptop. 'Whatever works, I guess.'

The sound of her unwrapping the chocolate bar was loud in the silence. Then he heard her approaching from behind, the soft *pfft, pfft, pfft* of her footsteps on the carpet reminding him of a stealthy cat. He smelt the fragrance of her perfume dance around his nostrils, the sweet peas and lilacs with an understory of honeysuckle—or was it jasmine?

'Is that one of your designs?' She was standing so close behind him every hair on the back of his neck lifted. Tensed. Tickled. Tightened.

'Yeah.'

She leaned over his shoulder, some of her hair brushing his face, and he had to call on every bit of self-control he possessed not to touch her. Her breath smelt of chocolate and temptation. In the soft light her skin had a luminous glow, the creamy perfection of her skin making him ache to run his finger down the slope of her cheek. He let out the breath he hadn't realised he'd been holding and clicked the computer mouse. 'Here. I'll give you a virtual tour.' He showed her the presentation he'd been working on for a client, trying to ignore the closeness of her body.

'Wow…' She smiled and glanced at him, her head still bent close to his. 'It's amazing.'

Max couldn't tear his eyes away from the curve of her mouth. Its plump ripeness, the top lip just as full as the lower one and the neat definition of the philtrum ridge below her nose. He met her gaze and something in the atmosphere changed. The silence so intense he was sure he could hear his blood pounding. He could certainly feel it—it was swelling his groin to a painful tightness. He put his hand down on hers where it was resting on the desk, holding it beneath the gentle but firm pressure of his. He felt her flinch as if his touch electrified her and her eyes widened into shimmering pools of cornflower blue.

The tip of her tongue swept over her lips, her breath coming out in a jagged stream. 'Max…' Her voice was whisper soft, tentative and uncertain.

He lifted her hand from the desk and toyed with her fingers, watching every micro-expression on her face. Her skin was velvet soft and he was getting off thinking about her hands stroking his body. Stroking *him*. Was she thinking about it? About the heat they generated? About the lust that swirled and simmered and sizzled between them? She kept glancing at his mouth, her throat rising and falling over a series of delicate swallows. Her breathing was uneven. He was still seated and she was standing, but because of the height ratio, he was just about at eye level with her breasts.

But the less he thought about her breasts the better.

Max released her hand and rose from the desk chair in an abrupt movement. 'Go back to bed, Sabrina.' He knew he sounded as stern as a schoolmaster but he had to get the damn genie back in the lamp. The genie of lust. The wicked genie that had been torturing him since he'd foolishly kissed Sabrina three weeks ago.

'I was sound asleep in bed before you started tapping away at your computer.' Sabrina's tone was tinged with resentment.

Max let out a long slow breath. 'I don't want to argue with you. Now go to—'

'Why don't you want to argue with me?' Her eyes flashed blue sparks. 'Because you might be tempted to kiss me again?'

He kept his expression under lockdown. 'We're not doing this, Sabrina.'

'Not doing what?' Her mouth was curved in a mocking manner. 'You were going to kiss me again, weren't you? Go on. Admit it.'

Max gave his own version of a smile and shook his head as if he was dealing with a misguided child. 'No. I was not going to kiss you.'

She straightened her shoulders and folded her arms. 'Liar.'

Max held her gaze, his body throbbing with need. No one could get him as worked up as her. No one. Their verbal banter was a type of foreplay. When had it started to become like that? For years, their arguments had just been arguments—the clash of two strong-willed personalities. But over the last few months something had changed. Was that why he'd gone to the dinner party of a mutual friend because he'd known she'd be there? Was that why he'd offered to drive her home because her car was being serviced? There had been other people at the dinner who could have taken her but, no, he'd insisted.

He couldn't even recall what they'd been arguing about on the way home or who had started it. But he remembered all too well how it had ended and he had to do everything in his power to make sure it never happened again. 'Why would I kiss you again? You don't want another dose of stubble rash, do you?'

Her combative expression floundered for a moment and her teeth snagged her lower lip. 'Okay…so I might have been lying about that…'

Max kept his gaze trained on hers. 'You're not asking me to kiss you, are you?'

The sparkling light of defiance was back in her eyes. 'Of course not.' She gave a spluttering laugh as if the idea was ludicrous. 'I would rather kiss a cane toad.'

'Good.' He slammed his lips shut on the word. 'Better keep it that way.'

CHAPTER THREE

SABRINA STALKED BACK to her bed, climbed in and pulled the covers up to her chin. Of course she'd wanted Max to kiss her. And she was positive he'd wanted to kiss her too. It secretly thrilled her that he found her so attractive. Why wouldn't it thrill her? She had all the usual female needs and she hadn't made love with a man since she was eighteen.

Not that what had happened back then could be called, by any stretch of the imagination, making love. It had been selfish one-sided sex. She had been little more than a vessel for her boyfriend to use to satisfy his base needs. She'd naively thought their relationship had been more than that. Much more. She had thought herself in love. She hadn't wanted her first time to be with someone who didn't care about her. She had been so sure Brad loved her. He'd even told her he loved her. But as soon as the deed was done he was gone. He'd dumped her and called her horrible names to his friends that still made her cringe and curl up in shame.

Sabrina heard Max preparing for bed. He went into the bathroom and brushed his teeth, coming out a few minutes later dressed in one of the hotel bathrobes. Was he naked under that robe? Her mind raced with images of his tanned and toned flesh, her body tingling at the thought of lying pinned beneath him in the throes of sizzling hot sex.

She couldn't imagine Max ever leaving a lover unsatisfied. He only had to look at her and she was halfway to an orgasm. It was embarrassing how much she wanted him. It was like lust had hijacked her body, turning her into a wanton woman who could think of nothing but earthly pleasures. Even now her body felt restless, every nerve taut with the need for touch. *His* touch. Was it possible to hate someone and want them at the same time? Or was there something wrong with her? Why was she so fiercely attracted to someone she could barely conduct a civil conversation with without it turning into a blistering argument?

But why *did* they always argue?

And why did she find it so…so stimulating?

It was a little lowering to realise how much she enjoyed their verbal spats. She looked forward to them. She got secretly excited when she knew he was going to be at a function she would be attending, even though she pretended otherwise to her family. No wonder she found joint family functions deadly boring if he didn't show up. Did she have some sort of disorder? Did she crave negative interaction with him because it was the only way she could get him to notice her?

Sabrina closed her eyes when Max walked past her bed, every pore of her body aware of him. She heard the sheets being pulled back and the sound of him slipping between them. She heard the click of the bedside lamp being switched off and then he let out a sigh that sounded bone-weary.

'I hope you don't snore.' The comment was out before she could stop herself.

He gave a sound that might have been a muttered curse but she couldn't quite tell. 'No one's complained so far.'

A silence ticked, ticked, ticked like an invisible clock.

'I probably should warn you I've been known to sleepwalk,' Sabrina said.

'I knew that. Your mother told me.'

She turned over so she was facing his bed. There was enough soft light coming in through the gap in the curtains for her to see him. He was lying on his back with his eyes closed, the sheets pulled to the level of his waist, the gloriously naked musculature of his chest making her mouth water. He looked like a sexy advertisement for luxury bed linen. His tanned skin a stark contrast to the white sheets. 'When did she tell you?'

'Years ago.'

Sabrina propped herself up on one elbow. 'How many years ago?'

He turned his head in her direction and opened one eye. 'I don't remember. What does it matter?'

She plucked at the sheet covering her breasts. What else had her mother told him about her? 'I don't like the thought of her discussing my private details with you.'

He closed his eye and turned his head back to lie flat on the pillow. 'Bit late for that, sweetheart.' His tone was so dry it could have soaked up an oil spill. 'Your parents have been citing your considerable assets to me ever since you hit puberty.'

Sabrina could feel her cheeks heating. She knew exactly how pushy her parents had been. But so too had his parents. Both families had engineered situations where she and Max would be forced together, especially since his fiancée Lydia had broken up with him just before their wedding six years ago. She even wondered if the family pressure had actually scared poor Lydia off. What woman wanted to marry a man whose parents staunchly believed she wasn't the right one for him? His parents had hardly been subtle about their hopes. It had been mildly embarrassing at first, but over the years it had become annoying. So annoying that Sabrina had stubbornly refused to acknowledge any of Max's good qualities.

And he had many now that she thought about it. He was steady in a crisis. He thought before he spoke. He was hard working and responsible and organised. He was a supremely talented architect and had won numerous awards for his designs. But she had never heard him boast about his achievements. She had only heard about them via his parents.

Sabrina lay back down with a sigh. 'Yeah, well, hate to tell you but your parents have been doing the same about you.' She kicked out the rumples in her bed linen with her feet and added, 'Anyone would think you were a saint.'

'I'm hardly that.'

There was another silence.

'Thanks for letting me share your room,' she said. 'I don't know what I would have done if you hadn't offered. I heard from other people at the cocktail party that just about everywhere else is full.'

'It's fine. Glad to help.'

She propped herself back on her elbow to look at him. 'Max?'

He made a sound that sounded like a *God, give me strength* groan. 'Mmm?'

'Why did you and Lydia break up?' Sabrina wasn't sure why she'd asked the question other than she had always wondered what had caused his fiancée to cancel their wedding at short notice. She'd heard the gossip over the children issue but she wanted to hear the truth from him.

The movement of his body against the bed linen sounded angry. And the air seemed to tighten in the room as if the walls and ceiling and the furniture had collectively taken a breath.

'Go to sleep, Sabrina.' His tone had an intractable *don't push it* edge.

Sabrina wanted to push it. She wanted to push him into revealing more about himself. There was so much she didn't know about him. There were things he never spoke about—like the death of his baby brother. But then neither did his parents speak about Daniel. The tragic loss of an infant was always devastating and even though Max had been only seven years old at the time, he too would have felt the loss, especially with his parents so distraught with grief. Sometimes she saw glimpses of his parents' grief even now. A certain look would be exchanged between Gillian and Bryce Firbank and their gazes would shadow as if they were remembering their baby boy. 'Someone told me it was because she wanted kids and you didn't. Is that true?'

He didn't answer for such a long moment she thought he must have fallen asleep. But then she heard the sound of the sheets rustling and his voice broke through the silence. 'That and other reasons.'

'Such as?'

He released a frustrated-sounding sigh. 'She fell in love with someone else.'

'Did you love her?'

'I was going to marry her, wasn't I?' His tone had an edge of impatience that made her wonder if he had been truly in love with his ex-fiancée. He had never seemed to her to be the falling-in-love type. He was too self-contained. Too private with his emotions. Sabrina remembered meeting Lydia a couple of times and feeling a little surprised she and Max were a couple about to be married. The chemistry between them had been on the mild instead of the wild side.

'Lydia's divorced now, isn't she?' Sabrina continued after a long moment. 'I wonder if she ever thinks she made the wrong decision.'

He didn't answer but she could tell from his breathing he wasn't asleep.

Sabrina closed her eyes, willing herself to relax, but sleep was frustratingly elusive. Her body was too strung out, too aware of Max lying so close by. She listened to the sound of him breathing and the slight rustle of the sheets when he changed position. After a while his breathing slowed and the rustling stopped and she realised he was finally asleep.

She settled back down against the pillows with a sigh...

Max could hear a baby crying...the sound making his skin prickle with cold dread. Where was the baby? What was wrong with it? Why was it crying? Why wasn't anyone going to it? Should he try and settle it? Then he saw the cot, his baby brother's cot...it was empty... Then he saw the tiny white coffin with the teddy bear perched on top. *No. No. No.*

'Max. Max.' Sabrina's voice broke through the nightmare. 'You're having a bad dream. Wake up, Max. Wake up.'

Max opened his eyes and realised with a shock he was holding her upper arms in a deathly grip. She was practically straddling him, her hair tousled from being in bed or from him manhandling her. He released her and let out a juddering breath, shame and guilt coursing through him like a rush of ice water. 'I'm sorry. Did I hurt you?' He winced when he saw the full set of his fingerprints on her arms.

She rubbed her hands up and down her arms, her cheeks flushed. 'I'm okay. But you scared the hell out of me.'

Max pushed back the sheets and swung his legs over the edge of the bed, his back facing her. He rested his hands on his thighs, trying to get his heart rate back to normal. Trying not to look at those marks on her arms. Trying not to reach for her.

Desperately trying not to reach for her.

'Max?' Her voice was as soft as the hand she laid on his shoulder.

'Go back to sleep.'

She was so close to him he could feel her breath on the back of his neck. He could feel her hair tickling his shoulder and he knew if he so much as turned his head to look at her he would be lost. It had been years since he'd had a nightmare. They weren't as frequent as in the early days but they still occasionally occurred. Catching him off guard, reminding him he would never be free from the pain of knowing he had failed his baby brother.

'Do you want to talk about your nightmare?' Sabrina said. 'It might help you to—'

'No.'

Sabrina's soft hand was moving up and down between his shoulder blades in soothing strokes. His skin lifted in a shiver, his blood surging to his groin. Her hand came up and began to massage the tight muscles of his neck and he suppressed a groan of pleasure. Why couldn't he be immune to her touch? Why couldn't he ignore the way she was leaning against him, one of her satin-covered breasts brushing against his left shoulder blade? He could smell her flowery fragrance; it teased and tantalised his senses. He felt drugged. Stoned by her closeness.

He drew in a breath and placed his hands on either side of his thighs, his fingers digging into the mattress. He would *not* touch her.

He. Would. Not.

Sabrina could feel the tension in his body. The muscles in his back and shoulders were set like concrete, even the muscles in his arms were bunched and the tendons of his hands white and prominent where he was gripping the mattress. His thrashing about his bed had woken her from a fitful sleep. She had been shocked at the sound of his anguish, his cries hadn't been all that loud but they had been raw and desperate and somehow that made them seem all the more tragic. What had he been dreaming about? And why wouldn't he talk about it? Or it had it just been one of those horrible dreams everyone had from time to time?

Sabrina moved her hand from massaging his neck to trail it through the thickness of his hair. 'You should try and get some sleep.'

'You're not helping.' His voice was hard bitten like he was spitting out each word.

She kept playing with his hair, somehow realising he was like a wounded dog, snipping and snarling at anyone who got too close. She was close. So close one of her breasts was pressing against the rock-hard plane of his shoulder blade. The contact, even through the satin of her nightie, made her breast tingle and her nipple tighten. 'Do you have nightmares often?'

'Sabrina, please…' He turned and looked at her, his eyes haunted.

She touched his jaw with the palm of her hand, gliding it down the rough stubble until she got to the cleft in his chin. She traced it with her finger and then did the same to the tight line of his mouth, exploring it in intimate detail, recalling how it felt clamped to hers. 'Do you ever think about that night? The night we kissed?' Her voice was barely more than a whisper.

He opened and closed his mouth, the lips pressing together as if he didn't trust himself to use them against hers. 'Kissing you was a mistake. I won't be repeating it.'

Sabrina frowned. 'It didn't feel like a mistake to me… It felt…amazing. The best kiss I've ever had, in fact.'

Something passed through his gaze—a flicker of heat, of longing, of self-control wavering. Then he raised a hand and gently cupped her cheek, his eyes dipping to her mouth, a shudder going through him like an aftershock. 'We shouldn't be doing this.' His voice was so gruff it sounded like he'd been gargling gravel.

'Why shouldn't we?' Sabrina leaned closer, drawn to him as if pulled by an invisible force.

He swallowed and slid his hand to the sensitive skin of her nape, his fingers tangling into her hair, sending her scalp into a tingling torrent of pleasure. 'Because it can't go anywhere.'

'Who said I wanted it to go anywhere?' Sabrina asked. 'I'm just asking you to kiss me, not marry me. You kiss other women, don't you?'

His breath came out and sent a tickling waft of air across the surface of her lips. 'The thing is… I'm not sure I can *just* kiss you.'

She stared at him in pleasant surprise. So pleasant her ego got out of the foetal position and did a victory dance. 'What are you saying?' She couldn't seem to speak louder than a whispery husk.

His eyes had a dark pulsing intensity that made her inner core contract. 'I want you. But I—'

'Can we skip the but?' Sabrina said. 'Let's go back

to the *I want you* bit. Thing is, I want you too. So, what are we going to do about it?'

His gaze drifted to her mouth and then back to her eyes, his eyes hardening as if he had called on some inner strength to keep his self-control in check. 'We're going to ignore it, that's what.' His tone had the same determined edge as his gaze.

Sabrina moistened her lips, watching as his gaze followed the movement of her tongue. 'What if I don't want to ignore it? What if I want you to kiss me? What if I want you to make love to me just this once? No one needs to know about it. It's just between us. It will get it out of our system once and for all and then we can go back to normal.'

She could hardly believe she had been so upfront. She had never been so brazen, so bold about her needs. But she could no longer ignore the pulsing ache of her body. The need that clawed and clenched. The need that only *he* triggered. Was that why she hadn't made love with anyone for all these years? No one made her feel this level of desire. No one even came close to stirring her flesh into a heated rush of longing.

'Sabrina…please…' His voice had a scraped-raw quality as if his throat had been scoured with a bristled brush.

'Please what? Don't tell it like it is?' Sabrina placed her hand on his chest where his heart was thud, thud, thudding so similar to her own. 'You want me. You said so. I felt it when you kissed me three weeks ago. And I know you want me now.'

Max took her by the hands, his fingers almost overlapping around her wrists. At first, she thought he was going to put her from him, but then his fingers tightened and he drew her closer. 'This is madness...' His smoky grey-blue gaze became hooded as it focussed on her mouth as if drawn to it by a magnetic force too powerful for his willpower.

'What is mad about two consenting adults having a one-night stand?' There she went again—such brazen words spilling out of her mouth, as if she'd swallowed the bad girl's guide to hook-up sex. Who was this person she had suddenly become since entering his hotel room? It wasn't anyone Sabrina recognised. But she wasn't going to stop now. She couldn't. If she didn't have sex with Max, someone she knew and trusted to take care of her, who else would she get to do the deed? No one, that's who.

Ten years had already passed and her confidence around men had gone backwards, not forwards. It was do or die—of sexual frustration. She wanted Max to cure her of her of her hang-ups...not that she was going to tell him about her lack of a love life. No flipping way. He'd get all knight-in-shining-armour about it and refuse to make love to her.

Max brushed the pad of his thumb over her bottom lip, pressing and then releasing until her senses were singing like the Philharmonic choir. 'A one-night stand? Is that really what you want?'

Sabrina fisted her hands into the thickness of his dark brown hair, the colour so similar to her own. She fixed her gaze on his troubled one. 'Make love to me, Max. Please?' *Gah*. Was she begging now? Was that how desperate she had become?

Yep. That desperate.

Max tipped up her chin, his eyes locking on hers. 'One night? No repeats? No happy ever after, right?'

Sabrina licked her lips—a mixture of nerves and feverish excitement. 'I want no one and I mean no one to find out about this. It will be our little secret. Agreed?'

One of his dark brows lifted above his sceptical gaze. But then his gaze flicked back to her mouth and he gave a shuddery sigh, as if the final restraint on his self-control had popped its bolts. 'Madness,' he said, so low she almost couldn't hear it. 'This is madness.' And then his mouth came down and set fire to hers.

CHAPTER FOUR

Six weeks later...

'So, ARE YOU still keeping mum about what happened between you and Max in Venice?' Holly asked when she came into Sabrina's studio for a wedding-dress fitting.

Sabrina made a zipping-the-lips motion. 'Yep. I promised.'

Holly's eyes were twinkling so much they rivalled the sparkly bridal tiaras in the display cabinet. 'You can't fool me. I know you slept with him. What I don't understand is why you haven't continued sleeping with him. Was he that bad a lover?'

Sabrina pressed her lips together to stop herself from spilling all. So many times over the last six weeks she'd longed to tell Holly about that amazing night. About Max's amazing lovemaking. How he had made her feel. Her body hadn't felt the same since. She couldn't even think of him without having a fluttery sensation in her stomach. She had relived every touch of his hands and lips and tongue. She had repeatedly, obsessively dreamed about his possession, the way his body had moved within hers with such intense passion and purpose.

She picked up the bolt of French lace her friend had chosen and unrolled it over the cutting table. 'I'm not going to kiss and tell. It's...demeaning.'

'You kiss and told when he kissed you after he drove you home that night a few weeks back. Why not now?'

'Because I made a promise.'

'What?' Holly's smiling expression was exchanged for a frown. 'You don't trust me to keep it a secret? I'm your best friend. I wouldn't tell a soul.'

Sabrina glanced across the table at her friend. 'What about Zack? You guys share everything, right?'

Holly gnawed at her lip. 'Yeah, well, that's what people in love do.'

She tried to ignore the little dart of jealousy she felt at Holly's happiness. Her friend was preparing for her wedding to Zack Knight in a matter of weeks and what did Sabrina have on her love radar? Nothing. *Nada.* Zilch.

A mild wave of nausea assailed her. Was it possible to be lovesick without actually being in love? Okay. She was in love. In love with Max's lovemaking. Deeply in love. She couldn't stop thinking about him and the things he had done to her. The things they had done together. The things she had done to him. She placed a hand on her squeamish tummy and swallowed. She had to get a grip. She couldn't be bitter and sick to her stomach about her best friend's joy at marrying the man she loved. So what if Holly was having the most amazing sex with Zack while all Sabrina had was memories of one night with Max?

Holly leaned across the worktable. 'Hey, are you okay? You've gone as white as that French lace.'

Sabrina grimaced as her stomach contents swished and swirled and soured. 'I'm just feeling a little…off.'

Holly did a double blink. 'Off? As in nauseous?'

She opened her mouth to answer but had to clamp her hand over it because a surge of sickness rose up from her stomach. 'Excuse me…' Her hand muffled her choked apology and she bolted to the bathroom, not even stopping to close the door.

Holly came in behind her and handed her some paper towels from the dispenser on the wall. 'Is that a dodgy curry or too much champagne?'

Sabrina looked up from the toilet bowl. 'Ack. Don't mention food.'

Holly bent down beside her and placed a hand on Sabrina's shoulder. 'How long have you been feeling unwell?'

'Just today…' Sabrina swallowed against another tide of excessive saliva. 'I must have a stomach bug… or something…'

'Would the "or something" have anything to do with your weekend in Venice with Max, which you, obstinately and totally out of character, refuse to discuss?'

Sabrina's scalp prickled like army ants on a military parade. Max had used a condom. He'd used three over the course of the night. She was taking the lowest dose of the Pill to regulate her cycle because the others she'd tried had messed with her mood. 'I can't possibly be pregnant…'

Holly helped her to her feet. 'Are you saying you didn't sleep with him?'

Sabrina pulled her hair back from her face and sighed. 'Okay, so I did sleep with him. But you have to promise you won't tell anyone. Not even Zack.'

'Honey, I can trust Zack to keep it quiet.' Holly stroked Sabrina's arm. 'Did Max use a condom?'

Sabrina nodded. 'Three.'

Holly's eyes bulged. 'At a time?'

'No, we made love three times.' She closed the toilet seat and pressed the flush button. 'We made a promise not to talk about it. To anyone. Ever.'

'But why?'

Sabrina turned to wash her hands and face at the basin. 'We both agreed it was the best thing considering how our families go on and on about us getting together. We had a one-night stand to get it out of our system. End of story. Neither of us wants be involved with the other.'

'Or so *you* say.' Holly's tone was so sceptical she could have moonlighted as a detective.

Sabrina made a business of drying her face and hands. 'It's true. We would be hopeless as a couple. We fight all the time.'

Holly leaned against the door jamb, arms folded. 'Clearly not all the time if you had sex three times. Unless it was combative sex?'

Sabrina glanced at her friend in the reflection of the mirror. 'No…it wasn't combative sex. It was…amazing sex.' She had to stop speaking as the tiny frisson of re-membered delight trickled over her flesh.

'Have you seen Max since that weekend?'

'No. We agreed to keep our distance as if nothing happened.' Sabrina sighed. 'He even checked out early from the hotel after our night together. He wasn't there when I woke up. He sent me a text from the airport to say he'd covered the bill for the suite and that's the last time I heard from him.' It had hurt to find the suite empty the next morning. Hurt badly. So much for her following the Fling Handbook guidelines. She'd fool-ishly expected a good morning kiss or two...or more.

'If you're not suffering from a stomach bug, then you'll have to see him sooner or later,' Holly said.

Sabrina put her hand on her abdomen, her heart be-ginning to pound with an echo of dread. She couldn't possibly be pregnant... *Could she?* What on earth would she say to Max? Max, who had already made it known he didn't want children. How could she announce *he* was the father of her child?

But wait, women had pregnancy scares all the time. Her cycle was crazy in any case. She had always planned to have kids, but not yet. She was still build-ing up her business. Still trying to prove to her family her career choice was as viable, rewarding and fulfill-ing as theirs.

She'd had it all planned: get her business well estab-lished, hopefully one day fall in love with a man who would treat her the way she had always longed to be treated. Not that she had actively gone looking for the love of her life. She had been too worried about a repeat of her embarrassing falling-in-love episode during her teens. But getting married and having babies was what she wanted. One day. How could she have got it so messed up by falling pregnant? Now? While being on the Pill and using condoms? She was still living in a poky little bedsit, for God's sake.

Sabrina moved past Holly to get out of the bathroom. 'I can't tell him until I know for sure. I need to get a test kit. I have to do it today because there's a Midhurst and Firbank family gathering tomorrow night and I can't do a no-show. It's Max's mother's birthday. She'd be hurt if I didn't go.'

'You could say you've got a stomach bug.'

Sabrina gave her a side-eye. 'My parents and brothers will be there and once they hear I've got a stomach bug, one or all of them will be on my doorstep with their doctor's bag.' She clutched two handfuls of her hair with her hands. 'Argh. Why am I such a disaster? This wasn't meant to happen. Not *no-o-o-w*.' To her shame, her last word came as a childish wail.

'Oh, sweetie, you're not a disaster. Falling pregnant to a guy you love is not a catastrophe. Not in this day and age in any case.'

Sabrina dropped her hands from her head and glared at her friend. 'Who said I was in love with Max? Why do you keep going on about it?'

Holly placed her hands on her hips in an *I know you better than you do yourself* pose. 'Hello? You haven't slept with anyone for ten years, and then you spend a night in bed with a man you've known since you were in nappies? You wouldn't have slept with him if you didn't feel something for him.'

Sabrina rolled her lips together and turned away to smooth the fabric out on the worktable. 'Okay, so maybe I don't hate him as much as I used to, but I'm not in love with him. I wouldn't be so…so…stupid.' *Would she?* She had promised herself she would never find herself in that situation again. Fancying herself in love with someone who might reject her in the end like her teenage boyfriend had. Falling in love with Max would be asking for the sort of trouble she could do without. More trouble, that was, because finding herself pregnant to him was surely trouble enough.

Holly touched Sabrina on the arm. 'Do you want me to stay with you while you do the test?'

Sabrina gulped back a sob. 'Oh…would you?'

Holly smiled. 'That's what best friends are for— through thick and thin, and sick and sin, right?'

If it hadn't been his mother's birthday Max would have found some excuse to not show up. Not that he didn't want to see Sabrina. He did, which was The Problem. Wanting to see her, wanting to touch her, wanting to kiss her, wanting, wanting, wanting to make love to her again. He had told himself one night and one night only and here he was six weeks later still replaying every minute of that stolen night of seriously hot sex. Sex so amazing he could still feel aftershocks when he so much as pictured her lying in his arms. Sex so planet-dislodging he hadn't bothered hooking up with anyone else and wondered in his darkest moments if he ever would.

He couldn't imagine touching another woman after making love with Sabrina. How could he kiss another mouth as sweet and responsive as hers? How could he slide his hands down a body so lush and ripe and feminine if it didn't belong to Sabrina?

Max arrived at his parents' gracious home in Hampton Court, and after greeting his mother and father took up his usual place at the back of the crowded room to do his people-watching thing. He searched the sea of faces to see if Sabrina was among them, more than a little shocked at how disappointed he was not to find her. But then a thought shot like a stray dart into his brain. What if she brought someone with her? Another man? A new date? A man she was now sleeping with and doing all the sexy red-hot things she had done with him?

Max took a tumbler of spirits off the tray of a passing waiter and downed it in one swallow. He had to get a hold of himself. He was thirty-four years old, not some hormone-driven teenager suffering his first crush. So what if Sabrina slept with someone else? What business was it of his? They'd made an agreement of one night to get the lust bug out of the way.

No repeats.

No replays.

No sequel.

No happy-ever-after.

Max turned to put his empty glass down on a table next to him and saw Sabrina greeting his mother on the other side of the room. The way his parents adored her was understandable given they hadn't had any children after the loss of Daniel. Sabrina, as their only godchild, had been lavished with love and attention. Max knew their affection for her had helped them to heal as much as was possible after the tragic loss of an infant. Not that his parents hadn't adored him too. They had been fabulous parents trying to do their best after such sad circumstances, which, in an ill-advised but no less understandable way, had fed their little fantasy of him and Sabrina one day getting together and playing happy families.

But it was a step too far.

Way, way too far.

Sabrina finally stepped out of his mother's bone-crushing hug and met his gaze. Her eyes widened and then flicked away, her cheeks going an intense shade of pink. She turned and hurriedly made her way through the knot of guests and disappeared through the door that led out to the gallery-wide corridor.

Max followed her, weaving his way through the crowd just in time to see Sabrina scuttling into the library further down the corridor, like a terrified mouse trying to escape a notoriously cruel cat. In spite of the background noise of the party, the sound of the key turning in the lock was like a rifle shot. Or a slap on the face.

Okay, so he had left her in Venice without saying goodbye in person but surely that didn't warrant *this* type of reaction?

Max knocked on the library door. 'Sabrina? Let me in.'

He could hear the sound of her breathing on the other side of the door—hectic and panicked as if she really was trying to avoid someone menacing. But after a moment the key turned in the lock and the door creaked open.

'Are you alone?' Sabrina's voice sounded as creaky as the door, her eyes wide and bluer than he had ever seen them. And, he realised with a jolt, reddened as if she'd been recently crying. A lot.

'Yes, but what's going on?' He stepped into the room before she could stop him and closed the door behind him.

Sabrina took a few steps back and hugged her arms around her middle, her eyes skittering away from his. 'I have something to tell you…'

Here we go. Max had been here so many times before. The *I want more than a one-night stand* speech. But this time he was okay with it. More than okay. He could think of nothing he wanted more than to have a longer fling with her. Longer than one night, that was. A week or two, a month or three. Long enough to scratch the itch but not long enough for her to get silly ideas about it being for ever. 'It's okay, Sabrina. You don't have to look so scared. I've been thinking along the same lines.'

Her smooth brow crinkled into a frown. 'The same… lines?'

Max gave a soft laugh, his blood already pumping at the thought of taking her in his arms. Maybe even here in the quiet of the library while the guests were partying in the ballroom. What could be sexier than a clandestine affair? 'We'd have to keep it a secret, of course. But a month or two would be fun.' He took a step towards her but she backed away as if he was carrying the Black Plague.

'No.' She held up her hands like stop signs, her expression couldn't have looked more horrified than if he'd drawn a gun.

No? Max hadn't heard that word from a woman for a long time. Weird, but hearing it from Sabrina was unusually disappointing. 'Okay. That's fine. We'll stick to the original agreement.'

She gave an audible swallow and her arms went back around her middle. 'Max…' She slowly lifted her gaze back to his, hers still wide as Christmas baubles. 'I don't know how to tell you this…'

His gut suddenly seized and he tried to control his breathing. So she'd found someone else. No wonder his offer of a temporary fling had been turned down. She was sleeping with someone else. Someone else was kissing that beautiful mouth, someone else was holding her gorgeous body in their arms.

'It's okay, Sabrina.' How had he got his voice to sound so level? So damn normal when his insides were churning with jealousy? Yes, jealousy—that thing he never felt. Ever. Not for anyone. The big green-eyed monster was having a pity party in his gut and there was nothing he could do about it.

One of Sabrina's hands crept to press against her stomach. She licked her lips and opened her mouth to speak but couldn't seem to get her voice to work.

Max called on every bit of willpower he possessed to stop himself from reaching for her and showing her why a temporary fling with him was much a better idea than her getting involved permanently with someone else. A hard sell to a fairytale girl, but still. His hands stayed resolutely by his sides, but his fingers were clenching and unclenching like his jaw. 'Who is it?' There. He'd asked the question his pride had forbidden him to ask.

Sabrina's brow creased into another puzzled frown. 'I… You think there's someone…*else*?'

Max shrugged as if it meant nothing to him what she did and whom she did it with. But on the inside he was slamming his fist into the wall in frustration. Bam. Bam. Bam. The imaginary punches were in time with the thud, thud, thud of his heart. 'That's what this is about, isn't it?'

'Have *you* found someone else?' Her voice was faint and hesitant as if it was struggling to get past a stricture in her throat.

'Not yet.'

She closed her eyes in a tight squint as if his answer had pained her. She opened her eyes again and took a deep breath. 'In a way, this is about someone else…' She laced her fingers together in front of her stomach, then released them and did it again like a nervous tic. 'Someone neither of us has met…yet…'

Max wanted to wring his own hands. He wanted to turn back time and go back to Venice and do things differently. He had to get control of himself. He couldn't allow his jealousy over a man who may or may not exist to mess with his head. He took a calming breath, released it slowly. They would both eventually find someone else. He would have to get used to seeing her with a husband one day. A man who would give her the family she wanted. The commitment and the love she wanted. And Max would move from woman to woman just as he had been doing for the last six years. 'So, you're saying you're not actually seeing someone else right at this moment?'

'No.' Her face screwed up in distaste. 'How could you think I would want to after what we shared?'

'It was just sex, Sabrina.' He kept his tone neutral even though his male ego was doing fist pumps. Damn good sex. Amazing sex. Awesome sex he wanted to repeat. Then a victory chant sounded in his head. *There isn't anyone else. There isn't anyone else.* The big green monster slunk away and relief flooded Max's system.

'Yeah, well, if only it had been just sex…' Something about her tone and her posture made the hairs of the back of his neck stand up. Her hand kept creeping over the flat plane of her belly, her throat rising and falling over a swallow that sounded more like a gulp.

Max was finding it hard to make sense of what she was saying. And why was she looking so flustered? 'I'm not sure where this conversation is heading, but how about you say what you want to say, okay? I promise I won't interrupt. Just spit it out, for God's sake.'

Her eyes came back to his and she straightened her spine as if girding herself for a firing squad. 'Max… I'm pregnant.'

CHAPTER FIVE

MAX STEPPED BACK as if she had stabbed him. His gut even clenched as if a dagger had gone through to his backbone. *Pregnant?* The word was like a poison spreading through his blood, leaving a trail of catastrophic destruction in its wake. His heart stopped and started in a sickening boom-skip-boom-skip-boom-skip rhythm, his lungs almost collapsing as he fought to take a breath. His skin went hot, then cold, and his scalp prickled and tightened as if every hair was shrinking away in dread.

'You're...pregnant?' His voice cracked like an egg thrown on concrete, his mind splintering into a thousand panicked thoughts. A baby. They had made a baby. Somehow, in spite of all the protection he had used, they had made a baby. 'Are you sure?'

She pressed her lips together and nodded, her chin wobbling. 'I've done a test. Actually, I've done five. They were all positive.'

Max scraped a hand through his hair so roughly he nearly scalped himself. 'Oh, God...' He turned away, a part of him vainly hoping that when he turned back he wouldn't find himself in the library of his parents' mansion with Sabrina telling him he was to be a father. It was like a bad dream. A nightmare.

His. Personal. Nightmare.

'Thanks for not asking if it's yours.' Sabrina's soft voice broke through his tortured reverie.

He swung back to face her; suddenly conscious of how appallingly he was taking her announcement. But nothing could have prepared him for this moment. He had never in his wildest imaginings ever thought he would be standing in front of a woman—any woman—bearing this bombshell news. Pregnant. A baby. *His* baby. 'I'm sorry, but it's such a shock.' Understatement. His heart was pounding so hard he wouldn't have been out of place on a critical care cardiac ward. Sweat was pouring down between his shoulder blades. Something was scrabbling and scratching like there was a frantic animal trapped in his guts.

He stepped towards her and held out his hands but she stepped back again. His hands fell back by his sides. 'So…what have you decided to do?'

Her small neat chin came up and her cornflower-blue eyes hardened with determination. 'I'm not having a termination. Please don't ask me to.'

Max flinched. 'Do you really think I'm the sort of man to do something like that? I'm firmly of the opinion that it's solely a woman's choice whether she continues with a pregnancy or not.'

Relief washed over her pinched features but there was still a cloud of worry in her gaze. 'I'm not against someone else making that difficult choice but I can't bring myself to do it. Not under these circumstances.

I don't expect you to be involved if that's not what you want. I know this is a terrible shock and not something you want, but I thought you should know about the pregnancy first, before it becomes obvious, I mean.' Her hand went protectively to her belly again. 'I won't even tell people it's yours if you'd rather not have them know.'

Max was ashamed that for a nanosecond he considered that as an option. But how could he call himself a man and ignore his own flesh and blood? It wasn't the child's fault so why should it be robbed of a relationship with its father? He had grown up with a loving and involved father and couldn't imagine how different his life might have been without the solid and dependable support of his dad.

No. He would do the right thing by Sabrina and the baby. He would try his hardest not to fail them like he had failed his baby brother and his parents. He stepped forward and captured her hands before she could escape. 'I want my child to have my name. We'll marry as soon as I can arrange it.'

Sabrina pulled out of his hold as if his hands had burned her. 'You don't have to be so old-fashioned about it, Max. I'm not asking you to marry me.'

'I'm not asking you. I'm telling you what's going to happen.' As proposals went, Max knew it wasn't flash. But he'd proposed in a past life and he had sworn he would never do it again. But this was different. This was about duty and responsibility, not foolish, fleeting, fickle feelings. 'We will marry next month.'

'Next month?' Her eyes went round in shock. 'Are you crazy? This is the twenty-first century. Couples don't have to marry because they happened to get pregnant. No one is holding a gun to your head.'

'Do you really think I would walk away from the responsibility to my own flesh and blood? We will marry and that's final.'

Sabrina's eyes flashed blue sparks of defiance and her hands clenched into fists. 'You could do with some work on your proposal, buddy. No way am I marrying you. You don't love me.'

'So? You don't love me either,' Max said. 'This is not about us. This is about the baby we've made. You need someone to support you and that someone is me. I won't take no for an answer.'

Her chin came up so high she could have given a herd of mules a master class in stubbornness. 'Then we're at an impasse because no way am I marrying a man who didn't even have the decency to say goodbye in person the night we…had sex.'

Max blew out a breath and shoved a hand back through his hair again. 'Okay, so my exit might have lacked a little finesse, but I didn't want you to get any crazy ideas about our one night turning into something else.'

'Oh, yeah? Well, because of the quality of your stupid condoms, our one-night has turned into something else—a damn baby!' She buried her face in her hands and promptly burst into tears.

Max winced and stepped towards her, gathering her close against his body. This time she didn't resist, and he wrapped his arms around her as the sobs racked her slim frame. He stroked the back of her silky head, his mind whirling with emotions he had no idea how to handle.

Regret, shame and blistering anger at himself. He had done this to her. He had got her pregnant. Had the condoms failed? He was always so careful. He always wore one. No exceptions. Had he left it on too long? At one point he had fallen asleep with her wrapped in his arms, his body still encased in the warm wet velvet of hers.

Was that when it had happened? He should never have given in to the temptation of touching her. He had acted on primal instinct, ruled by his hormones instead of his head. 'I'm sorry. So sorry. But I thought you said you were on the Pill?'

She eased away from his chest to look up at him through tear-washed eyes. 'I'm on a low dose one but I was so caught up with nerves about the expo, I had an upset tummy the day before I left for Venice. Plus, I was sick after having that champagne at the cocktail party.' She tried to suppress a hiccup but didn't quite manage it.

Max brushed the hair back from her face. 'Look, no one is to blame for this other than me. I shouldn't have touched you. I shouldn't have kissed you that first time and I definitely shouldn't have booked you into my room and—'

'Do you really regret what happened between us that night?' Her expression reminded him of a wounded puppy—big eyes, long face, fragile hope.

He cradled her face in his hands. 'That's the whole trouble. I don't regret it. Not a minute of it. I've thought of that night thousands of times since then.' He brushed his thumbs over her cheeks while still cupping her face. 'We'll make this work, Sabrina. We might not love each other in the traditional way, but we can make do.'

She tugged his hands away from her face and stepped a metre away to stand in front of the floor-to-ceiling bookshelves. 'Make do? Is that all you want out of life? To...' she waved her hand in a sweeping gesture '... *make do*? What about love? Isn't that an essential ingredient of a good marriage?'

'I'm not offering you that sort of marriage.'

Her eyes flashed and she planted her hands on her hips. 'Well, guess what? I'm not accepting *that* sort of proposal.'

'Would you prefer me to lie to you?' Max tried to keep his voice steady but he could feel ridges of anger lining his throat. 'To get down on bended knee and say a whole lot of flowery words we both know I don't mean?'

'Did you say them to Lydia?'

'Let's keep Lydia out of this.' This time the anger nearly choked him. He hated thinking about his proposal six years ago to his ex-fiancée. He hated thinking about his failure to see the relationship for what it had been—a mistake from start to finish. It had occurred to him only recently that he had asked Lydia to marry him so his parents would back off about Sabrina. Not the best reason, by anyone's measure.

'You still have feelings for her, don't you? That's why you can't commit to anyone else.'

Max rolled his eyes and gave a short bark of a laugh. 'Oh, please spare me the pop psychoanalysis. No, I do not still love Lydia. In fact, I never loved her.'

Sabrina blinked rapidly. 'Then why did you ask her to marry you?'

He walked over to the leather-topped mahogany desk

and picked up the paperweight he had given his father when he was ten. He passed it from hand to hand, wondering how to answer. 'Good question,' he said, putting the paperweight down and turning to look at her. 'When we first dated, she seemed fine with my decision not to have kids. We had stuff in common, books, movies, that sort of thing.' He gave a quick open-close movement of his lips. 'But clearly it wasn't enough for her.'

'It might not have been about the kid thing. It might have been because she knew you didn't love her. I never thought your chemistry with her was all that good.'

Max moved closer to her, drawn by a force he couldn't resist. 'Unlike ours, you mean?' He traced a line from below her ear to her chin with his finger, watching as her pupils darkened and her breath hitched. Her spring flowers perfume danced around his nostrils, her warm womanly body making his blood thrum and hum and drum with lust. *Don't touch her.* His conscience pinged with a reminder but he ignored it.

Her hands came up to rest against his chest, the tip of her tongue sweeping over her rosebud lips. But then her eyes hardened and she pushed back from him and put some distance between them. 'I know what you're trying to do but it won't work. I will not be seduced into marrying you.'

'For God's sake, Sabrina,' Max said. 'This is not about seducing you into changing your mind. You're having my baby. I would never leave you to fend for yourself. That's not the sort of man I am.'

'Look, I know you mean well, but I can't marry you. I'm only just pregnant. I can't bear the thought of everyone talking about me, judging me for falling pregnant after a one-night stand, especially to you when I've done nothing but criticise you for years. Anyway, what if I were to have a miscarriage or something before the twelve-week mark? Then you'd hate me for sure for trapping you in a marriage neither of us wanted in the first place.'

The mention of miscarriage gave him pause. He had seen his mother go through several of them before and after the death of Daniel. It had been torture to watch her suffer not just physically but emotionally. The endless tears, the longing looks at passing prams or pregnant women. He had been young, but not too young to notice the despair on his mother's face. 'Okay. So we will wait until the twelve-week mark. But I'm only compromising because it makes sense to keep this news to ourselves until then.'

Sabrina bit her lower lip and it made him want to kiss away the indentation her teeth made when she released it. 'I've kind of told Holly. She was with me when I did the test.'

'Can you trust her to keep it to herself?'

'She'll probably tell Zack, but she assures me he won't blab either.'

Max stepped closer again and took her hands, stroking the backs of them with his thumbs. 'How are you feeling? I'm sorry I didn't ask earlier. Not just about how you're feeling about being pregnant but are you sick? Is there anything you need?'

Fresh tears pooled in her eyes and she swallowed a couple of times. 'I'm a bit sick and my breasts are a little tender.'

'Is it too early to have a scan?'

'I'm not sure, I haven't been to see the doctor yet.'

'I'll go with you to all of your appointments, that is, if you want me there?' Who knew he could be such a model father-to-be? But, then, he figured he'd had a great role model in his own dad. Even so, he wanted to be involved for the child's sake.

'Do you want to be there or would you only be doing it out of duty?'

'I want to be there to see our baby for the first time.' Max was a little surprised to realise how much he meant it. But he needed to see the baby to believe this pregnancy had really happened. He still felt as if he'd stepped into a parallel universe. Could his and Sabrina's DNAs really be getting it on inside her womb? A baby. A little person who would look like one or the other, or a combination of both of them. A child who would grow up and look to him for protection and nurturing. Did he trust himself to do a good job? How could he when he had let his baby brother down so badly?

The door suddenly opened behind them and Max glanced over his shoulder to see his mother standing there. 'Oh, there you two are.' Her warm brown eyes sparkled with fairy godmother delight.

Sabrina sprang away from Max but she bumped into the mahogany desk behind her and yelped. 'Ouch!'

Max reached for Sabrina, steadying her by bringing her close to his side. 'Are you okay?'

She rubbed her left hip, her cheeks a vivid shade of pink. 'Yes...'

'Did I startle you?' Max's mother asked. 'Sorry,

darling, but I was wondering where you'd gone. You seemed a little upset earlier.'

'I'm not upset,' Sabrina said, biting her lip.

His mother raised her eyebrows and then glanced at Max. 'I hope you two aren't fighting again? No wonder the poor girl gets upset with you glaring at her all the time. I don't want my party spoilt by your boorish behaviour. Why can't you just kiss and make up for a change?'

Max could have laughed at the irony of the situation if his sense of humour hadn't already been on life support. He'd done way more than kiss Sabrina and now there were consequences he would be dealing with for the rest of his life. But there was no way he could tell his mother what had gone on between them. No way he could say anything until she was through the first trimester of her pregnancy. It would get everybody's hopes up and the pressure would be unbearable—even more unbearable than it already was.

'It's fine, Aunty Gillian. Max is being perfectly civil to me,' Sabrina said, carefully avoiding his gaze.

Max's mother shifted her lips from side to side. 'Mmm, I'm not sure it's safe to leave you two alone for more than five minutes. Who knows what might happen?'

Who knew, indeed?

As soon as the door closed behind Gillian Firbank, Sabrina swung her gaze to Max. 'Do you think she suspects anything?'

'I don't think so. But we have to keep our relationship quiet until you get through the first trimester. Then we can tell everyone we're marrying.'

She stared at him, still not sure how to handle this change in him. So much for the one night and one night only stance he'd taken before. Now he was insisting on marrying her and wouldn't take no for an answer.

She blew out a breath, whirled away and crossed her arms over her middle. 'You're being ridiculous, Max. We can't do this. We can't get married just because I'm pregnant. We'd end up hating each other even more than we do now.'

'When have I ever said I hated you?' Max's jaw looked like it was set in stone. A muscle moved in and out next to his flattened mouth as if he was mentally counting to ten. And his smoky blue eyes smouldered, making something fizz at the back of her knees like sherbet.

'You don't have to say it. It's in your actions. You can barely speak to me without criticising something about me.'

He came to her and before she could move away he took her by the upper arms in a gentle but firm hold. Deep down, Sabrina knew she'd had plenty of time to escape those warm strong fingers, but right then her body was craving his touch. Six long weeks had passed since their stolen night of passion and now she was alone with him, her senses were firing, her needs clamouring, her resolve to resist him faltering. 'I don't hate you, Sabrina.'

But you don't love me either.

She didn't say the words out loud but the silence seemed to ring with their echo. 'We'd better get back to the party otherwise people will start talking.'

His hands tightened. 'Not yet.' His voice was low and deep and husky, his eyes flicking to her mouth as if drawn by a force he couldn't counteract.

Sabrina breathed in the clean male scent of him, the hint of musk, the base note of bergamot and a top note of lemon. She leaned towards him, pushed by the need to feel him close against her, to feel his body respond to hers. He stirred against her, the tempting hardness of his body reminding hers of everything that had passed between them six weeks ago. 'Max... I can't think straight when you touch me.'

'Then don't think.'

She stepped out of his hold with a willpower she hadn't known she possessed. 'I need a couple of weeks to get my head around this...situation. It's been such a shock and I don't want to rush into anything I might later regret.'

She didn't want to think about all the madly-in-love brides who came to her for their wedding dresses. She didn't want to think about Max's offer, which had come out of a sense of duty instead of love. But she didn't want to think about bringing up a baby on her own either. She walked to the library door, knowing that if she stayed a minute longer she would end up in his arms.

'Where are you going?' Max asked.

She glanced over her shoulder. 'The party, remember?'

He dragged a hand over his face and scowled. 'I hate parties.'

CHAPTER SIX

BY THE TIME Max dragged himself out of the library to re-join the party there was no sign of Sabrina. He moved through the house, pretending an interest in the other guests he was nowhere near feeling, surreptitiously sweeping his gaze through the crowd to catch a glimpse of her. He didn't want to make it too obvious he was looking for her, but he didn't want her to leave his parents' house until he was sure she was okay.

He was having enough trouble dealing with the shock news of her pregnancy, so he could only imagine how it was impacting on her. Even though he knew she had always wanted children, she wanted them at the right time with the right guy. He wasn't that guy. But it was too late to turn back the clock. He was the father of her child and there was no way he was going to abandon her, even if he had to drag her kicking, screaming and swearing to the altar.

Max wandered out into the garden where large scented candles were burning in stands next to the formal garden beds. There was no silky honey-brown head in the crowd gathered outside. The sting of disappoint-

ment soured his mood even further. The only way to
survive one of his parents' parties was to spar with Sabrina. He hadn't realised until then how much he looked
forward to it. Was he weird or what? Looking forward
to their unfriendly fire was not healthy. It was sick.

And so too was wanting to make love to a woman
you got pregnant six weeks ago. But he couldn't deny
the longing that was pounding through him. He'd
wanted to kiss her so badly back in the library. Kiss
her and hold her and remind her of the chemistry they
shared. Hadn't it always been there? The tension that
vibrated between them whenever their gazes locked.
How the slightest touch of her hand sent a rocket charge
through his flesh. That first kiss all those weeks ago
had set in motion a ferocious longing that refused to
be suppressed.

But it *had* to be suppressed. It *must* be suppressed.
He was no expert on pregnancy, having avoided the
topic for most of his adult life, but wasn't sex between
the parents dangerous to the baby under some circumstances? Particularly if the pregnancy was a high-risk
one? How could he live with himself if he harmed the
baby before it even got a chance to be born? Besides,
he didn't want their families to get too excited about
him and Sabrina seeing each other. He could only imagine his mother's disappointment if she thought she was
going to be a grandmother only to have it snatched away
from her if Sabrina's pregnancy failed.

No. He would do the noble thing. He would resist
the temptation and get her safely through to the twelve-
week mark. Even if it damn near killed him.

Max's mother came towards him with half a glass of champagne in her hand. 'Are you looking for Sabrina?'

'No.' *Shoot*. He'd delivered his flat denial far too quickly.

'Well, if you are, then you're wasting your time. She went home half an hour ago. Said she wasn't feeling well. I hope it wasn't your fault?' The accusatory note in his mother's voice grated along his already frayed nerves.

Yep, it was definitely his fault.

Big time.

Sabrina managed to make it back to her tiny flat without being sick. The nausea kept coming and going in waves and she'd been worried it might grip her in the middle of the party celebrations. She had decided it was safer to make her excuses and leave. Besides, it might have looked suspicious if her mother or Max's noticed she wasn't drinking the champagne. After all, the party girl with a glass of bubbles in her hand and a dazzling smile on her face whilst working the room was her signature style.

But it seemed Sabrina had left one party to come home to another. The loud music coming from the upstairs flat was making the walls shake. How would she ever get to sleep with that atrocious racket going on? She only hoped the party wouldn't go on past midnight. Last time the neighbours had held a party the police had been called because a scuffle had broken out on the street as some of the guests had been leaving.

It wasn't the nicest neighbourhood to live in—certainly nowhere as genteel as the suburbs where her parents and two older brothers lived and where she had spent her childhood. But until she felt more financially stable she didn't feel she had a choice. Rents in London were continually on the rise, and with the sharing economy going from strength to strength, it meant there was a reduced number of properties available for mid- to long-term rent.

She peeled off her clothes and slipped her nightgown over her head. She went to the bathroom and took off her makeup but then wished she hadn't. Was it possible to look that pale whilst still having a functioning pulse?

Sabrina went back to her bedroom and climbed into bed and pulled the covers over her head, but the sound of heavy footsteps clattering up and down the stairs would have made a herd of elephants sound like fairies' feet. Then, to add insult to injury, someone began to pound on her front door.

'Argh.' She threw off the covers and grabbed her wrap to cover her satin nightgown and padded out to check who was there through the peephole. No way was she going to open the door if it was a drunken stranger. But a familiar tall figure stood there with a brooding expression. 'Max?'

'Let me in.' His voice contained the thread of steel she had come to always associate with him.

She unlocked the door and he was inside her flat almost before she could step out of the way. 'What are you doing here?'

He glanced around the front room of her flat like a construction official inspecting a condemned building.

'I'm not letting you stay here. There isn't even an inter-com on this place. It's not safe.'

Pride stiffened her spine and she folded her arms across her middle. 'I don't plan to stay here for ever but it's all I can afford. Anyway, you didn't seem to think it was too unsafe when you kissed me that time you brought me home.'

'My mind was on other things that night.' There was the sound of a bottle breaking in the stairwell and he winced. 'Right. That settles it. Get dressed and pack a bag. You're coming with me.'

Sabrina unfolded her arms and placed them on her hips. 'You can't just barge into my home and tell me what to do.'

'Watch me, sweetheart.' He moved past her and went to her bedroom, opening drawers and cupboards and throwing a collection of clothes on the bed.

Sabrina followed him into her bedroom. 'Hey, what the hell do you think you're doing?'

'If you won't pack, then I'll do it for you.' He opened another cupboard and found her overnight bag and, placing it on the bed, began stuffing her clothes into it.

Sabrina grabbed at the sweater he'd picked up and pulled on it like a dog playing tug-of-war. 'Give it back.' *Tug. Tug. Tug.* 'You're stretching it out of shape.'

He whipped it out of her hands and tossed it in the bag on the bed. 'I'll buy you a new one.' He slammed the lid of the bag down and zipped it up with a savage movement. 'I'm not letting you stay another minute in this hovel.'

'Hovel?' Sabrina snorted. 'Did you hear that clanging noise? Oh, yes, that must be the noise of all those silver spoons hanging out of your mouth.'

His grey-blue eyes were as dark as storm clouds with lightning flashes of anger. 'Why do you live like this when you could live with your parents until you get on your feet?'

'Hello? I'm twenty-eight years old,' Sabrina said. 'I haven't lived with my parents for a decade. And nor would I want to. They'd bombard me constantly with all of your amazingly wonderful assets until I went stark certifiably crazy.'

There was the sound of someone shouting and swearing in the stairwell and Max's jaw turned to marble. 'I can't let you stay here, Sabrina. Surely you can understand that?'

She sent him a glare. 'I understand you want to take control.'

'This is not about control. This is about your safety.' He scraped a hand through his hair. 'And the baby's safety too.'

Sabrina was becoming too tired to argue. The noise from upstairs was getting worse and there would be no hope of sleeping even if by some remote chance she convinced Max to leave her be. Besides, she secretly hated living here. The landlord was a creep and kept threatening to put up the rent.

Sabrina was too proud, too determined to prove to her parents she didn't need their help. But it wasn't just herself she had to think about now. She had to take care of the baby. She'd read how important it was for mothers-to-be to keep stress levels down and get plenty of rest for the sake of the developing foetus. Was Max thinking along the same lines? 'Why did you come here tonight?' she asked.

'I was worried about you. You left the party early and I worried you might be sick or faint whilst driving home. I'm sorry. I should have offered to drive you but I was still reeling from your news and—'

'It's okay.' She tossed her hair back over one shoulder. 'As you see, I managed to get home in one piece.'

He stepped closer and took her hands in his. His touch made every nerve in her skin fizz, his concerned gaze striking a lethal blow to her stubborn pride. 'Let me look after you, Sabrina. Come home with me.'

Her insides quivered, her inner core recalling his intimate presence. The memories of that night seemed to be swirling in the air they shared. Her body was so aware of his proximity she could feel every fibre of her satin nightgown against her flesh. Was he remembering every moment of that night? Was his body undergoing the same little pulses and flickers of remembered pleasure? 'Live with you, you mean?'

'We'll have separate rooms.'

She frowned. 'You don't want to…?'

'I don't think it's a good idea.' He released her hands and stepped back. 'Not until you get through the first trimester. Then we'll reassess.' His tone was so matter-of-fact he could have been reading a financial report.

Sabrina couldn't quell her acute sense of disappointment. He didn't want her any more? Or maybe he did but he was denying himself because he'd set conditions on their relationship. 'But how will we keep our…erm…

relationship or whatever we're now calling it a secret from our families if we're living under the same roof?'

'In some ways, it'll make it easier. We won't be seen out and about together in public. And I travel a lot for work so we won't be on top of each other.'

Doubts flitted through her mind like frenzied moths. Sharing a house with him was potentially dangerous. Her body was aflame with lust as soon as he came near, living with him would only make it a thousand times worse. She ached to feel his arms around her, his kiss on her mouth, his body buried within hers. What if she made a fool of herself? Wanting him so badly she begged him to make love to her?

What if she fell in love with him?

He wasn't offering her love, only his protection. Food and shelter and a roof over her head. And a stable but loveless marriage if the pregnancy continued. But wasn't that a pathway to heartbreak? How could she short-change herself by marrying someone who wasn't truly in love with her?

Max came closer again and took her hands. 'This is the best way forward. It will ensure your safety and my peace of mind.'

She looked down at their joined hands, his skin so tanned compared to the creamy whiteness of hers. It reminded her of the miracle occurring inside her body, the cells dividing, DNA being exchanged, traits and features from them both being switched on or off to make a whole new little person. A little person she was already starting to love. 'I don't know…'

His hands gave hers a small squeeze. 'Let's give it a try for the next few weeks, okay?'

Sabrina let out a sigh and gave him a wry glance. 'You know, you're kind of scaring me at how convincing you can be when you put your mind to it.'

He released her hands and stepped back with an unreadable expression. 'I'll wait for you out here while you get changed out of your nightgown. Any toiletries you need from the bathroom before we get going?'

She sighed and turned back for the bedroom. 'I'll get them once I've got changed.'

Max waited for Sabrina while she gathered her makeup and skincare products from the bathroom. He would have paced the floor but there wasn't the space for it. He would have taken out a window with his elbow each time he turned. It was true that he hadn't noticed how appalling her flat was when he'd brought her home that night all those weeks ago. The flat wasn't so bad inside—she had done her best to tart things up with brightly coloured scatter cushions and throw rugs over the cheap sofa, cute little knick-knacks positioned here and there and prints of artwork on the walls. There was even a bunch of fresh flowers, presumably supplied by her best friend Holly, who was a florist.

But it was what was on the outside of Sabrina's front door that worried him. Apart from the stale cooking smells, there were no security cameras, no intercom to screen the people coming in and out of the building. How could he sleep at night if he left her here with who knew what type of people milling past? Criminals? Drug dealers? Violent thugs?

No. It was safer for her at his house. Well, safe in one sense, dangerous in another. He had made a promise to himself that he would keep his hands off her. He knew he was locking the stable door even though the horse was well on its way to the maternity ward, but he had to be sensible about this. Sleeping with her before the three-month mark would make it even harder to end their relationship if the pregnancy failed.

Something tightened in his gut at the thought of her losing that baby. *His* baby. He had never imagined himself as a father. For most of his life he had blocked it out of his mind. He wasn't the type of man who was comfortable around kids. He actively avoided babies. One of his friends from university had asked him to be godfather to his firstborn son. Max had almost had a panic attack at the church when his friend's wife had handed him the baby to hold.

But now *he* was going to be a father.

Sabrina came out after a few minutes dressed in skinny jeans and a dove-grey boyfriend sweater that draped sensually over her bra-less breasts. On her feet she was wearing ballet slippers, and on her face an expression that was one part resignation and one part defiance. He tore his gaze away from the tempting globes of her breasts, remembering how soft they had felt in his hands, how tightly her nipples had peaked when he'd sucked on them. In a few months her body would be ripe with his child.

A child *he* had planted in her womb.

He had never considered pregnancy to be sexy but somehow with Sabrina it was. Damn it, everything about her was sexy. Wasn't that why he'd crossed the line and made love to her last month in Venice?

But now he had drawn a new line and there was no way he was stepping over it.

No. Freaking. Way.

Sabrina hadn't realised she had slept during the drive from her flat to Max's house in Notting Hill. She woke up when the car stopped and straightened from her slumped position in the passenger seat. She hadn't been to this new house of his before—but not for want of trying by his and her parents. She had walked past it once or twice but was always so keen to avoid him that she had stopped coming to the Portobello Road markets for fear of running into him.

The house was one in a long row of grand four-storey white terrace houses. Each one had a black wrought-iron balustrade on the second-floor balcony and the same glossy black decorative fencing at street level.

When Max led the way inside, she got a sense of what Lizzie Bennet in *Pride and Prejudice* had felt when seeing Pemberley, Mr Darcy's estate, for the first time. *This could be your home if you marry him.*

She turned in a circle in the black and white tiled foyer, marvelling at the décor that was stylish and elegant without being over the top. The walls and ceiling were a bone white but the chandelier overhead was a black one with sparkling crystal pendants that tinkled with the movement of air. There was a staircase leading to the upper floors, carpeted with a classic Persian runner with brass rods running along the back of each step to hold it in place. Works of art hung at various points, which she could only presume were originals. He didn't strike her as the sort of man to be content with a couple of cheap knock-offs to adorn his walls, like she had done at her flat.

'I'll show you to your room,' Max said. 'Or would you like something to eat and drink first?'

Sabrina tried to smother a yawn. 'No, I think I'll go straight to bed. I'm exhausted.'

He carried her small bag and led the way up the stairs, glancing back at her every few steps to make sure she was managing okay. It would have been touching if it hadn't been for how awkward the situation between them was. She was very much aware of how she had rocked his neat and ordered life with her bombshell news. She was still trying to come to terms with it herself. How was she going to run her business and look after a baby? What was she going to say to her parents and brothers?

Oh, by the way, I got myself knocked up by my mortal enemy Max Firbank.

'I'll show you around tomorrow, but the main bathroom is on the ground floor, along with the kitchen and living areas,' Max said. 'On this floor there's my study, second door on the left, and the guest bedrooms, each with its own bathroom. My room is on the third floor. There's a gym on the top floor.'

Sabrina stopped on the second-floor landing to catch her breath. 'Who needs a gym with all these stairs?'

He frowned and touched her on the arm. 'Are you okay?'

'Max, I'm fine. Please stop fussing.'

He drew in a breath and released it in a whoosh, his hand falling away from her forearm. 'Tomorrow I'll have the rest of your things brought over from your flat.'

'How am I going to explain why I'm not at home if my parents or brothers drop by? Where will I say I'm staying?'

'Tell them you're staying with a friend.'

Sabrina arched her eyebrows. 'Is that what you are now? My…friend?'

He glanced at her mouth before meeting her gaze with his inscrutable one. 'If we're going to be bringing up a child together then we'd damn well better not be enemies.'

She had a feeling he was fighting hard not to touch her. One of his hands was clenching and unclenching and his chiselled jaw was set in a taut line. 'This is your worst nightmare, isn't it? Having me here, pregnant with a baby you didn't want.'

'Let's not talk any more tonight. We're both tired and—'

'I'm not so tired that I can't see how much you're hating this. Hating *me*.' She banged her fist against her chest for emphasis. 'I didn't do it deliberately, you know.'

'I never said you did.'

Sabrina was struggling to contain her overwrought emotions. Her life was spiralling out of her control and there was nothing she could do about it. She swallowed a sob but another one followed it. She turned away and squeezed her eyes shut to stop the sting of tears.

Max put the bag down and placed his hands on her shoulders, gently turning her to face him, his expression etched with concern. 'Hey...' His finger lifted her face so her eyes met his. 'Listen to me, Sabrina. I do not hate you. Neither do I blame you for what's happened. I take full responsibility. And because of that, I want to take care of you in whatever way you need.'

But I need you. The words stayed silent on her tongue. She would not beg him to make love to her again. She wanted him to own his desire for her. To own it instead of denying it. She blinked the moisture away from her eyes. 'I'm worried about how I'll cope with my work and a baby. What if I lose my business? I've worked so hard to get it to this stage.'

His hands tightened on her shoulders. 'You will not lose your business. You can appoint a manager or outsource some work. The golden rule in running a business is only to do the stuff that only you can do.'

'I've been trying to do that by hiring a part-time assistant but she messed up my booking for Venice,' Sabrina said.

'It takes time to build up your confidence in your staff but if you train them to do things the way you want them done, and check in occasionally to see if they're on track, then things will eventually run the way you want them to.' He removed his hands from her shoulders and picked up her bag again. 'Now, young lady, it's time for you to get some shut-eye.'

He led her to one of the guest bedrooms further down

the corridor. It was beautifully decorated in cream and white with touches of gold. The queen-sized bed was made up with snowy white bedlinen, the collection of standard and European pillows looking as soft as clouds. The cream carpet threatened to swallow her feet up to the ankle and she slipped off her shoes and sighed as her toes curled against the exquisite comfort of luxury fibres.

Max put Sabrina's bag on a knee-high chest near the built-in wardrobes. 'I'll leave you to settle in. The bathroom is through there. I'll see you in the morning.' His tone was so clipped he could have trimmed a hedge. He walked the door to leave and she wondered if he was thinking about the last time they had been alone together in a room with a bed. Did he regret their lovemaking so much that he couldn't bear the thought of repeating it? It felt uncomfortably like her boyfriend walking away, rejecting her. Hurting her.

'Max?'

He turned back to face her. 'Yes?'

Sabrina had to interlace her fingers in front of her body to keep from reaching out to him. She couldn't beg him to stay with her. Wouldn't beg him. The risk of him rejecting her would be too painful. 'Nothing…' A weak smile flickered across her lips. 'Goodnight.'

''Night.' And then he left and closed the door with a firm click.

CHAPTER SEVEN

MAX WENT DOWNSTAIRS before he was tempted to join Sabrina in that damn bed. What was wrong with him? Hadn't he done enough damage? He wanted slip in between those sheets with her, even if just to hold her against his body. He hadn't forgotten how it felt to have her satin-soft skin against his. He hadn't forgotten how it felt to glide his hands over her gorgeous breasts or how it felt to bury himself deep into her velvet warmth.

But he must *not* think about her like that. He had to keep his distance otherwise things could get even more complicated than they already were. Relationships got complicated when feelings were involved and he was already fighting more feelings than he wanted to admit. Everything was different about his relationship with Sabrina. Everything. And if that wasn't enough of a warning for him to back off in the feelings department, he didn't know what was.

He couldn't remember the last time he'd had a sleepover with a lover. It hadn't been in this house as he'd only moved in a few months ago once the renovations had been completed. He hadn't even shared his previous house with Lydia in spite of her broad hints to move in with him.

Max sat at his desk in his study and sighed. For the next six weeks he would have to make sure he kept his relationship with Sabrina completely platonic. Since when had he found it sexy to make love to a pregnant woman? But now he couldn't stop thinking about the changes her body was undergoing.

Changes *he* had caused.

His gaze went to the framed photograph of his family on his desk. It had been taken just days before Daniel had died. His mother and father were sitting either side of him and he was holding his brother across his lap. Everyone was smiling, even Daniel.

Max wondered if he would ever be able to look at that photograph without regret and guilt gnawing at his insides. Regret and guilt and anger at himself for not doing more to help his little brother. It had taken many years for his parents to smile again, especially his mother.

Would the birth of his parents' first grandchild heal some of the pain of the past?

When Sabrina woke the next morning, it took her a moment to realise where she was. The room was bathed in golden sunlight, and she stretched like a lazy cat against the marshmallow-soft pillows. It was a Sunday so there was no rush to get out of bed...although staying in bed would be a whole lot more tempting if Max was lying here beside her. She'd heard him come up the stairs to his room on the floor above hers in the early hours of the morning. Didn't the man need more than three or four hours of sleep?

There was a tap at the door and she sat up in the bed. 'Come in.'

Max opened the door, deftly balancing a tray on one hand as he came in. 'Good morning. I thought you might like some tea and toast.'

'Oh, lovely, I haven't had breakfast in bed in ages.'

He came over to the bed and placed the tray, which had fold-down legs, across her lap. This close she could smell his freshly shampooed hair and the citrus fragrance of his aftershave. He straightened and gave his version of a smile. 'How are you feeling?'

'So far, so good,' Sabrina said. 'Sometimes the nausea hits when I first stand up.'

'Good reason to stay where you are, then.'

She picked up the steaming cup of tea and took a sip. 'Mmm…perfect. How did you know I take it black?'

His expression was wry. 'I think it's safe to say your parents have told me just about everything there is to know about you over the years.'

Not quite everything.

Sabrina had never told her parents about her first sexual experience. The only person she'd told was Holly. It was too embarrassing, too painful to recall the shame she'd felt to hear such horrible rumours spread about her after giving herself to her boyfriend. 'Seriously, they told you how I take my tea?'

He gave a half smile. 'Only joking. No, I've been observing you myself.'

She put her tea back on the tray and picked up a slice

of toast and peeped at him from half-lowered lashes. 'I've noticed.'

'Oh?'

'Yep. You got really annoyed when I danced with one of the guys at that party at my parents' house a few months back.' She nibbled on the toast and watched his expression go from that mercurial smile to a brooding frown. She pointed the toast at him. 'There. That's exactly how you looked that night.'

He rearranged his features back into a smile but it didn't involve his eyes. 'You imagined it. I was probably frowning about something else entirely.'

Sabrina examined her slice of toast as if it were the most interesting thing in the world. 'Thing is… I've never been all that comfortable with the dating scene.'

'But you're always going on dates.' Max's frown was one of confusion. 'You've nearly always got someone with you when you go to family gatherings.'

So, he'd noticed that too, had he? Interesting. Sabrina shrugged. 'So? I didn't want everyone to think I was a freak.' She hadn't intended to tell him about her past. It hadn't seemed necessary the night they'd made love. Max's magical touch had dissolved all of her fears of physical intimacy. Well, most of them. But it wasn't physical intimacy that was her problem now. Emotional intimacy was the issue. What if she developed feelings for him that weren't reciprocated? Real feelings. Lasting feelings. *Love* feelings.

'When was the last time you had sex with a guy?' His voice had a raw quality to it.

She looked at the toast in her hand rather than meet his gaze. 'Other than with you? Ten years.'

'*Ten years?*' The words all but exploded from his mouth.

Sabrina could feel her colour rising. 'I'm sure that seems like a long time to someone like you, who has sex every ten minutes, but I had a bad experience and it put me off.'

He took the toast out of her hand and held her hand in both of his. 'Sabrina…' His thumbs began a gentle stroking of her wrist, his eyes meshing with hers. 'The bad experience you mentioned…' His throat rose and fell as if he was trying to swallow a boulder. 'Were you—?'

'No, it was completely consensual,' Sabrina said. 'I was eighteen and fancied myself in love and felt ready to have sex for the first time. I never wanted my first time to be outside the context of a loving relationship. But my so-called boyfriend had another agenda. He just wanted to crow to his friends about getting it on with me. I overheard him telling his friends I was hopeless in bed. The gossip and rumours did the rounds of my friendship group. It was humiliating and I wanted to die from shame. Up until you, I hadn't been brave enough to sleep with anyone else.' She chanced a glance at him from beneath her lowered lashes. 'Go on, say it. Tell me I'm a frigid freak.'

His frown carved a deep V into his forehead, his hands so soft around hers it was as if he were cradling a baby bird. 'No…' His voice had that raw edge again. 'You're no such thing. That guy was a jerk to do that to you. You're gorgeous, sensual and so responsive I can barely keep my hands off you.'

His words were like a healing balm to her wounded self-esteem. So what if he didn't love her? He desired her and that would have to be enough for now. His gentle touch made her body ache to have him even closer, skin on skin. She leaned in and pressed a soft-as-air kiss to his mouth, just a brush of her lips against his. 'Thank you...'

His mouth flickered as if her light kiss had set off an electric current in his lips. He drew her closer, one of his hands going to the back of her head, the other to glide along the curve of her cheek, his mouth coming down to within a breath of hers. But then he suddenly pulled back to frown at her again. 'But that night we made love... My God, I probably hurt you. Did I?'

Sabrina wound her arms around his neck, sending her fingers into the thickness of his hair. 'Of course you didn't. You were amazingly gentle.'

'But you were practically a virgin.' His expression was etched with tension. 'I should have taken more time. I shouldn't have made love to you more than once. Were you sore? Did I do anything you didn't like?'

She shook her head. 'No, Max. I enjoyed every second of our lovemaking. I just wish...' She bit her lip and lowered her gaze.

'Wish what?'

'Nothing. I'm being silly.'

Max inched up her chin with the end of his finger. 'Tell me.'

Sabrina took a breath. 'I've only had sex four times

in my life, one time I don't want to even think about any more. The other three times were so amazing that I sometimes wonder if I imagined how amazing they were.'

'What are you saying?'

'I'm asking you to make love to me again.'

His eyes searched hers. 'Is that really what you want?'

She looked into his smouldering eyes. 'I want you. You want me too…don't you?'

His hand slid under the curtain of her hair. 'It scares me how much I want you. But I don't want to complicate things between us.'

'How will it complicate things if we sleep together? It's not as if I'm going to get pregnant.' Her attempt at humour fell flat if his reaction was anything to go by.

He closed his eyes in a slow blink, then he removed her hand from him and stood up. 'I'm sorry, Sabrina, but I can't. It wouldn't be fair to you.' He scraped a hand through his still-damp-from-a-shower hair. 'You're not thinking straight. It's probably baby brain or something.'

'Baby brain?' Sabrina choked out a humourless laugh. 'Is that what you think? Really? Don't you remember how amazing that night in Venice was?'

'Sabrina.' His stern schoolmaster tone was another blow to her flagging self-esteem.

She pushed the tea tray off her legs and set it on the other side of the bed. 'Or maybe sex is always that amazing for you. Maybe you can't even distinguish that night from the numerous other hook-ups you've had since.' She threw him a glance. 'How many have there been, Max?' Tears smarted in her eyes but she couldn't seem to stop herself from throwing the questions at him, questions she didn't really want answered. 'Is that why you've refused to sleep me with since that night? How many have you had since then? One or two a week? More?'

He drew in a long breath and then released it. 'None.'

'None?'

He came and sat beside her legs on the bed and took her hand again, his fingers warm and strong around hers. 'None.'

Sabrina used the back of her free hand to swipe at her tears. 'Are you just saying that to make me feel better?'

'It's the truth. There hasn't been anyone because…' He looked down at her hand in the cage of his, a frown pulling at his forehead.

'Because?'

His gaze met hers and a wry smile flickered across his mouth. 'I'm not sure.'

Sabrina moistened her dry lips. 'Was it…amazing for you too? That night in Venice, I mean?'

He gave her hand a squeeze. 'How can you doubt it? You were there. You saw what you did to me.'

She lowered her gaze and looked at their joined hands, thinking of their joined bodies and the sounds of their cries of pleasure that night. His deep groans and whole-body shudders. 'It's not like I have much experience to draw on…'

He brought up her chin with the end of his finger. 'It was amazing for me, sweetheart. You were everything a man could ask for in a lover.' His frown came back, deeper than before. 'I just wish I'd known you were so inexperienced. Are you sure I didn't hurt you?'

Sabrina placed her other hand on top of his. 'Max, listen to me. You didn't hurt me.'

He brought her hand up to his mouth, pressing his lips against the back of her knuckles, his gaze locked on hers. 'When I saw you at my mother's party last night I was considering offering you more than a one-night fling.' He lowered her hand to rest it against his chest. 'I would've been breaking all of my rules about relationships in doing so, but I couldn't get you out of my mind. Or stop thinking about how good we were together.'

'Then why won't you make love to me again?'

His irises were a deep smoky grey, his pupils wide and ink black, and they flicked to her mouth and back to her gaze. 'You're making this so difficult for me.' His voice was gravel rough and he leaned closer until his lips were just above hers. 'So very difficult...' And then his mouth came down and set hers aflame.

It was a soft kiss at first, slow and languorous, his lips rediscovering the contours of her mouth. But it soon changed when his tongue stroked across her bottom lip. She opened to him and his tongue met hers, his groan of satisfaction as breathless as her own. His hands came up to cradle her face, his fingers splaying across her cheeks, his mouth working its mesmerising magic on hers. The movement of his tongue against hers set off fireworks in her blood. Her pulse raced, her heart thumped, her need for him rising in a hot tide of longing that left no part of her body unaffected. Her breasts tingled at the close contact as he drew her closer, the satin of her nightgown sliding sensually over her flesh.

He lifted his mouth to blaze a hot trail of kisses along her neck to the scaffold of her left clavicle. 'God, I want you so damn much...' His voice came out as a growl, the warmth in his lips as hot as fire. He was making her burn for him. She could feel it smouldering between her legs, the slow burn of lust that he had awakened in her.

'I want you too.' She breathed the words against his lips, her tongue stroking his lower lip, tasting him, teasing him.

He sealed her mouth with his, massaging her lips in a tantalising motion that made her pulse and ache with feverish desire. His tongue danced with hers, an erotic choreography that made her senses sing. One of his hands slipped the shoestring strap of her nightgown down her shoulder, uncovering her right breast. He brought his mouth down to its rosy peak, his caress so gentle it made her shiver with delight. His teeth lightly grazed her nipple, his tongue rolling over and around it until she gave a gasp of pleasure. He lowered the other strap off her left shoulder, the satin nightgown slithering down to her waist, revealing her body to his feasting gaze.

'You are so damn beautiful.'

Sabrina began to lift his T-shirt, desperate to touch his warm male skin. 'I want to touch you.'

He pulled back to haul his T-shirt over his head, tossing it to the floor. He stood and came over to remove the tea tray from the bed and set it on top of a chest of drawers. He came back to her. 'Are you sure about this?'

'Never surer.' Sabrina wriggled out of her night-gown, a part of her a little shocked at her lack of shy-ness. But hadn't he already seen all there was to see? She loved the way he looked at her with eyes blazing with lust. It was the most ego-boosting thing to see him struggle to keep control. No one had ever made her feel as beautiful as he did. No one had ever made her feel proud to be a woman, proud of her curves, proud of her sounds as desire shuddered through her.

Max swallowed and stared at her for a long moment, seemingly still struggling with the tug-of-war between his body and his brain. Sabrina drank in the sight of him naked, his taut and tanned torso cut and carved with well-defined muscles that would have made Mi-chelangelo drool and sharpen his chisel. She had never thought of a man as being beautiful before—it was a term usually applied to women. But in Max's case it was entirely appropriate. There was a classical beauty about the structure of his face and body, the aristocratic lines and planes and contours reminding her of heroes—both fictional and historical—from times past.

Max gathered her close, his touch as gentle as if he were handling priceless porcelain. It made her skin lift and shiver in a shower of goose-bumps. 'Are you cold?' He frowned and glided his hand over her thigh.

Sabrina smiled and brushed her hand down the wall of his chest, suddenly feeling shy about touching him. But she ached to touch him. To caress him. 'I'm not cold. I'm just enjoying being touched. You have such incredible hands.'

He brought his mouth back to hers in a lingering

kiss that made her need of him throb deep in her core. Every movement of his lips, every touch of his tongue, every contact point of his body with hers made her desire build to the point of pain. There was a storm gathering in her feminine flesh, a tight turbulence that spread from her core to each of her limbs like all her nerves were on fire. There was a deep throbbing ache between her legs and every time his tongue flicked against hers, it triggered another pulse of lust that made it throb all the more. She moved against him restively, wanting more but not sure how to ask for it.

Perhaps he sensed her shyness, for he took one of her hands and brought it down between their bodies. 'You can touch me.' His voice was so deep and husky it made her skin tingle to think she was having such an effect on him.

Sabrina stroked him with her fingers, enjoying the satin-wrapped steel of his male flesh. He drew in a sharp breath as if her touch thrilled him as much as his thrilled her. 'Am I doing it right?'

'Everything you're doing is perfect.' His breathing increased its pace, his eyes dark and glittering with need.

She moved her hand up and down his shaft, enjoying the feel of him without the barrier of a condom. Skin on skin. The smoothness and strength of him making everything that was female in her do cartwheels of delight.

After a moment, he removed her hand and pressed her down so he was balanced above her on his elbows. 'I don't want to rush you.'

'Rush me?' Sabrina gave a soft laugh. 'I'm practically dying here I want you so much.'

His slow smile made her heart trip and kick. 'Slow is better. It makes it more enjoyable for both of us.'

She reached down to stroke him again. 'Isn't it killing you to hold on so long?'

His jaw worked as if he was reining in his response to her touch. 'I want this to be good for you. Better than good.'

Sabrina's heart was asking for more room inside her chest. He was the dream lover, the lover she had fantasised about for most of her adult life. A lover who put her needs ahead of his own. A lover who respected her and made sure she enjoyed every second of their lovemaking.

But she wanted more. More of him. All of him. He moved over her, gathering her close, nudging her entrance with his erection, taking his time to move, waiting for her to get used to him before going further.

It was so different from her first time as a teenager. So very different it made her chest tighten with emotion. If only *he* had been her first lover. Her body responded to him like fuel to fire. It erupted into sensations, fiery, pulsating sensations that rippled through her entire body. She welcomed him into her with a breathless gasp of pleasure, her inner muscles wrapping tightly around him, moving with him as he began to slowly thrust. Her need built and built within her, his rhythmic movements triggering electrifying sensations that made every cell of her body vibrate. Tension gathered again in her core, a teasing tantalising tension that was more powerful than before. It was taking over her body, taking over her mind, pulling her into one point of exquisite feeling...

But she couldn't quite complete the journey. Her body was poised on a vertiginous precipice, needing, *aching* to fall but unable to fly.

Max brought his hand down to her tender flesh, caressing, providing that blessed friction she needed to finally break free. And fly she did, in waves and ripples and pulses that left no part of her body unaffected. It was like being tossed into a whirlpool, her senses scattering as shockwave after shockwave rocketed through her. Sabrina heard someone gasping and crying in a breathless voice and realised with a jolt that those primal and earthy sounds had come from her.

Max waited until her storm had eased before he increased his pace, bringing himself to his own release with a series of shuddering movements that made her wonder if he had been as affected by their lovemaking as she. Or was this normal for him? Was sex simply sex for him and nothing else? The physical satiation of primal needs that could be met with any willing female? Or had he been as moved as she had been by the flow and ebb of sensations that were still lingering in her body like waves gently washing against a shore?

He began to play with her hair, running his fingers through the tousled strands, the slight pull on her scalp sending a frisson down her spine. How could one person's touch be so powerful? Evoke such incredible sensations in her body?

After a long moment, he raised his head to look down

at her, his hand now cradling the back of her head. His expression was confusing to read, it was as if he had pulled down an emotional screen on his face but it hadn't gone all the way down, leaving a gap where a narrow beam of light shone through. The contours of his mouth that hinted at a smile, the smoky grey-blue of his eyes, the pleated brow that wasn't quite a frown made her wonder if he—like her—was privately a little shocked at how good they were together. 'You were wonderful.' His voice had that gravel and honey thing going on. 'Truly wonderful.'

Sabrina let out a shuddery sigh—just thinking about the sensations he had caused made her shiver in delight. 'Is it like that for you all the time?'

He didn't answer for a moment and she wished she hadn't gone fishing for compliments. Stupid. Stupid. Stupid. Of course it wasn't different for him. Of course it wasn't special. Of course it wasn't unique.

She wasn't special.

She wasn't unique.

Max's hand cupped the side of her face, his gaze more blue than grey—a dark, intense blue that made her think of a midnight sky. 'It's not often as good as that. Rarely, in fact.'

Sabrina's heart lifted like it was attached to helium balloons. 'But it sometimes is?' Why couldn't she just let it drop? But she had to know. She longed to know if he felt even a portion of what she'd felt. Her body would never be the same. How could it? It had experienced a maelstrom of sensations that even now were lingering in her flesh in tiny tingles and fizzes.

A small frown appeared on his brow and his eyes moved between each of hers in a back and forth motion as if he were searching for something he didn't really want to find. 'Sabrina…' He released a short sigh. 'Let's not make this any more complicated than it already is.'

Sabrina knew she was wading into the deep end but couldn't seem to stop herself. 'What's complicated about asking you if the sex we just had was run-of-the-mill for you?'

He held her gaze for a beat and then pushed himself away. He got off the bed and rubbed a hand over the back of his neck, tilting his head from side to side as if to ease a knot of tension.

He let out another sigh and turned back to face her, a twisted smile ghosting his mouth. 'Okay, you win. It was great sex. Awesome. The best I've had in years, which was why I was going to offer you a longer fling yesterday at my mother's party.'

Sabrina searched his expression, wondering whether to believe him or not. How silly was she to push for a confession from him only to doubt it when he gave it to her? 'Do you mean it?' Her voice was as soft as a whispered secret, uncertain and desperately seeking reassurance.

Max came back to sit on the bed beside her. He took one of her hands and brought it up to his mouth, kissing each of her fingertips in turn, his eyes holding hers. 'You're a beautiful and sexy woman. I can't remember a time when I've enjoyed sex more.' He gave another rueful twist of his mouth. 'Maybe I've been dating the wrong type of woman.'

Sabrina lowered her gaze and chewed one side of her mouth. 'Better than not dating at all, I suppose…' She didn't want to think about him dating other women. Now that they'd made love again, it made her sick to think of him kissing and caressing someone else. Thank God he hadn't been with anyone since their night in Venice, but how would she feel if he had? But if she didn't marry him, he would be at liberty to sleep with whomever he wished.

It was her call.

Max tipped up her chin with his finger, meshing his gaze with hers. 'What happened to you when you were eighteen would be enough to put most people off dating for a decade. But you have no need to feel insecure. You're one hell of a sexy partner, sweetheart. That night we first kissed? I wanted you so badly it was all I could do to tear myself away.'

'Really?'

His smile made something in her chest ping. He leaned down to press a soft kiss to her mouth. 'Couldn't you tell?'

Sabrina smiled against his mouth. 'It was kind of an enthusiastic kiss now that I think about it.'

He kissed her again, a longer kiss this time, the movement of his lips stirring her senses into overdrive. He lifted his mouth just above hers, his eyes sexily hooded. 'Is that enthusiastic enough for you?'

She traced the line of his mouth with her finger, her body tingling with excitement at the way his hard body was pressing against her. 'Getting there.'

He captured her finger with his teeth, holding it in a soft bite, his eyes pulsating with lust. 'I want you.'

Sabrina shivered in anticipation and looped her arms around his neck. 'I want you too.'

He brought his mouth back down to hers, kissing her long and deep, his tongue gliding into her mouth with a slow thrust that made her body tremble. His hands cradled her face, his upper body pressing down on her breasts, the skin-on-skin contact thrilling her senses all over again. She could feel the swollen ridge of his erection against her lower body, and her inner core responding with tight contractions and clenches. The sweet tension was building, all her pleasure points in heightened awareness of his touch. One of his hands went to her breast in a slow caress that made her skin tighten and tingle. His thumb rolled over her nipple, back and forth until it was a hard pebble of pleasure. The sensations travelled from her breasts to her belly and below as if transmitted by a sensual network of nerves, each one triggered and tantalised by his spine-tingling touch. He went lower to caress her intimately, his clever fingers wreaking havoc on her senses, driving up her need until she was breathless with it.

But he coaxed her only so far, leaving her hanging in that torturous zone that made her wild with longing. Wild and wanton and racked with primitive urges she'd had no idea she possessed. She felt like she would *die* if he didn't let her come. The need was like a pressure cooker inside her flesh. Building. Building. Building.

He gently pressed her down with his weight, his body entering hers with a smooth deep thrust that made her gasp and groan in delight. Her body welcomed him, worshipped him, wrapped around him in tight coils of need that sent pulses of pleasure ricocheting through her flesh.

He set a slow rhythm at first, but then he gradually increased his pace and she went with him, holding him, stroking his back and shoulders, her body so finely tuned to his that she was aware of every breath he took, every sound he made, every movement of his body within hers.

He rolled her so she was lying on top of him, his hands gripping her hips, encouraging her to move with him in an erotic rhythm that intensified her pleasure. She should have felt exposed and vulnerable but she didn't, instead she felt sexy and desirable. His eyes gleamed with delight as she rode him, naked flesh to naked flesh, hers soft and yielding, his hard and commanding.

Sabrina could feel the tight tingle in the core of her being; the slow build was now a rush of heady sensation threatening to consume her like a swamping wave. It was terrifying and yet tantalising as her body swept her up into a tumult of powerful pulses of pleasure, blissful, frightening pleasure that stole her breath and blanked out her thoughts. She heard herself cry out, a high wail that sounded almost primitive, but she was beyond caring. Her body was riding out a cataclysmic storm that made every pore of her skin tingle and tighten as the waves of orgasm washed over her.

Max continued to move within her, his hands holding her by the hips now, his face screwed up in in-

tense pleasure as he pumped his way to paradise. It was
as thrilling as the orgasm she'd just had to watch him
shudder through his. The way his hands tightened on
her almost to the point of pain, the clench of the toned
muscles of his abdomen, the momentary pause before
he allowed himself to fly. The raw sexiness of his response made her feel proud of her femininity in a way
she had never before.

He arched his head back on the pillow and let out
a ragged-sounding sigh as his whole body relaxed. He
ran a light hand up and down her right arm, his touch
like an electrical current on her sensitised-by-sex skin.

His eyes meshed with hers, holding them in a lock
that communicated on another level—a level she could
feel deep in her flesh. Their bodies were still connected,
neither of them had moved. She hadn't been able to.
Hadn't wanted to.

He gave a crooked smile and gathered her close so
she was sprawled across his chest. She laid her head
against the thud of his heart, and sighed as his hand
went to the back of her head in a slow-moving caress
that made every hair on her scalp shiver at the roots.

Words didn't seem necessary, although Sabrina
had plenty she wanted to say. But she kept her mouth
closed. He might hold her like a romantic lover but
this was not a love match. She had to keep her head.
She had to keep her heart out of this. She closed her
eyes and nestled against him, breathing in the musky
scent of their coupling. For so long Max had been her
enemy. The man she actively avoided or if she couldn't
avoid him, she fought with him. But how would she

be able to conceal her body's involuntary response to him? How would she stop herself from betraying how he made her feel?

Max wasn't her ideal husband. How could he be when he'd always made it clear he didn't want children? He'd been prepared to marry his ex-fiancée but only on the proviso that the marriage would be childless. He didn't want the things Sabrina wanted, the things she'd wanted since she was a little girl. But now circumstances had forced them together because he refused to walk away from her and their child.

Max moved so he was lying beside her and leaning on one elbow. His free hand moved from her face in a slow caress down between her breasts to rest against the flat plane of her belly. There was a faintly disturbing gravitas about his expression that made her wonder if he was already regretting making love to her. Regretting the child they had made.

Sabrina searched his tense features, noted the shadows behind his eyes. 'Does your decision never to have children have something to do with what happened to your brother Daniel?' She knew she was crossing a line by bringing up the subject of his baby brother. Some of the tiny muscles on his face flinched as if she'd slapped him with the pain of the past.

His hand fell away from her belly and he rolled away and got off the bed, his back turned towards her. 'I was the last person to see him alive.' The words were delivered in a hollow tone that echoed with sadness. 'You didn't know that, did you?' His glance over his shoulder was almost accusing.

Sabrina pressed her lips together and shook her head. 'No…no, I didn't…'

He turned back around and drew in a savage-sounding breath, releasing it in a gust. 'No. Because my parents wanted to protect me from blame.' Guilt was etched on his features and shadowing his gaze in smoky clouds.

She frowned in confusion. Why was he blaming himself for his baby brother's death? 'But Daniel died of SIDS, didn't he?'

'Yes, but I can't help blaming myself.' His throat rose and fell. 'I was seven years old. Surely that's old enough to know if something was wrong with my baby brother? But I must have missed it. I thought he was asleep. If only I had acted earlier, called Mum to check on him or something.'

Sabrina thought of Max as a young child, confused and distraught by the death of his baby brother. Even adults blamed themselves, particularly mothers, when a baby tragically died of Sudden Infant Death Syndrome, so how much more would Max shoulder the blame from his immature and somewhat ignorant perspective as a young child?

'But, Max, you were so young. You shouldn't be blaming yourself for Daniel's death. It was a tragic thing but no way was it your fault. Your parents don't blame you, surely?' She had heard nothing of this from his parents or her own, who were such close friends of Gillian and Bryce Firbank.

'No, of course they don't,' Max said in the same grim tone. 'They were in shock and grieving terribly at the time but they were always careful to make sure I was shielded from any sense of responsibility for Daniel's death. But I couldn't stop blaming myself. Still can't, to be perfectly honest.' He gave a twisted movement of his mouth that was as sad to see as the shadows in his eyes.

'Oh, Max...' Sabrina got off the bed and went to him, put her arms around him and hugged him close. After a moment, she leaned back to look up into his eyes. 'I don't know what to say... I can't bear the thought of you blaming yourself all this time. Have you talked to your parents about it?'

He shook his head, his shoulders going down on a sigh. 'We hardly ever mention Daniel's name now. It upsets Mum too much.'

'Understandable, I guess.'

Max's arms fell away from around her body and he stepped back, his expression difficult to read. 'My mother had several miscarriages before and after Daniel died. That's why there was such a gap between Daniel and me. She desperately wanted another child after he died, but each time another pregnancy ended, I saw another piece of her fade away.' Something flickered in his gaze. 'I've always felt guilty about my decision not to have children. My parents would love grandchildren. But I realised I can't tell them about this baby of ours until we're through the danger period. It would destroy them to have their hopes raised and then dashed.'

'Your poor mum. I'm not sure I knew about the miscarriages,' Sabrina said. 'Mum's never mentioned it. Neither has your mum.'

'She doesn't talk about it. Hasn't for decades. She's always so upbeat and positive but I know she must still think about it.' He sighed again. 'And that's another thing I blame myself for. My parents' marriage has been tested way too much because of my failure to protect my brother.'

'But your parents are happy together, aren't they? I mean, they always look like they are. Your dad adores your mum and she adores him.'

His mouth gave a twisted movement, his eyes shadowed. 'But how much happier would they have been if I hadn't let them down?'

Sabrina placed her hand on his arm. 'Max, you haven't let them down. It's not your fault. They're amazingly proud of you. They love you.'

He covered her hand with his and attempted a smile. 'You're a sweet girl, Sabrina. But I have a habit of letting people down in the end. That's why I keep my relationships simple. But nothing about us is simple now, is it? We've made a baby.'

Sabrina hadn't realised until now how deeply sensitive Max was. He was aware of the pain his mother had suffered and was doing all he could to protect Sabrina during the early days of her pregnancy. But marrying him was a big step. Sleeping with him six weeks ago had changed her life in more ways than she had thought possible. 'Max…this offer of yours to marry me…'

His hands came up to cradle her face, his eyes moving back and forth from her gaze to her mouth. His breathing had altered, so too had hers. Their breaths mingled in the small space between their mouths, weaving an intoxicating spell on her senses. 'Maybe I need to work a little harder to convince you, hmm?'

His mouth came down and covered hers, his lips moving in soft massaging movements that made every bone in her body feel like it had been dissolved. She swayed against him, dizzy with need, her body on fire with every spine-tingling stroke and glide of his tongue. The dance of their mouths was like sophisticated choreography, no one else could have kissed her with such exquisite expertise. No one else could have made her mouth feel so alive, so vibrantly, feverishly alive. Her heart picked up its pace, sending blood in a fiery rush to all the erogenous zones of her body, making her acutely aware of pleasure spots that ached to be touched, longed to be caressed. Longed to be filled with his intimate invasion.

Max lifted his mouth off hers, his eyes still gleaming with arousal. 'That one night was never going to be enough. We both know that.'

'Then why didn't you contact me afterwards?'

His mouth shifted in a rueful manner. 'We agreed to stay clear of each other but there wasn't a day that went past that I didn't regret agreeing to that rule.'

Sabrina hadn't been too enamoured with that rule either. Every day of those six weeks she'd ached to see him. Ached to touch him. Ached to give herself to him. But that was how she'd got in to this mess in the first place. Max and she had made a child together from their one night of passion.

Passion but not love.

Max didn't love her and was only offering to marry her because of their child. Her dreams of a romantic happily ever after with a man who adored her were fast disappearing.

'Do you regret this?' Sabrina couldn't hold back the question. 'Taking our relationship to this level?'

His frown deepened and his hand stilled on her hair. 'No.' He released a jagged sigh and added, 'But I don't want you to get hurt. I'm offering you marriage. Not quite the sort you're after but it's all I can offer.'

Sabrina aimed her gaze at his Adam's apple. 'I know what you're offering, Max... I'm just not sure I can accept it...'

He brought her chin up with his finger and did that back and forth thing again with his eyes, searching hers for any trace of ambiguity. 'We're good together, Sabrina. You know that. We can make a go of this. We've both come from stable backgrounds so we know it'll be the best thing for our child to have both its parents together.'

She felt torn because there was nothing she wanted more than to give her baby a stable upbringing like the ones she and Max had experienced. Didn't every mother want that for her baby? But would marrying a man who didn't love her be enough in the long run? He might come to love their child, but would he ever come to love her as well? And why was she even asking such a question? She wasn't in love with Max. *Was she?* She had to keep her feelings out of it. If she fell for him it would make her even more vulnerable than she already was.

But she couldn't ignore the chemistry between them when her body was still tingling from head to foot from his lovemaking. Neither could she ignore the dread that if she refused to marry him, he would be free to go back to his playboy life. Sure, he would be an involved father but not permanently on site like hers had been. Sabrina released a sigh and rested her hand against his thudding heart.

'Okay, I will marry you, but we can't tell anyone until after the twelve-week mark. We'll have to keep our relationship secret from our families until then, because no way am I going to be subject to pressure and well-meaning but unsolicited advice from our families.'

The frown relaxed slightly on his forehead but it seemed to lurk in the grey shadows of his eyes. He brushed back her hair from her face and pressed a soft kiss to her lips. 'They won't hear about it from me.'

CHAPTER EIGHT

Two weeks passed and Sabrina's noisy and cramped flat became a distant memory. All of her things had now been moved and were either in storage or at Max's house. She was touched by his attention to detail, the way he made sure everything was perfectly set up for her. Nothing seemed too much trouble for him, but she couldn't help wondering if he was finding the rapid change in his neat and ordered life a little confronting.

But for her, living with him showed her how seriously she had misjudged him in the past. It made it harder and harder to remember exactly why she had hated him so much. Or had that been a defence mechanism on her part? Somehow her heart had recognised that he was the one man who could make her fall for him and fall hard.

Each time Holly came in for a fitting, Sabrina had to quell her own feelings of disappointment that her wedding wasn't going to be as she had dreamed and planned for most of her life.

But Holly wasn't Sabrina's best friend for nothing and it didn't take her long to pick up on Sabrina's mood at her fitting that afternoon. 'You don't seem yourself today, Sabrina. Is something wrong?'

Sabrina placed another pin in the skirt of Holly's gown to mark where she needed to take it in. 'Other than my husband-to-be is only marrying me out of duty because I'm pregnant with his baby?'

'Oh, honey,' Holly sighed. 'Do you really think Max doesn't care about you? Personally, I think he's been in love with you for months.'

Sabrina sat back on her heels and looked up at her friend. 'What makes you think that?'

Holly lifted one shoulder. 'It's just a vibe I got when I saw him at that party a few months ago. He was acting all dog-in-the-manger when you were dancing with that other guy.'

'So? He was probably just annoyed with me for drawing attention to myself.' Sabrina picked up another pin. 'Turn a little to the left. That's it.' She inserted the pin at Holly's waistline. 'Have you been dieting? This is the third time I've had to take this dress in.'

Holly laughed. 'Wedding nerves. Or excitement more like.'

There was a silence broken only by the rustle of fabric as Sabrina fiddled with the alterations on the dress.

'Have you and Max set a date for the wedding?' Holly asked.

Sabrina scrambled to her feet and stabbed the pins back in her pincushion. 'Not yet…' she sighed. 'I can't see him wanting a big one. He's never been one for large gatherings. He missed out on the Firbank party animal gene.'

Holly's look was as probing as a spotlight. 'Have you decided what you feel about him?'

Sabrina made a business of tidying up her dressmaking tools. She had been deliberately avoiding thinking about her feelings for Max. They were confusing and bewildering, to say the least. He was the last person she had thought she would fall in love with, but how could she not lose her heart to such a wonderful man? He was everything she wanted in a life partner. He was stable and strong and dependable. He had good family values, he was hard working and supportive.

Yes, he was nervous about becoming a father, which was understandable given what had happened to his baby brother. But she wished he would open up more to her about his concerns. To let her in to his innermost doubts and fears. She had hated him for so long, loathed and resented him, and yet these days she only had to think of him and her heart would flutter and a warm feeling spread through her body. 'It's complicated...' She glanced at her friend. 'I used to think I hated him but now I wonder if I ever did. Was it like that for you with Zack?'

Holly's toffee-brown eyes melted at the sound of her fiancé's name. 'It was exactly like that. I hated him when I first met him but as soon as he kissed me...' she gave a dreamy smile '... I think that's when I fell completely and hopelessly in love.'

Sabrina knew from earlier conversations with Holly that handsome playboy Zack Knight had fallen in love with Holly the moment he'd met her. With Zack's reputation as a celebrity divorce lawyer and Holly a twice-jilted wedding florist, their romance had been the talk of London. And while Sabrina was thrilled Holly and Zack were so in love and looking forward to their wedding in a few weeks' time, it made her situation all the more heart-wrenching. She longed for Max to love her the way she had come to love him. Her feelings for him—now that she'd acknowledged them—were intense and irreversible.

But would she be happy knowing, deep down, he was only marrying her out of a sense of duty?

Max was still privately congratulating himself on keeping his relationship with Sabrina a secret from his family. There was something deeply intimate about keeping their involvement quiet. The bubble of secrecy made every moment with her intensely special, as if they were the only two people left on the planet. He had never felt that close to anyone else before and it was both terrifying and tempting. Tempting to think it could grow and develop into something he had told himself never to aspire to because he didn't deserve it.

Worried he would somehow jinx it, destroy it.

It was still too early for Sabrina to be showing her pregnancy, but just knowing his baby was nestled inside her womb made him feel things he had never expected to feel. Not just fear, although that was there big-time, but flickers of excitement, anticipation, wonder. He caught himself wondering what their child would look like, who it would take after, what traits or quirks of personality it would inherit. He had even stopped avoiding people with prams and now took covert glances at the babies inside.

And he had gone to London's most famous toyshop and bought two handmade teddy bears—one with a blue ribbon and one wearing a pink tutu, because, for some reason, he couldn't get the idea of a tiny little girl just like Sabrina out of his mind. He was keeping the bears for when he and Sabrina came home from their first ultrasound appointment.

The day of the appointment, Max cleared his diary for the whole day because he was in no fit state to work even though it would only take up half an hour or so. He was barely able to speak on the way to the radiography centre as he was so lost in his tangled thoughts. His stomach pitched and pinched, his heart raced and his pulse rioted. What if there was something wrong with the baby?

He hadn't realised until now how much he cared about that little bunch of cells. The feelings ambushed him, making him wonder if other fathers felt like this. Men were mostly at arm's length from a pregnancy, distant from what was going on in their partner's body as it nurtured and sustained new life. But he felt an overwhelming sense of love for the child that was growing in Sabrina's womb. What was ahead for their child? What sort of person would they become? How could he as its father make sure it had everything it needed for a long and fulfilling and healthy life?

Max sat beside Sabrina in the waiting room, took her hand and rested it on his thigh. 'Nervous?'

She gave a wobbly smile. 'A little. Are you? You've been awfully quiet.'

He squeezed her hand. 'Sorry. I'm still getting my head around everything.'

A flicker of worry passed through her blue gaze and she looked down at their joined hands. 'I'm sorry about all of this... I can't help feeling it's my fault we're in this situation.'

'Sabrina.' He tipped up her chin and locked his eyes with hers. 'It's not your fault. If it's anyone's fault it's mine.'

Max was relieved Sabrina had finally agreed to marry him. He wanted nothing more than to provide a stable and loving home for their child. And it would be a loving relationship, though perhaps not in the most romantic sense. He genuinely cared about Sabrina, she had been a part of his life for so long, and yet it had only been recently that he had found out the more complex layers to her personality.

He had been deeply touched when she'd revealed to him what had happened to her as a teenager. He wished she had told him that night in Venice but she hadn't and he had to accept it. Would he have still made love to her? He couldn't answer that question. The need between them was so strong and seemed to be getting stronger.

Sabrina's name was called and they were led into the examination room. Max continued to hold her hand as the sonographer moved the probe over Sabrina's still flat abdomen. How could a baby—his baby—be growing inside her? It didn't seem real until he saw the image of the foetus come up on the screen. He could barely register what the sonographer was saying. All he could think was that was his child floating around in the amniotic sac that would feed and nurture it until it was born in seven months' time.

His chest suddenly felt tight with emotion, his heart thumping with a combination of dread and wonder. What sort of father would he be? How could he trust that he would always do the right thing by his child? He had never thought this day would occur and yet here he was sitting with his wife-to-be and staring at a 3D image of their baby.

His wife-to-be. Sabrina, his fiancée. The mother of his child.

Sabrina's hand grasped his tighter. 'Isn't it incredible?' Her eyes shone with the same wonder he was feeling. 'That's our baby.'

Max squeezed her hand and smiled. 'It sure is.'

'You have a few more weeks to decide if you want to know the sex,' the sonographer said. 'It's usually pretty clear from about eighteen to twenty weeks.'

'Do you want to know the sex of the baby?' Sabrina asked Max after the scan was completed.

'Do you?'

'I asked you first.'

'I'm not a great one for surprises, as you probably know,' Max said. 'But I'll go with what you decide. It's your call.'

Her teeth did that lip-chewing thing that never failed to make him want to kiss away the teeth marks on her pillow-soft lips. 'I kind of want to know but I kind of don't. Does that make sense?'

He smiled and brought her hand up to his lips, kissing her bent knuckles. 'It makes perfect sense. At least you've got a bit of time to make up your mind.'

She nodded and gave a fleeting smile. 'It's a little scary now that I've seen the baby… I mean, it makes it so…so real, doesn't it?'

Max kept her hand in his. 'You don't have to be afraid, sweetie. I'll be with you every step of the way.'

She looked at the printed photo of their baby that the sonographer had given them. 'I wonder who it will take after? You or me? Or maybe a bit of both of us.'

'As long as it's healthy, that's all that matters,' Max said. And even then things could happen. Bad things. Tragic things. His gut churned at the thought and his heart started tripping and hammering again. Boom. Trip. Boom. Trip. Boom. Trip. Boom.

Sabrina must have sensed his disquiet and placed her other hand over their joined ones. 'You'll be a wonderful father, Max. I know you will.'

He tried to smile but it didn't quite work. 'Come on. Let's get you home so you can rest.'

Sabrina wasn't tired when they got home but she was concerned about Max. He had seemed preoccupied at the appointment and he'd kept looking at the photo of the baby since then with a frown pulling at his brow. Was he thinking of all the things that could go wrong even after a healthy baby was born? There were no words to settle his fears because no one could guarantee that nothing would happen to their baby. Even after gestation and infancy, there was still the treacherous landscape of childhood and adolescence. But worrying about it wouldn't change what fate had decided—or so she kept telling herself.

Max came into the bedroom where she was resting a short time later, carrying two shopping bags. He sat on the edge of the bed and passed them to her. 'For the baby, whatever sex it is.'

Sabrina opened the first bag to find a handmade teddy bear wearing a blue ribbon. 'So you think it's a boy?'

He gave a one-shoulder shrug. 'I'm hedging my bets. Open the other bag.'

She opened the bag and pulled out another teddy bear but this one was wearing a pink tutu. It touched her that Max had already gone shopping for their baby. It made her wonder if his growing feelings for the baby would somehow, one day, include her. 'They're so cute, Max. That was so thoughtful of you.'

He picked up the blue-ribboned teddy bear and balanced it on his knee, his finger absently flicking the ribbon around its neck. 'Both Daniel and I had one of these. Our grandparents gave them to us.' Something drifted over his features like a shadow across the sky. 'Daniel's was buried with him; it sat on the top of his coffin during the service. I'm not sure if Mum kept mine or not. I think she found it hard to look at it once Daniel had died.'

Her heart ached at what Max must have felt at his baby brother's funeral. And she felt deeply moved that he had shared with her a little more about his childhood and the sadness he still carried. Sabrina took the bear out of Max's hands and set it beside the pink-tutu-dressed one by her side. She took his hand in hers and stroked the strong tendons running over the back of his hand. 'I have a feeling this baby is going to bring a lot of joy to both our families, but especially to yours. You'll be a fabulous dad. I just know it.'

He gave a ghost of a smile and lifted her hand up to his mouth, pressing a soft kiss to the backs of her knuckles. 'I wish I had your confidence.' He lowered her hand to his lap and circled one of her knuckles with his thumb, a frown settling between his eyebrows. 'I'll do my best to protect you and the baby. But what if I fail?'

Sabrina grasped his hand, squeezing it. 'You won't fail. Don't even think like that, Max. Everyone feels a bit daunted by the prospect of parenthood. It's normal.'

He gave another fleeting smile but a shadow remained in his gaze. 'That reminds me...' He let go of her hand and pulled a small velvet box out of his trouser pocket. 'I have something else for you.' He handed the box to her. 'Open it. If you don't like it we can change it for something else.'

Sabrina took the box and prised open the lid. Inside was an exquisite diamond ring that glinted as the light caught all its facets. Being in the business she was in, she saw lots of engagement rings but none had been as gorgeous as this one. 'Oh, Max, it's beautiful...' She glanced up at him. 'But it looks frightfully expensive.'

'And why wouldn't I buy you an expensive ring?'

Because you don't love me.

She didn't have to say it out loud. It was loud enough

in her conscience to deafen her. She looked back at the ring and carefully took it out of its velvet home.

Max suddenly took the ring from her and lifted her hand and slipped it over her ring finger. 'There. What about that? A perfect fit.'

'How did you guess my size? Or is that another thing my parents have told you over the years?'

He gave a twisted smile. 'They might well have. But, no, this time I guessed.'

Sabrina looked down at the ring winking on her finger. She tried not to think about how different this moment might have been if they were like any other normal couple. A couple who had met and fallen in love the old-fashioned way. 'It's a gorgeous ring, Max. Truly gorgeous.'

A frown appeared on his forehead. 'Would you have preferred to choose one yourself?'

'No. This one's perfect.' She glanced at him again. 'But I'll have to only wear it in secret for another month because if either of our parents see this giant sparkler on my hand—'

'Maybe we should tell them.'

Sabrina frowned. 'But I thought we agreed to keep it quiet until the twelve-week mark?'

He took her hand and toyed with the ring on her finger, his inscrutable gaze meshing with hers. 'I know but we've had the first ultrasound and everything looks healthy so—'

She tugged her hand out of his and held it close to her body. 'No, Max. I think we should wait. It's only another month and then we can tell everyone about the baby and…and set a date for the wedding.' Every time she thought about the wedding she had a panic attack. How was she going to get a dress made in time? What if she ballooned and looked nothing like the picture she had in her mind of the bride she had always wanted to be?

But it wasn't just about looking the part…what if Max *never* came to love her? People who genuinely loved you never deserted you. It was love that sheltered and sustained a relationship, not an overblown sense of duty.

Max captured her hand again and stroked it in warm, soothing motions. 'I don't want you to think I'm hiding you from my parents out of shame or embarrassment, like we're having some tawdry little affair. I'm proud to be your partner.'

Sabrina squeezed his hand. 'Oh, Max, that's so sweet of you. But I'm kind of enjoying our little secret. I'm surprised we've managed to keep it quiet this long. But I'm sure that's only because my mum and dad are away on holiday at the moment. I told Mum when she phoned me that I was moving out of my flat to stay with a friend. Unusually for her, she didn't ask which one, but it won't be long before she does.'

'But would it be such a problem to tell her you're staying with me? I don't want to come between you and your parents, especially your mother. And especially now you're pregnant.'

Sabrina rolled her eyes. 'You know what my parents are like, always telling me what I should do. I know they mean well, but as soon as they know I'm pregnant they'll whip out their medical bags and whisk me off to have every test under the sun. I just want to have time to get used to it myself. I'm enjoying the secrecy and the privacy for now.'

Max turned her hand over and traced a lazy circle in her palm. 'I'm enjoying it too.'

'You are?'

His eyes glinted. 'So much so, I think we should go away for the weekend.'

A bubble of excitement formed in her chest. 'Where to?'

'It's a secret.'

Sabrina gave him a coy look. 'You kind of like your secrets, don't you?'

He gave a quick grin that transformed his face. 'More than I realised. Can you take the time off work? I know you usually work on a Saturday but—'

'It's fine. My assistant Harriet is getting better all the time so she can take over while I'm away. I figured she's going to have to do more and more for me the further along I get with the pregnancy.'

Max stroked his hand over the back of her head. 'How long will you work? I can support you if you'd like to take more time off and—'

'I love my job, Max. Pregnancy isn't a disease. I'm perfectly healthy and—'

'I just worry about you doing too much. Running a business more or less singlehandedly is not an easy task. You need to outsource so you're not overburdened with unnecessary work. We have a wedding to plan and a baby on the way and that needs to take priority, surely?'

How could he suggest she take time out from the

business she loved as if it was nothing more than a fill-in job? Sabrina swung her legs over the edge of the bed and stood. 'Will you stop lecturing me about what I should do? You're starting to sound like my parents.'

'Yeah, well, maybe your parents are onto something.' Max's tone tightened.

She glared at him, stung by his betrayal in siding with her parents. 'What's that supposed to mean?'

He released a rough-sounding breath. 'Look, I don't want to argue with you. I'm just saying you need to do things a little differently. You're a talented designer, no question about that, but you can't possibly make every single dress yourself.'

'I don't make every one myself. I have a small team of seamstresses but I do all the hand-sewing myself because that's my signature touch.'

'Would it help if I set up a workroom for you here?' Max asked. 'You could work from home and get your assistant to run the shop so you can rest when you need to.'

It was a tempting offer. She had often thought of working from home without the distraction of phones and walk-ins who were 'just browsing'. Some of her hand sewing was complicated and painstaking work and she needed to concentrate. And truth be told, she had been feeling a little overwhelmed with it all even before she'd found out she was pregnant. 'You wouldn't mind?'

'Why would I mind?'

'I don't know… I just thought weddings weren't your thing.'

He came back to take her hands in his. 'There is only one wedding I'm interested in right now and that's ours. And the sooner it happens the better.'

Sabrina chewed the side of her mouth. 'But I need time to make myself a dress.'

'Don't you have one in stock you could use?'

She rolled her eyes and pulled her hands away. 'Duh. I've been planning my wedding since I was four years old. No. I cannot wear a dress from stock. I want to make it myself.'

He frowned. 'How long will it take to make one?'

'I usually have a six-month lead time for most of my clients. I'm only doing Holly's in a shorter time frame because she's my best friend.'

'Six months?' His tone was so shocked she might have well as said it would take a century.

'I might be able to rustle something up a little earlier but I want my dress to be something I can be proud of when I look back on our wedding day.' Not to mention her relationship with Max. But would she look back on that with pride or despair?

'You're stalling.' The note of schoolmaster censure was back in his tone. 'I don't want to wait for months on end to get married. We've made the decision so let's get on with it.'

'I am not stalling,' Sabrina said. 'Weddings are not dinner parties where you invite a few guests, cook some food and open some wine. It takes months of planning and—'

'So we'll hire a wedding planner.'

'Max, you're not listening to me,' Sabrina said. 'I

want to plan my own wedding. I want to make my own dress. I don't want it to be a rushed shotgun affair.'

His jaw worked for a moment. 'I'd like to be married before the baby is born. I want it to have my name.'

'The baby will have your name regardless.' Sabrina sighed and came over to him, touching him on the forearm. 'Maybe we can compromise a bit. I can't say I want to walk up the aisle with a big baby bump on show. That's not quite what I envisaged for myself when I was growing up.'

His hands came to rest on the tops of her shoulders, his eyes searching hers. 'Would you be happy with a small and simple wedding, just family and a few close friends?'

She would have to be happy with it because she was starting to realise there wasn't time for her to plan anything else. How far from her childhood dreams had she come? 'Is that what you would like? Something small and intimate?'

One of his hands went to the nape of her neck, the other to cradle the side of her face. 'I'm sorry I can't give you exactly what you want but we can make do.'

Make do. There was that annoying phrase again. But Sabrina was increasingly aware of her habit of idealising stuff and ending up disappointed when nothing met her standards. Maybe it was better this way. To lower her expectations and be pleasantly surprised when it worked out better than she thought. She pasted on a smile. 'Then that's what we'll do. Make do.'

CHAPTER NINE

By the time the weekend came, Sabrina had almost convinced herself her relationship with Max was just like that of any other young couple in love and preparing for their marriage and a baby. Almost. He whisked her out of London on Friday afternoon, with their weekend bags loaded in the boot of his car, and drove a couple of hours into the countryside to a gorgeous Georgian mansion a few kilometres from a quiet village.

The mansion had been recently renovated for the garden was still showing signs of having had tradesmen's workboots and ladders and other construction paraphernalia all over it. But even in the muted late evening summer light she could see the neglected garden's potential. Roses bloomed in messy abundance, clematis and fragrant honeysuckle climbed rampantly over a stone wall, and along the pathway leading to the front door she could see sweet alyssum filling every crack and crevice in a carpet of white and purple.

'What a gorgeous place,' Sabrina said, glancing at him as helped her out of the car. 'Is it yours?'

'Yes. Do you like it?'

'I love it.' She breathed in the clove-like scent of night stocks and sighed with pleasure. 'Wow. It's just like out of a fairytale. I'm almost expecting fairies or goblins to come dancing out of that back section of the wild garden.'

Max took her hand. 'Come on. I'll show you around.' He led her to the front door, taking care she didn't trip over the cracked pathway. 'I bought it a while back. I've been coming down when I can to do some of the work myself.'

She gave him a sideways glance. 'Well, I know from personal experience how good you are with your hands.'

He grinned back and squeezed her hand. 'Cheeky minx. Careful, the sandstone step here is a bit uneven. I was going to replace it but I quite like the fact it's been worn down over the years.'

It was becoming more and more apparent to Sabrina that Max was a traditionalist at heart. He was always careful in his designs to respect a building's history and incorporate it cleverly into any new development on the same site, just as he had done with his house in Notting Hill. And wasn't his determination to marry her because of the baby another indication of his commitment to his strong values?

Max unlocked the door and led her inside the house, switching on lights as he went. The interior had been tastefully decorated in mostly neutral colours, which brought in more light. The furniture was a mixture of old and new and she wondered if he'd chosen it himself or got an interior decorator to do it for him. He would

certainly know plenty in the course of running his architectural firm. Most of whom would be female.

Sabrina swung her gaze back to his. 'You have excellent taste. Or did you get someone to do the decorating for you?'

He kicked at the crooked fringe on the rug on the
floor with his foot to straighten it out. 'There's a woman
I use now and again. She's good at listening to what I
want and getting on with it.'

The big green-eyed monster was back and poking
at Sabrina's self-esteem. 'Is that all you use her for?'

Max frowned. 'Pardon?'

Sabrina wished she hadn't spoken. She turned away
and ran her hand over a beautiful walnut side table.
'Nothing…'

He came up behind her and placed his hands on her
shoulders and turned her to face him. 'Sabrina. Listen
to me.' His voice was gentle but firm. 'You and I are in
a committed relationship. You don't have to worry that
I'll be looking at any other woman. Ever. Understood?'

She chewed at her lower lip. 'I'm sorry but I can't
help feeling a little insecure. It's not like we're in love
or anything. How can you be so certain you won't fall
in love with someone else?'

His hands tightened on her shoulders. 'Stop torturing yourself with unlikely scenarios. I realise this is a
tricky time for you. You have crazy hormonal stuff happening and a lot has happened in a short period of time.
But believe me when I say I'll remain faithful to our
marriage vows. You have my word on that, sweetheart.'

Sabrina looked into his grey-blue eyes and wished there

was a magic spell she could cast that would make him fall in love with her. It would be so much easier to relax and enjoy every facet of their relationship if she thought it was founded on the things that were most important to her.

He was offering commitment without love. Other men offered love and then reneged on the commitment. Could she continue to hope and pray Max would find the courage to relax the guard around his heart and love her as she longed to be loved? She stretched her mouth into a smile. 'Thank you.'

He inched up her chin and planted a kiss on her lips. 'Come on. I'll show you upstairs.'

Sabrina followed him up the staircase to the landing, where eight bedrooms each with their own bathroom were situated. The master bedroom was huge with a gorgeous window seat that overlooked the rambling garden and the landscape beyond. Sabrina knelt on the chintz-covered cushioned seat and looked at the wonderful view of rolling fields and the dark green fringe of forest and wondered if she had ever seen such a beautiful setting. 'Gosh, it's so private. Are there any neighbours?'

'Not close by,' Max said. 'That's why I bought it. It's nice to get away from the hustle and bustle every now and again.'

Sabrina rose from the window seat. 'Do you plan to live here one day? It's a big house for one person. I mean, you weren't planning on settling down and all.'

He reached past her to open the window to let in some fresh air. 'It's more of a weekender. I find it relaxing to be surrounded by nature instead of noise. It clears my head so I can work on my designs.'

Sabrina bit her lip and fiddled with the brass knob the curtains were held back by. 'As big as this place is, you might not get much head space when there's a wailing baby in the house…'

He took her hands in his, his thumbs stroking the backs of her hands. 'Are you nervous about being a mum?'

'A little…yeah, actually a lot.' She sighed. 'I know women have been having babies for ever but it's my first baby and I can't help feeling a little worried I won't be good enough.'

He cut back an incredulous laugh and squeezed her hands. 'Not good enough? You'll be the best mum in the world. You're a natural nurturer.'

'But don't you worry about how this baby is going to change both our lives? I mean, a bit over a month ago we were both single and hating each other. Now we're having a baby and getting married.'

'I have never hated you.' His tone had a strong chord of gravitas.

But what did he feel for her? 'You certainly gave me that impression. Not that I can talk, of course.'

His expression was cast in rueful lines. 'Yes, well, with our parents watching us like hawks for any sign of a melting of the ice between us, I guess we both did or said things we regret now.'

Sabrina moved closer as his hands went to her hips. It never ceased to amaze her how neatly they fitted together like two pieces of a puzzle. 'You're being far too gracious, Max. I seem to remember being an absolute cow to you on a number of occasions.'

He dropped a kiss to the tip of her nose and smiled. 'You're forgiven.'

She smiled back, struck again by how much a smile transformed his features. She lifted her hand to his face and traced the contours of his mouth. 'You have such a nice smile. I don't think I ever saw you smile at me before a few weeks ago.'

'Maybe you're teaching me to lighten up a bit.'

'By accidentally falling pregnant? Yeah, like that's the way to do it.'

He brushed her hair back from her forehead. 'What's done is done. We're moving forward now and it won't help either of us to focus on the negatives about how we got together.' He stepped back with a brief flash of a smile. 'I'm going to bring in our things while you settle in. I've brought some supper for us.'

Sabrina sat on the end of the bed once he'd gone, her thoughts in a messy tangle. Was she being too negative about their situation? She was a lot better off than many young women who suddenly found themselves pregnant after a one-night stand. Max was determined to stand by her and support her. He was bending over backwards and turning himself inside out to be the best partner he could be.

She was grateful he was standing by her, but it didn't stop her hoping his concern for her and the baby would grow and develop into lasting love.

When Sabrina came downstairs, Max had unpacked the car and loaded the fridge with the food he had brought. She was touched by how much effort he had put into making their weekend away so stress-free for her. She hadn't had to do anything but pack her overnight bag.

He came back into the sitting room with a glass of fresh orange juice and some nibbles on a plate. 'Here you go. I've just got to warm up the dinner.'

Sabrina took the juice and smiled. 'Who knew you were so domesticated?'

'Who indeed?'

He sat down beside her and slung his arm along the back of the sofa near her shoulders. His fingers played with the loose strands of her hair, making her scalp tingle and her skin lift in a frisson of delight. 'Not too tired?' he asked.

She leaned forward to put her juice on the coffee table in front of the sofa, then sat back to look at him. 'Not too tired for what?'

His eyes did that sexy glinting thing. 'No way am I making love to you until you've had something to eat, young lady.'

Sabrina shifted so she was straddling his lap, her arms going around his neck. 'But what if all I want right now is you?'

He ran his hands down the length of her arms, his touch lighting fires along her flesh. 'Those pregnancy hormones really are going crazy, hey?'

She had a feeling it had nothing to do with her hormones. It had everything to do with him. How he made her feel. 'Could be.' She brought her mouth down to his, meeting his lips in a kiss that sent a river of flame straight to her core. She could feel the pulsing ache of her body pressed so close to the burgeoning heat of his.

The surge of his male flesh reminding her of the erotic intimacy to come.

He drew in a harsh breath as if the leash on his self-control had snapped. One of his hands going to the back of her head to keep her mouth crushed to his. His tongue thrust between her lips, meeting hers in a hot sexy tangle that sent another shiver racing down her spine.

Sabrina set to work on undoing the buttons on his shirt, peeling it away from his body so she could touch his warm hard flesh. He slid his hands under her top, the glide of his slightly calloused hands on her naked skin making her ache for his possession. He deftly unclipped her bra and brought his hands around the front of her body to cradle her breasts. His thumbs stroked back and forth over her nipples, turning them into achingly hard peaks that sent fiery shivers to her core.

'God, you're so damn sexy I can hardly control myself.' His voice was deep and sounded like it had been dragged over a rough surface.

'Don't control yourself, then.' Sabrina licked his lower lip, relishing in the way he shuddered at her touch. 'You can do what you want to me if you'll let me do what I want to you, okay?'

He didn't answer but drew in a ragged breath and brought his mouth back to hers in a long drugging kiss that involved tongues and teeth and lips and mutual desire so ferocious it threatened to engulf them both.

Sabrina wrenched at his belt fastening, finally getting it undone and tugging it through the lugs of his trousers. She tossed it to the floor over her shoulder and it landed in a snake-like slither on the carpeted floor.

She wriggled down off his lap, quickly removing the rest of her clothes, a frisson passing over her flesh when she saw his eyes feasting on her. It amazed her how quickly his body responded to hers and how quickly hers responded to his. Even now she could feel the tight pulses and flickers of need deep in the core of her womanhood, the tender flesh swelling in high arousal, the blood pumping through her veins at breakneck speed.

'Take your trousers off.' Sabrina was a little shocked at how forthright she was being. Shocked but thrilled to be discovering her sensual power. For so many years she had doubted herself, felt ashamed and insecure. But with Max she felt powerfully sexy and feminine. There was no room for shame, only room for the celebration of her sensual awakening.

He stood and stepped out of his trousers, his expression a mixture of rampaging desire and caution at what she might do to him. She pushed him back down on the sofa, bending down on her knees in front of his seated form. 'Now I get to play naughty girl with you.'

Max sucked in another breath and put his hands on her shoulders. 'You don't have to do that—'

'I want to.'

'Oh, God…' He groaned as her hands encased him, moving up and down in massaging strokes the way he had taught her. But she wanted more. She wanted to taste him the way he had tasted her.

Sabrina gave him one long stroke with her tongue from base to tip, delighting in the whole-body shudder he gave. It gave her the impetus to keep going, to torture him with her tongue the way he had done to her.

She stroked him again with her tongue, back and forth like she was enjoying her favourite ice cream, casting him wicked temptress glances from beneath half-mast lashes. His breathing rate increased, his body grew more and more tense, every muscle and sinew struggling to keep control. Sabrina opened her mouth over him, drawing him in, sucking and stroking until he was groaning in blissful agony.

Max pulled himself away before he came, breathing hard, his eyes glazed with lust. 'Not all the way, sweetheart.'

'Why won't you let me?'

He got to his feet and picked her up in his arms. 'Because I have other plans for you.'

She linked her arms around his neck and shivered in anticipation. 'Ooh, that sounds exciting.'

He gave her a glinting smile and walked up the stairs, carrying her as if she weighed no more than one of the cushions off the sofa. When they got to the master bedroom, he laid her on the bed and came down beside her, his thighs in an erotic tangle with hers. He cupped one of her breasts in his hands, bringing his mouth down to take her tight nipple into his mouth. He swirled his tongue around its pointed tip, then gently drew on her with a light sucking motion that sent arrows of heat to her core. He moved to her other breast, pleasuring her with the gentle scrape of his teeth and the flick and stroke of his tongue.

Sabrina moved restlessly beneath him. 'Please. I want you *so* much…' Her body was throbbing with the need to feel him inside her. The hollow ache between her legs was unbearable, every nerve primed and poised for the erotic friction it craved.

'I want you too, so damn much, I'm nearly crazy with it.' He moved down her body, holding her hips with his hands as he kissed her abdomen from her belly button down to the top of her mound. She drew in a sharp breath as his mouth came to the heart of her desire. He separated her with the stroke of his tongue, moving along her sensitive flesh in a series of cat-like licks that made every hair on her head shiver at the roots.

It was too much and it wasn't quite enough. Her nerves were tight as an over-tuned cello string, vibrating with the need for release. And then she was suddenly there, falling apart under the ministrations of his lips and tongue, shattering into a million pieces as the tumult of sensations swept through her. She cried, she laughed, she bucked and moaned and clutched at his hair, but still he kept at her until the very last aftershock left her body. She flung her head back against the bed, her breathing still hectic. 'Oh, my God…that was incredible.'

Max placed a hand on her belly, a triumphant smile curving his mouth. 'But wait. There's more.' He moved back over her, careful not to crush her with his weight, and entered her with a smooth, thick thrust, making her gasp all over again.

He set a slow rhythm at first, but then he increased the pace at her urging. She wanted him as undone as she had been. She moved her hands up and down the bunched muscles of his arms, then placed them on his taut buttocks, kneading and stroking the toned flesh as his body moved intimately within hers.

'You feel so damn good.' His voice was part moan, part groan as his mouth came back to hers.

Sabrina kissed him back, using her lips and tongue and even her teeth at one point. The intensity of his passion for her was thrilling. The movement of his body, the touch and taste of him delighting her senses into an intoxicating stupor. She arched her spine, desperate to get closer, to trigger the orgasm she could feel building in her body.

He slipped a hand underneath her left hip, lifting her pelvis and shifting slightly to change the contact of their hard-pressed bodies. And just like that she was off again in a heart-stopping release that sent shockwaves through every inch of her flesh. It was like fireworks exploding, fizzing and flickering with blinding light and bursts of colour like a shaken kaleidoscope.

Sabrina was conscious of the exact moment he let go. She felt every shudder, every quake, felt the spill of his essence and held him in the aftermath, listening to the sound of his breathing slowly return to normal. There was something almost sacred about the silence that fell between them. The quiet relaxation of their bodies, the synchronisation of their breathing, the mingling of their sensual fragrances and intimate body secretions was so far removed from her first experience of sex it made her love for Max deepen even further.

Max leaned on one elbow and placed his other hand on her thigh. 'Was that exciting enough for you?'

Sabrina smiled a twisted smile and touched his stubbly jaw in a light caress. 'You know it was.'

He captured her hand and kissed her fingertips, holding her gaze with his. 'I've never been with a more responsive partner. Every time we make love you surprise me.'

She aimed her gaze at his Adam's apple, feeling suddenly emotional. 'I know I've said it before, but I wish you'd been my first lover. I can't believe I let that jerk mess with my head so much and for so long.'

He cradled her close, his hand gently brushed back her hair from her forehead. 'Sweetie, if I were ever to find myself alone with that creep I would delight in giving him a lesson on how to respect women. What he did to you was disgusting and unforgiveable.'

Sabrina couldn't help feeling touched by the flare of righteous anger in his eyes. It was wonderful to have someone stand up for her, someone who respected and cared about her welfare. Even if he didn't love her the way she wanted to be loved, surely it was enough that he would move heaven and earth to take care of her and their baby? 'You're such a good man, Max.'

He pressed a soft kiss to her lips and then lifted himself off the bed. 'Stay here and rest. I'll bring supper up in few minutes.'

Sabrina propped herself up on the elbows. 'Are you sure you don't want some help?'

He pointed a finger at her but there was a smile in his eyes. 'Stay. That's an order.'

She gave him a mock-defiant look. 'You know how

obstreperous I get when you issue you with me orders. Are you sure you want to take that risk?'

His eyes ran over her naked form in a lustful rove that made her want him all over again. 'Are you spoiling for a fight, young lady?' His voice was a low deep growl that did strange things to the hairs on the back of her neck.

Sabrina got off the bed and sashayed across to him with a sultry smile. She sent her hand from the top of his sternum to the proud bulge of his erection. 'I was thinking more along the lines of making love, not war. Are you on?'

He shuddered at her touch and pulled her closer. 'I'm on.' And his mouth came down on hers.

CHAPTER TEN

AN HOUR OR SO later, Max sat across from Sabrina in the cosy kitchen of the cottage and watched as she devoured the supper of soup and fresh bread and fruit he'd brought with him. He wondered if he would ever get tired of looking at her. Her hair was all tousled where his hands had been in it, her lips were swollen from his kisses and her cheeks had a beautiful creamy glow.

She looked up to see him looking at her and her cheeks went a faint shade of pink. She licked her lips and then, finding a crumb or two, reached for her napkin and dabbed at her mouth. 'What?'

Max smiled and pushed his untouched bread roll towards her. 'I like watching you eat. You remind me of a bird.'

'Yeah? What type? A vulture?' She picked up the bread roll and tore it into pieces. 'Seriously, I can't believe my appetite just now. I'm starving.'

'Must be the hormones.'

She gave him a sheepish look. 'Or the exercise.'

His body was still tingling from said exercise. And that was another thing he wondered if he'd ever tire

of—making love with her. 'I should have fed you earlier. It's almost midnight.'

'I love midnight feasts.' She popped another piece of
bread in her mouth, chewed and swallowed, and then
frowned when she saw his water glass. 'Hey, didn't you
bring any wine with you? I'm the one who isn't drinking while I'm pregnant, not you.'

'That hardly seems fair,' Max said. 'I'm not a big
drinker in any case.'

'Oh, Max, that's so thoughtful of you. But I don't
mind if you have a glass of wine or two.'

'It's not a problem.' He passed her the selection of
fruit. 'Here, have one of these peaches.'

After a while, she finished her peach and sat back
with a contented sigh. 'That was delicious.'

He got up to clear the table. 'Time for bed?'

She smothered a yawn. 'Not before I help you clear
this away.' She pushed back her chair and reached for
the plates.

'I'll sort it out. You go up and get comfortable.'

She was halfway to the door when she turned around
to look at him with a small frown wrinkling her forehead. 'Max?'

'What's up, sweetie?'

'Have you brought anyone else down here? Another
woman, I mean?'

'No. I've only just finished the renovations.' He
picked up the plates and cutlery and added, 'I wasn't
going to share it with anyone, to be perfectly honest.
Even my parents don't know about it.'

'Why haven't you told them?'

'There are some things I like to keep private.'

She chewed at her lip. 'I've been thinking… It must have been hard for Lydia, knowing your parents didn't think she was right for you.'

Funny, but Max could barely recall what his ex-fiancée looked like now. 'Yes, it probably was hard for her.' He frowned and continued. 'I sometimes wonder if I only got engaged to her to stop them banging on about you.'

Something flickered through her gaze. 'Not the best reason to get engaged.'

'No.'

'Have you seen her since?'

'No. What would be the point? We've both moved on.'

She gave him a thoughtful look. 'But have you?'

'Have I what?'

'Moved on.'

Max turned and loaded the dishwasher. 'You can rest easy, Sabrina. I have no lingering feelings for Lydia. You're my priority now.'

'But in a way, it's the same, isn't it?'

He closed the dishwasher with a snap. 'What's the same?'

'The way you felt about her is similar to how you feel about me. You weren't in love with her and you're not in love with me.'

Max didn't like where this conversation was heading. He wasn't incapable of love. He just chose not to love in *that* way. It wasn't called 'falling in love' for nothing. You lost all control when you loved someone to that degree. He was worried that if he fell in love he would eventually let the person down. Hadn't he always done so? His parents? His baby brother? Even Lydia had been short-changed and had gone off looking for someone who could love her the way she wanted.

'Sabrina.' He let out a long sigh. 'Let's not have this discussion this late at night. You're tired and—'

'What are you afraid of?'

He gave a short laugh to lighten the atmosphere. 'I'm not afraid of anything. Now, be a good girl and go upstairs and I'll be up in a second.'

She looked like she was going to argue, but then she let out a sigh and turned and headed upstairs.

Max leaned his hands on the kitchen counter and wondered if this was always going to be a stumbling block in their relationship. But he assured himself that Sabrina wasn't in love with him so what was the problem? If she had been, wouldn't she have said so? No, they were two people forced together because of circumstance and they were both committed to making the best of the situation. They had put their enmity aside, they liked each other, desired each other and respected each other. If that wasn't a positive thing, what was? Their relationship had a lot more going for it than others he'd seen. And it was certainly better than any relationship he'd had in the past.

Way better.

Sabrina spent the rest of the weekend with her mouth firmly closed on the subject of Max's feelings for her. She didn't want to spoil the relaxing time together because she could see how hard he was trying to do everything right by her. Her feelings weren't the top priority right now. They had a baby on the way and she had to somehow reassure Max he would be a wonderful father. She knew it still troubled him and she ached to ease that painful burden for him.

She consoled herself that in time he might relax the guard around his heart, open himself to loving her once he fell in love with their baby. Didn't most new parents say the experience of bringing a child into the world was a defining moment? A time when overwhelming love flooded their beings? It was her hope, her dream and unceasing prayer that Max would feel that groundbreaking love for their child and include her in it.

A few days later, Max left for a brief trip to Denmark, where he had a project on the go. Sabrina could sense his reluctance to leave her but she assured him she would be fine as she had work aplenty of her own to see to. Most days her nausea was only mild and if she was sensible about getting enough rest she was able to cope with the demands of her job.

Living at his house had far more benefits than she had first realised, not least the warm protective shelter of Max's arms when she went to sleep each night and when she woke each morning. Staying at his house was like living in a luxury hotel but much less impersonal. There were reminders of him everywhere—books, architectural journals he was reading, one with a feature article on him—and even the house itself with its stylish renovation that perfectly married the old with the new.

There was that word again—*marriage*.

But she couldn't bring herself to regret her acceptance of his proposal. She had to concentrate on what was best for the baby and put her own issues aside. Max cared about her otherwise he wouldn't have made such a fuss over her, looking after her, insisting on her living with him and doing a hundred other things for her that no one had ever done for her before.

The evening he was due to come back, Sabrina found a photo of him with his family in the study, taken before his baby brother had died. She had seen the photo at his parents' house in the past but somehow she hadn't really looked at it in any detail before. She traced her finger over Max's bright and happy smile as a seven-year-old boy and wondered if the birth of their baby would heal some of the pain of the past. There was no doubt in her mind that he would make an excellent father.

The sound of the doorbell ringing almost made her drop the photo frame. Max was due home any minute, but surely if it was him he would use his key rather than the doorbell? She placed the photo back on Max's desk and went out to check the security monitor in the foyer to see who was at the door. Her heart nearly jumped out of her chest when she saw it was her mother standing there with Max's mother Gillian. She had thought her mother would be away for another week in France…or had she got the dates wrong?

Sabrina stepped backwards away from the monitor, hoping Gillian Firbank and her mother hadn't heard her footsteps on the black and white tiles of the foyer, but in her haste she stumbled and bumped against the hall table. She watched in horror as the priceless vase that was sitting there wobbled and then crashed to the floor, shattering into pieces.

'Max?' Gillian said, rapping firmly at the door. 'Is that you? Are you okay?'

Sabrina stood surrounded by the detritus of the vase, her heart hammering faster than that of a rabbit on the run. Should she open the door? But how could she explain why she was at Max's house? They were supposed to be keeping their relationship a secret. But if their mothers found her in situ at Max's home...

'Perhaps it's a burglar,' Sabrina's mother said. 'We'd better call the police.'

Sabrina had no choice but to open the door before her mother summoned half of London's constabulary to Max's house. 'Hi,' she said. 'I'm...erm...housesitting for Max.'

Gillian's and Sabrina's mother's eyes widened and then they exchanged a twinkly-eyed glance.

'Housesitting? For... Max?' Her mother's voice rose in a mixture of disbelief and hope.

'Yes. Just while he's in Denmark. He's coming back tonight. In fact, I thought he would be home before this. Perhaps his flight's been delayed.'

Gillian's mouth was tilted in a knowing smile. 'I knew something was going on with you two at my party.'

'Nothing's going on,' Sabrina lied, not very well by the look on the two women's faces.

'I wanted to show your mother Max's new renovations,' Gillian said. 'We were in the area and saw the lights on and thought we'd pop in. But if Max isn't home we'll come back another time.'

'You told me the other day you were staying at a friend's house.' Her mother's expression was one part accusatory, one part delighted.

'Yes, well, that's sort of true,' Sabrina said.

'So you two are friends now?' Her mother's eyes danced like they were auditioning for a part in *La Cage aux Folles*.

'Mum, it's not what you think—'

'Actually, it is what you think,' Max said as he came up the path to the front door carrying his travel bag with his laptop case slung over his shoulder. 'Sabrina and I are getting married.'

'Married?' The mothers spoke in unison, their faces so aglow with unmitigated joy they could have lit up the whole of London.

Max put his arm around Sabrina's waist and drew her close to his side. 'Yes. We haven't set a date yet but we'll get around to it soon.'

Sabrina glanced at him with a question in her eyes but he simply smiled and bent down to kiss her. 'Miss me, darling?' he said.

'You have no idea how much.' Sabrina bit her lip. 'I'm sorry about your vase...'

'What vase?'

She pointed to the shattered pieces of porcelain strewn over the foyer behind them. 'I bumped it when I was checking the security monitor. Please tell me it wasn't valuable.'

'Not as valuable as you,' he said, and kissed her again.

'Oh, look at you two gorgeous things.' Gillian grabbed

Sabrina's mother's arm to lead her inside Max's house. 'We need to celebrate. Let's open some champagne.'

Sabrina gave him a *what do we do now?* look, but his expression remained calm. 'They had to find out sooner or later,' he said, sotto voce, and led her inside behind the older women.

Before she knew it, Max had efficiently cleaned up the pieces of the vase and Sabrina found herself sitting beside him on one of the sofas in the main sitting room. Her mother and Gillian were sitting opposite with glasses of champagne raised in a toast.

'Why aren't you drinking yours, Sabrina?' her mother asked after everyone else had sipped theirs. Max had only taken a token sip, however.

Sabrina cradled her glass in her hands, her cheeks feeling so hot she could have stripped the paint off the walls. 'Erm…'

'Oh, my God!' Gillian shot to her feet as if a spring in the sofa had jabbed her. 'You're pregnant?'

Max looked like he was the one suffering morning sickness. Sabrina's mother Ellen looked like she didn't know whether to laugh or cry.

Sabrina decided there was no point denying it. Besides, she wanted her mother to be one of the first to know and not find out some other way. 'Yes, I am pregnant but only eight weeks. We're not telling everyone until the twelve-week mark.'

There were hugs and kisses and hearty congratulations all round and finally, after promising they would only tell their husbands and Sabrina's brothers about the pregnancy, the mothers left.

Max closed the door on their exit with a sigh. 'I'm sorry. I forgot I told my mother to drop in sometime to see the completed renovations.'

Sabrina frowned. 'But why did you have to tell them we're getting married? Why not just say we're having a fling or something? You know how I feel about this. Now they'll be in full on wedding fever mode, telling everyone our business and—'

'I was thinking about it while I was away,' Max said. 'Trying to keep our involvement a secret is going to cause you more stress than you need right now. I figured it was safer to get this out in the open. I didn't realise my mother would twig about the pregnancy, though.'

Sabrina sank back into the sofa and hugged one of the scatter cushions, eyeing her untouched glass of champagne as if it had personally insulted her. 'If I hadn't broken that damn vase, trying to avoid them, we might still have kept our secret safe. Argh. I hate how out of control my life is right now.'

He hunkered down next to her and grazed his knuckles across her cheek, his eyes warm and tender. 'It was going to come out sooner or later. And there's no reason to think your pregnancy isn't going to continue.'

'Would you prefer it if I lost the baby?'

He flinched. 'No. How can you ask that?'

She shrugged one shoulder and tossed the cushion to one side. 'I've done a pretty good job of stuffing up your neatly controlled life.'

He straightened and then came to sit beside her on the sofa, his hand slipping under the curtain of her hair to the nape of her neck, his expression wry. 'Maybe it needed shaking up a bit.'

Sabrina could feel every inch of her body responding to his touch. She placed her arms around his waist, loving the strength and warmth of his body so close to hers. She rested her head against his chest and sighed. 'At least our families are happy for us.'

He lifted her face off his chest and meshed his gaze with hers. 'It's a good start.'

'But what if we make each other miserable? I mean, further down the track?'

He brushed an imaginary hair away from her face. 'We're both mature adults. We can handle the odd difference of opinion, surely? Besides, I quite like arguing with you.'

A smile tugged at her mouth, a hot tide of longing pooling in her core. 'Do you fancy a fight now?'

His eyes glinted. 'Bring it on.' And he scooped her up in his arms and carried her to the bedroom.

CHAPTER ELEVEN

A FEW DAYS LATER, Sabrina had left the shop early, leaving Harriet in charge so she could get home to make a special dinner. They had been eating out mostly but she wanted to have a night at home for once. She suspected he took her out for dinner so often so she wouldn't have to cook but she enjoyed cooking and wanted to do something for him for a change.

Max's once-a-week housekeeper had been through the house and left it spotless. Holly had given Sabrina some fresh flowers and she placed them in the new vase she'd bought to replace the one she'd broken.

He came in just as she was stirring the Provençale chicken casserole on the cooktop and she put the spoon down and smiled. How could a man look so traffic-stopping gorgeous after a long day at work? 'How was your day?'

'Long.' He came over and planted a kiss on the top of her head. 'Mmm…something smells nice.'

Sabrina held up the spoon for him to have a taste. 'It's one of your favourites. Your mum told me.'

He tasted the casserole and raised his brows in approval. 'Delicious. But why are you cooking? Shouldn't you be resting as much as possible?'

'I like cooking.'

'I know, but you don't have to wait on me. I could have picked up a takeaway to save you the bother.'

Sabrina popped the lid back on the pot. 'I'm not waiting on you. I just wanted to do something for you for a change. You've been so good about everything and I—'

'Hey.' He placed his hands on her shoulders and turned her so she was facing him. 'I like doing things for you. I want to make this relationship work.'

She bit down on her lip. 'I know. For the baby's sake, right?'

His hands gave her shoulders a gentle squeeze. 'Not just for the baby. For you. I care about you, Sabrina. Surely you know that?'

She gave an on-off smile. Would caring be enough for her? 'I know but—'

He placed a finger over her lips. 'No buts. I care about you and will do everything in my power to make you happy.' He lowered his hand and brought his mouth to hers instead, kissing her leisurely, beguilingly until she melted into his arms.

Sabrina wound her arms around his neck, pressing herself closer to the tempting hard heat of his body. Her inner core already tingling with sensation, his mouth triggering a tumultuous storm in her flesh. His tongue met hers and she made a sound of approval, her senses dazzled by the taste of him, the familiar and yet exotic taste that she craved like a potent drug. His hands cradled her face as he deepened the kiss, his lips and tongue wreaking sensual havoc, ramping up her desire like fuel tossed on a naked flame. It whooshed and whirled and rocketed through her body, making her aware of every point of contact of his body on hers.

With a groan Max lifted his mouth from hers. 'How long can dinner wait?'

Sabrina pulled his head back down. 'Long enough for you to make love to me.'

He kissed her again, deeply and passionately. Then he took her hand and led her upstairs, stopping to kiss her along the way. 'I've been thinking about doing this all day.'

'Me too,' Sabrina said, planting a series of kisses on his lips. 'I'm wild for you.'

He smiled against her mouth. 'Then what's my excuse? I've been wild for you for months.'

He led her to the master bedroom, peeling away her clothes and his with a deftness of movement that made her breathless with excitement. The touch of his warm strong hands on her naked skin made her gasp and whimper, his hands cupping her breasts, his lips and tongue caressing them, teasing her nipples into tight peaks of pleasure. The same tightly budded pleasure that was growing in her core, the most sensitive part of her hungry, aching for the sexy friction of his body.

Max worked his way down her body, gently pushing her back against the mattress so she was lying on her back and open to him. It was shockingly intimate and yet she didn't have time to feel shy. Her orgasm was upon her as soon as his tongue flicked against the heart of her and she came apart in a frenzied rush that travelled through her entire body like an earthquake.

He waited until she came down from the stratosphere to move over her, entering her with a deep but gentle thrust, a husky groan forced from his lips as her body wrapped around him. Sabrina held him to her, riding another storm of sensation, delighting in the rocking motion of his body as he increased his pace. Delighting in the strength and potency of him, delighting in the knowledge that she could do this to him—make him breathless and shuddering with ecstasy.

Max collapsed over her, his breathing hard and uneven against the side of her neck. 'You've rendered me speechless.'

Sabrina stroked her hands over his lower back. 'Same.'

He propped himself up on his elbows, his eyes still dark and glittering with spent passion. 'I mean it, sweetie. I don't think I've ever enjoyed sex as much as I have with you.'

She couldn't imagine making love with anyone but him. The thought appalled her. Sickened her. She snuggled closer, her arms around his middle, wondering if it were possible to feel closer to him than she did right now.

After a long pause he stroked a strand of hair away from her face, his eyes dark with renewed desire. 'How do you think dinner is holding up?'

She rubbed her lower body against his pelvis and smiled her best sexy siren smile. 'It'll keep.' And she lifted her mouth to the descent of his.

* * *

Max had a run of projects that urgently needed his attention. He'd been neglecting his work in order to take care of Sabrina, making sure she had everything she needed in the early weeks of her pregnancy. But his work could no longer be postponed. He had big clients who expected the service they paid good money for. He hated leaving Sabrina but he had a business to run and people relying on him.

Travelling out of town meant he would have to stay overnight and that's what he hated the most. Not waking up next to her. Not having her sexy body curled up in his arms, the sweet smell of her teasing his nostrils until he was almost drunk on it. He informed her of his business trip over breakfast and she looked up from buttering her toast with disappointed eyes. So disappointed it drove a stake through his chest.

Her smile looked forced. 'Oh... Thanks for telling me.'

He scraped a hand through his hair. Clearly he had some work to do on his communication skills. And his timing. 'I'm sorry. I should have told you days ago. I thought I could manage it at a distance but the client is getting restless.'

She got up from the table and took her uneaten toast to the rubbish bin and tossed it in. 'I know you have a business to run. So do I.'

'Why aren't you eating? Do you feel sick?'

She turned from the bin with a combative look her on face. 'I'm fine, Max. Stop fussing.'

He came over to her and took her stiff little hands

in his. 'Do you think I really want to leave you? I hate staying in hotels. I would much rather wake up with you beside me.'

Her tight expression softened. 'How long will you be away?'

'Two nights,' Max said, stroking the backs of her hands. 'I'd ask you to come with me but I know you're busy with Holly's dress. Which reminds me, we need to set a wedding date. My mother has been on my back just about every day to—'

'Yeah, mine too.' Her mouth twisted. 'But I don't want to get married close to Holly's wedding day. But neither do I want to be showing too much baby bump on ours. I don't know what to do. Ever since I was a little girl, I've dreamed of my wedding day. Not once in those dreams did I picture myself waddling up the aisle pregnant. I'm stressing about it all the time. Whenever I think about it I just about have a panic attack.'

He cupped her cheek in his hand. 'Oh, sweetie, try not to stress too much. We'll talk some more when I get back, okay?'

She sighed. 'Okay…'

Max kissed her on the forehead, breathing in her summer flowers scent. 'I'll call you tonight.' He touched her downturned mouth with his fingertip. 'Why don't you ask Holly to stay with you while I'm away? I'm sure she wouldn't mind.'

'She spends every spare minute with Zack.' A spark of annoyance lit her gaze. 'Besides, I don't need flipping babysitting.'

'I can't help worrying about you.'

She slipped out of his hold and picked up her tote bag where it was hanging off the back of a chair. 'You worry too much. I'll be fine. I have plenty to keep me occupied.'

Max placed his hands on her shoulders, turning her to face him. 'You'll have to be patient with me, Sabrina. I'm not the world's best communicator. I'm used to going away for work at a moment's notice. But obviously that's going to have to change once we become parents.'

She let out a soft sigh. 'I'm sorry for being so snippy. I'm just feeling a little overwhelmed.'

He brought up her chin with his finger, meshing his gaze with her cornflower-blue one. 'It's perfectly understandable. We'll get through this, sweetheart. I know we will.'

She gave another fleeting smile but there was a shadow of uncertainty behind her eyes. 'I have to run. I have a dress fitting first thing.'

He pressed a kiss to her lips. 'I'll miss you.'

'I'll miss you too.'

Sabrina was ten minutes late to her fitting with her client, which was embarrassing as it had never happened before. But she couldn't seem to get herself into gear. Ever since she'd found out Max was going away, she'd felt agitated and out of sorts. It wasn't that she wanted to live in his pocket. She had her own commitments and responsibilities, but she had come to look forward to their evenings together each day. She loved discussing the events of the day with him over dinner, or curling up on the sofa watching television. She had even got him hooked on one of her favourite TV series. She loved the companionship of their relationship. It reminded her of her parents' relationship, which, in spite of the passage of years, seemed to get stronger.

And then there was the amazing sex.

Not just amazing sex, but magical lovemaking. Every time they made love, she felt closer to him. Not just physically, but emotionally. It was like their bodies were doing the talking that neither of them had the courage to express out loud. She longed to tell him she loved him, but worried that if she did so he would push her away. She couldn't go through another humiliation of rejection. Not after what had happened when she was eighteen. But even so, she had to be careful not to read too much into Max's attentive behaviour towards her. He cared for her and he cared about their baby.

That was what she had to be grateful for.

Holly came in for her final fitting later that afternoon just on closing time. 'Hiya.' She swept in, carrying a bunch of flowers, but then noticing Sabrina's expression frowned. 'Hey, what's up?'

Sabrina tried to smile. 'Nothing.'

Holly put the flowers down. 'Yeah, right. Come on, fess up.'

Sabrina was glad Harriet had left for the day. She closed the shop front door and turned the 'Closed' sign to face the street. 'Come out the back and I'll do your fitting while we chat.'

'Forget about the fitting—we can do that another

day,' Holly said, once they were out the back. 'The wedding isn't for another few weeks. What's wrong?'

Sabrina put her hand on her belly. Was it her imagination or had she just felt a cramp? 'I'm just feeling a bit all over the place.'

'Are you feeling unwell?'

'Sort of…' She winced as another cramp gripped her abdomen.

Holly's eyes widened. 'Maybe you should sit down. Here…' She pulled out a chair. 'Do you feel faint?'

Sabrina ignored the chair and headed straight to the bathroom. 'I need to pee.'

She closed the bathroom door, taking a breath to calm herself. Tummy troubles were part and parcel of the first weeks of pregnancy. Nausea, vomiting, constipation—they were a result of the shifting hormones. But when she checked her underwear, her heart juddered to a halt. The unmistakable spots of blood signalled something was wrong. She tried to stifle a gasp of despair as a giant wave of emotion swamped her.

Was she about to lose the baby?

Holly knocked on the bathroom door. 'Sabrina? Are you okay?'

Sabrina came out a short time later. 'I think I need to go to hospital.'

Max was in a meeting with his client when he felt his phone vibrating in his pocket. Normally he would have ignored it—clients didn't always appreciate their time with him being interrupted. Especially this client, by far the most difficult and pedantic he had ever had on his books. But when he excused himself and pulled out his phone, he didn't recognise the number. He slipped the phone back into his pocket, figuring whoever it was could call back or leave a message. But he only had just sat back down with his client when his phone pinged with a text message. He pulled the phone out again and read the text.

Max, it's Holly. Can you call me ASAP?

Max's chest gave a painful spasm, his heart leaping and lodging in his throat until he could scarcely draw breath. There could only be one reason Sabrina's friend was calling him. Something must be wrong. Terribly wrong. He pushed back his chair and mumbled another apology to his client and strode out of the room. He dialled the number on the screen and pinched the bridge of his nose to contain his emotions. 'Come on, come on, come on. Pick up.'

'Max?'

'What's happened?' Max was gripping the phone so tightly he was sure it would splinter into a hundred pieces. 'Is Sabrina okay?'

'She's fine. She's had a slight show of blood but nothing since so that's good—'

Guilt rained down on him like hailstones. He should never have left her. This was *his* fault. She'd been out of sorts this morning and he'd made it a whole lot worse by springing his trip on her without warning. What sort of job was he doing of looking after her when the first time he turned his back she ended up in hospital? Was there something wrong with him? Was there a curse on all his relationships, especially the most important one of all? His guts churned at the thought of her losing the baby. Of *him* losing her. Dread froze his scalp and churned his guts and turned his legs to water.

'Are you sure she's okay? Can I speak to her?'

'She's still with the doctor but I'll get her to call you when she's finished. She didn't want to worry you but I thought you should know.'

Damn right he should know. But he still shouldn't have left her. He had let her down and now he had to live with his old friend, guilt. 'Thanks for calling. I'll be back as soon as I can.'

'You're free to go home now, Sabrina,' the doctor said, stripping off her gloves. 'The cervix looks fine and the scan shows the placenta is intact. A break-through bleed at this stage, especially one as small as yours, is not unusual. Some women have spotting right through the pregnancy. Just make sure you rest for a day or two and if you have any concerns let us know.'

Sabrina tried to take comfort in what the doctor had said but her emotions were still all over the place. 'I'm not going to lose the baby?'

'I can't guarantee that. But, as I said, things look fine.' The doctor glanced at the engagement ring on Sabrina's hand and smiled. 'Get your fiancé to take extra-special care of you for the next few days.'

Her fiancé...

Sabrina wished Max were waiting outside instead of Holly. Her friend was fabulous and had swung into action as if she had been handling fretting pregnant women all her life. But the person Sabrina most wanted by her side was Max. She felt so alone facing the panic of a possible miscarriage. What if she had lost the baby? What if she *still* lost it? The doctor was right, there were no guarantees. Nature was unpredictable.

Holly swished the curtain aside on the cubicle. 'The doctor said you're fine to go home. Max is on his way.'

'You called him? How did you get his number?'

Holly patted Sabrina's tote bag, which was hanging from Holly's shoulder. 'I found his number on your phone. I didn't feel comfortable calling him on your phone so I called him on mine. I know you didn't want to worry him but if something had happened, imagine how he'd feel?'

Sabrina got off the bed, testing her legs to see if they were as shaky as they had been earlier when panic had flooded her system. 'He would probably feel relieved.'

'What? Do you really think so?'

'I know so.' Sabrina cast her friend a weary glance. 'The only reason we're together is because of the baby.'

Holly frowned. 'But he cares about you. I could hear it in his voice. He was so worried about you and—'

'Worrying about someone doesn't mean you love them,' Sabrina said. 'It means you feel responsible for them.'

'You're splitting hairs. That poor man almost had a heart attack when I told him you were in hospital.'

'I wish I had what you have with Zack,' Sabrina said. 'I wish Max loved me the way Zack loves you. But wishing doesn't make it happen.'

'Oh, honey, I'm sure you're mistaken about Max. You're feeling emotional just now and this has been a huge scare. You might feel better once he's back home with you.'

But what if she didn't?

Max risked speeding tickets and any number of traffic violations on the way back to London. He'd called Sabrina several times but she must have turned her phone off. He called Holly and she told him Sabrina was back at his house, resting.

'Can you stay with her until I get back?' Max glanced at the dashboard clock. 'I'm about an hour away.'

'Sure.'

'Thanks. You're a gem.' He clicked off the call and tried to get his breathing under control. But every time he thought of what could have happened to Sabrina he felt sick to his guts. Miscarriages were dangerous if help wasn't at hand. It might be the twenty-first century but women could still haemorrhage to death. He couldn't get the picture of a coffin out of his mind. Two coffins. One for Sabrina and another for the baby. How could he have let this happen? How could he have put his work before his responsibilities towards her and their child?

It felt like an entire millennium later by the time Max opened his front door. Holly had obviously been waiting for him as she had her bag over her shoulder and her jacket over her arm.

'She's upstairs,' Holly said.

'Thanks for staying with her.'

'No problem.' She slipped out and Max was halfway up the stairs before the door closed.

Sabrina was standing in front of the windows with her back to him, her arms across her middle. She turned when she heard his footfalls but he couldn't read her expression.

Max wanted to rush over to her and enfold her in his arms but instead it was like concrete had filled his blood and deadened his limbs. He opened and closed his mouth, trying to find his voice, but even that had deserted him. His throat was raw and tight, blocked with emotions he couldn't express.

'You're back.' Her voice was as cold as the cruel icy hand gripping his throat.

'I came as fast as I could. Are you all right?'

She was holding herself almost as stiffly as he was but he couldn't take a step towards her. His legs felt bolted to the floor, his guts still twisting and turning at what might have been.

'I'm fine.'

'And the baby?' He swallowed convulsively. 'It's still—?'

'I'm still pregnant.'

Relief swept through him but still he kept his distance. He didn't trust his legs to work. He didn't trust his spiralling emotions. They were messing with his head, blocking his ability to do and say the things he should be saying. Things he wasn't even able to express to himself, let alone to her. 'Why aren't you in bed? You need to rest.'

A shuttered look came over her eyes. 'Max, we need to talk.'

He went to swallow again but his throat was too dry. Something was squeezing his chest until he could barely breathe. 'You scared the hell out of me. When I got that call from Holly...' His chest tightened another notch. 'I thought... I thought...' In his mind he could see that tiny white coffin again and another bigger one next to it. Flowers everywhere. People crying. He could feel the hammering of his heartbeat in time with the pulse of his guilt.

Your fault. Your fault. Your fault.

'Max, I can't marry you.'

He went to reach for her but she stepped back, her expression rigid with determination. 'You're upset, sweetie. You've had a big shock and you'll feel better once you've—'

'You're not listening to me.' Her voice with its note of gravity made a chill run down his neck.

'Okay.' He took a breath and got himself into some sort of order. 'I'm listening.'

She rolled her lips together until they almost disappeared. 'I can't marry you, Max. What happened today confirmed it for me.'

'For God's sake, do you think I would have left town if I thought you were going to have a miscarriage? What sort of man do you think I am?'

Her expression remained calm. Frighteningly calm. 'It's not about the miscarriage scare. You could have been right beside me at the hospital and I would still have come to the same decision eventually. You were wrong to force your proposal on me when you can't give your whole self to the relationship.'

'Forced?' Max choked back a humourless laugh. 'You're having my baby so why wouldn't I want you to marry me?'

'But if I had lost the baby, what then?' Her gaze was as penetrating as an industrial drill. 'Would you still want to marry me?'

Max rubbed a hand down his face. He had a headache that was threatening to split his skull in half. Why did she have to do this now? He wasn't over the shock of the last few hours. Adrenaline was still coursing through him in juddering pulses. 'Let's not talk about this now, Sabrina.'

'When will we talk about it? The day of the damn wedding? Is that what you'd prefer me to do? To jilt you like Lydia did?' Her words came at him like bullets. *Bang. Bang. Bang.*

Max released a long, slow breath, fighting to keep his frustration in check. He couldn't talk about this now, not with his head so scrambled, thoughts and fears and memories causing a toxic poison that made it impossible for him to think straight. Impossible for him to access the emotions that went into automatic lockdown just as they had done all those years ago when he'd seen his mother carrying the tiny limp body of his baby brother. It felt like he was a dead man standing. A robot. A lifeless, emotionless robot.

'I put marriage on the table because of the baby. It would be pointless to go ahead with it if you were no longer pregnant.'

Nothing showed on her face but he saw her take a swallow. 'I guess I should be grateful you were honest with me.'

'Sabrina, I'm not the sort of man to say a whole bunch of words I can't back up with actions.'

Tears shone in her eyes. 'You act like you love me. But I can't trust that it's true. I need to hear you say it, but you won't, will you?'

'Are you saying you love me?'

Her bottom lip quivered. 'Of course I love you. But I can't allow myself to be in a one-sided relationship. Not again. Not after what happened when I was eighteen.'

Anger whipped through him like a tornado. 'Please do me the favour of not associating anything I do or say with how that creep treated you. You know I care about you. I only want the best for you and the baby.'

'But that's my point. If there wasn't a baby there wouldn't be an us.' She turned to the walk-in wardrobe.

'Hey, what are you doing?'

'I'm packing a bag.'

Max caught her by the arm. 'No, you're damn well not.'

She shook off his hold, her eyes going hard as if a steel curtain had come down behind her gaze. 'I can't stay with you, Max. Consider our engagement over. I'm not marrying you.'

'You're being ridiculous.' Panic was battering inside his chest like a loose shutter in a windstorm. 'I won't let you walk away.'

She peeled off his fingers one by one. 'You're a good man, Max. A really lovely man. But you have serious issues with love. You hold everyone at a distance. You're scared of losing control of your emotions so you lock them away.'

'Spare me the psychology session.' Max couldn't keep the sarcasm in check. 'I've tried to do everything I can to support you. I've bent over backwards to—'

'I know you have but it's not enough. You don't love me the way I want to be loved. And that's why I can't be with you.'

Max considered saying the words to keep her with him. How hard could it be? Three little words that other people said so casually. But he hadn't told anyone he loved them since he'd told his baby brother, and look how that turned out. He felt chilled to the marrow even thinking about saying those words again. He had let her down and there was nothing he could do to change it. He wasn't good enough for her. He had never been good enough and he'd been a fool to think he ever could be. 'Will you at least stay here for a bit longer till I find you somewhere to live?'

A sad smile pulled at her mouth. 'No, Max, I don't think that would be wise. I'll stay with my parents for bit until I find somewhere suitable.'

Later, Max could barely recall how he'd felt as Sabrina packed an overnight bag and handed him back the engagement ring. He hadn't even said, *No, you keep it.* He'd been incapable of speech. He drove her to her parents' house in a silence so thick he could almost taste it. His emotions were still in an emergency lockdown that made him act like an automaton, stripping every expression off his face, sending his voice into a monotone.

* * *

It was only days later, when he got back home to his empty house after work, where the lingering fragrance of her perfume haunted him, that he wondered if he should have done more to convince her to stay. But what? Say words she knew he didn't mean? He would be no better than that lowlife scum who'd hurt her so badly all those years ago.

But why did his house seem so empty without her there? He had got used to the sound of her pottering about. Damn it, he'd even got used to the mindless drivel she watched on television. He would have happily watched a test pattern if he could just sit with his arm around her. He could get through watching just about anything if he could hear the sound of her laughter and her sighs, and patiently hand her his handkerchief when she got teary over the sad bits of a movie.

But he would have to get used to not having her around.

Sabrina dragged herself through the next few days, worn down by sadness that her life wasn't turning out like that of the dewy-faced brides that filed through her shop. It was like having salt rubbed into an open and festering wound to see everyone else experiencing the joy and happiness of preparing for a wedding when her dreams were shattered. Why was her life destined to fall short of her expectations? Was there something wrong with her? Was she too idealistic? Too uncompromising?

But how could she compromise on the issue of love? Moving back in with her parents might not have been the wisest move, Sabrina decided. She was engulfed by their disappointment as well as her own. It seemed everyone thought Max was the perfect partner for her except Max himself. But she couldn't regret her decision to end their engagement. She couldn't remain in a one-sided relationship. The one who loved the most was always the one who got hurt in the end. She wanted an equal partnership with love flowing like a current between them. Like it flowed between both sets of parents, long and lasting and able to withstand calamity.

No. This was the new normal for her. Alone.

And the sooner she got used to it the better.

A few miserable days later, Max went into his study and sat at his desk. He found himself sitting there every night, unable to face that empty bed upstairs. He sighed and dragged a hand over his face. His skull was permanently tight with a headache and his eyes felt gritty.

His eyes went to the photograph of his family before Daniel had died. There was nothing he could do to bring his brother back. Nothing he could do to repair the heartache he had caused his parents by not being more vigilant. His phone rang and he took it out of his pocket and swore when he saw it was his mother. The gossip network was back at work after a few days' reprieve. No doubt Sabrina's mother Ellen had called his mum to tell her the wedding was off. He was surprised Ellen hadn't done so the moment it had happened but maybe Sabrina had wanted things kept quiet for a bit. He answered the phone. 'Mum, now's not a good time.'

'Oh, Max. Ellen told me Sabrina called off the engagement.'

'Yep. She did.'

'And you let her?'

'She's an adult, Mum. I can't force her to be with me.' Even though he'd damn well given it a good shot.

'Oh, darling, I'm so upset for you and for her,' his mum said. 'I can't help thinking your father, Ellen, Jim and I have been putting too much pressure on you both. We just wanted you to be happy. You're perfect for each other.'

'I'm not perfect for anyone. That's the problem.' He let out a jagged sigh. 'I can't seem to help letting down the people I care about. You, Dad and Daniel, for instance. I do it without even trying. It's like I'm hardwired to ruin everyone's lives.'

'Max, you haven't ruined anyone's lives,' his mother said after a small silence. 'I know you find it hard to allow people close to you. You weren't like that as a young child, but since we lost Daniel you've stopped being so open with your feelings. It was like a part of you died with him. I blame myself for not being there for you but I was so overwhelmed by my own grief I didn't see what was happening to you until it was too late. But you weren't to blame for what happened, you know that, don't you?'

Max leaned forward to rest one elbow on the desk and leaned his forehead against his hand. 'I should have known something was wrong. You asked me to check on him and he seemed fine.'

'That's because he *was* fine when you checked on

him. Max, the coroner said it was SIDS. Daniel might have died in the next ten minutes and there was nothing you could have done to change that.' She sighed and he heard the catch in her voice. 'Darling, do you think I haven't blamed myself? Not a day goes past that I don't think of him. But it would be an even bigger tragedy if I thought you weren't living a fulfilling life because you didn't think you deserved to love and be loved in return.'

'Look, I know you mean well, Mum, but I can't give Sabrina what she wants. What she deserves. I'm not capable of it.'

'Are you sure about that, Max? Totally sure?'

Max ended the call and sat back in his chair with a thump. It was slowly dawning on him that he had made the biggest blunder of his life. His feelings for Sabrina had always been confusing to him. For years he'd held her at arm's length with wisecracking banter, but hadn't that been because he was too frightened to own up to what was going on in his heart? She had always got under his skin. She had always rattled the cage he had constructed around his heart.

And up until he'd kissed her he'd done a damn fine job of keeping her out. But that one kiss had changed everything. That kiss had led to that night in Venice and many nights since of the most earth-shattering sex of his life. But it wasn't just about amazing sex. There was way more to their relationship than that.

He *felt* different with her.

He felt alive. Awakened.

Hopeful.

His sexual response to her was a physical manifestation of what was going on in his heart. He was inexorably drawn to her warm and generous nature. Every time he touched her, he felt a connection that was unlike any he'd experienced before. Layer by layer, piece by piece, every barricade he'd erected had been sloughed away by her smile, her touch. Her love. How could he let her walk away without telling her the truth? The truth that had been locked away until now. The truth he had shied away from out of fear and cowardice.

He loved her.

He loved her with every fibre of his being. His love for her was the only thing that could protect her. Love was what had kept his family together against impossible odds. Love was what would protect their baby, just as he had been protected. His and her parents were right—he and Sabrina were perfect for each other. And if he didn't exactly feel perfect enough, he would work damn hard on it so he did.

Because he loved her enough to change. To own the feelings he had been too fearful to name. Feelings that he needed to express to her because they were bubbling up inside him like a dam about to break.

Sabrina's parents fussed over her so much each night when she came home from work that she found it claustrophobic. They were doing it with good intentions but she just wanted to be alone to contemplate her future without Max. Thankfully, that night her parents had an important medical function to attend, which left Sabrina to have a pity party all by herself.

The doorbell rang just as she was deciding whether she could be bothered eating the nutritious meal her mother had left for her. She glanced at the security monitor in the kitchen and her heart nearly stopped when she saw Max standing there. But before she allowed herself to get too excited, she took a deep calming breath. He was probably just checking up on her. Making sure she'd settled in okay.

She opened the door with her expression cool and composed. 'Max.' Even so, her voice caught on his name.

'I need to talk to you.' His voice was deep and hoarse, as if he had swallowed the bristly welcome mat.

'Come in.' Sabrina stepped away from the door to allow him to follow but she didn't get far into the foyer before he reached for her, taking her by the hands.

'Sabrina, my darling, I can't believe it has taken me this long to realise what I feel about you.' His hands tightened on hers as if he was worried she would pull away. 'You've been in my life for so long that I was blind or maybe too damn stubborn to see you're exactly what our parents have said all this time. You're perfect for me. Perfect because you've taught me how to feel again. How to love. I love you.'

Sabrina stepped a little closer or maybe he tugged her to him, she wasn't sure. All she knew was hearing him say those words made something in her chest explode with joy like fireworks. She could feel fizzes and tingles running right through her as she saw the look of devotion on his face. 'Oh, Max, do you mean it? You're not just saying it to get me back?'

He wrapped one arm around her like a tight band, the other hand cupped one side of her face, his eyes shining like wet paint. 'I mean it with every breath and bone and blood cell in my body. I love you so much. I've been fighting it because on some level I knew you were the only one who could make me feel love again and I was so worried about letting you down. And then I went and did it in the worst way possible. I can't believe I stood there like a damn robot instead of reaching for you and telling you I loved you that night you came home from hospital. Please marry me, my darling. Marry me and let's raise our baby together.'

She threw her arms around his neck and rose up on tiptoe so she could kiss him. 'Of course I'll marry you. I love you. I think I might have always loved you.'

Max squeezed her so tightly she thought her ribs would crack. He released her slightly to look at her. 'Oh, baby girl, I can't believe I nearly lost you. I've been such a fool, letting you leave like that. How devastated you must have felt when you told me you loved me and I just stood there frozen like a statue.'

Sabrina gazed into his tender eyes. 'You're forgiven, as long as you forgive me for being such a cow to you for all those years.'

He cradled her face with his hands and brushed his thumbs across her cheeks. 'There's nothing to forgive. I enjoyed every one of those insults because they've brought us here. You are the most adorable person in the world. I wish I could be a better man than I am for you, but I give you my word I'll do my best.'

Sabrina blinked back tears of happiness. 'You are the

best, Max. The best man for me. The only man I want. You're perfect just the way you are.'

He gave her a lingering kiss, rocking her from side to side in his arms. After a while, he lifted his head to look at her, his eyes moist with his own tears of joy. 'Hang on, I forgot something.' He reached into his trouser pocket and took out her engagement ring and slipped it on her finger. 'There. Back where it belongs.'

Sabrina smiled and looped her arms around his neck again. 'We are both back where we belong. Together. Ready to raise our little baby.'

He hugged her close again, smiling down at her. 'I'm more than ready. I can't wait to be a father. You've taught me that loving someone is the best way of protecting them and I can safely say you and our baby are not going to be short of my love.' He kissed her again and added, 'My forever love.'

EPILOGUE

A FEW WEEKS LATER, Max stood at the end of the aisle at the same church in which he and his baby brother had been christened, and looked out at the sea of smiling faces, his friends and family. He saw Zack sitting with Sabrina's family with a grin from ear to ear, having just got back from his honeymoon. Holly was the maid of honour so Zack would have to do without his new bride by his side while the ceremony was conducted.

Max drew in a breath to settle his nerves of excitement. The church was awash with flowers thanks to Holly. He couldn't believe how hard everyone had worked to get this wedding under way in the short time frame. But wasn't that what friends and family were for? They pulled together and the power of all that love overcame seemingly impossible odds.

The organ began playing 'The Bridal March' and Holly, as Sabrina's only bridesmaid, and the cute little flower girl, the three-year-old daughter of one of Max's friends from University, began their procession.

And then it was time for his bride to appear. Max's heart leapt into his throat and he blinked back a sudden rush of tears. Sabrina was stunning in a beautiful organza gown that floated around her, not quite disguising the tiny bump of their baby. She looked like a fairytale princess and her smile lit up the church and sent a warm spreading glow to his chest.

She was wearing something borrowed and something blue, but when she came to stand in front of him he saw the pink diamond earrings he had bought her after they had found out at the eighteen-week ultrasound they were expecting a baby girl. They had decided to keep it a secret between themselves and it thrilled him to share this private message with her on this most important of days. One day they would tell their little daughter of the magic of how she brought her parents together in a bond of mutual and lasting love.

Sabrina came to stand beside him, her eyes twinkling as bright as the diamonds she was wearing, and the rush of love he felt for her almost knocked him off his feet. He took her hands and smiled. 'You look beautiful.' His voice broke but he didn't care. He wasn't ashamed of feeling emotional. He was proud to stand and own his love for her in front of all these people. In front of the world.

Her eyes shone. 'Oh, Max, I can't believe my dream came true. We're here about to be married.'

He smiled back. 'Our dream wedding.' He gave her hands a little squeeze. 'My dream girl.'

* * * * *

LET'S TALK
Romance

For exclusive extracts, competitions and special offers, find us online:

- facebook.com/millsandboon
- @MillsandBoon
- @MillsandBoonUK

Get in touch on 01413 063232

For all the latest titles coming soon, visit
millsandboon.co.uk/nextmonth

MILLS & BOON

THE HEART OF ROMANCE

A ROMANCE FOR EVERY READER

MODERN
Prepare to be swept off your feet by sophisticated, sexy and seductive heroes, in some of the world's most glamourous and romantic locations, where power and passion collide.

HISTORICAL
Escape with historical heroes from time gone by. Whether your passion is for wicked Regency Rakes, muscled Vikings or rugged Highlanders, awak the romance of the past.

MEDICAL
Set your pulse racing with dedicated, delectable doctors in the high-pressure world of medicine, where emotions run high and passion, comfort a love are the best medicine.

True Love
Celebrate true love with tender stories of heartfelt romance, from the rush of falling in love to the joy a new baby can bring, and a focus on th emotional heart of a relationship.

Desire
Indulge in secrets and scandal, intense drama and plenty of sizzling hot action with powerful and passionate heroes who have it all: wealth, statu good looks…everything but the right woman.

HEROES
Experience all the excitement of a gripping thriller, with an intense romance at its heart. Resourceful, true-to-life women and strong, fearless face danger and desire - a killer combination!

To see which titles are coming soon, please visit
millsandboon.co.uk/nextmonth

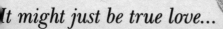